W9-AYO-386

02/2012

WHERE THERE'S SMOKE

PALM BEACH COUNTY
LIBRARY SYSTEM
3650 Summit Boulevard
West Palm Beach, FL 33406-4198

WHERE THERE'S SMOKE

TERRA LITTLE

www.urbanbooks.net

Urban Books
1199 Straight Path
West Babylon, NY 11704

Where There's Smoke copyright © 2009 Terra Little

All rights reserved. No part of this book may be reproduced in any form or by any means without prior consent of the Publisher, excepting brief quotes used in reviews.

ISBN- 13: 978-1-933967-78-3
ISBN- 10: 1-933967-78-1

First Printing January 2009
Printed in the United States of America

10 9 8 7 6 5 4

This is a work of fiction. Any references or similarities to actual events, real people, living, or dead, or to real locales are intended to give the novel a sense of reality. Any similarity in other names, characters, places, and incidents is entirely coincidental.

Distributed by Kensington Publishing Corp.
Submit Wholesale Orders to:
Kensington Publishing Corp.
C/O Penguin Group (USA) Inc.
Attention: Order Processing
405 Murray Hill Parkway
East Rutherford, NJ 07073-2316
Phone: 1-800-526-0275
Fax: 1-800-227-9604

Acknowledgments:

Before I lure you into the midst of the upcoming tale, I need you to know that I appreciate your support and I thank you for taking the time to get to know me and my work. I'm referring to all of you—everyone, everywhere.

Dedication:

This book is dedicated to all the women who have struggled with drug addiction and prevailed; to all the women who are going through the struggle right now; and to all the women who are working on getting over their fear of the struggle, so they can take that first step. I might not know your struggle, but I feel your pain.

Prologue

ALEC

I was erasing yesterday's lecture material from the blackboard when the process server walked into my classroom. I thought he was one of my students' parents, and I automatically put on my best welcome-to-my-classroom smile.

"Can I help you?" I asked. Several of my students were struggling in my class, and if this was a concerned parent wanting to know how he could help, I was more than willing to discuss his son's or daughter's progress at length.

"Are you Alec Avery?" the man asked.

I looked at the lanky white man curiously. He was short with bushy looking hair, and wore middle of the road clothes, and heavy soled, thick leather shoes laced too tightly. I thought he might be Byron Tardell's father, a kid in my fifth hour with a propensity toward sneaking his iPod past me and sitting in the very back of the class, listening to it while I lectured. Just yesterday I had finally confiscated it, and I had to admit, the kid had some smooth grooves on that thing, if the sampling I'd treated myself to was any indication.

"Let me guess, you're Byron's dad, and you're here to pick up his iPod, right?" I moved from the board to my desk, pulled out a drawer, and dug around under some papers. "I have to tell you, this thing is very disruptive in class. I've asked Byron to leave it at home on several occasions, but—"

"I'm not Byron's father, Mr. Avery," the man said, coming toward me with a thick envelope extended. Reflexively, I took it. "In fact, I don't have any children. Never really cared for them, you know? Anyway, I'm a process server and you should consider yourself served. Have a nice day."

With that, he was gone. I looked down at the envelope in my hand as if I had no idea how it got there. *Served?* I'd never been served with anything in my life. Oh, yeah, divorce papers, but that was different. I had been expecting them, elated with the prospect of finally receiving them even. This was something else altogether.

I tossed the envelope on my desk and returned to the board. Five seconds later I was back at my desk, staring at the envelope. I couldn't think of anyone I owed money to, and as far as I knew, I didn't have any wives left to divorce. So what the hell was this? I sat at my desk and ripped open the envelope, unable to wait another minute. I scanned the cover sheet carefully, my eyes growing wider and wider as the seconds passed. After about five minutes of reading, I mentally reminded myself to breathe.

In my hand I was holding a petition for child support. Some woman, whom I had no knowledge or recollection of, was claiming that I had fathered a child with her over sixteen years ago, and after all these years, she wanted financial compensation. *What the hell?*

I read the plaintiff's name again and searched my memory. Breanne Phillips. The name didn't ring a bell with me, not even remotely. I had done more than my share of traveling while I was in the marines, and, of course, I'd sampled some of the ladies, but I hadn't left any babies behind that I knew of. But that was how things worked, wasn't it? You didn't know you'd left babies behind until you got hit for child support out of the blue. Like this. Like now. Possibly this was a case of mistaken identity. There were stories of women who had nothing to go on except the name of their child's father. Every guy in the state with the name in question was summoned to appear, so that the woman could point out the right one, the man she had screwed without bothering to learn anything other than his name. This might be one of those situations. It had to be.

I was in the military for twelve years and married for nine of those years. There was no way I had fathered a child. Well, I mean, there was a *way*, but this had to be a mistake.

My students began trickling into class, each looking more harried and harassed than the last, and none of them looking like they were in the mood for Geometry. I shoved the papers in a drawer, put on my game face, and went to stand at the door. The first bell of the day would be ringing shortly.

"Miss Jacobs, I thought I asked you to start giving serious thought to the types of shirts you wear to school from now on," I reminded a female student as she sidled past me wearing a sheer looking shirt, unbuttoned to show ample cleavage. Where was her mother when this girl was buying or stealing her clothing?

"You lucky I didn't wear the first one I put on, Mr. Avery," she came back.

"No, I think you might be the lucky one. Go to the office and see if they have a sweater in the lost and found you can borrow, please, Miss Jacobs." The rest of the class burst out laughing and I couldn't resist chuckling myself. The look on her face was truly a Kodak moment.

"You kidding, right?"

"I wish I was. You'd better hurry up, because I'm not giving you a pass. You get caught roaming the halls, and it's an automatic detention. Go." I pointed out the door and raised my eyebrows meaningfully. As soon as she huffed out the door, breasts bouncing all over the place, I pulled it closed and lifted a silencing hand. "Turn to page 188 in your books, class."

A resounding aawww filled the room and I silently commiserated as I scooped up the teaching manual and turned to the board, chalk in hand. Whoever this child was that I didn't know, and that I was supposed to have fathered, wouldn't be too much older than the hooligans I taught on a daily basis. *God, please let this whole thing be a terrible mistake*, I prayed.

It wasn't until the end of the day when I was picking up wads of paper from the classroom floor and using them to toss free throws at the trashcan that I remembered where I knew the name Breanne Phillips. I froze like a poster of Jordan, flying midair, in the midst of a slam-dunk, and rolled the name around on my tongue for long seconds. It couldn't be. I hoped like hell it wasn't. But it would be just my luck if it was.

Damn.

You can run from the past, but you sure as hell can't hide, I thought as I cruised through the Robinwood Housing Projects. The place looked even worse than it had the last time I passed by, which was just last week. I made a quick right between two multi-story tenements, then made a U-turn in the back parking lot. I drove back the way I came, this time pulling to a stop in front of a vacant building. Back in the day an unchecked kitchen fire had spread from one unit to another until half the building was ruined. It was never repaired, but I knew that it was as occupied as any of the other buildings. I pressed the horn—two quick taps followed by one long one—and waited patiently.

A few minutes later Deeter came stumbling outside wearing the same clothes he always wore—faded and dirty jeans and a thin T-shirt. I pressed a button to lower my window and sucked in as much fresh air as I could before he walked up to my truck. After that it was all over. Deeter probably hadn't taken a bath since I was around ten or eleven, and I was now thirty-six.

"What's up, Dee?" I did the hand shake, fist pump Deeter still liked to do even though it had gone out with platform shoes the first time around. He'd been around for as long as I could remember, probably was as old as the dirt caked on his ass, and he was a reliable source of information. He was one of my best customers back when these projects were my kingdom. I figured if anybody would know what I needed to know, Deeter would. I reached over and picked up a McDonald's bag from the passenger seat and handed it out the window to him. "You been staying out of trouble?" I asked.

As Deeter approached my truck, he rubbed his eyes and yawned expansively. I was supposed to take the hint that I had disturbed his nap, but I ignored it.

"You tell them fools extra special sauce and heavy salt on the fries?" he wanted to know. He opened the bag and shoved a few fries in his mouth.

"Yeah, I told them," I lied. "Have you given any more thought to the shelter I was telling you about, Deet?"

"Hell with a shelter, Smoke. I got all I need right inside that building there. It ain't the Holiday Inn, but it's enough. You got a smoke?"

I reached back over in the passenger seat and handed him a carton of Kools.

"You know those things will kill you, right?" I asked.

He gave me a toothless grin. Crack cocaine had long since rotted his teeth and I couldn't help but grin back. I had sold him more than enough of the shit myself.

"So, what, I quit smoking and then tomorrow I step my pretty ass off the curb and get ran over by a tobacco truck? I don't think so. What the hell you doing here anyway? Today ain't Friday."

Friday was the day I made my weekly stop to check up on Deeter and brought him a Big Mac and fries or whatever else he requested. He wouldn't take money, and I stopped offering it to him because I didn't want to buy drugs or liquor for him. But he did accept the food and the clothes I lied and told him I couldn't use anymore. I was hoping Deeter's name came up when I stood before my maker on Judgment Day, although that wasn't really the reason I did the things I did for him. I did most of it because he was my cousin, and the rest of it I did because he was but one of the people I'd hurt back when I didn't know any better.

"I know it's not Friday, Deet, but I had a situation come up," I said. "What do you think about these?" I handed him a new pair of jeans and watched while he shook them out and held them against him to see if they were long enough.

"They'll do, I guess. What kind of situation? You running from one-time again?" He looked at me hopefully, like he was desperate to be in the thick of some real live action again.

"You know I don't get down like that anymore. I keep trying to tell you that one-time is your friend, everybody's friend. Embrace them," I joked.

"*Sheeiiit*, you embrace them sons-of-bitches. I'm a'ight myself. Bring me some fish next week." I nodded.

"Listen, Deet, you remember a little chick named Breanne Phillips from back in the day?"

"Seems like I do, but it's been a long time, Smoke. Back then everybody was naming they kids shit like Brianna and Tiara and Ciara—all that crazy shit. Then they started in with the cars—Porsche and Mercedes. Now which Brianna you talking 'bout, 'cause it's one on every corner, for real."

"This would've been before I left, when I was still in the game. I'm thinking she was from around here. A customer, Deet." That jogged his memory.

"Oh, you talking 'bout that little dark thang with the uppity mama and sister? Yeah, I think I do remember her. Not real clear, though. Didn't you used to run around with her for a minute?"

I shook my head as I chuckled ruefully.

"I don't think so. I just told you she was a customer. You ever know me to run around with my customers?"

"Naw," Deeter admitted. "Then it must not be the same little gal. Or maybe I'm getting mixed up in my old age. You had a chickenhead running after you every time I looked up. Hell, who could keep up? She still owe you some money or something?"

"I was just wondering, that's all."

"Well they been gone from around here for some years, that uppity woman and her daughters, the ones I'm thinking 'bout. But I think it's still an uncle or two running around here somewhere. You want me to see what I can find out?"

"Nah, I'm cool. I was just wondering. OK, so fish next Friday. Anything else you need?"

"Naw, Smoke, I'm easy. Tell ya mama I said hey, and don't forget about my sweet potato pie, either."

Deeter refused to consider leaving his burned out building in the projects, and I had given up on trying to force him out. I kept him updated on the various rehab programs that were available to him, and left it at that. I watched him until he was out of sight. As I drove home, I was thinking hard enough to give myself a headache.

He was one of the few people I allowed to call me by my nickname—Smoke. The name was part of the life I'd left behind when the police finally caught up to me and hauled my ass off in handcuffs. I was twenty years old then, cocky and full of illusions of joining the ranks of the big-time drug cartel. As it was, I had the Robinwood Projects on lock. I was like a god there, slinging dope from one corner to the next and stacking cash like it was going out of style. Then it all came crashing down when one of my minions messed up and sold some product to an undercover cop. A deal was made, and I was set up.

It was the best thing that ever happened to me.

The impending situation with Breanne Phillips might well be the worst. The more I thought about it, the more I remembered about her, and none of it was particularly pleasant. If I was picturing the right girl, she was a faithful customer, strung out on crack cocaine and certainly not the type of girl I had gone for back then. I never mixed business with pleasure, so I was sure that I hadn't fathered a child with a junky. The girls I had selected for myself never indulged in anything past the luxury of helping me spend the money I made.

I was more convinced than ever that this was all a big mistake. *Breanne Phillips, I am not your baby's daddy*, I thought cryptically.

As soon as I got home I sat down with the papers again. All of the woman's identifying information had been blacked out, otherwise I would've knocked on her door myself and politely asked her what the hell she was trying to do. She obviously knew where I was, so why couldn't I know the same about her? I had the right to cross-examine an adverse witness, didn't I?

Intent on doing just that, I reached for the phone and

punched in a number I knew by rote, although I didn't dial it very often. But desperate times called for desperate measures, and this was definitely a desperate time.

If I had my way, very shortly I would be knocking on Breanne Phillips's door, wherever she was, and asking her what the hell she thought she was doing. What I wanted to know couldn't wait for a court date that was two months away.

I had served twelve years in the United States Marines, and during that time I'd made a good number of lifelong friends. One of them was now a mover and shaker, a high powered attorney based in Houston, Texas by the name of Angelo Pallazolo. I called in a favor, and two days later I had an address and phone number for Breanne Phillips. She was living outside of Chicago, Illinois in a suburb called Hartford. Had been for the last four years. I seriously thought about calling her, but then I had a better idea. I bought a plane ticket to Chicago. Miss Phillips and I were about to have a come-to-Jesus meeting.

Chapter 1

ANNE

Sometimes I wondered why women as a whole fell for the conspiracy of childbirth and motherhood in the first place. After babies stopped smelling good enough to eat, after they learned how to talk and started thinking for themselves, and after their skin turned rough instead of smooth, they stopped being worth the trouble. And no one understood that better than a mother. Before you had children everyone looked askance at you and wondered why you were bucking the natural order of things. What was taking you so long to have a bundle of joy, they wondered? Two weeks, hell, two hours with my son and nobody would ever wonder again. Lately the boy was driving me crazy.

I dumped a basket of clean laundry in the middle of his full-sized bed and looked across the room at him. He was sitting in his recliner, leaned all the way back, with a pair of headphones glued to his ears. I could hear rap music blaring from where I was standing, could even make out the words. Bitch this, whore that. I marched over, flipped off the stereo, and stood over him like the warden I was fast becoming. Whatever happened to the sweet little boy who'd done whatever I asked him to do in a timely fashion?

"Ma, you tripping. I was listening to that," he said, clearly irritated.

"I asked you to fold your laundry and put it away," I reminded him sweetly. "An hour ago."

"And I told you I was gone do it."

"Who are you raising your voice to?"

"I wasn't raising my voice." But he was mumbling as he brought the chair to an upright position and came to his feet. I tipped my head back and looked in his face. He was just over six feet compared to my own five-three, but I was nowhere near intimidated.

I folded my arms under my breasts and shifted my weight to one side.

"Sounded like it to me. What were you doing then?"

"I was just making sure you heard me," he said.

"Well hear this. Get this laundry folded right now, because after that the yard awaits. Don't make me have to come tell you again."

I was walking out of his room when he decided to kick the empty laundry basket with his size thirteen foot and send it flying across the room. I turned around in shock.

"Why do I have to do anything around here?" my son demanded to know. "Folding laundry is women's work. I'm a man."

"You start cooking and cleaning up after yourself and then you can call yourself a man. What's your problem, boy?" I narrowed my eyes and glared at him, waiting for a response.

"I ain't got no problem."

"Oh, yeah, you do, starting with the fact that your grammar is atrocious. Now I'm not going to kiss your ass because you came out of mine, OK? I shouldn't even have to ask you to help out around here, Isaiah. Kick something else and you'll be hanging out at home this weekend while everyone else is out running the streets. Comprende?" I left him mumbling and grumbling and went to fold my own laundry.

When my son was two minutes old I named him Lucifer because pushing him out of me had hurt like hell. Then, after I came to my senses, I decided that he wasn't demonic at all, and changed his name to Isaiah. That one stuck. Now, sixteen years later, I was wondering if Lucifer might've been more appropriate after all. I couldn't put my finger on it, but somewhere between his fourteenth and sixteenth birthdays he had changed. He used to be easygoing and well mannered, and we'd always gotten along like gangbusters. We never had to fight about him doing his chores, and I hardly had to raise my voice. I guess I should've known the good times wouldn't last, but still, I wasn't entirely convinced that his sudden change had everything to do with his becoming a full-fledged teenager. I was certain there was more to the story than him simply smelling himself. I could feel it in the air around him, hear it in his voice when he talked to me. Something important was different.

I thought I knew what at least part of his problem was, although we hadn't discussed it in years. I wanted to discuss my theory with him now, but I was afraid. He pretended that it didn't matter, and for a while I did too. But it did matter, at least to him. For my part, it was old news, part of a past that I'd buried many years ago. I never thought I'd have to resurrect even the minutest detail of my past once I buried it, and I never wanted to.

Around the time Isaiah was three years old, I learned that people do lots of things they don't want to do in the name of love. Parents do all kinds of things they would never have believed themselves capable of doing for their children. I was no different back then, and I wasn't to this day—starting with the trash I collected and took out. It was one of Isaiah's usual chores, but I decided to take pity on him and do it for him. I even went so far as to drag the trashcans to the curb for him, not that he would notice and appreciate it.

As I looked up and down the quiet street I lived on, I waved to a few neighbors and checked my mail. I noticed a black car parked at the curb a few houses down, with tinted windows and out-of-state license plates, but it wasn't out of place enough for me to linger on it. I mostly noticed it because it was one of the new Chrysler luxury models and I was considering trading in my SUV for one just like it. Not black, though, maybe pearl white, something more feminine and suited to my personal style.

I plucked a particularly interesting envelope from the stack and eyed it suspiciously as I walked back up the driveway and into the house.

"Isaiah," I called out as I closed and locked the storm door behind me, "the grass is waiting!"

Oh, yeah, another thing I did for my son in the name of love. I had put the wheels in motion to track down his father. That was something I never thought I would do, but I did it anyway. My son was rapidly changing into someone I didn't recognize, and I was hoping Smoke Avery had grown up enough to help me straighten him out.

I was hoping he would even want to.

When I found out I was pregnant I didn't factor Smoke Avery into the equation. It wasn't like we'd had some big love affair or something. Actually, it was quite the opposite. Smoke was the boy I bought my drugs from. He was the boy I handed my virginity to in exchange for crack cocaine. I had long since forgotten how much crack it was, but I know it was a trifling amount, certainly not worth what I paid for it in the long run. But since when does a crackhead possess superior powers of reasoning?

That was what I used to be—a crackhead. And that was how I happened upon the love of my life—my son, Isaiah Avery Phillips. Smoke wasn't somebody I loved, although I did have a crush on him. He was a means to an end. I wanted to get high, and he was the neighborhood pusher. That he had planted a baby inside of me was my little secret, one I never intended to divulge to him, and the idea wouldn't have crossed my mind a few months ago if my son hadn't suddenly decided that not having a father in his life was cause to start showing his ass.

I thought he was just going through a phase when he brought home that first report card with all the Cs and Ds on it. I chalked it up to his spending too much time concentrating on sports and girls. He played both football and basketball, and he played them well. He was MVP time after time, had all the pretty little cheerleaders running after him, fanning between their legs, and I figured that he was getting a little full of himself. He loved sports and he loved the attention from the girls, and the importance of school was becoming blurry to him.

I sat him down and had *the talk* with him. He was thirteen at the time, and I knew it was a little late in coming, but I gave it to him straight anyway. I told him everything I knew about the birds and the bees, relationship issues, respecting women, and I told him everything I knew about drugs. I confessed to him that I was a reformed crack cocaine addict and I told him that I had started using when I wasn't much older than he was. I told him about how drugs had nearly ruined my life, and about how hard it was to get clean.

Some would say that I shouldn't have told my son all that I did, but I was always honest with him, and I didn't see a need to lie about something so serious and life threatening. Drugs were fighting a war with today's children, and as a casualty of that war, I wanted my son to be prepared to fight for himself as I never was.

In the beginning, I used my lunch money and the extra cash I made babysitting to buy drugs. I was a freshman in high school then, fourteen and completely clueless. It didn't take me long to graduate from scraping up quarters and crumpled dollar bills to snatching purses and stealing to get high. Somehow, some way, I managed to get the money to feed my addiction. A lot of the things I did I couldn't really remember clearly now, but I do remember when the money stopped being so accessible and I started offering Smoke my body in exchange for the magic rocks he had. Before my savior rolled into town and snatched me up by the collar, I had dropped out of school and given up on any hope for a future beyond my addiction. It was a powerful thing, a horrible, horrible thing.

I shared that part of my past with my son, minus all the immoral things I did, so that he would know not to ever think himself infallible or invulnerable to anything, so that his eyes and mind would be open to reality.

I did everything I could to make sure that Isaiah knew the importance of education. I yelled and screamed when his grades went from As and Bs to Cs and Ds. I preached, attended parent-teacher jeopardy conferences, grounded him, took away all the creature comforts I could think of taking, and still nothing. He claimed he didn't care about school or grades, and now he had this wild notion in his head that he was going to be the next big rap star, the next overnight success who lacked a basic high school education and gave credence to the idiocy of Ebonics.

I was ashamed to admit that I gave up for a while. He wore me down with his talking back and sneaking out of the house. I got tired of talking to his teachers and to him. I decided that he wasn't going to cause me to start growing gray hair and developing wrinkles. It was his life, and if he wanted to ignore everything that I had tried to teach him, if he wanted to ruin his life, then so be it. After all, I could only do so much, right?

Then I found weed in his drawer. And Ecstasy pills in his pants pockets while I was sorting laundry. The weed and the pills took me back in time to the days when I was using, and no one seemed to notice. I knew where it could lead, not that it necessarily *would*, but that it *could*, and I knew what I had to do.

I had to save my son.

ISAIAH

I didn't know what the fuck my old lady's problem was. I wished she would get off my back and stop hounding me about school and shit like that. I kept telling her that I had everything under control, but did she listen? *No*. And I kept telling her to stop calling me Isaiah. My friends called me Zay. Isaiah was a punk's name, and I ain't no punk.

I would be if she had her way, though, running around switching like a girl and hanging on to her shirt tail, looking up to her for all the answers to my questions. *Mama, what's this? What's that?* I used to do that shit when I was a kid, like she knew everything about everything.

Then I found out that she wasn't all that smart. Anybody with an ounce of sense, *one freaking ounce of sense*, would've known better than to get strung out on crack. That right there proved that my mama was just about as dumb as a box of rocks. She talked a good game, but she wasn't really no better than anybody else. She couldn't even tell me who my daddy was when I asked her. Just stood there looking all crazy, like she was 'bout to cry. She didn't even know!

There was this crackhead that came around school sometimes. Helen, that was her name. Helen the Ho, me and my boys called her. Everybody knew she came around after school looking for my boy, Hood. He was pushing weight so tough the nigga was riding in a brand new convertible while the principal was pushing a Chevy. One time he let me watch while he made Helen give him brain for a rock, and that shit almost blew my mind!

Almost, I said. Until I thought about my mama, walking up and down the street looking for the dopeman, strung out and needing a fix. Ain't shit funny about having a mama who used to be a crackhead. How many niggas you know got a mama who used to suck a glass dick? And probably real dicks to get to the glass dick? What the fuck? She never told me how she got her drugs, but how else could she have gotten them?

I was kind of young when she explained everything to me, tried to make me understand how hard she worked to get where she was now. And I had to admit, my mama got some bank. She running thangs and shit. But still, ain't too much of shit she could really tell me right about now. My mama and Helen. Helen and my mama. Running around in my head, bumping into each other, one looking like the other. They one and the same, as far as I was concerned. My daddy was probably some nigga just like Hood.

"Isaiah, the grass is waiting!" my mama yelled.

There she go, like the grass gone get up and walk the hell off. I was gone go ahead and cut the grass so she could stop nagging at me, though. 'Cause I didn't want to hear no lip when Hood and the rest of my boys swooped through and picked me up later on. It was on tonight, and I was getting out of the house come hell or high water.

ALEC

I was starting to feel like a real gumshoe, a private investigator of the highest order. I'd been in the Chicago area for two days and, as far as I knew, Breanne Phillips had no idea I was following her. The first day, a Thursday, I sat in my rental, hiding behind blacked out windows, getting my bearings, checking out her spread, and digesting all that there was to see, which wasn't much.

Breanne Phillips had come up in the world. She lived in a two-story ranch style house with trimmed hedges and picture windows along the front, a little under an hour outside of Chicago. A two-car garage and a double-wide driveway completed the picture of wholesome domesticity, as did the shiny black mailbox sitting at the curb with the number six on it. It was a handsome house, half-brick and half cream-colored siding—spacious looking. I wondered if she was married or had a live-in lover to help her use up the space. Or maybe the rest of her family lived in the house with her and her child. I vaguely remembered Breanne's mother and sister. Both, as Deeter had hinted, light-skinned and haughty, even though back then we were all living in what people now called the ghetto. Perhaps they were inside right now, soaking up life outside of the Robinwood Projects, and being one big happy family.

I was considering going to find some food to put in my stomach when the front door opened. Having rented a car at the airport and driven straight to my destination, I was starving and my ass was almost asleep from sitting for so long. I had the key in the ignition, ready to shift into drive, when Breanne stepped out on the small front porch.

I froze and stared.

Black Breanne, hair so thick, hair so wild, looks like a Zulu child. I remembered the childhood chant the kids had tortured her with, myself included, when we were in grade school and junior high. She was dark skinned, like a Hershey bar, with thick, coarse hair that was always in disarray, either from neglect or from the many fights she was always in the middle of. She hadn't faired well, I recalled. Always crying because the other girls talked about her clothes and shoes, her dark skin and nappy hair.

By the time she came to the high school I was already making a name for myself in the drug game, and I barely noticed her, aside from noticing her little onion shaped butt. She was dark and we tended to favor the high yella chicks with long hair back then, and she was still the butt of many cruel jokes about her clothes and her hair.

Sometime around the middle of her freshman year and my junior year I started noticing her more, but for all the wrong reasons. She became a customer, one of the many addicts I sold crack cocaine to. A few times she bought other things, sampling and experimenting, but eventually she settled on crack as her drug of choice, and I was just money hungry enough to oblige her.

I had plenty of ego, too. When she didn't have the money for the product she wanted, I put her on her back and spread her legs, made her work it off. I think I did that because I could, and because power was a heady, dangerous thing. Desire never entered into the equation. She wasn't someone to be desired, with her tangly hair and dry skin. She was nothing to me, no one. I couldn't even lie and say that I had thought about her over the years and wondered what had ever become of her. I suppose I'd relegated her to the part of my mind that wanted to bury the past and deny that it had ever happened. I forgot all about Breanne Phillips until I was served with a petition for child support.

Until I saw her again.

Shame came first. Heavy, stifling shame, because of what

I'd done to her, of how I'd treated her. Then anger came, because of what she was trying to do to me. I stewed in it for a minute and felt it float away even though I tried to hold it to me like a vice. But shock and reluctant surprise edged the anger out of the way and overtook me. I'd seen a lot of things in my life, and done just as much, but the instant she stepped out on the porch and made her way down the driveway, I realized that I could still be caught off guard.

She rolled two trashcans to the curb, then collected her mail from the box. She stood still for a moment, flipping through a stack of envelopes, and I took complete stock of the enemy. The first thing I noticed was that she had locked her hair. It brushed her shoulders in a riot of thin, twisted, licorice looking strands. They were pushed back from her forehead with a wide headband, giving me a clear view of her face. She looked toward where I sat in the car hiding and I gasped.

Toward the end, before she stopped coming around, she was thin and emaciated, sunken looking. But she was none of that now. Her face was heart shaped and clear. She had the direct look of someone who knows herself, and because of that fact, can read the next person like a book. Her eyes were still large and overpowering, but now they were bright and focused, intelligent looking. They were still too big for her face, I thought. At least that hadn't changed.

She couldn't have known that she was staring directly into my face as she pursed her lips and admired my rental car. Expertly arched brows met in the middle of her forehead for the slightest of seconds, and I wondered what she was thinking just then. I knew what I was thinking. *She isn't wearing a bra.* Her breasts could barely be considered decent handfuls, but they were seriously saluting me through the white T-shirt she wore, and I couldn't be mad at them. The little onion ass I remembered was hidden inside snug fitting faded jeans.

Everything else was new. The poise with which she walked was new. The lean healthiness of her body was new. She wasn't stooped over, appearing humble and defeated, the way I was used to seeing her, the way I had expected to see her now. She all but pranced back up the driveway in her high-heel sandals and disappeared into the house, calling out to someone. I waited for my first glimpse of her husband or lover.

I didn't know why I wasn't expecting the child to emerge from the house, but I wasn't. It seemed too simple, too easy. Too storybook. I thought I would have to work to catch a glimpse of the child she was trying to pin on me, maybe barge up to the door and demand to see him or her, cause a scene of some kind.

I was saved from that kind of drama, though. Apparently he was being made to mow the lawn, and I had a front row seat for the performance. I watched him drag the lawnmower from the depths of the garage, his lips moving the entire time, probably cursing. I lifted unsteady hands from the steering wheel and extended them in front of me as I darted back and forth between looking at his bare arms and my own. We were the exact same shade of caramel brown, which meant exactly nothing. Plenty of brothas were caramel brown. Plenty were tall too, and I told myself that these coincidences were strictly circumstantial.

Plenty of brothas didn't have thick eyebrows that spread across their foreheads like eagle's wings, though. They didn't have light brown eyes that caught the sun and turned gray. Most might not have a birthmark that sat just to the left of their noses like a period, and many would not have a slightly squared cleft chin. All those things I had.

The youngblood busy yanking on the lawnmower cord

and mumbling under his breath had all those things, too. Along with ears that stuck out from the sides of his head and a slight gap between his front teeth. I knew this because once the lawnmower growled to life, I started the car and inched along the curb until I was just about in front of him. I leaned across the passenger seat to stare at him at the exact moment something across the street caught his attention. He looked up and smiled.

I shot off down the street like a race car driver. I caught him watching the car through the rearview mirror, and didn't give a shit. That little motherfucker had my mother's eyes, her nose, and her mouth. He had my father's ears, his long legs, big feet, and his birthmark. He had my face, the one I rightfully owned and one he had no business having. I hadn't given him permission to share it with me, and I hadn't given Breanne Phillips permission to take it from me to give to him.

I found a dingy restaurant not too far from Breanne's subdivision and decided it would have to do. Not only was I starving, but I didn't think I could drive any farther. My head was messed up and I didn't want to risk the chance of crashing into another car and killing someone. I was angrier than I'd ever been in my life. In thirty-six years I couldn't remember ever feeling the way I felt right at that moment. Not even when the police were slapping handcuffs on me and hauling my ass to jail. Not even when the judge decided that he would be doing me a favor by giving me the choice that wasn't really a choice—serve your country in prison or in the military. That wasn't a fucking choice. And neither was some woman having a child and, sixteen years later, demanding that you pay her money for the privilege.

I barely tasted the sandwich and iced tea the waitress slid in front of me, but somehow I managed to eat. I snatched my cell phone from my pocket and called the airline to arrange for a seat on the next flight home. I dropped the phone on the tabletop and watched it bounce around like a jumping bean. It was on vibrate and I had an incoming call. I looked at the caller-ID and cursed. I was massaging the bridge of my nose as I pressed a button to reject the call and send it to my voicemail. The last thing I needed was to have to deal with another female, even if that female was the woman I had been seeing steadily for the past six months. I wasn't in the mood to answer questions or offer platitudes. I could've killed someone with my bare hands, but I couldn't have had a civil conversation just then, so I decided to avert disaster and let her leave a message.

I sat in a booth in the restaurant for another hour, then drove off the lot headed for the airport. Twenty minutes later I was parked down the street from Breanne Phillips's house again.

She was behind the wheel of a burgundy Lexus SUV when it cruised down the driveway after ten o'clock that night. It streaked past me and disappeared around a corner, well above the speed limit. I debated following her, but a few minutes later, something more interesting caught my attention. Or rather, *someone* more interesting.

A car full of shady looking young hooligans swerved around the corner from the opposite direction and screeched to a halt in front of Breanne's house. The music was blasting, bass thumping, and heads were bobbing in time to the beat. He tipped out of the garage, trotted down the driveway, and hopped in the backseat. My car shook from the intensity of the music as they passed.

In a daze, I wondered if he'd thought to lock the door behind him. I wondered why, if he was sneaking out, he hadn't closed the garage door behind him and put things back like he found them, so as not to arouse undue suspicion. I wondered who the clowns were he was rolling with, where they were going, and when he'd be back.

Then I wondered what the hell kind of mother Breanne Phillips was if she was leaving the house after ten at night and leaving her son unattended to run wild.

Except for a quick trip to a gas station around the corner and down the street, I didn't move from my surveillance spot for the next several hours. I was still sitting in the car, sipping from a twenty-ounce bottle of soda when she came home at close to midnight. I watched her unload ten bags of groceries from the back of her SUV and cart them into the house. I imagined that she called out to him for some assistance, and finding him gone, the shit would hit the fan any minute. I expected her to come running from the house, distressed and obviously upset, and I timed her.

The lights came on inside. I knew she walked from room to room switching them on, because I followed the progression with which they came on. First the living room and another downstairs room. Then all the windows on the second level, across the front of the house, one at a time. She was searching each room, probably hoping that he was in there somewhere. I could've told her he was long gone, but she didn't ask me. All she wanted from me was money, so I stayed in the car and kept my mouth shut.

He rolled up sometime after two in the morning. This time there was no music to announce his arrival and the driver of the sporty little Mustang convertible he was riding shotgun in had had the foresight to turn off the headlights. I watched him creep up to the door on unsteady feet and shook my head. High as a kite, or drunk as hell—one of the two, I guessed. I grunted and sat back in my seat, chewed on my thumbnail absently while he took forever to unlock the door and stumble inside the dark house.

I caught myself laughing when a light suddenly switched on inside the house and the sound of a blaring alarm system reached my ears. She had set a trap for him. And he was busted.

Lack of forethought and planning were definitely not traits he'd inherited from me.

By Friday afternoon I knew a little more about the enemy. She jogged early in the morning, in short shorts and a clingy tank top, and still no bra. And she didn't mind breaking a sweat. She left for work at seven-thirty, dressed in a tailored pantsuit, carting a bottle of the liquid yogurt breakfast drink women seemed to be crazy about, and shooting off rapid-fire instructions to the boy. He looked no worse for wear after last night's debacle, even had on pressed khakis, a short sleeved polo shirt, and rugged soled leather shoes. She dropped him off at school and then put the pedal to the metal all the way down the freeway.

I cruised by the single level building Breanne disappeared into, wondering what the hell she did at the Olive Branch Wellness Center, but I didn't park and get out to see for myself. Plenty of time for that later, when I was certain I wouldn't slay her on the spot. I was content, for the time being, just knowing where she lived and where she worked, that I could find her again when I needed to.

A little after three I cruised by the school. I just wanted to see the place without all the distractions from that morning—moving traffic and gangs of kids all over the place. I was mildly surprised to see that it was a Lutheran school, affiliated with a family of schools that were frequently noted for academic excellence. The tuition wasn't cheap, and I wondered again if that was why Breanne suddenly needed monetary assistance.

I parked around the back of the building and watched a group of boys shoot hoops like they were in the NBA. It took me several minutes of gawking at the speed and skill of the boys to realize that one of them was Breanne's son.

When he slam dunked, I grinned. When he moved in for a lay-up, I hissed appreciatively. When he fouled another player, I shook my head. I got so caught up in watching them that you couldn't have told me I wasn't watching the pros play. The boy was good, powerful and quick, even if he was a little bit of a show off. I had been at that age, too.

Four or five of them piled their sweaty asses into the Mustang from last night and drove off in a haze of loud music. But not before I noticed that the boy did a double take when he noticed my rental sitting at the curb not far away.

"Yeah, I'm watching you, youngblood," I said to myself. I dug my cell phone from my pocket and glanced at my watch. It was twenty after six and I figured Breanne would be home from work or wherever she'd gone that morning. He did another double take just before he lifted a forty-ounce bottle to his mouth and took a long swig. I noticed that, too.

It was time to contact the enemy and find out exactly what the hell was going on. I punched in Breanne's home number and waited for her to pick up.

Chapter 2

ANNE

Just last night I'd told Isaiah that he was grounded for two weeks. Straight home from school every day and no television or phone privileges. So why did I come home from work and he was nowhere to be found? He had my cell phone and I called it, and immediately got the voice-mail, which meant that either the phone was turned off, or he had rejected my call because he knew his behind was supposed to be in the house. I looked at the kitchen trash, then at the sink. The trash hadn't been taken out, and the dishes hadn't been washed. Again. A quick trip upstairs confirmed that his room looked like a tornado had whipped through it, and he'd left a pair of his funky drawers in the middle of the floor.

I sat at the kitchen table nursing a glass of lemonade and wondering what the hell I was going to do about my son. He was spinning out of control and I was getting more and more tired of dealing with his crap. The scene from last night had nearly moved me to violence as it was. He clearly had no earthly idea who he was messing with, and I had almost shown him before I caught myself.

He came stumbling into my house in the middle of the night, smelling like a brewery and looking even worse. Pupils dilated to the point that the whites of his eyes were barely visible and marijuana smoke thick in his clothes. I wanted to slap him and hurt him the way he was hurting me, but I hadn't done that. I had simply informed him that he was grounded, laid out the rules for his grounding, and took myself to bed. What else could I do?

I thought he'd gotten the message last night that I meant business, but after two hours passed tonight, and he still wasn't home, I conceded the fact that he simply didn't give a shit. I tried the cell again. Still no answer. Then I got up and took a package of chicken breasts out of the freezer. I put them in the microwave to thaw, and snatched the phone up when it rang.

"Isaiah?" I barked. Whoever was on the other end said nothing for several seconds, which further convinced me that it was my son. I started in. "You're supposed to be home doing your chores, boy. Where the hell are you?" I took a breath as alternate possibilities floated through my mind. "Are you all right?"

"This isn't Isaiah," the caller said. It was a man, but damned if I could catch his voice. Not many men called me, and if this was one of the select few, I would've recognized the voice instantly. I didn't recognize this one.

"Then who is this? Has something happened to my son?"

"Your son is fine, unless you factor in the forty ounce I just saw him pulling from. This is Smoke, Breanne."

"Smoke?" My voice went high and strange sounding. *Smoke?*

"Smoke," he said definitively. "I got your little greeting card and I thought we should talk."

"Oh . . . well, now isn't a good time," I stalled. "I'm waiting for my son to come home, and then I have to kill him. He was supposed to come straight home after school but—"

"But he hung out at school, shooting hoops and guzzling beer straight from the bottle. No class, your boy. I'm coming over."

"Smoke, listen . . ."

"I'll be happy to once you open the door and let me in."

"What?"

"I'm pulling into your driveway now. Daddy's home. Open the door, Breanne."

He hung up on me and I raced to the living room and pushed the drapes back to look outside. I recognized the car instantly, the one from the other day, the one I had admired without realizing that it belonged to him. The man had been sitting in front of my house, staking me out like I was a common criminal.

I was insulted and it showed on my face as I marched to the door and swung it open. We stood on opposite sides of the storm door staring at each other before I finally turned the brass knob and let him into my home. This was my sanctuary, and Smoke Avery was about to violate it.

"I can't believe you've been sitting outside my house stalking me." I backed away from the door one step at a time. Smoke stepped into my house and sucked up all the free space around him. I looked in his face for the first time in almost seventeen years.

"I can't believe you had me served with child support papers." The look in his eyes told me that he wasn't quite as calm as his voice suggested, and I took another step backward. "I haven't seen you in I don't know how long, and suddenly you want me to be your baby's daddy?"

"It's not what you think. I didn't want any of this, Smoke."

"And stop calling me Smoke," he snapped irritably. The next thing I knew he was brushing past me and walking through the living room toward the kitchen. Walking through my house like he had every right to do so. I closed the door and hurried to catch up with him.

"You identified yourself as Smoke when you called," I reminded him as I came into the kitchen behind him. I busied myself with taking the chicken from the microwave and setting it in the sink.

"Momentary lapse of memory. Smoke is dead, Breanne."

"So is Breanne. I never liked that country ass name anyway. I go by Anne now, so please call me that from now on."

"Fine, *Anne*." He rolled the name around on his tongue, took a seat at the kitchen table and watched me intently. "How did this happen, *Anne*?"

"You mean how did you end up with a child by a crackhead?"

"We haven't established that your son is mine."

"Yet," I snapped. "You don't think I know who my son's father is, Smoke? You think I was so cracked out that I didn't know who I was fucking?" He had the grace to wince.

"You have to factor in room for error here, and under the circumstances the boy could easily be another man's son. You were—"

I'd heard enough. I whirled around to face him.

"I know what I was, and I know what I am now. I also know what you were, so don't try to run that holier than thou shit on me, OK?" I picked up a hand towel and wiped chicken slime from my hands, thought about my next words carefully. I'd tracked Smoke down because I needed help with my son, not because I needed another negative influence to expose him to. "I'll tell you what. Why don't you leave now and first thing in the morning I'll contact my attorney and call the whole thing off? Accept my apologies for the inconvenience, and we'll pretend that this never happened. I'll even reimburse you for your travel expenses. Does that sound all right to you?" He didn't respond, and I took that as a yes. "Let me get my purse."

I left the kitchen and returned a few minutes later, short of breath from jogging up the stairs in a hurry and digging through my purse furiously for my checkbook. I slapped it on the table and flipped through the carbons for a blank check, pen poised.

"What do you think, four hundred?" I looked him in his eyes.

"Woman, what the hell are you doing?"

"Oh, I'm a woman now? Just a minute ago you were doing your damnedest to take that distinction away from me. Wait, I think maybe five hundred since you rented that pretty little car and all. It couldn't have been cheap."

"Would you hold up a minute?" He reached across the table and dropped a hand on top of mine, then plucked the pen from between my fingers. "You always did have a bad attitude."

"Keep telling me what I always was, and it'll get worse. I don't take shit in my own house, Smoke. From anybody."

"Seems to me you're taking plenty of it from your son," he drawled.

"Excuse me?"

"Didn't you say he was supposed to be home doing chores? Where is he now, or do you even know?"

"I think I have a pretty good idea."

"The same idea you had last night?"

I blew out a breath and held out my hand.

"Give me back my pen. I need to write this check so you can get the hell out of here."

"I need some answers before I take your check and get the hell out of here."

"I don't owe you any explanations."

"You don't?" Smoke stood and came around the table toward me. "You served me with papers *at my job*, claiming that I owe you child support for a kid I never knew existed. I took time off work to come here from Indiana to see you, not to mention sitting in a car for damn near two days, and you don't owe me any explanations? Girl, I think you better think again."

He came so close I had to tip my head back to hold his stare.

"I'm not afraid of you," I said.

"You should be."

We both started when the door opened and Isaiah came strolling into the house like it was any other day and he wasn't grounded. I elbowed Smoke in the stomach, trying to signal him to step back, but he ignored me. He was still hovering over me when Isaiah walked into the kitchen, looking from me to Smoke slowly.

"That's your car in the driveway?" he asked Smoke.

I actually heard Smoke swallow before he spoke.

"It's a rental. You like it?"

"It's kinda sweet. Let me ask you this, though, why you been following me? I saw you at the school today."

I shifted and looked at Smoke. His eyes flickered away from Isaiah's face long enough to lock with mine. We stared each other down.

"You've been following my son?"

"Yeah, I wanted to see what all the fuss was about." He turned his attention back to Isaiah. "How long you been drinking?"

"What?" Isaiah was incredulous. "Who is this dude, Ma?"

I looked at my son and then at his father, convinced I was seeing double. They were nearly the same height, had the same coloring and the same face. One had a little more life stamped on his face than the other, but I could easily see what my son would look like in ten or fifteen years. Easily.

Smoke Avery hadn't changed very much in the years since I last saw him. The boyish roundness in his face was gone, replaced by lean jaws and a sculpted jaw line. His brows spread across his forehead like a bird in flight, and underneath them, his wide eyes still went from hazel to smoke in mere seconds. My son's did too, when he was working up to a temper. He'd given my son his lips, too. They were full and the top lip was perpetually ashy so that it was necessary for him to touch the tip of his tongue to it periodically, to moisturize it. Isaiah kept ChapStick for such occasions and he was always rubbing his lips together to smooth it out. They were nearly carbon copies of each other, right down to the gap between their front teeth and the curved pinkie finger on both of their left hands.

It was almost too much to absorb. I waved Isaiah's question away nervously and pointed a finger at him.

"I thought we agreed that you were grounded? Where have you been?"

Isaiah flailed his arms dramatically and had the nerve to go bug-eyed on me, and in front of company no less.

"We didn't agree on nothing, Ma. As usual, *you* did all the talking and *I* was barely listening. I must'a forgot about being grounded. Anyway, I was out playing ball with Hood and them."

He turned to leave the kitchen, but Smoke's words stopped him cold.

"So you were out playing ball, drinking beer, *and* smoking weed?"

"Smoke, please," I begged just as Isaiah turned back around and came forward aggressively.

"Is that this cat's name? Smoke? Well, *Smoke*, why don't

you get to stepping? Who is this dude, Ma, and why you got him all up in my business?"

"Let's start with the fact that *dude* isn't my name, and then let's move on to the fact that you don't *have* any business. Then let's get around to me telling you that I think I might decide to get all up in your business in a real way, very, very soon, son. You ain't seen nothing like me up in your business yet, believe me. Apologize to your mother for the way you just talked to her."

"Smoke . . ."

"Man, kiss my ass. This is my house, you just a guest, and an uninvited one at that. Like I said, *step*."

Smoke tried to nudge me to the side, but I stood firm.

"Let me step around you for a minute, Anne. I just need to . . ."

He stepped around me and I stepped right with him, blocking his path.

"Enough," I bit out through clenched teeth. I flattened a hand against Smoke's chest and glared at my son. "Isaiah, this is my house, and in my house we don't disrespect guests. Nor do you disrespect me. I think I told you that before. You just added two more weeks to your punishment, so congratulate yourself for your industriousness and go to your room." He stood there ignoring me and staring at Smoke. "*Now*."

"Your son is getting out of control, Anne," Smoke told me after Isaiah had stomped up the stairs and slammed the door to his room loud enough for us to hear in the kitchen.

I ran shaky hands through my locks and met his eyes.

"*Your* son is getting out of control, Smoke. He's smoking weed, and I think popping pills. What are those things called, the ones that have you hugging everybody and trying to stick your tongue down everybody's throat?"

"Ecstasy," he supplied with a grin.

"Right. Those things." I paced in front of him. "I found them in his pocket. He's sneaking out and ignoring curfews, which you know already, and I'm seriously thinking about strangling him in his sleep. You heard for yourself how he talks to me and his grades are bad now. I'm about to lose it. I actually thought about having a glass of wine with lunch this afternoon, if that tells you anything."

"What's wrong with that?" He regarded me curiously.

"I don't put any controlled substances in my body. Haven't for over sixteen years, and I refuse to let him drive me to it now."

"Not even a beer every now and again?"

"Nothing. Ever again."

"Well maybe you need to get a bottle of beer, pour it out, and use the bottle to smack youngblood upside the head once or twice."

I stopped pacing and shot him a look. He was dead serious.

"Could you see me wrestling with that fool? And when he's drunk and high, too? It would be a blood bath."

"Whose blood?"

"Smoke, this is not the time for corny ass jokes, OK?" But I thought about it for a second. "His, definitely. I've fought much stronger shit than his little narrow behind, that's for sure. I think I could take him."

"Right. Why now, Anne? Why wait sixteen years to tell me I have a son?" He propped his hands on his hips and stared down at me.

"Because you were never supposed to know, Smoke. All these years he's been *my* son. The way I see it, it was a fair trade. I traded you sex for drugs, and that was the end of it. I wasn't supposed to get pregnant, but I did. That was my situation to deal with, and I've been doing just fine. Until . . ." I lifted a hand and gestured toward the empty doorway wearily. I smoothed a hand over my head and looked at Smoke over my shoulder. "He was an easy child, he really was. Always smiling and laughing, laid back and easy to get along with. Did you know that he's been on the honor roll every school year until the last couple of years? He was never a problem, and he was such a sweet boy. Now I don't know who the hell he is half the time."

"Imagine how I feel," Smoke said. "I don't know who he is at all."

"You're right," I said. "I should've thought this through more before I started looking for you. I had no right to barge into your life and try to force your hand. I'm sorry." I went back to the table, picked up the pen he'd dropped there, and started filling out the check. "I'll give you this and let you get on with your life." He leaned against the counter and watched me.

"Do you actually think I can just turn around and walk out after finding out I have a son, Anne?"

"Why shouldn't you be able to?" I was genuinely surprised by the question and it showed on my face. "He's *my* son and *my* problem. I didn't even ask, do you have other children? A wife?" It was just occurring to me the spot I'd put him in with my petition for child support.

"No and no," he said, "but if I did this would've caused some serious problems."

"Serious as hell." I tore off the check and handed it to him. "I said I was sorry."

"What about the child support? I mean, I'm sure we can come up with a fair amount and I could—"

"I don't need your money, Smoke. That wasn't what this was about."

"What was it about then?"

"It was about the weed and the Ecstasy and the liquor. I guess it was about me, too."

"Come again?" He studied the check carefully, nodded,

and slipped it in his pocket. I watched five hundred dollars of my hard earned money disappear.

"You reminded me earlier of what I used to be. My son knows what I used to be, too," I said.

"You told him?"

"I have no secrets from Isaiah." I flushed when his eyebrows rose. "Except for you, of course, but other than that, none. He knows that I was addicted to crack, and he knows how hard I struggled to build the life I have. I can't understand why he's choosing to follow that path, knowing what I've told him, and it scares the shit out of me. If anybody knows about drugs and how one drug can lead to using another one, it's you and me. Especially me, and I don't want that kind of life for my son."

"So you thought hitting me with child support would help the situation?"

"No, I thought that if I hit you with child support you'd demand visitation rights and start spending time with Isaiah. I was hoping that I wasn't the only one who had changed for the better, and that maybe you could help me put him back on the right track."

ISAIAH

They thought I went to my room, but I didn't. I slammed the door and came to sit on the step to listen to what they were saying. And I was getting madder and madder with every minute that passed. I was more convinced than ever that my mama was a trick.

My daddy? *That nigga down there was my daddy?* What the hell? He just shows up out of the blue, trying to put the smack down on a brotha, like he running thangs and shit. And she just stood there, looking all crazy, saying nothing when she should'a been telling that buster to step, right along with me. Who did he think he was anyway, with his crazy ass name? *Smoke*. What the fuck kind of name was *Smoke*?

I didn't care what his damn name was, he ain't no daddy of mine. If he tried to step to me again I would show his ass that too. Why niggas always wanna show up out of the blue, when they kids damn near grown, trying to whip some ass? That cat got me messed up, got some serious shit twisted. He ain't never did shit for me. Nothing. My mama been taking care of me all these years, and she could keep right on doing it. Period. End of discussion.

I listened long enough to verify one crucial fact. My mama was a crack whore and my supposed daddy was a crack pimp. She paid for a rock with some ass and got me by that motherfucker. The more I thought about it, the madder I got until it seemed like smoke was coming out of my ears. Everybody else's mama was respectable and clean. Why did I have to get stuck with a crackhead for a mama? She always clowned me about smoking a little weed, but hitting a joint wasn't shit like smoking crack. Any day of the week that shit wasn't nothing alike. And she wouldn't be so uptight about drinking if she wasn't a damn junkie. Who the hell didn't drink a damn beer every now and again? A junkie didn't because they didn't have no damn control, that's who.

This shit was just too much. She was down there begging that nigga to be a daddy to me, like I really needed his sorry, absentee ass. And then again, she wouldn't have to be begging if she would'a told him about me in the first place. I could'a already had a daddy if it wasn't for her. Everything always came back to her and her bullshit.

I was down the steps and in the kitchen before I knew what I was doing. I could tell they wasn't expecting me to come back down by the crazy surprised expressions on their faces. My mama looked like she was 'bout to cry, but

I didn't care. I was 'bout to cry too. But I wasn't sad. I was mad as a motherfucker.

"Look, dude, don't pay no attention to my mama, a'ight? She think I need you, but I don't, OK?" I stared at the nigga, standing there looking like me and shit. I peeped that out. If he wasn't my daddy, he was some damn body, my cousin or some shit. "So you can leave, a'ight? It's too fucking late for all that daddy shit now, and I don't want y'ass even if it wasn't. You feel me?"

"Isaiah!" my mama shouted. She had the nerve to let a few tears fall. I flapped a hand at her.

"It's cool, Ma. I see how this shit went down. You was buying crack and bought me too, right? It's cool. You should gone ahead and add a few more dollars to that check you gave his sorry ass and see if he got a few rocks in his pocket. Then you wouldn't need to be thinking about drinking and shit because of me."

I wasn't through saying what I wanted to say, but that was all I got a chance to say.

ALEC

Before I knew what I was doing, I had the boy by his neck, pressed against the wall, damn near choking his scrawny ass. He was almost as tall as I was, but nowhere near as strong. I heard him choking, but the sound didn't penetrate the wall of black that suddenly dropped over my eyes. I couldn't believe the shit coming out of his mouth. If I had ever dreamed of talking to my mother like he'd just talked to Anne, I would've still been looking for my teeth, all these years later. I thought about knocking out a few of his, just on GP.

He was grasping at my arm, trying to pull my fingers

from around his neck, and I hardly felt him touching me. I locked eyes with him. Hard.

"Check it, youngblood," I growled. "You might not want me, but you're stuck with me anyway. And don't think that I'm checking the shit out of you just because I'm your *sorry ass* daddy. The fact is, any man with a dick in his pants would be on your head whether he was your daddy or not. You don't talk to women the way you were just talking to your mother. It's not nice, and it's not very manly of you, either. I don't want to ever hear it again. Understand?"

He nodded stiffly, eyes bugged out. I took pity on him and loosened my grip. Slightly.

"You got something to say to your mother?" I asked. He nodded again and I let him go, stepped back expectantly.

"Yeah, I got something to say," my son croaked. I tilted my head to the side, waiting. "Crack kills," he said and ran out of the kitchen.

I dropped my head and massaged the bridge of my nose. Then I looked at Anne. She was sitting at the table, staring at me through shocked eyes.

"I could go after him and pop him in the mouth," I offered.

"You already half killed him. I think that's enough excitement for one night."

"I didn't see you doing anything," I snapped. I just knew she wasn't getting ready to make all this shit my fault.

"What could I do, Smoke? This is what I was talking about. Where is all this coming from?"

"You could try standing up for yourself every once in a while. That might help."

"I'm tired," she said, and looking at her I could see that she was. "I'm too tired to stand up for myself. All I want to do now is go somewhere and sit down."

"He said some hurtful things." I pushed my hands in my pockets and rocked back on my heels, searching her face.

"He's said worse, and I've heard worse. The words themselves stopped hurting me a long time ago. The fact that he feels whatever he's feeling strongly enough to say them is the thing that gets me every time. That and the fact that he feels that it's OK to say them to my face. You want something to eat or drink? You said you've been in your car for two days."

I shook my head and moved closer.

"I got a hotel room a few hours ago, and food before that. Ask me how I knew I needed to come here with a full stomach."

She cracked a smile and dropped her head in her hand. Her nails were nicely manicured, oval shaped, and painted a soft shade of pink.

"You can still walk away, you know. In fact, I wouldn't blame you if you did."

I thought about the boy. My son. With my mother's mouth and my ears, my father's height and big feet. My forehead and eyes, my gap between his front teeth. He was me fifteen years ago. Another me and then again he was another chance to do something right. I knew him even if he didn't think I did. I knew the little punk swigging beer and smoking weed, running with the wrong crowd and thinking it was cool. It was how I'd started slinging dope like there was no tomorrow. One step led to another and to another until, before I knew it, I was no longer Alec but Smoke. *Smoke the Dopeman.*

I felt something bloom in the center of my chest, where I used to have a heart. Then I chuckled despite myself.

"Who would've ever thought that the two of us would be parents, let alone parents of the same child? I'm still a little pissed about that, by the way."

"Come on, then, I'll walk you to the door," Anne told me

as she got to her feet. I planted my hands on her shoulders, and pushed her back down in the chair. "Smoke . . ."

"Nah, I think I'll stick around for a while. I've changed a lot over the years, Anne, but I never did like to be openly challenged. Youngblood just challenged the hell out of me, and you know I can't walk away from that."

"Smoke . . ."

"I thought I told you to stop calling me Smoke?" She ignored my question.

"I don't want this to get any uglier than it already has."

"It's probably a little late for that. It was on when he called me *dude* for the third or fourth time. You and me, though, we need to talk."

Chapter 3

ALEC

I offered to pick up Anne and take her to lunch on Saturday, but she had other ideas. Instead of sitting down to a nice meal and having a civilized conversation, I found myself following her around the Olive Branch like I was her administrative assistant. Every half-hour or so she seemed to remember that I was there, and promised to feed me soon. I had arrived promptly at noon, and by two o'clock, I stopped believing her. I let myself be put to work moving boxes from the entryway into a large storage room at the rear of the building while she disappeared into an office to speak with a thin white man with two strands of hair on his head.

A little after three, Anne came to find me. I was in the employee lunchroom eagerly sharing a sandwich with an attractive woman named Vonetta. I was working my way around to answering *the question*, the one most single women eventually asked men they were eyeing: *Why aren't you married?* when she stuck her head in the door and motioned for me to follow her with a simple lift of her eyebrows. I thanked Vonetta—call me Von—and brought the last few bites of my sandwich with me.

"I thought you were supposed to be moving boxes?" she asked as soon as we were alone. She tossed the question over her shoulder casually as she led the way to yet another office. I watched her hips sway from side to side inside the short skirt she was wearing and chewed thoughtfully.

"I did move the boxes. I thought we were supposed to be eating?" I leaned against the doorjamb and watched her sprint around the office, shutting down the computer, looking for her purse and changing shoes. She kicked black flats off her feet and slipped them into a pair of tan high-heels that matched her skirt and blazer.

"We will, as soon as I get my hands on a file I'm looking for." She sent me a distracted glance as she began digging through a stack of files on the desktop. "Smoke, would you look over on the coffee table and see if you see a file labeled TAXES?"

I looked around the office slowly, really seeing it for the first time. It was more long than wide, with a wooden desk and leather chair at one end, and comfortable looking furniture grouped at the other. Midway between the two extremes was a round table with five chairs pushed up to it and a bowl of candy in the center. Blinds were at the windows and inspirational posters in black frames adorned the walls. Platitudes like HAVE COURAGE and START YOUR JOURNEY jumped out at me as I made my way farther into the office and headed toward the coffee table in question. I switched on a floor lamp and started digging through the files there.

"What am I looking for exactly? I mean, besides a Big Mac?"

She didn't think I saw her roll her eyes, but I did.

"It's a manila folder with a little sticker on it that says TAXES. Do you think you can handle that?" she droned. I thought it must be the voice she used with Isaiah when he was playing dumb. I found the folder in five seconds flat and took it over to her. She snatched it gratefully and blew out a relieved breath.

"What kind of place is this anyway that you have to work all day on a Saturday?"

"It's a wellness center, mainly centered around women's issues, but we do have a few male clients."

"Oh, you mean like yoga and Pilates classes?"

"No, I mean like drug education classes and counseling," she informed me, all business. "We also have support groups for victims of sexual assault and for persons with disabilities, both adults and teens. Mondays, Wednesdays, and Fridays, we have a community health nurse come in to speak to teens about taking care of themselves, nutrition, and hygiene and stuff, and on Tuesdays and Thursdays we have jazzercise classes. I'm thinking about adding another AA meeting on Friday evenings if I can talk someone into agreeing to work that evening."

"Ah." I stuck my hands in my pockets and looked around the office again, paying more attention this time. "So the boss is at home relaxing while all the little people bust their asses making it happen, huh?"

"Do I look like I'm at home relaxing to you?" She scanned the contents of the file quickly and snapped it closed, glancing at me in the process. "Chinese or Italian?"

"I'm thinking Italian," I said.

"Good, 'cause that's what I was thinking. I was hoping you wouldn't say Chinese. Give me five minutes and I'll be ready to roll." She held up one slender finger and skipped out of the office.

I stood there, processing what she'd said while I waited

for her to come back. After a few minutes, I got antsy and began scanning the titles on the bookshelves adjacent to her desk. All social work stuff, and I yawned on GP. I moved on down the wall and came to a grouping of framed photos. Several of them instantly caught my attention and I lingered, staring at one for long seconds before shifting to look at the next one. Portraits of Isaiah in various stages of growth showed me myself all over again. I grinned despite the twisting sensation in my gut and shook my head. He really was the spitting image of me. That he could be so eerily like me floored me all over again. I picked up an eight by ten of my son flanked by two women at his kindergarten graduation. He wore a crisp black robe and a tilted hat with a white tassel dangling to one side, and he looked like he was ready to conquer the world, missing teeth and all. Anne stood to the right of him, looking fierce in a fitted black dress that stopped just short of her knees, and strappy black heels. I didn't have any trouble determining that she wasn't wearing a bra. *What is it with her and the bras?* The woman on my son's left was older, matronly looking, and beaming with pride. The color of her skin told me she wasn't Anne's mother, and I wondered who she was.

I put the picture back where it was and studied a few more, ones of Anne alone or with women friends, laughing and having a good time, one of her shooting hoops with Isaiah, and one of her in a bright red cap and gown, holding some sort of certificate in front of her like a badge of honor. I thought the smile on her face in that particular picture sparkled just a bit brighter than in any of the others.

I left the bookshelf and ventured behind her desk. She kept a personal heater underneath her desk to warm her feet, and two extra pairs of flats besides the ones she'd kicked off a few minutes ago—brown ones and white ones, covering all the bases no matter what she was wearing. An embroidered banner suspended from a silver thumbtack on the wall to my right caught my attention. ONE LIFE AT A TIME, it said. I crossed my arms over my chest, took my eyes higher up on the wall, and stared at what I found there.

"OK, I'm ready," Anne announced, striding into the office and plucking her keys from the desktop. She dangled them from one finger and looked at me curiously. I suppose the expression on my face did look a little strange. "Smoke?"

"You've been busy."

"I'm guessing you have too. Can we eat now?"

"I know you're not getting testy and I've been running around here working like a slave and starving my ass off."

"Yes, I am getting testy. I always do when I'm hungry, and thank you for all your help today. We're getting ready for a guest speaker. I wasn't expecting it to take so long, though. Are you driving, or am I?"

"I am," I decided. "I've seen the way you drive your SUV, and it ain't pretty." She rolled her eyes again and walked out of the office, turning off the lights as she went, and leaving me in the dark. Several seconds later, I followed.

We talked about general things during the drive to the restaurant, which was fine with me because I had some pretty specific things I wanted to know, and I was formulating my questions even as I told her about the weather back home in Indiana and about the hotel I was staying in. Was it comfortable? Yes. Was it reasonably priced? No, but I didn't skimp on my personal comfort. Who was the guest speaker? An eating disorder survivor who was a former client of the center. She'd written a best selling book and insisted on having a book signing at the center to give back.

I drove carefully and only glanced at Anne when it was safe to do so, at stoplights. But there seemed to be fifty million of them, so I was glancing at her frequently, and not minding a bit. She was nice to look at, attractive in a fresh scrubbed way. No makeup, except for a light sheen of lip-gloss, and probably mascara. She didn't need makeup, though. Her skin was impressively clear and tight, like a teenager's. Teeth white and perfectly aligned so that she used her tongue a lot when she pronounced words. I remembered that her teeth were always nice, even when she was at her worst.

"Tell me what happened," I said as soon as we sat down across from each other in a booth by a large picture window.

"With what? Isaiah?"

"With you. Bring me up to speed on what I've missed since we last saw each other."

"You didn't miss anything, Smoke. Hell, you wouldn't even be here if my son wasn't showing his ass right now."

I let the *my son* comment ride. For now.

"So you were really never going to tell me?"

"No. What would've been the point?"

"What's the point now?"

"I don't want him to end up screwing up his life. That's the point now."

"That would've been the point sixteen years ago, too. Did he ever want to know about his father?" I sat back and drummed my fingers on the table, watched her watch me.

"He did, when he was around eleven or twelve. He started asking questions that I couldn't answer, so I told him that his father wasn't around anymore. He had me and Aunt Bobbi, and that was enough."

I spied a waiter coming toward our table.

"Or so you thought," I murmured. She would've hissed

at me if the waiter hadn't arrived just then. "I'll have the lobster linguini and garlic cheese bread, and please bring me the coldest beer you can find. You mind?" I looked at Anne, remembering her no alcohol policy.

"No, I don't mind." She leaned forward and the front of her shirt gapped. "I'll have the eggplant parmesan and cheese bread, too. And the coldest iced tea you can find, please."

"How come you don't wear a bra?" I asked immediately after the waiter was gone.

"What?"

"You don't wear a bra. Why not?" My eyes traveled from her face to her breasts and back again. She seemed unfazed by the question, and looked down at her breasts as if she was just noticing she had them. I chuckled when she cupped them lightly and glanced at me.

"These things would make a bra mad. Plus, I like the fact that they still salute, you know? Well I guess you wouldn't know. Does it bother you that I don't wear a bra?"

"Not at all. I was just wondering." We considered each other for long seconds and then I made myself look away. "You surprise me."

"How so?"

"Just not what I expected, I guess."

"What did you expect? For me to still be killing myself, living in a hovel and expecting you to be my ticket to the good life?"

"The truth?"

"Please."

"I was expecting something like that, yeah. And then I was expecting to be able to unequivocally deny that your son was my son."

"You could still do that." She sat back to make room for

her iced tea and smiled sweetly at the waiter, said thank you softly, like she really meant it.

I picked up my beer and took a sip.

"Could I?"

"It's all about choices, Smoke. You can do whatever you want to do. It's your world. I'm just a squirrel trying to get a nut."

"You think you're hip, don't you? Squirrel trying to get a nut. That's some stuff I haven't heard since Robinwood." I laughed at the phrase she used and nodded appreciatively. "What's the nut?"

"A better life for my son," she said simply.

"What about your own life? Tell me what you did to better yourself."

"Everything I did, I did for my son." She thought about what she'd said and held up a finger as she drank her tea. "Except for getting clean. I did that strictly for myself. The rest was nothing compared to that."

"Was it as hard as they say it is?"

She looked at me, surprised.

"You never tried your own stuff?"

"Rule number one—don't get high off your own supply. I smoked a little weed here and there, though. I saw what the other stuff did to . . ." I trailed off, realizing where I was going and feeling funny about it.

"To people like me," she finished. "But you kept right on selling it."

"The dope game is a mentality, Anne. A bunch of unevolved brothas refusing to see past the noses on their faces. The easy money and the bling-bling sucks you in, and before you know it, you're a slave to it. I was as guilty as the next brotha, I admit that."

"Well, since you can admit that, then I'll admit that getting clean was the hardest thing I've ever done in my life.

Many times I thought I wouldn't make it, but I didn't have a choice. I had to get myself together so I could start living my life."

Our food arrived and we both dug in.

"From what I can see, you've done pretty well for yourself." I wanted to know more about her, but so far she managed to deflect my questions. I was trying to be tactful, but curiosity was eating me up.

"There's always more to do. What's your life like these days, Smoke?"

"I thought I told you not to call me Smoke?"

"That was your first mistake. You *told* me when you should've been *asking* me." She pointed her fork across the table at me. "Answer my question, *Smoke*."

"My life is good. I work when I have to, play when I want to, and do whatever else I want to do in the meantime."

"Not necessarily conducive to instant fatherhood. What kind of work do you do? Please don't tell me you still sell drugs."

I sent her a retiring look and forked up pasta, chewing slowly.

"You think you're the only one who can change?"

"I don't know many working stiffs who wear Rolex watches." She nodded toward my wrist.

"I was smarter with the money I made than most, believe that. I manage to do all right with some investments I made and a few other things that are none of your business. I teach math to a bunch of hardheaded high school kids in my spare time. Does that answer your question?"

She sat back and roared with laughter, exposing the column of her neck to me and pressing a hand to her breasts.

"Math? You're kidding, right? You didn't even graduate from high school. When did all this happen?"

"I earned a GED while I was in the military, and then I went to college. A lot of things can happen in sixteen years, as you know." I popped the last bite of bread in my mouth and followed it with a mouthful of beer. She had laughed at me. Damn, I was a little stung.

"An army man?"

"Marines. Twelve years. I figure I was joining up around the time you were giving birth," I told her. "Which brings me back around to my original question. What happened to you? Where did you go to secretly give birth to my son?"

"That's the first time you've referred to Isaiah as your son."

"How can I deny that when he looks exactly like me? Did you think I wouldn't notice? I'll be damned if he doesn't have my crooked pinkie, too. It's some humbling shit, that's for damn sure." I pointed my fork across the table at her. "Answer my question, *Anne*."

ANNE

Smoke unnerved me. I could admit that to myself even as I sat there, cool as a cucumber. What kind of man went from selling drugs to teenagers to teaching them math? I couldn't put it together so that it made sense to me, although I was greatly relieved to learn that he was living a legitimate lifestyle. I wondered for a split second if he was lying to me, then I dismissed the thought as quickly as it came. The Smoke I used to know wasn't a liar. He'd always said what he meant, and meant what he said. Once, he'd told a boy who owed him money that he would break his jaw if the boy didn't pay the money within a certain amount of time. I remembered seeing the boy with his mouth wired shut a few days later. Everyone knew that

Smoke had dispatched one of his minions to take care of the task. It amounted to the same thing as telling the boy that he would do it himself, but there was one crucial factor not to be overlooked. It was probably why the boy hadn't taken him too seriously. Smoke's hands were always manicured and smooth, like the rest of him. He couldn't be bothered with scraping his knuckles or injuring himself. There were plenty of lackeys to do his dirty work for him.

We had come up in a time when territory and turf rules were, for the most part, respected. Smoke's territory was the Robinwood Housing Projects, all fourteen buildings, all one hundred and twelve stories combined. He stood out from the griminess and decay of the buildings like a sore thumb, in his casually expensive clothing and understated accessories. I could believe that he'd squirreled away money because he never wasted it on meaningless things like gaudy jewelry and over the top cars. His one extravagance had been the ridiculously expensive sneakers he'd always worn with his pressed khakis or Levi's, and he'd driven a constantly washed and waxed late model SUV.

Part of me had been expecting to find Smoke withering away in prison somewhere, a shell of the handsome boy he once was, and I was immeasurably glad that he was whole and here to help me with my son.

Even if he did unnerve me.

"I lived in Jackson, Mississippi up until four years ago," I said suddenly. Smoke froze in the process of lifting his glass. It was suspended in midair as he stared at me with his mouth open in disbelief.

"Mississippi?"

"That's what I said. That's where Isaiah grew up. Me, too."

"How the hell did you end up in Mississippi?"

"I'll save that story for another time," I said and finished my tea.

"A mystery woman, huh? I like that. So tell me about the Olive Branch Wellness Center. Why does it mainly service women?"

"Because I'm a woman, and I say so. There's a few men."

"Around to carry boxes and shit?" He grinned knowingly and I rolled my eyes at him, caught.

"When they can do that right." He sucked his teeth and slanted a hooded gaze at me as he shifted and slid his wallet from a back pocket. "I started it as a way to give back to the community, and it just kind of mushroomed from there."

"You want some dessert? Because I do." He lifted a hand to signal the waiter. "What does it cost to finance a place like that?"

"Most of our income comes from government grants and subsidies, but we do operate on a sliding scale fee basis for clients who can pay. It's a nonprofit. Chocolate cheesecake," I told the waiter. "I'm going to have to run three extra laps in the morning."

"Wear a bra while you do it. Vanilla bean cheesecake."

The waiter took our dishes, snickered under his breath, and moved away. I gaped at Smoke.

"Not funny."

"Funny as hell. You started the center all by yourself?"

"Me and another recovering addict who, luckily, was quite experienced in writing grants and proposals for funding. Before she hit rock bottom, she was a corporate big whig."

"Who was in Mississippi?"

"I told you, that's a story for another day."

"All right, well then where's your man? I'm assuming you have one."

I was not willing to go there, especially not with Smoke. I turned it around on him.

"Where's your woman? You're too good looking not to have one . . . or two."

"You think I'm good looking?"

"Smoke . . ."

"Damn, you're not giving an inch, are you? The woman I'm currently seeing is back home. Now you."

"What exactly does this have to do with Isaiah?" I eyed him suspiciously. I pulled the fork out of the hunk of cheesecake the waiter placed in front of me, and proceeded to take a hunk of Smoke's cheesecake. He didn't seem to mind, so I took another forkful.

"Not a damn thing. This is strictly me being nosy. Eat your own dessert."

"Yours looks like it tastes better. I should've ordered the same thing." I licked the back of my fork decadently.

"You should have, but since you didn't, eat your own." He reached over and dug into mine. "You meet a man in Mississippi?"

"Several of them, actually." I smiled when his eyebrows shot up. "But they were all counselors and gatekeepers, and that's all I'm going to say about that. There is no man in my life, other than Isaiah."

"And he's not a man, which may be part of his problem. You letting him think he is."

I was instantly offended. I waved an irritated hand and locked eyes with him.

"Look, don't start, Smoke. I'm having a decent day so far. I don't need shit from you to screw it up, OK?"

"I'm just saying, Anne. He's doing the shit he's doing because he knows he can get away with it. You don't need to be grounding him like he's Greg Brady."

"And what do I need?"

"A broomstick," he joked.

"Screw you, Smoke." I pushed my half-eaten cheesecake to the middle of the table and slid my purse across the seat toward me.

"That's already been accomplished, and it's the reason we're here now. Because you screwed me and got pregnant and neglected to mention that fact to me. Shall we move on?"

"I was the last person you would have wanted a child with, and you know it." Where the hell was my wallet? I finally found it and snatched a twenty out to pay for my lunch. I looked up and found Smoke staring me down. "What?"

"You're right," he said after several seconds had passed with us staring at each other. "You were the last person I would've wanted a child with, and that's assuming I ever wanted a child, by the way, because I'm not sure I ever did. You were always spaced out and flaky looking, and you had a bad habit, so no I wouldn't have considered making a child with you. But there is a child and I'm trying to make myself do the right thing here, Anne."

"I wasn't too spaced out and flaky looking to sleep with, though, was I, Smoke?"

"We didn't do much sleeping, as I recall. I think I already told you about egos and power trips, too. And we can talk about whose idea it was, if you like."

"You found me a time or two," I snapped.

"Because I knew I could," he snapped back.

I tossed my money on the table and slid out of the booth, stood next to the table, fighting back tears.

"Take me back to my car, please."

"Not so fast. What's our game plan for dealing with Isaiah?"

"I don't know what *your* game plan is, but *mine* is to go back to my car and go home to my son. You just go on back to your life, Smoke, and forget we exist. It'll probably be easier that way anyway. I think I can handle things from here on out." I slung my purse over my shoulder and shifted my weight onto one foot to wait. He was deliberately taking his time selecting a bill from his wallet. "Look, don't make me cause a scene. It doesn't take that long to pull out a twenty and stand your ass up."

His eyes crawled up to mine slowly and held.

"Don't be rushing me now, woman. You butted into my life long enough to drag me across state lines and surprise me with a long lost son. Seems like you can wait for me to pay for lunch now that I'm here. Matter of fact, don't be rushing me out of town either. I'll leave when I feel like leaving."

"Is that the kind of English you teach your students? Don't *be* rushing me?" I stepped back when he stood and came toward me.

"I teach math, smart ass," he said, leaning close enough to slip my twenty into the vee of my shirt. "If you were wearing a bra, it would hold that. Catch it before it hits the floor. You ready?"

I stomped out of the restaurant ahead of him and tapped my foot by the car, waiting for him to unlock the passenger door. He took his time doing that, too, and I thought about scratching him. I rolled my eyes and got in the car when he held the door open, smiling like a Cheshire cat. I sat back with my arms folded across my chest.

I was silent during the drive back to the center. When he pulled to a stop next to my SUV, I opened the door and dropped a foot to the pavement. I looked at Smoke over my shoulder.

"I'm sorry I contacted you, Smoke."

"So am I, Anne. I'm sorry I made you pregnant, too."

That jabbed at me in a deep place, and I gasped in shock.

"I'm not," I choked out as I stepped out and closed the door. I leaned down and looked at him through the window. "I think you gave me the best part of you in Isaiah. My son and I will make it through this thing he's going through. Thanks for lunch, and have a nice life."

I climbed into my Lexus and drove off without a backward glance.

It was after seven in the evening and Isaiah still wasn't home. I was starting to get worried. Furthermore, I was starting to get angry. I gave up on attempting to throw something together for dinner, and went to change into my gown and housecoat. If this was going to be a repeat performance of the other night, I had no intention of staying up until the wee hours of the morning worrying myself to death. If he came in stumbling and hungry, that was too damn bad for him. You could lead a horse to water, but you couldn't make him drink. Isaiah wouldn't drink and I was growing weary of leading.

I made myself a mug of green tea and took it with me to sit in front of the television in the family room. A few hours of mindless entertainment, and then I was going to bed, Isaiah be damned. I loved my son to near distraction, but I was not about to sacrifice my sanity for his madness, particularly if it meant I had to do it all by my lonesome.

I figured that by now Smoke was on a plane back to Indiana, to his tidy little life, leaving me and my son high and dry. And that was fine, it really was. Finding him and telling him about Isaiah was a last ditch effort anyway. I hadn't really believed anything substantial would come out of it. We weren't talking about two star-crossed lovers who'd somehow been separated and then reunited. My situation with Smoke was much grittier than that. The fact of the matter was that an addict and a pusher had made a child during a twenty-minute encounter. There was nothing storybook about it. So why should Smoke give a damn, and why should I expect him to?

No, this thing Isaiah was going through was my problem to deal with. Or not to deal with, as the case was rapidly becoming. All the experts said that at some point, children went their own way and did their own thing, regardless of what their parents had tried to teach them. Isaiah certainly seemed to be going his own way, and I was working hard to make that fact be fine with me. It had to be, didn't it?

It didn't take a degree in rocket science for me to know what my son thought of me. I had been relegated to the dregs of society in his young mind. Instead of absorbing the point of my divulging my past to him—how hard I'd worked and how devastating drug addiction could be—he'd grabbed hold to all the pauses and empty spaces in the discussion and shaped them into meanings that suited him. I accepted that he thought of me as a crackhead. I lamented the fact that he didn't factor in everything I had worked to give him, but I accepted that, too. Kids were selfish like that. What I couldn't accept was the manner in which he spoke to me, the names he called me, out loud and to my face. Maybe finding a broomstick wasn't such a bad idea after all. It had to stop, I decided. Even if I had to start punching him in the mouth every time he got riled up and started in.

I knew that I wasn't being as firm with Isaiah as I should've been, and I also knew that something had to give. Either I had to bust my ass and force my son back on the right track, or the something that had to give would be me. Giving up was right around the corner. I could watch Isaiah destroy his life, I could sit back and let him use drugs with the potential for addiction, and I could pretend that I didn't notice anything amiss with him. I could fall at the feet of the policemen when they arrested my son one day, and scream and rail about the injustices done to my poor baby. I could rally against the justice system and enable him in his behavior. All of that I could do, but at the end of the day, it would make me no better than my own mother.

In fact, it would make me less than a mother, a real one anyway. But Isaiah was leaving me no choice. And Smoke wasn't even a factor.

Isaiah still hadn't come home after eleven o'clock, so I went to bed.

ISAIAH

I thought the Colt 45 was going to my head. Thought I was seeing things, for real. I was sitting in the passenger seat of Hood's ride, bobbing my head to track number seven on Jay Z's second CD, when dude strolled over to the car like he was planning on hopping in. He stood by the passenger door, staring at me. Hood reached over and turned down the music and we all got quiet. It was me, Hood, and one of his flunkies named Marcus. Hood brought him along because he had a bag full of fire ass weed, ripe for the rolling. That shit was so pungent I could smell it as soon as Marcus spread out in the backseat and started rolling a blunt as thick as my thumb. When dude walked up we all froze like, *what the fuck?*

He was dressed in black slacks and a matching blazer, with a crew neck dress shirt underneath, looking like one-time for real. Hood started inching his hand under his seat, going for his piece. We was parked on a back street in the park ten blocks over from my house, behind some trees. Wasn't nobody around, and Hood must've thought he could get a few shots off if he needed to, without too much of a risk. Hood was crazy like that.

Dude noticed the direction of Hood's hand and stopped staring at me long enough to stare at him.

"I wouldn't do that if I were you, youngblood," dude said. Hood looked at him like he was crazy, but he sat back.

"Man, who the hell is you?" Hood asked dude. He tapped me on the arm and tipped his head. "Zay, you know this cat?"

"Nah," I said and took another swig of Colt. "I don't know shit about this dude. He ain't one-time, though."

"If you don't know this motherfucker, then how you know he ain't one-time?"

"Trust me on this." I looked up at dude. "You want some of this, old man?"

"I was about to ask you the same thing, *Zay*. You want some of this?"

I shook my head and laughed.

"Hood, you believe this dude's name is Smoke? Who the fuck is named Smoke? That's some of that old *Super Fly* shit there. Whatchu want with me anyway, and why you following me around and shit? Ain't that against the law?"

"Uh, excuse me," Marcus butted in, sounding silly. I turned around and looked at him. "Anybody mind if I fire this bitch up?" He held up a thick ass blunt in one hand and a lighter in the other. He was a straight up weed head.

"You can light it up, but it'll fall apart in your hands before you get a good toke off it," dude said. "You didn't pinch the head tight enough."

I stared at dude like he was an alien from outer space. Hood started laughing, covering his mouth like he was about to cough.

"Wait a minute, Zay. This the dude you was telling me about, the one from Indiana?"

I had told Hood about dude busting up in my house trying to clown me and shit, but I didn't tell him that dude was my long lost daddy. He didn't need to know all that.

"Yeah, this that cat," I said. "Running a brotha down and shit. Whatchu say you wanted?"

"A little of this, little of that. I'm on my way back home. Thought maybe you might want to talk a minute before I left." Behind me Marcus fired up the blunt, and smoke slammed into the back of my head like a mutha. I started coughing just on GP. That fool was puffing hard as hell.

Hood took the blunt, pulled on it twice, and handed it to me. I shook my head and waved it away. For some reason I didn't want dude to see me doing my do.

"Talk about what?" I asked.

"A little of this, little of that." Dude slid his hands in his pockets and grinned at me. Next thing I knew he was shaking his head like I was a bad joke. That made me mad.

"What's so damn funny?"

"You are. You think you've got it all figured out, don't you?"

"I know you ain't got shit figured out. 'Cause if you did, you would disappear right about now. Vanish like smoke, Smoke." I thought that was pretty funny and grinned back at his ass. "You feel me?"

"Unfortunately, I do. Check this out, Zay." He leaned down and spread his hands over the top of the door, staring me down. "I'm thinking I might be back. Are you ready for what I might bring with me?"

"Man, for the last time, you ain't my daddy, and I don't give a shit if you never come back, OK? If you planning on coming back next weekend, I ain't gone have time to be bothered with your shit anyway, 'cause I got a game on Saturday. So don't waste your time."

"What kind of game on Saturday?"

"Basketball. Why?"

"Where is it?"

"At the school. Why?"

"What time does it start?"

"Seven-thirty. Why? You ain't coming no way."

"Maybe, maybe not. You any good?"

"I might be. Why?"

"What's up with this dude, Zay? This your daddy or something?" Hood choked out around a mouthful of smoke. Didn't he just hear me tell dude he wasn't my daddy?

I felt dude staring at me. Hard. But I wouldn't look at him. I took a swig of Colt, wiped my mouth with the back of my hand, and looked at Hood a long time. Then I said, "Yeah."

"Oh snap," Marcus said from the backseat.

"Damn, y'all do look alike now that you mention it," Hood cracked. He handed Marcus the blunt and looked at dude. "You say you from Indiana. Where bout?"

"I don't recall saying I was from Indiana, but since you asked, Indianapolis."

"I got some cousins that live there. You know any people with the last name Knight?"

I looked at Hood like he'd lost his damn mind. No this fool wasn't getting ready to turn this shit into a family reunion. And why black folks always wanting to know if you know somebody else? Who gave a shit?

"I might. I used to know a few people named Knight years ago. Yogi and Pat from Robinwood. That was before your time, though."

Hood actually started getting excited. I ain't never seen that fool smile like that before. Not even when he was getting a blowjob.

"Hold up. I had a cousin named Yogi. He got killed a few years back, though. That cat was straight crazy. You knew him?"

Dude nodded slowly. "Vaguely."

Hood was on a roll. "His mama is my mama's sister. I came up there a few times in the summer when I was little. Used to follow that fool around everywhere he went. That was back when Yogi was banking and shit. He was slinging dope like it wasn't no tomorrow, working for this nigga named—"

"Zeus," dude said. My head snapped around quick as hell and we stared at each other.

"That's some wild shit," Hood was saying. "You know Zeus? Man, I heard all kinda shit about that cat back in the day. Dude," he looked at Marcus, "Zeus was like a god or some shit."

"Or Satan," dude said. Before I knew what he was doing, he snatched my door open and stepped back. "Get out."

"*What?*"

"Get out." I didn't move and his eyebrows raised. "You need me to help you get out?"

I got out.

Chapter 4

ALEC

"A son?" It was a shriek more than a question.

I stopped packing long enough to look at Diana over my shoulder. She was standing behind me, arms folded across her chest, leaning on one foot. She was a pretty woman, even when she was pissed, and I was certain she was aware of that fact. My eyes swept her from head to toe, then I smiled engagingly. She was tall, almost as tall as me, and always on a diet to maintain her slim figure. I secretly thought a few more pounds wouldn't hurt, but who had asked me? We'd finished making love an hour ago, and she was still prancing around naked.

I reached out and flicked one of her nipples with the tip of my finger, watched it rise and harden, and looked into her wide brown eyes. She was as fine as she wanted to be.

"A son," I confirmed in a grave voice.

"And you're just now telling me this?" She pushed her long, relaxed hair from around her shoulders and held it away from her face with both hands. I took advantage of her pose and moved close to cup her breasts in my hands. I kissed her on her forehead softly.

"I just found out myself last weekend. His name is Isaiah, and he's sixteen years old. It's funny how much he looks like me." I squeezed her breasts for a moment longer, then reluctantly eased around her to get to my closet. As much as the idea of taking her back to bed appealed to me, I had a plane to catch and a basketball game to attend.

"What kind of woman doesn't tell a man he's a father until sixteen years later? That's what I want to know." She plopped down in the middle of my bed and stretched out luxuriously. "And who is this woman, anyway?"

"Just a girl I used to know over sixteen years ago, so stop wigging out." I figured the circumstances of my relationship with Anne didn't need to be disclosed. It wasn't really my business to tell. Plus, I wouldn't exactly come out looking like Mr. Clean in the aftermath. There were many things Diana didn't know about me, and I preferred to keep it that way.

"You still haven't told me what kind of woman she is, Alec. I mean, should I be packing a bag, too?"

"You jealous?" I folded a pair of Levi's and laid them in the suitcase. I was taking a few pairs of boxers from a drawer when it occurred to me that she hadn't answered my question. I meant it as a joke, but her silence told me that it wasn't one. I looked at her curiously.

"Should I be?"

By comparison, Diana was *Vogue* material to Anne's *Health & Fitness* type flair. She was like a sleek sports car while Anne brought to mind a sturdy sedan with luxury options. Diana was everything I liked in a woman—always well groomed and sweet smelling, soft and ultra feminine. I didn't think I'd ever seen her sweat, even though she taught PE at my school and professed to work out on a daily basis. An image of Anne huffing down the street, jogging with no bra crossed my mind, but I pushed it away and focused on the soft bush of hair between Diana's thighs. Should she be jealous? *Hell no*.

"I'm going to see my son, to spend time with him, so I would have to say the answer to your question is no. His mother and I aren't interested in each other like that."

"Still, maybe I should go with you."

"Not this time, OK? I need to focus on Isaiah right now. We're still feeling each other out. And you, my dear, would be a distraction."

"When will you be back then?"

"Sunday night," I said. *Or maybe Monday*, I thought. Isaiah had mentioned something to me about the two of us possibly hanging out on Sunday. Actually, I had mentioned it, but he hadn't refused me outright, and I chose to take that as a definite maybe.

"You sure you don't need a little something-something to tide you over until then?" She smiled seductively and parted her thighs for my viewing pleasure.

I took the sight in leisurely. Then I glanced at my watch.

"I would love to, baby, but my flight leaves in two hours. I need to get a move on." She wasn't pleased with my response, but I had visions of witnessing jump shots and slam-dunks dancing through my head. Missing my flight and having to catch a later one was not an option, no matter how good the pussy was.

And it was good. I conceded that, but I was never the kind of man to get waylaid by something as simple as good sex. I'd had all kinds of sex during my thirty-six years on earth, and by now I knew the answer to the great mystery many women still labored over to this day. Good sex and a pretty smile did not keep a man if he didn't want to be kept. He might linger for a time, but ultimately he could be lured away if it looked like something better had come along.

After six months of dallying with Diana Daniels, I had

come to the conclusion that she was still laboring over the great mystery. My students called her a dime-piece, which meant she was extremely good looking. Whenever she drummed up an excuse to strut into my classroom, it was always a production, and the boys usually went on full alert while the girls resorted to teeth sucking and darting meaningful glances at each other. I sat back and watched the dynamics, secretly amused and slightly put off. She was a siren and her sexuality walked ten feet ahead of her like a sultry prelude to the real thing.

Diana was a near carbon copy of my wife. Excuse me, my *ex*-wife. At twenty-three, I'd married a sleeker version of Diana because the great mystery was still a mystery to me, and nine years of high maintenance headaches was what I got for my trouble. She hadn't wanted children because pregnancy would ruin her figure. She hadn't wanted to work outside of the home because it was beneath her, even though she was constantly pushing me to earn more money. She liked to spend her days shopping and socializing with the other military wives, and she would not even consider the possibility that I would eventually sever ties with Uncle Sam and join the civilian world. She couldn't understand why I would pursue something as mundane as a teaching degree when I could be doing something more exciting and lucrative, like finance or law. But the sex was hotter than hot, and for a time I was blinded to everything except the mind numbing orgasms I enjoyed on a regular basis. Then I got my sight back, miraculously, and decided I needed a divorce.

My marriage ended right around the time my third tour of duty ended. She decided that she liked being a military wife, and I decided that she should continue to pursue that ambition for herself. Meanwhile, I was out. The trouble was, somehow, I'd managed to get myself back in. With Diana. I knew she wanted more from our fledgling relationship, and probably even expected it. By now I should've been simpering at her feet and doing my best to hold on tightly to a good thing while I had it. And I did hold tight to it, while it was in my bed, but I had no trouble releasing it when the sun came up.

It sounded callous, but in reality, I cared about Diana, and the thought of cheating on her never crossed my mind. Well, hardly ever anyway. I just didn't allow my second head to cloud my judgment where she was concerned. It hadn't escaped my notice that she was eerily similar in looks and personality to my ex-wife, which suggested that I wasn't quite as evolved as I liked to think. But every day was a work in progress, right?

I listened to the sound of Diana's blaring silence during the drive to the airport. She was pouting because I hadn't invited her along, and I wasn't caring. I sent her off with a generous kiss and boarded my flight with something like anticipation rolling around in my gut. My thoughts were already just outside of Chicago, wondering what my son would say to me when he saw me again. I was almost looking forward to another verbal sparring.

Last Sunday he'd lit into me good after I made him get out of the car with his no good buddies. He was embarrassed and mad as hell, and no sooner than we were ten feet away from the car he had started in, talking pure bullshit to me. I let him rant and rave about how I had no right to interfere in his life or to tell him what to do. I listened patiently while he assured me that if I ever tried to put my hands on him again, I would regret it. I think I might've even smiled at that point, envisioning myself putting his little ass in a sleeper hold and taking him down real quick. He was absolutely livid, and I couldn't blame him. I would've been just as indignant if my mother had suddenly sprung a father on me that late in the game, and I said that to him. Then I said something else that still humbled me every time I thought about it. And I had thought about it many times over the last week.

"Can I talk now?" I asked Isaiah. He was still huffing and puffing, looking so much like my mother that I wanted to kiss him. I was past due for a visit with her, and with him standing there frowning exactly like she did when she was pissed, guilt washed over me. I'd missed the past two Sunday dinners and I needed to call her soon for atonement. She would get the shock of her life when she set eyes on him. That she would set eyes on my son was a foregone conclusion. He just didn't know it yet.

"You can talk, but that don't mean I have to listen," Isaiah said. He looked off toward the street and kept his eyes there. I kept my eyes on his face. He knew I was staring at him, and it made him uncomfortable. After a while he met my eyes defiantly. "What?"

"I didn't know about you," I said.

"I got that."

"If I had known about you, I would've been in your life from day one."

"So it's all my mama's fault?"

I thought about that for a few seconds and shook my head.

"Not all her fault. It was a crazy time, a complicated situation. She didn't know what to do, and I—"

"She was cracked out. You ain't gotta sugar coat the shit for me. I know the deal."

"You ain't gotta curse at me either," I told him. "I know you're angry. Hell, I'm angry too. But as men we need to figure out a way to deal with this situation." I doubt he was aware that there were tears in his eyes. I stopped myself from reaching out to him, knowing that wasn't what he needed right then. He wanted me to, though. I could feel it coming off of him in waves, and I told myself that one day soon I would give him what he wanted. When he was ready to accept it.

"You mad 'cause you got a kid you didn't want by a crackhead?" His voice lowered noticeably and he shot a nervous glance toward the car. I had my first peep into what part of his problem was.

"I never liked that word." I let that statement hang out there between us. "I'm mad, as you put it, because I've got a son that I didn't have the privilege of seeing grow up. I'm mad because I don't know what your favorite color is. Or what your favorite food is, or even if you have a girlfriend that I should be pulling your coattail about." I stepped closer to him, close enough that he could smell the onions on my breath, leftover from the burger I'd wolfed down for lunch. "I'm mad because it was my job to take you for haircuts and talk to you about the birds and the bees and to knock you upside the head when you got out of line. All that shit and more. That's what I'm mad about."

"My mama handled her business."

"So she's not just a crackhead?" My eyebrows rose as I studied him. He blushed and shuffled his feet in the grass. Silence stretched out and I knew I'd made my point. Still, I said, "One of these days I'll take you to see some *real* crackheads, and then you can see for yourself what the dope life is like. You can see all the little dirty, hungry children and the filth. I promise you you'll come home and kiss your mother's feet."

He heard what he wanted to hear.

"Man, you ain't taking me no place, and you know it."

"Oh, but I am. That is, if you want to go. I don't want to force myself on you, Isaiah."

"Zay."

"What?"

"My friends call me Zay."

"We're friends now?"

"Nah," he waved a nonchalant hand. "I don't know you like that."

"You want to know me like that?"

"Why you wanna know me? That's what I want to know."

"Well, it's not because of your winning personality, that's for sure. I'll be back next weekend. Let me think about that question during the week and I'll have an answer for you when I get back."

"You gotta think about it?" He was outdone, looking at me suspiciously.

"I've got a lot of shit to think about, just like you do." I slipped a folded piece of paper from my pocket and held it out to him. "These are my home, work, and cell numbers. Call me if you want to talk before then." He made no move to take the paper from me, but I wouldn't take it back. Couldn't. "Take the paper, Zay," I said softly.

He took it, but he hadn't used it during the week. I knew because I was monitoring all three phones diligently, checking for messages every free second I had, and there were none.

The plane was circling around Chicago, preparing to land when my cell phone rang. A passing stewardess shot me a veiled look and I shook my head at her. *No, I'm not going to answer it when you just told us to turn off our cell phones and make sure our seatbelts are secure. I'm a good little passenger*, my look told her. She moved on down the aisle.

A good little passenger who suddenly had to pee. I hurried to the restroom at the rear of the plane and pulled out my cell phone as soon as I closed the door behind me.

"Hello?" I mumbled into the phone. The reception was shitty, but I could still make out the sound of a woman's voice in the background, something about taking the trash out before it started stinking up the whole house. Anne. Which meant that my caller was . . . "Isaiah?"

"I'm playing ball tonight. You coming?"

"My plane is about to land now. What's up with the trash?" I leaned against the steel sink and listened to him groan theatrically, and smiled.

"I'm 'bout to take it out. I keep telling her to give me a minute, but she thinks a minute is ten seconds."

"Consider yourself lucky. My mother thought a minute was five seconds." Actually, to my mother a minute was a minute, but telling her to give me one was unthinkable. She said do it, and I did it. Period. "Take it out so she can stop fussing."

"Whatever. Why you talking all low?"

"Because I'm not supposed to be on the phone while the plane is landing. I don't know what the hell difference it makes, though. Why are you mumbling?"

"Because I'm not supposed to be on the phone at all. She catches me and that's another two weeks added on. I risked it to call you. Don't you feel special?"

"We're going to have to do something about that mouth of yours," I said.

"Whatever. You coming to the house?"

"Do you want me to?"

"You do what you want to do. I'ma be here till about six, and then I gotta jet to the school for practice before the game."

I wondered if he really thought he was being slick. Then I remembered that he was sixteen, so probably so. I filed the particulars of his agenda in the back of my mind and checked the time. It was a little after three.

"I still need to pick up my rental and drive out there, so it may be around six or so when I get to my hotel."

"Isaiah!" Anne shrieked in the background. Another theatrical groan.

"Cool," he said. "I'll see you when I see you."

"Whatever, youngblood. I'll be there in a little while. Take out the trash." He did just what I was expecting him to do and hung up on me. I slipped out of the restroom and resumed my seat.

"I was beginning to think you'd fallen in," the stewardess drawled as she came to lean over me. I sat still while she unnecessarily checked my seatbelt. Her breasts were practically in my mouth.

"I had to take an important phone call," I told her.

"Oh? Your wife or girlfriend?"

"My son," I said with more than a little pride. I was starting to like the feel of those two words on my tongue, starting to like the sound of them coming out of my mouth.

It was a little past seven when I finally made it to Isaiah's school. I waited a ridiculous amount of time while my rental was detailed and then traffic was heavier than I had anticipated. Then I drove around for another ten minutes, looking for a parking space because the school's lot was packed. I finally rolled up behind a car that was backing out of a space not far from the gymnasium doors, and pulled in gratefully.

I joined the line at the door and passed the perky little blonde three one-dollar bills when it was my turn, let her stamp my hand with some sort of glow-in-the-dark stamp, and ventured into the fray. The scent of musk and teenagers blasted me as I stepped inside the gym and took stock. It was huge and filled to the brim with chatty students and anxious looking parents, of which I was now one. I didn't realize that I was searching for any sign of

Anne until I concluded that she wasn't there. At least, I didn't see her if she was, and I had looked thoroughly.

I spotted a stretch of empty seating on the top row of the bleachers against the wall and navigated my way up the steps, weaved in and out of clusters of people, and claimed it for myself. Ten minutes and counting. The crowd was chanting back and forth across the width of the gym, one side against the other. I looked around quickly, making sure that I was sitting on the right side. Concluding that I was, I leaned back against the wall and settled in to see some ball playing, to see my son play ball for the first time.

The crowd went wild as the teams emerged from separate doors and began their warm-ups. Cheerleaders kicked and jumped and clapped for the players as their names were announced. I heard my son's name, saw him exchange high-fives with his teammates, and then let his eyes sweep the length of the bleachers. Seconds later, our eyes locked and I nodded slightly. After that, he pretended to ignore me and I pretended not to be wounded. It was a flesh wound, though.

The score was eighteen to sixteen, in favor of Isaiah's team, and the buzzer signaling the end of the first quarter had just sounded when Anne walked into the gym. I noticed her immediately. The expression on her face said that she was feeling rushed and irritated. She stood by the doors for a few minutes, looking around the gym. I knew the instant she found Isaiah because her face relaxed and a small smile involuntarily tilted her lips. I was struck by the many pleasing aspects of her face. Her locks were pulled back and secured at the nape of her neck with a clip, giving her the appearance of youthfulness.

But there was nothing youthful about the glittery lipgloss on her lips, or the knowing sparkle in her big, slanted eyes. She noticed someone she knew and treated them to a full smile, her nose crinkling and her teeth sparkling. Then Isaiah broke away from the sidelines where his team was huddled and jogged over to her. The coach blew his whistle sharply, motioning for him to return, and he held up one long finger in response to the command. I wondered what they were talking about, him towering over her like a giant, and her fiddling with his jersey, picking off imaginary lint only mothers seemed to see. She looked more like she could be his girlfriend than his mother in her snug fitting, flare-leg jeans and high-heels. I noticed that her toenails were bright red, and that she wasn't wearing a bra. The cropped black leather blazer she was wearing parted on one side when she pushed her purse back and propped a hand on her hip, revealing a form fitting black tee shirt and the unmistakable imprint of the tip of an erect nipple. *What is it with the bras?*

The whistle shrieked again, Isaiah mumbled something to her and then jogged back to his team. Balls slammed against the floor and the crowd geared up for more action. Oblivious to it all, Anne tipped along the front row of bleachers, searching for a seat. I watched her squeeze her ass into a tight space and set her purse on the floor between her feet. The dangly silver earrings in her ears slapped against her neck as she turned her head to respond to something that the man sitting next to her said. I wondered what the hell he suddenly had to talk about. Then I wondered why the hell I was wondering and turned my attention back to the game.

At half time Anne slipped away from the crowd and disappeared through the gym doors. After what I thought was a decent interval, I followed her. She was in line at the concession stand set up farther down the corridor when I stepped up behind her and cleared my throat. She kept digging around in her purse, so I moved closer and leaned over her shoulder to make my presence known. She stepped back, startled, and did a double take.

"Smoke, what are you doing here?"

"I came to see Isaiah play."

"He invited you?" She was clearly surprised.

"In a roundabout way. You didn't, though." I tipped my head to let her know she was next in line, and stepped up behind her as she approached the counter. She ordered a can of Coke and asked for a straw, and I held up two fingers to let the attendant know to give her two straws.

"I didn't think you'd be interested in stuff like this. Where the hell is my money?" she asked, jerking her purse in irritation.

While she dug around looking for money, I handed the attendant a five-dollar bill, took my change, and picked up the soda and straws.

"Stuff like watching my son play basketball?" She jumped as my hand settled on her waist. "You're holding up the line," I explained.

"I need to pay for my soda."

"I got it."

"Well, I guess I owe you this then."

I looked from the bills she held out to her face and chuckled softly. I took them from her, folded them, and pulled the check she'd given me the previous weekend from my pocket to fold in with the bills.

"You're still not wearing a bra, so catch this before it hits the floor," I drawled close to her ear as I tucked the wad inside her shirt. She looked around quickly to see if anyone was watching, then walked off in a huff.

I caught up with her just inside the doors and settled my hand on her waist again.

"Sit with me."

"Why, because you have two straws and you think you're getting some of my soda?"

"Because I *have* the soda, and if you want it you'll have to sit with me to get it." I left her there and started climbing back up to my seat. I knew she would follow, if for nothing else than to claim her soda. I scooted over and made room for her to sit next to me.

She plopped down and set her purse between her feet.

"My soda, please?" Instead of giving it to her, I popped the tab and took a long swallow directly from the can. I belched quietly as I passed it to her. She punched me on my thigh. "You should've bought your own, you pig."

"I bought that one. Stop fussing, woman, and pay attention. The cheerleaders are 'bout to shake some booty."

"That one on the end, the one with the weave ponytail is the one Isaiah has his eye on," Anne told me, leaning in conspiratorially. "She calls the house fifty-leven times a day."

"What's her name?"

"Aisha. What the hell kind of name is that?" I slid a glance over to her.

"So what I'm hearing you say is that you don't like her?"

"She's a skank." She rolled her eyes and tilted the can to her lips.

"Spoken like a mother. My mother didn't like any of my girlfriends either."

"All your girlfriends *were* skanks, Smoke. At least the ones I knew of anyway. Mothers know these things. Trust me."

"Well she's got one thing going for her," I baited Anne, tongue in cheek.

"What's that?"

"She's wearing a bra." I took another punch in the thigh. "You hit like a girl. Pass the soda."

Third quarter whizzed by with Isaiah racking up fifteen more points. At one point he slammed dunked and Anne jumped to her feet, pushed two fingers into her mouth, and whistled like a pro. Then he fouled another player and she would've left the bleachers to confront the referee if I hadn't laid a hand on her arm before she could get away. I was enjoying the show she was putting on just as much as the one taking place on the floor.

"If you yell 'shake it off, Isaiah' one more time, I swear to God," I told her after about the fifth time.

"What? The ref is blind in one eye and can't see out the other. Did you see that play? That was *not* a foul."

"I'm sorry, but it *was* a foul." I tugged on the back of her jacket. "Sit down, Anne. You can't go down there and kick nobody's ass."

"I could probably take that ref," she said, resuming her seat. She saw my look and rolled her neck. "You don't think I can?"

"I think *you* need to shake it off. Tell me about Mississippi." I could see that I'd caught her off guard with the abrupt change of subject, but I was dying to know. I had planned to wait until later or tomorrow to pin her down, but I was too impatient to wait even that long. I wouldn't go so far as to say that I was fascinated by Anne, but I was extremely curious to know how she'd come to be the woman sitting next to me. I wanted to know more about who my son's mother was, as a person.

"It's ancient history, Smoke."

Her eyes were trained on the game, so I took mine there too.

"Just give me a hint."

"OK," she said slowly. "I lived there with an aunt until Isaiah was twelve, and then I moved here. Satisfied?"

"No. Did you decide to move there when you found out you were pregnant?"

"My aunt found out I was pregnant and decided that I would live there with her. She knew my . . . situation, and she showed up one day and told me to pack a bag. Next thing I knew, I was in Mississippi. She dragged me on a Greyhound bus with her and off we went."

"And you stayed," I prompted her when she fell silent. She took a few seconds to clap when someone made a basket, then shifted to look at me. We stared at each other.

"I didn't have a choice. As soon as we got there she started a bedside vigil. Wouldn't let me out of the house unless I was with her, and she shoved food down my throat every time I opened my mouth. I swear I gained ten pounds every month I was there. That woman could cook like you wouldn't believe, and she would ask me every day what I was craving—besides crack, that is. I'd tell her and she'd make it for me. She sat with me when I was going through withdrawal, and put up with my shit when I was fiending. I look back on that time in my life and think she must've been a living angel. I'd be pacing the floor and cursing up a storm, threatening to do all kinds of shit, and she'd just sit there and smile, keep on reading her Bible like I'd just said 'good morning' instead of 'kiss my ass.' She scared the shit out of me."

"So you just sat around the house eating all day?"

"And studying for my GED. She insisted on that. I took the test three times and finally passed it when I was twenty. The math portion kicked my ass every time. Isaiah was two then."

"Wait a minute." I held up a finger. "You went from eating up everything in the house to Isaiah being two. What are you leaving out? You had Isaiah, and then what?"

"I went into labor one night while I was sitting in the kitchen, pigging out on any and everything. I remember my water breaking just as I was scraping the bottom of a quart of butter pecan ice cream. Think I was a little pissed about being interrupted, too. Anyway, I had to wake her up so we could get to the hospital. I was in labor for twenty-one hours with Isaiah, and then he finally popped out, screaming at the top of his lungs. I thought when I left the hospital that I was going back to her house, but she had other plans."

"Is she the woman in the picture in your office?"

"Yeah, that's her. Aunt Bobbi. She took my son and signed me into an inpatient drug treatment program. I stayed there for a year. I hated her for that at the time."

"You didn't see Isaiah for a whole year?" I searched her face to see if she was joking.

"Yes, I did. She brought him to see me every weekend, faithfully. She wasn't cruel, and she made a point of telling me, quite often, that she wasn't looking for any kids to raise, so I had better get my shit together so I could take my son. I was eighteen when I went in, nineteen when I graduated from the program, and I had every intention of taking my son and getting on the first bus back to Indiana the minute they let me out. But things didn't quite work out that way."

"A year of treatment, Anne?" She nodded seriously.

"The best year of my life."

"So you were, what, twenty by then? What happened next?"

"You know, you're kind of nosey, Smoke."

"I thought I told you to stop calling me Smoke?"

"When I knew you, you were Smoke."

"And when I knew you, you were Breanne. What's your point?"

"Since you put it like that, I don't guess I have one. Breanne is dead, though."

"What killed her?" She hopped to her feet.

"Shake it off, Isaiah!" She sat back down. "Self-awareness and education killed the shit out of her, choked her to death, and gave her a proper burial. It wasn't pretty."

"Did you like Mississippi? Is that why you stayed so many years?"

"I liked it OK, but Isaiah thrived there. He had lots of friends and my aunt spoiled him rotten, so I decided to stay a little while longer. Before I knew it, years had passed and people were treating us like we'd been there all the time. Plus, I liked the small town community feel of it. After a while, it just seemed too complicated to pack up and move back to Indiana. I had a part-time job in a library that I really loved because I could read all the books I wanted, whenever I wanted to, and I could pick Isaiah up from school and bring him to work with me in the afternoons. Plus, my aunt was sick by then, and I couldn't see packing up and leaving her when she needed me, after everything she did for me. I owed it to her to help her the way she helped me, so we stayed until she died. End of story."

"Is that a nice way of telling me to shut up and mind my own business?" I grinned at her and she grinned back.

"Something like that."

"What about all the degrees?" I'd seen them on the wall in her office.

"What about them?"

"You earned them."

"I did," she said slowly.

"I'm impressed. Why social work and African studies?"

"Because it's a thankless job, but somebody has to do it, and who better than a previously thankless person? African studies because it was interesting. Did you know that I traced my lineage back to a tribe in Africa that was renowned for its superior tribal warfare? Learning about where I came from helped me see where I was going. Why did you decide to teach?"

"Probably for the same reason you just stated. I think I

needed to give something back because I had taken so much from society."

"Do you like it? Teaching?"

"I love it."

"I love my son."

"Is that a warning?"

"Should it be?"

"If it is, it isn't necessary. Can I ask you something?"

"You will anyway, but I'm not promising an answer."

"All right. Why did you take that first hit of crack?" I saw her face shut down and close for business, but I didn't regret the question. It had been at the back of my mind since last Friday.

"I'll save that story for another time," she said.

"What if I never ask again?"

"You will. You're too busy trying to fit me into the category you think I should fit into, but you can't because I don't fit anymore. I changed my shape so I would never fit again. You ask questions because you're looking for some reason to discredit me and make me be a fake. Do I sneak off and light up? Am I secretly an alcoholic? What? I can't simply be a woman who straightened her shit up and moved on, can I? If I were a man, you'd be slapping me on my back and welcoming me back into the fold. You wouldn't have so many questions because the particulars wouldn't be nearly as important. So, you *will* ask again, and I may or may not give you the third installment to my saga at that time. It depends on whether I'm PMSing at the time. And on whether I feel like it's any of your business. So far you've managed to catch me in good moods."

Having been neatly and efficiently put in my place, I could do nothing but stare at her with my mouth slightly hanging open. I finally snapped out of my trance and noticed that the game was coming to an end. My son's team had won by a slippery two points, and people were starting to file out of the gym a little at a time. I looked for Isaiah and didn't see him. A few seconds later, I found my voice.

"I didn't mean to make you angry, Anne. Or to hurt your feelings. I was just—"

She treated me to one of those dazzling, crinkled nose smiles and laid a hand on my thigh. If she felt me tense up, she didn't show it.

"I'm not angry, Smoke, and my feelings aren't hurt, either. I stopped giving people the power to hurt me a long time ago. I can't seem to make it stick where Isaiah is concerned, though."

"Now I'm insulted," I half-joked. She'd basically told me that I meant nothing to her. I wasn't quite sure how I felt about that, but I put a smile on my face anyway.

"Oh, well, sorry, I guess." She shrugged and tossed her purse over her shoulder. "The game's over. I should go find Isaiah."

ANNE

I got the hell away from Smoke as fast as my heels would allow me. It was surprising enough to run into him, at Isaiah's school of all places, but he started in with the questions and threw me off my game. Seriously. Why was he so interested in my life, anyway?

I was always skittish around Smoke, even way back when I was in the third grade and he was in the fifth. I was new to the school and he was already one of the popular kids, one of the ones who thought I was a creature from outer space. Hell, all the kids thought that, now that I was thinking about it. I walked around like a period at the end of a sentence—small, black, and wholly unnoticeable. I might've faded into the walls if it hadn't been for the thick, coarse hair standing out from my head like a mop, and the hand-me-down clothes calling attention to me. And, of course, the color of my skin.

There were other dark-skinned kids who would've made just as worthy targets as I was, but their make up was different from mine. They didn't seem to be pre-conditioned to accept ridicule and harassment the way I was. I walked around with my head hung low, and my eyes constantly averted. I might as well have had a sign on my back telling people to kick me because I was already down. The other kids had picked up on the fact that I was a walking victim and made me their poster child, an assignment I didn't have the wherewithal to rebel against.

I was telling the truth when I told Smoke that he didn't have the power to hurt me now. Not many people did. In fact, there were only two people that I knew of who could bring me to my knees, and that was Isaiah and myself. My son could devastate me, and I could harm myself, but no one else held that privilege. I had taken my power back just before I murdered silly little, destructive Breanne Phillips.

She was the one who cared what people said about her and what they felt for her. She was the one who had listened when people told her that she was black and ugly, and she believed it wholeheartedly. It was such a damn shame, too. If people had never said those things to her, she might've been able to look them in the eye when she passed them, and she might've been able to feel good about herself. The crack might've never been an issue.

They say the Lord doesn't give you more than you can bear. I used to wonder what his thought process was when he gave me my mother and sister. How had he figured I could bear to live with them and not try to destroy myself just to escape?

Smoke was a conduit for my self-destruction, although

he didn't know that was my mission at the time. Probably didn't give a shit, either. His focus had been on making as much money as he could, any way he could, like a lot of misguided, young black men, and my money was green, just like everybody else's.

He never focused on me long enough to see that I had stars in my eyes whenever I was close to him. The adolescent crush I'd harbored for him was my secret, and I held it to me like it was worth a million bucks. It was the reason I only purchased my drugs from him when I could've just as easily gone somewhere else. It was the reason I gave him my virginity when I could've just as easily given it to someone else for a rock or two. He was the finest, smoothest boy I'd ever seen, and I desired him with a fourteen-year-old's intensity. In other words, irrationally.

It seemed strange, all these years later, to admit to myself that I had desired Smoke sexually. It felt almost wrong to think it even now. Yet some things didn't change regardless of what the mitigating circumstances were. Although I was fourteen when I took my first hit of crack cocaine and felt the zing of it course through my system, I was still a teenager. I was aware of my vagina when my jeans were too tight, of my breasts when I accidentally brushed my nipples and caused them to stiffen. I knew what it was to watch and wonder about the opposite sex. I watched and wondered about Smoke Avery, the same as a lot of other girls, and sixteen years later, I was skittish around him because he forced me to remember that.

I stood by my SUV, waiting for Isaiah to come out of the school. The bus carrying the visiting school's team had lumbered off a few minutes ago, so I guessed he would be emerging any minute. He usually spent several minutes bullshitting around in the locker room before he finally decided to grace me with his presence. I looked around the parking lot, which was almost empty, and hoped I wouldn't have to barge into the locker room and drag his butt out of there. I'd actually done that once before.

A few seconds later I jumped a full three feet when a hand touched my shoulder. I whirled around with a hand pressed to my chest, and let out a relieved breath when I saw that it was Isaiah's coach who'd touched me, and not some lunatic I would have to fight off.

"Leonard, you scared the shit out of me. Wait a minute and let me catch my breath." I bent at the waist and breathed deeply. A scream was lodged in my chest, begging to be released, but I fought against indulging it. He stood there chuckling, and the sound of it made me chuckle, too.

"I'm sorry, Anne. You know my sense of humor is slightly skewed. You want to punch me or something?" He was a big man, tall and wide with muscle that had mellowed slightly with age and nonuse. His skin was white enough to glow in the dark, and he perpetually sported a military style crew cut. He reminded me of a character from the Beetle Bailey comic strip, except he was younger and more feral looking. Isaiah always called him a bulldog behind his back.

"No, I'm fine now. But I think I might punch Isaiah when he comes out for making me wait so long. Did you need to speak with me about anything in particular? Isaiah showing his ass, for instance?" This was what I had been reduced to, thinking that everything was bad news about Isaiah.

"Actually, this past week was a really good week for him. As long as he keeps it up, he should be OK, I think. I just wanted to say hello, see how you were."

"I'm good. You?"

"Well, my boys kicked some ass tonight, so I can't complain. You look good, Anne, but then you always do."

I couldn't help blushing. Leonard always managed to

slip in some sort of compliment whenever I encountered him, which was often. I hadn't decided yet if he was flirting with me.

"Thanks, Leonard. I appreciate that." I shifted into the beam of a parking lot light and glanced at my watch. "What is taking Isaiah so long?"

"I'll go in and send him on out," he offered. He slid past me and headed toward the building. A few feet from my car, he stopped and turned back. I looked at him expectantly. "One of these evenings, maybe after a game or something, I'd like it if we could go for coffee or grab a bite to eat, Anne. Does that sound OK to you?" My eyes widened.

"You *are* flirting with me. I wondered about that."

"I wondered if you'd caught on by now. I must be out of practice if it took you this long. Will you think about it?"

"I promise I will," I said. I watched him disappear into the building and pulled my keys from my jacket pocket. I climbed into the driver's seat and locked the doors. One scare a night was enough. I turned the key and switched on the radio, sat back, and let myself be soothed by India Arie's fluid voice. I started twitching my shoulders to the beat and singing along with the bridge, thought I was sounding good. A tap on the passenger side window broke my rhythm and brought the scream back to the center of my chest. I glared at Smoke through the glass and slammed my finger down on the power lock.

He pulled open the door and climbed in. I waited until he was settled with the door closed and we were all nice and cozy. Then I screamed at the top of my lungs.

"What the hell is wrong with you?" he asked.

"I'm sorry. I needed to let that out. That's the second time somebody's sneaked up on me tonight. The first time I didn't scream, but I had to this time. Why are you still here?"

"I was waiting for Isaiah. I thought maybe he might want to get some dinner or something. You think he will?"

"He might. Leonard went in to get him, so you can ask him yourself in a few minutes." I turned the music down and drummed my fingers on the steering wheel, looked out the windshield at nothing. "I'm knocking him upside the head first. This waiting stuff is getting ridiculous."

"Leonard, huh?"

"Yeah, Leonard is his coach."

"Leonard was pushing up on you a minute ago, too."

"You still stalking me?" I narrowed my eyes on his face and stared him down.

"Stalking is a strong word. I was standing outside my car and I just happened to see *Leonard* over here getting his mack on. It was completely harmless. You're into white men, huh?"

"You never had a white woman?"

"Once or twice, just long enough to figure out that it wasn't my flavor. There's something about a sista that can't be touched. I don't know what it is, though. I can't put my finger on it."

"Well maybe you should spend more time trying to figure out what it is, and less time dipping into my business. Where is that boy?"

Smoke looked out his window and spotted Isaiah coming across the parking lot with his duffel bag slung over his shoulder.

"Here he comes now, and don't start that nagging and shit the minute he gets in the car, Anne. It's nerve wracking."

"Kiss my ass, Smoke," I said and pressed a button to unlock the doors. He was still laughing when Isaiah pulled the back door open on my side. I paid no attention to Smoke and started right in as soon as I heard the door close. "Do you have any idea how long I've been waiting out here, boy? You act like you got a personal chauffeur or something. What were you doing in there, taking a bubble bath?"

"Mama, please . . ."

"Don't give me that 'Mama, please' mess. Anything could've happened to me out here." I turned the motor over and reached up to tilt the rearview mirror so I could see his face. "You didn't think about that, did you?"

"Yeah, Coach Leonard's old horny butt could've grabbed you and ran off," Isaiah drawled, and Smoke laid his head back and howled with laughter. I slanted him a glance and rolled my eyes.

"Neither of you is funny. Smoke, didn't you have something to do?" I raised my eyebrows at him.

"Oh, it's like that?"

"It's like that."

"You want to come with us, Anne?"

"No. I think I've had about all I can take of you for one night, but thanks anyway."

"Wait, who is us, and where are we going?" Isaiah pushed his head between the front seats and looked from me to Smoke suspiciously.

I opened my mouth, but Smoke beat me to it, and, as usual, he was very eloquent.

"Us is me and you, youngblood. I'm hungry. Let's go get something to eat."

"I ain't all that hungry."

"Get out anyway," Smoke said, pushing his door open and stepping out. He aimed a meaningful look into the backseat and closed his door with a flick of his wrist.

I turned around in my seat and looked back at a mutinous Isaiah.

"You getting out?"

"If I don't, he'll probably come around here and try to choke a brotha to death. That dude is something else. Where did he say we was going?"

"I don't know, but you'd better eat something because I'm not cooking tonight," I told him.

ISAIAH

I thought he was gone take me someplace like McDonald's or something, but he got me good. We went to a fancy seafood restaurant, where all the waiters were dressed up and the tables had white tablecloths on them. It was almost ten o'clock, so the place wasn't crowded, and we got a good table by the window. I sat down and looked at the lighted waterfall outside while he pinched his creases and sat down across from me. Was this dude for real?

"I ain't exactly dressed for fine dining," I said. I had on my jeans and Nautica shirt from earlier. Good thing I took a shower in the locker room.

"Me neither, but I'm in the mood for it, so what the hell? Check the menu out and see what you think you want. I already know I want a beer."

"Me, too."

He looked at me like I had two heads, then shook his head, laughing.

"Nice try. Anyway, I'm having an Irish Ale, not that weak shit you guzzle by the gallon. You need to chill on that, by the way."

"You need to chill on telling me what I need to chill on." I picked up a menu and slammed it open in front of me.

"How long you been smoking weed?"

"How long did you smoke weed?"

"I smoked it maybe four or five times in my life. I always liked to be in control of my faculties and weed skews your perception of reality."

"You didn't smoke it? You just sold it."

"Nope, never sold weed."

"Just crack, and to my mama." He didn't have a chance to say anything back to me because the waiter walked up. I handed him my menu and told him I wanted the shrimp feast and a glass of root beer. Dude ordered stuffed mahi-mahi and his beer, then sat back and looked at me.

"Is that why you're acting so ignorant? Because your mother was once addicted to crack, and I was the one who sold it to her? Do you think either she or I are proud of it?"

"I ain't acting ignorant."

"Yeah, you are. I think she lets you get away with it, though, because she feels guilty over having lost your respect."

"I don't know what you talking about, dude. I respect my mama."

"So you show respect by yelling at her and calling her names, abusing drugs, drinking, and fucking up in school? That's an ingenious tactic."

"You don't know nothing about it, so don't come at me with that daddy knows best routine. You ain't gotta look at your mama and think about when she was a drug addict and out there walking the streets, turning tricks. That shit ain't cool."

"Is that what you really think she was like?"

He propped his chin on his fist and stared at me long enough for me to scoot around in my chair. Dude's eyes were something else, like freaking missiles or something. I wondered if that was why Sierra Hughes was always twitching around in her desk whenever I looked at her in class, because I looked at her like he was looking at me. I shrugged and looked around the restaurant to keep from looking at him. Sierra's breasts were too damn big not to look at, but I didn't know what his deal was.

"She was young and sad looking all the time. I remember that much. Skinny little knock-kneed thing, too."

"She ain't knock-kneed no more, though, is she?" I watched our waiter come toward our table with food. Thank God, 'cause I was starving. "All my boys say my mama is a dime-piece. Especially Hood. I think that fool actually tried to talk to her once and she had to check him."

"We agree there. Hood is a fool. And no, she's not knock-kneed anymore. You're right about that too. But that's all you're right about. She never prowled around the streets looking for a hit. Doesn't sound pretty, but she only came to me for what she wanted back then."

"So she turned tricks for you then."

"It wasn't quite like that, I don't think. It's complicated, but it wasn't as simple as that. Don't tell her I said this because I'll deny it until I die, but I think she had a crush on me. I took advantage of that."

We both got quiet and sat back when our food came. I unfolded my napkin and spread it across my lap, then bowed my head to say grace. I remembered to do that even when I was high, although I never remembered what I thanked God for then. You couldn't sit at the table with my Aunt Bobbi and not say grace unless you wanted a smack on the back of your head.

I ate like I didn't know what food was. I had fried shrimp, scampi, pasta with shrimp in it, and beer battered shrimp. I saved those for last since it was the only beer I was going to get tonight. I almost forgot dude was there, because the food was so good. I looked up when I had three shrimp left and saw him grinning at me.

"What?"

"You worked up quite an appetite on the court tonight. Scored, what, thirty-five points?"

"Yeah," I mumbled and went back to my plate. I was surprised he was keeping up with my shots.

"I was impressed. Your mother was too. I had to hold her back from jumping on the ref a time or two."

"She's always clowning at my games, whistling and carrying on." I had to laugh and shake my head. My mama was more than a little bit. "Then if she ain't whistling, she's picking lint off my jersey, embarrassing the hell out of me. You need to tell her to stop doing that."

"I told her not to start nagging when you came out tonight but she did it anyway."

"She don't listen."

"Nah, she doesn't."

We grinned at each other and I got a funny feeling in my chest.

"Why did you take advantage of my mama?" I didn't know I wanted to ask him that question until it was out there and it was too late to take it back. I held my breath.

"Your friend Hood, he sells drugs. Am I right?" Wasn't no sense in lying.

"Yeah, he does a little something."

"You ever sit back and watch the way he operates, like he can do anything he wants to do and get away with it. Like he's untouchable?" He didn't wait for me to answer. "I had a fucked up mentality like that when I was heavy in the game. People stopped being people and money started being everything. I stopped looking into people's eyes when I talked to them."

I thought about what he said, rolled it around in my head for a minute, and nodded. I got that he was telling me he used to be stupid.

"What do you do now? You still slinging?"

"These days I'm slinging textbooks and worksheets around. I teach high school math."

"How you go from knowing a god to teaching math?"

"By the grace of God."

"Can I bring you anything else?" The waiter appeared from out of nowhere.

"You want something else, some dessert, fifty more shrimp?" he asked me, grinning. The waiter had the nerve to laugh too.

"Some of that Bananas Foster sounds good," I said.

"That's what I'm talking about. Bring two."

"What you gone eat?" I asked dude, playing with him. The waiter laughed then too.

We was in the car, a sweet little Cadillac Coupe, nodding our heads to some R. Kelly when dude went all deep on me again.

"I was arrested when I was nineteen, almost twenty. You would've been a newborn then, if I'm figuring correctly. I was looking at some serious prison time, too. Scared as a hell. Didn't feel nothing like a god then."

"You did a bid?" This shit was getting better and better. First a drug addict mama, and now a convict father. What the hell else could happen?

"I did a couple of months in the workhouse, until my court date. Then I went before the judge to find out how many years he was going to give me. The only person who came to court to support me was my mother. She cried and shouted out to God, fell in the aisle, and started speaking in tongues, all that shit."

I cracked up. I couldn't help myself. I was picturing this little old lady lying on the floor, talking crazy and looking even worse. I could see my mama doing some out of control shit like that. Dude was laughing too. I almost choked because I was cracking up so hard.

"I'm serious," he said. "She showed her natural ass, and all because of me. Begged the judge not to send me away. Told him I was too pretty to go to prison, which, don't get me wrong, is true, but I'm getting off the point. You asked me how I came to be a teacher."

We rolled to a stop at a red light and sat through it in silence. When the light turned green and he still hadn't said nothing, I looked at him.

"What happened?"

"He gave me an ultimatum. I could either go to prison or I could enlist in the military. It was my first time ever being arrested, and he said he would expunge my record if I chose door number two and never saw the inside of a courtroom again, so I did."

It was my turn to be impressed.

"Which branch?"

"Marines. Twelve years. I was probably in Germany around the time you were learning how to walk."

I was quiet for the rest of the drive to my house. I was thinking about everything he said, processing it. I didn't want to like him, but I was starting to. Even though I was mad as hell about the fact that he wasn't around when I was growing up, I was starting to like him. He was like this smooth, debonair type dude with a little bit of street mixed in, so you knew he didn't forget where he came from. I dug the way he dressed, the way he talked, and even the way he walked. I wondered what he thought of me, if he thought I looked like him or took anything else after him.

Dude pulled up in front of my house and shut off the car. I stared out at my house, looking at the front room window, where a light was on. The dashboard clock said it was after midnight. Past my curfew. I thought dude was going to push me out of the car and shove off, but he sat there with me, being quiet and looking at me as I looked at the house. I could feel the heat from his eyes, but I didn't turn around and look at him.

I knew my mama would be in the kitchen, making up excuses for staying awake and waiting up for me. One time I came home after three in the morning and she was in the kitchen baking a cake, talking about she had a craving for something sweet. She was probably taking some cookies out of the oven right now.

"Why she have to do drugs?" I asked suddenly. "I mean, I know she don't really have nothing to do with Aunt Laverne and Grandma Alice, but was shit *that* bad she had to *do drugs*?"

I did look at dude then. If he used to know what my mama was like when she was using, maybe he could tell me what the deal was. All she ever said was that she felt bad about herself, which didn't mean shit to me. That was like saying you didn't like what size shoe you wore. But you didn't go out and shoot up because you had big feet, did you?

Dude looked at me for a long time. Then he snatched the key out of the ignition and opened his door.

"I've been wondering that myself. Let's go ask her," he told me. I had to run to catch up with him before he walked up on the porch and rang the doorbell.

Just like I suspected, my mama was in the kitchen cooking. All that talk about not cooking dinner was right out the window. If my nose was telling me right, she had made some beef stew. She could put her foot in some beef stew, made it just like my Aunt Bobbi used to make it.

She was wearing a long, silk robe and matching house shoes, the kind with tall pointy heels, and I rolled my eyes. She was always wearing something like that around the house at night. No wonder my friends called her a dime-piece. I couldn't make her see that she was too old to dress like that. I shot a glance at dude and saw that he was checking her out as she walked back into the kitchen and left us standing in the foyer. Naw, she wasn't knocked-kneed no more, that was for sure. I wanted to tell dude to stop looking at my mama like that, but I didn't say nothing, just shook my head and led the way to the kitchen where she was.

"Please don't tell me you took my son to a burger shack for dinner, Smoke," my mama said. She didn't even ask where we went to eat, just assumed we had burgers, getting ready to start nagging again.

"I took my son, *our son*, out for a sit down dinner, Anne." Dude winked at me while she was busy pouring stew from a pot into a plastic bowl. "We could've brought you back something, so you wouldn't be cooking this time of night."

"It's fine. Isaiah knows I cook when I'm restless. He'll have this gone by tomorrow night anyway. You want something to drink?"

"Thanks anyway. Um, I think Isaiah has something he wants to ask you, Anne."

She was suspicious right off the bat. She took the bowl over to the refrigerator, pulled the door open and looked at me over her shoulder.

"If this is about spending the night at that idiot Hood's house, the answer is still *no*. Although I don't know why you're bothering to ask since you're out all night with him anyway. But still, he's—"

I jumped right in before she went off on one of her tangents and I lost my nerve.

"I was wondering why you started using drugs."

My mama froze like an ice cube, standing in the refrigerator door. For the longest time she just stood there, looking lost in space. Then her head fell to her chest and she took two deep breaths.

"Smoke, I told you—"

"He asked me, and I didn't know what to tell him. It seems to me you're the only one qualified to answer that question." He caught my look and cleared his throat. "We were *both* wondering," I said.

I didn't think she was going to answer me. She closed the refrigerator and started wiping down the counter and stove. Five, then ten minutes passed.

"Do you remember when you were in the seventh grade and your class was learning about slavery, Isaiah? I took it upon myself to fill in the blanks where the bullshit in your textbook left off. I explained to you about the various social issues that sprang up and about how blacks were divided and pitted against each other. The light-skinned slaves were put to work in the house and the dark-skinned slaves were put to work in the fields, right? You remember that?"

I realized that she was tearing up by the sound of her voice. The last time I saw my mama really *cry* cry was when I was nine and I was getting baptized. It was some humbling shit then, but it was even worse now. I looked at dude, hoping he knew what to do for her if she suddenly started screaming and calling out, because I sure as hell didn't. But he was staring at her, so he wasn't no help at all. *Damn.*

"Well, Aunt Laverne and Grandma Alice would've been house slaves because they're light-skinned and considered to be attractive, whereas I would've been made to work in the fields because dark skin wasn't considered as desirable. It was like that growing up in my house. They ganged up on me and called me ugly names because I wasn't pretty like them and I believed everything they said, the same way you believed that the tooth fairy actually came and got your little smelly teeth and put bo-dollars under your pillow for you to find the next morning. It was really me sneaking into your room after you finally went to sleep and I could get my hand under your pillow without waking you up. You always were a light sleeper." She must've realized she was getting a little off track, because she stopped and shook her head to clear it.

"Anyway, I listened to all this crazy bullshit at home, and then I went to school and got it all over again. My hair was nappy and my skin was too dark. The kids would whisper about me and say things when I walked down the hallways, about my clothes, my shoes, shit, anything they could find to make fun of me about. I thought, well, hell, it's a consensus, so they must be right. Something is really wrong with me."

"You always told me not to pay attention to what other kids said about me, unless they were saying I was mean, because maybe then I needed to take stock," I reminded her. She had drilled that shit into my head for so long that I forgot when she actually stopped drilling and I started remembering on my own. "That time you caught me making fun of Larry Jones's funky old jacket, you made me give him my new one. You said the greatest compliment somebody could give me was to say that I was a good person." I tried to keep from sounding like I was accusing her, but, shit, how could she tell me those things and then fall for the okey-doke herself?

"I told you that because I didn't ever want you to be the kind of person who could make someone feel the way other kids made me feel."

"But you said—"

She stopped wiping the stove and held up a hand. That was my cue to shut up.

"Isaiah, please. You asked me a question and I'm trying to answer it. I know what I told you, and I also know that I told you that stuff when I was fully grown and knew it to be true. When I was a kid, I soaked stuff up like a sponge, just like you did. It took me forever to convince you that that damn purple dinosaur wasn't real, but you soaked it up and you believed it with all your heart. Running around the house saying shimbaree, shimbarah all damn day and night. Do you see him anywhere now? That's what I thought. Stop interrupting me, so I can finish. It's past my bedtime.

"Where was I? Oh, OK, so I thought I was the ugliest person alive and I would sit outside and cry until I probably *was* the ugliest person alive from crying so much. Now on this one particular day, I had a really bad argument with your Aunt Laverne. I think she threw a canister of sugar at me and I pulled a knife on her. It was crazy. So I'm outside, right? And this guy walks up and tells me that he has something that will make me feel better. So much better that I wouldn't believe it. I knew him from around the neighborhood, so I went with him to see what it was, and I got lost. That's how I ended up in Mississippi with Aunt Bobbi. She came and found me and helped me get my shit together. Does that answer your question? And yours, Smoke? That's your third and last installment, by the way."

She walked out of the kitchen and left us standing there. Said something about locking up the house and for us to have a good night. Then she disappeared. Dude and me stood there staring at each other for the longest.

Chapter 5

ISAIAH

I was supposed to be hanging out with that fool Hood on Sunday, a repeat of last Sunday's activities in the park, but dude had said something about swinging by to pick me up so we could do something before he left. I sneaked and called Hood on his cell to tell him I couldn't make it, and then I beat my mama to the nagging she was about to start and got my chores done real quick. I didn't want no problems when dude showed up.

He said around noon, so I hopped out of bed after nine and jumped in the shower. I picked out khakis and a striped polo shirt to wear, and decided against putting on my Jordans in favor of the Bass loafers my mama insisted I needed when we went school shopping. They was sitting in my closet, looking lonely, and I decided to take pity on them. Plus, dude was always dressed to a tee, and I wasn't about to be following him around all day looking like a buster. I brushed my waves and dabbed on a little Cool Water cologne before I went to see what my mama was up to.

She was in the front room, going crazy on the tables

with a can of Pledge and her dusting rag, which was really a pair of Underoos with Superman on the front that I used to wear about a trillion damn years ago. She had the music blasting, rolling her hips along with Prince, singing about wanting to be some chick's lover. I stood in the doorway watching her bounce around in her running shorts and tee shirt, acting like she was the one really doing the singing instead of the dude with all the money. She didn't know she had an audience yet.

She killed a high note and flung back her locks so she could pump her hips harder. I didn't know what her locks had to do with her hips, but she was working it. I laughed and shook my head, left her to her dancing. I went in the kitchen and grabbed a soda from the fridge. Prince went off and I waited, with my soda halfway to my mouth, to see what the next CD in rotation was. A few seconds later, the Gap Band came on and I knew she was really getting ready to clown. "Early in the Morning" was her all-time jam, and it was the first song to start up. Oh, it was on now.

I noticed dude standing on the porch as I came out of the kitchen. I sneaked a look in the front room to make sure my mama was still getting her groove on, and she was. She didn't hear the doorbell, and now she was doing the snake while she dusted the pictures and other miscellaneous shit on the wall unit. I looked at dude as I crept down the hall toward the door.

I opened the storm door and held up a finger for him to be quiet. He stepped in, wearing tan slacks and a blazer, and pointed to the front room.

"You been out there long?" I whispered, standing close to him. Damned if he wasn't wearing Cool Water, too.

"Nah, just walked up. Who's having a party?"

"My mama does this every time she starts cleaning. You ever see her do the Cabbage Patch?" His eyebrows shot up and a smile crossed his face. I motioned for him to follow me as I tipped back down the hall. I stood on one side of the entry to the front room and dude leaned against the other side. She was grooving real tough by now, had her hands in her hair, pumping her hips like she was putting it on somebody. The can of Pledge and my drawers were sitting on a shelf. Me and dude slid looks at each other at the same time.

We watched her for about thirty seconds before she finally turned around and saw us standing there. She jumped like she was having a seizure, ran over to the stereo, and switched it off. I had to give it to her, she didn't act embarrassed because we saw her dancing. She just picked up my drawers and the Pledge, and came over to us. I knew she was embarrassed, though, because even though she had smooth, Hershey bar skin, she was blushing.

"Smoke, I didn't know you were coming," she said, looking up at dude. Then she aimed a killer look at me and I cracked up.

"I thought youngblood would've told you. We're hanging out, doing some stuff today before I leave. Is that OK with you? Because if you've got some chimneys for him to sweep, or some grout for him to clean, I can come back."

"You're funny." She reached out and tugged on the waistband of my khakis. "Go and put on a belt. A brown one since you've got on brown shoes. And what's this? You're actually wearing something other than those funky sneakers? Praise be to God. Go on."

I stood still as she adjusted the collar of my shirt and started picking at lint. I knew there wasn't none on my shirt because it was brand new. She just liked to fuss. "I don't need a belt. My pants ain't falling down."

"If you have belt loops, you wear a belt, whether you need one or not."

"Mama, please don't start nagging," I said. Dude chuckled and put his fist to his mouth like he was covering a cough when my mama gave him one of her looks.

"One of these days I'm going to pop you one for saying that to me. Go on now."

"You probably need to grow about five or six more inches to reach me." I held a hand over her head so she could see how short she was. She swatted it away and I took off toward the stairs before she could pop me one like she said. Height ain't never been a disadvantage where my mama was concerned.

I didn't know why, but I was feeling pretty good.

ALEC

I watched Isaiah jog up the stairs and disappear, then I took my eyes back to Anne.

"Woman, do you even own a bra?" She rolled her eyes at me and went back to her dusting, giving me her back.

"What is it about my breasts that offends you so much?"

"Hey, I have absolutely no problem with breasts." I walked through the room, over to her. I took a minute to look around and nodded approvingly. So far what I'd seen of Anne's house was nicely decorated, with plush furnishings in muted colors, and quality woods polished to a high sheen. I recognized good taste when I saw it. I walked up behind her at the wall unit. She was wiping a shelf and her ass was twitching with the effort. I didn't have an issue with asses either. "But are your nipples ever *not* hard?"

She went completely still and gave me her profile.

"Smoke . . ."

"Forget I said that. How do you feel about me taking Isaiah to Indiana?"

"*Today*?" She whirled around to look at me, shocked.

"I was thinking more like next weekend. I spoke to my mother this morning, and she wants to meet her grandson, as soon as possible, she said."

"Your mother wants to meet my son?"

"Apparently. She's planning a small scale family reunion. Says I can't show my face at her house unless I have Isaiah with me. Would that be all right with you?"

"A family reunion? In Indiana?" She looked shell-shocked, and spoke slowly.

I thought I knew what she was thinking.

"Anne, you know I'll take care of him. He'll stay with me at my house, and he—"

"It's not that, Smoke," she said. She waved a hand and stepped around me. She was wiping the palms of her hands on the back of her shorts as she walked out of the living room.

What the hell just happened here? I heard a door close nearby, waited ten seconds, and then went to see where the door was. I ran into Isaiah in the hallway.

"Give me a minute," I told him, shooting him a don't-ask-me look.

I found the door just off the hallway in a small alcove and knocked softly. No response came, so I turned the knob and stuck my head inside. It was a guest bathroom, with just a sink and toilet, decorated in earth tones. There was a wicker basket in one corner containing a variety of magazines, and a matching shelf on the wall over the toilet with neatly folded hand towels stacked on it. A faintly floral scent jumped out at me and I searched with my eyes for the potpourri that I knew was somewhere in the room. I found it in a bowl sitting on the vanity. I found Anne there, too, gripping the edge of the sink, crying softly.

I closed the door behind me and moved up behind her.

"You wouldn't know this, but crying women make me nervous as hell, so is there any chance you could stop any time soon?" She kept right on crying and I settled my hands on her shoulders and turned her around to face me. "What's the problem, Anne?"

"You want to take my son to Indiana." She wiped at her tears and looked up at me with those big eyes of hers. A watery smile curved her lips before she ducked her head. "It's stupid to be crying and carrying on. I guess I didn't really think about you having a family and the possibility of them wanting to meet Isaiah. That changes everything."

"How so?"

She was so out of sorts she put her hands on my arms and squeezed, and left them there. I looked in the mirror over the vanity and sized up the scene, knew I was in trouble. She was leaning back against the vanity and I was standing close enough to her that if I took a half step in her direction, our middles would be touching. My hands were still on her shoulders, and hers were now on my forearms. Under a different set of circumstances, it would've been an intimate embrace. I dropped my eyes and saw her ass perched on the edge of the vanity.

"He'll have cousins and aunts and uncles and a grandma," she whispered.

"He has an aunt and a grandmother now, doesn't he?" I took my eyes away from the mirror and put them back on her face, where they belonged.

"Not really. We send cards and short letters, pictures and stuff like that, but he hasn't seen Alice or Laverne since he was eleven, and that was at my Aunt Bobbi's funeral. They send him birthday and Christmas gifts, and there's the occasional phone call, but nothing like what family should be, Smoke. This is different."

"Then this'll be good for him."

"I know." We stared at each other.

"Tell me what you're really thinking," I said.

"I don't want him hurt. I don't want him to get his hopes

up and then you suddenly decide you don't want to be bothered with him after all. That would just make things worse. I mean, I don't care how hard he acts, I know my son, and he'll be hurt if you disappear again."

"I didn't disappear in the first place, Anne. I didn't know about him. But I know about him now, and I'm telling you I'm not going anywhere. You need me to promise or pinky swear or some silly shit like that?"

"Pinky swear is not silly," she said, smiling. She sucked in a deep breath and let it out slowly. I should've stepped back when she moved in and rested her forehead against my chest, but I didn't. What I did was take my hands to her waist and pull her in closer. "Have you mentioned this to him?"

"Not yet. I was planning on doing it while we were out today." I watched my fingers spread out around her waist in the mirror.

"Don't let him talk his way out of it, Smoke. He needs this."

"I hadn't planned on taking no for an answer. Plus, you'd probably have Beverly Avery knocking on your door in the middle of the night if I did. If you let him miss next Friday from school, I plan on driving down Thursday and taking him back with me Friday morning. I'll send him back on a plane Sunday night."

"That's fine, but if one hair is out of place on his head when he gets back here, I'll have to kill you. Do you understand the terms and conditions of this agreement?"

"Perfectly." Outside the door, I heard a loud meaningful groan. I grinned and shook my head. That boy was something else. "I should go."

"Thank you, Smoke."

"For what?"

"For everything. I appreciate it."

"No thanks necessary, but remember you said that

when he gets back from Indiana. I'm planning on introducing him to Deeter, too." I watched her search her memory, trying to remember who Deeter was. Apparently she remembered, because a few seconds later she threw her head back and burst out laughing.

"Deeter was a mess," she said when she could talk again.

"Still is. He'll have stories to tell when he returns, I guarantee you that. Come here and give me a hug. You look like you need one."

Now what the hell did I say that for? I didn't stop to examine my reasoning. I just slid my arms around her waist and hugged her tightly to my chest. She tucked her arms inside my blazer and spread her hands out on my back. We stayed like that for a minute.

"Your breasts are pressing against my chest," I whispered close to her ear. That made her giggle, so I walked my hands up her back to the spot where I thought the hooks of a bra should be and held her there. She started pulling away, and I eased the grip I had on her. I pressed a kiss to the curve of her shoulder, then to the edge of her jaw. Her lips were next. Just quick little pecks, lips firmly shut, and purely platonic. They were meant to cheer her up, nothing more. But she gasped and that caught my attention. I stared at her mouth, at the little pink tongue hiding inside, and dove in.

I just wanted to see what she tasted like. The sixteen-year-old waiting for me in the hall was proof enough that we had been intimate before, that, at some point, my penis had been inside her vagina. But nothing about what we'd done years ago was the least bit romantic or soulful. I had vague recollections of fumbling with her against a wall, sitting in a chair as she rode me amateurishly, and, once or twice, we'd had sex on a couch in somebody's apartment. Maybe that was why I was so fascinated with her braless breasts. I'd never seen them before. I didn't know what they looked like, what any part of her body looked like, really. My curiosity had more to do with wanting to know about her as a woman, and not the skinny little thing she used to be. So I tasted her. I tilted my head and made her taste me back.

I pushed my fingers through her locks, cupped the back of her head, and tongued her deep. She was a timid kisser, almost like she hadn't done it in a while and was out of practice. I groaned when I became frustrated with the limitations her lips placed on the kiss, and pressed in closer with more tongue. She had no choice but to open her mouth as wide as her skin would allow and take me in. I teased her tongue, taunted it nonstop, and made it come out to play with mine. Then she was kissing me back and my vision went a little fuzzy.

Anne turned the kiss into a minor scrimmage and I was more than willing to step into the ring with her. I sucked on her tongue, let her suck on mine, let her think she was choking me, and then tried to choke her. The kiss was wild and hot and so damn deep I didn't know where her lips stopped and mine started. I pressed her back against the vanity and fit myself between her legs, took her head back on her neck.

Isaiah's ill-timed knock on the door had us jumping apart like guilty teenagers.

"I'm *hungrrrry*," he called out in a sing-songy voice. I closed my eyes and massaged the bridge of my nose as I collected my thoughts and put them back in order.

"That was good," I said a few humming seconds later. Anne shot me a quelling look and wiped my spit from under her bottom lip with a shaky hand. Her nipples were straining against the front of her shirt and I thought about my own private strain.

"That was bad, Smoke."

“Excuse me?” I asked, ego on full alert.

“Don’t play with me. You know what I mean. You better go.”

I thought that sounded like a good idea, and I did just that. I stepped out into the hallway and cuffed my son around his neck, damn near dragged him to the door.

Three hours later, we were coming out of the movie theater and I was wiping butter from the popcorn we’d murdered from my fingers with a paper napkin, when I told him what had been on my mind all through the movie. Asking him what he thought had never crossed my mind. I just told him what our plans were for the following weekend.

“I’m driving down Thursday and driving back to Indiana Friday morning. So you need to be ready to roll, probably around ten or so,” I said, watching his face carefully. It was so exactly like mine that I still couldn’t believe it. I unlocked the passenger door for him and walked around the car. We dropped into the car at the same time, spread our legs out under the dash, and looked at each other.

“You taking me to Indiana with you?”

“Yeah.” I started the car and backed out of the parking space. “You got a problem with that?”

“For what? What’s in Indiana?”

“Your grandmother, for one thing. Cousins and aunts and uncles, for another. I told her about you and she wants to meet you. Looking forward to it, actually. She wanted to know everything about you, and I told her what little you’ve told me. You’ll have to tell her the rest. I have a nephew around your age, too. I think you might like him.”

“She wants to meet me?”

A car horn blared and I looked around. I’d forgotten I was driving after backing out of the parking space. We were sitting in the middle of the aisle, blocking traffic. I shifted the car into *drive* and navigated past the car waiting for my space.

"Told me not to darken her doorstep without you," I said.

"Dude, what did you tell her about me?"

I pretended to think about the question. I wasn't sure how much to tell him. Should I admit that I'd broken down and cried as I was describing him to my mother? Or that I had talked for an hour about his skill on the basketball court? That I had told her about him bowing his head and saying grace before he ate, spreading his napkin on his lap? I'd asked him about that at one point during dinner, and he told me that Anne had enrolled him in an etiquette class when he was ten. I was impressed with her all over again, and told my mother so. The details I gave her on Anne were sketchy, just that she was from Robinwood and that I hadn't known she'd given birth to my son, hadn't even known she was pregnant until just recently. But I boasted about my handsome son and she had listened attentively, and then demanded that I return with a picture of him immediately.

"I told her that you were my son and that I was very proud to say that, even if you do insist on calling me *dude*," I said. "Told her your ears were big, just like mine used to be, and that you like to smoke weed and drink, even though shit like that is beneath you." I concentrated on driving as he glared at me.

"You smoked weed, and don't even tell me you didn't drink, 'cause I ain't gone believe it."

"I was young and hardheaded, and a little on the wild side, Zay. Matter of fact, a lot on the wild side. You don't have to be."

"You told your mother that shit about me?"

"Yes, I told your grandmother that shit about you, and I believe I mentioned something to you about that gutter mouth of yours once before. It's the truth, isn't it?"

"Dude, you tripping. What's her name?"

"Beverly Avery, but don't even think about calling her Beverly or Bev or anything like that. She'll take your head off and hand it to you on a platter. The other grandkids call her Big Mama, and she'll tell you to call her that too." I let him sit on that for a while. Then I had a thought. "And for the record, my name is Alec Avery. Not Alex, *Alec*," I said, stressing the C on the end, lest there be any confusion. "I like that name better than I do dude."

"You want me to call you daddy now?" He was being sarcastic, knuckle headed little thunder-cat that he was.

"You can call me whatever you feel comfortable with, son." I lifted a hand and started ticking shit off. "Long as it's not motherfucker, dude, shithead, or asshole, or any variation therein. What sounds good to eat?"

He shrugged indifferently. "I wouldn't mind a steak."

"Point me in the right direction," I said. He gave me directions to a steak house and I pulled into the parking lot a few minutes later. I glanced at my watch and shut off the car.

"You got somewhere else to be? Because if you do . . ."

"Now where else would I rather be than with my *easy* going, *sweet* natured son, seeing as how he's such a *joy* to be around?"

"Dude, you tripping," he said and climbed out the car.

I caught up with him inside the restaurant and came to stand beside him at the hostess's podium. She was a good-looking sistah, somewhere around three or four years older than Isaiah, but I watched him turn on the charm anyway. I chuckled softly and looked away while he did his thing, pushed my hands in my pockets, and jingled loose change.

She led us to a table with a little more sashay in her

step than I thought was natural. He swiveled around in his chair to watch her walk away, and locked eyes with me across the table when he turned back around.

"She's cute."

"You're right. Too old for you, though."

"I could handle her. She might not be able to handle me, though."

I tucked my tongue in my cheek and studied the menu. "Should we start with appetizers?"

"I like the blooming onion," he said evenly. "My mama calls you Smoke." We looked at each other.

"Smoke is dead," I said, borrowing one of Anne's lines. I watched my son's eyes go from cool hazel to smoky gray in a matter of seconds. Knew mine were doing the same thing.

He knew it too. He laughed and used his menu to point across the table at me.

"No, he ain't."

After dinner I took my son back to the hotel with me so I could pack and get ready to head to the airport. I poked and prodded at him until he finally dropped his guard a little more and opened up to me. I asked him the questions I'd been wanting answers to since I first laid eyes on him in his yard wrestling with the lawnmower. I found out that he was partial to the color purple. Not that weak, watered down purple, he said, but the deep, intense purple that made you think of royalty. He sat at the small table in my room while I showered quickly and told me that, when he was younger, he wanted to be an astronaut and then a fire fighter. Somewhere along the way he had started scribbling, messing around with plots and characters, and now he wanted to be a writer. Horror stories or murder mysteries, he said. I left the bathroom door open so I could hear every word.

Pot roast with carrots and potatoes and brown gravy was his favorite meal. He hated okra and beets. I told him that I did too. We swapped stories about our mothers forcing us to eat the shit when we were younger. I sneaked in a comment or two about Anne, slid in the fact that from what I had seen so far, she'd done a good job raising him. I felt I owed her at least that much. He went to hemming and hawing, but he eventually admitted that she was a little flaky sometimes, but that she was a decent old lady. That's what he said, a decent old lady. I told him I had been married before and he wanted to know if I had other children. I told him no and thought I could almost hear his sigh of relief.

Who were his friends, I wanted to know. What were they like? There was Jerome, who was so damn smart the boy could be a doctor someday. And some cat named Bo-Bo, who was the next Cedric the Entertainer, for real. I laughed at a few of Bo-Bo's more infamous jokes and circled the conversation around to that little nigga, Hood.

"Bad news," I said. I tilted my head up and looked at myself in the mirror, swiped a Gillette Mach IV up my neck expertly. He didn't reply and I stepped back and caught his eyes from the bathroom doorway. "Hood is trouble, Zay. You feeling me on that?"

"Hood's all right. He don't act like you saw him acting all the time."

"Anybody you've got to sneak out of the house to hang with can't be up to any good, son. Plus, he sells drugs."

"Sometimes."

"Ain't no such thing as a part-time drug dealer. Either you're in or you're out. What are you going to do when he gets stopped by one-time and there's drugs in the car, right up under the seat you're sitting in? Because you know they'll suddenly be yours, right?" I went back to shaving.

"Why you shaving this time of the day?"

I looked at him, standing in the bathroom doorway frowning at me. I guessed he was tired of talking about sorry ass Hood and I decided to leave it alone. For now.

"Rule number one," I said to his reflection, "never leave the house half-assed. Always keep your shit tight because you never know what opportunities will present themselves. That's along the same lines as wearing a belt even if you don't need one. Plus, ladies like a brotha who's well turned out. Remember that." I splashed water on my face, patted it dry and followed up with aftershave. Cool Water.

He laughed and left the doorway.

"You think you GQ or somebody?"

I came out of the bathroom with nothing but a towel slung around my hips.

"GQ ain't got shit on me." I pulled a pair of Levi's and a T-shirt from the suitcase on the bed, then took a pair of boxers back into the bathroom. No sense in giving my son a preview of what he had to look forward to. His head was already big enough. I smoothed on deodorant, moisturized appropriately, and tossed my toiletries in a carrying case, then looked around to make sure I wasn't leaving anything.

"Why you want to fuck up your life by using drugs and hanging around with bullshit people?" I asked Isaiah as I came out of the bathroom and shook out my T-shirt. I pinned him with my eyes and wouldn't let him look away from me.

"I don't use drugs all the time."

"Some of the time is too much." And that, I thought, was that. "You can't think straight to write a complete sentence if your head is all messed up. Do me a favor anyway, Zay. Lay off the drugs and the drinking for the next little while. See if it makes as much of a difference as I think it will. You think you can do that?"

I managed to get a slight nod out of him and I let it ride. I finished getting dressed and took him home so I could make my flight. On the plane, I settled into a window seat, relaxed, and closed my eyes. As the plane taxied and took off, I let myself relive the kiss.

Chapter 6

ANNE

Smoke showed up Thursday evening, just like he said he would, and busted up in my house like he'd been doing it for years. Isaiah took him up to his room and they stayed in there with the door closed the rest of the night. I fell asleep after midnight, and Smoke had to wake me up to tell me that they were leaving. He was taking Isaiah back to his hotel with him to spend the night so they could jump on the road first thing in the morning.

I looked at Smoke, sitting on my bed, leaning over me, and shook myself. I always woke up muddle headed and talking crazy. I was surprised I didn't come to talking about moving chairs around and eating mashed potatoes while I was doing it. Crazy stuff like that. I must've said something halfway funny because Smoke chuckled and shook his head as he stood up and walked out of my room.

Now that the time had come, I was having mixed feelings about my baby leaving me, even if it was just for a weekend. We hadn't been apart more than a night since he was small enough for me to hold in my arms and balance on my hip. What was I supposed to do with myself without him around the house? I asked Smoke this as we were standing at the front door, waiting for Isaiah to come back with the pictures he'd picked out to take to his grandmother. I wrapped my robe tighter around me and looked up at him.

"I don't know, Anne. Maybe you could get a facial or a pedicure. Get fitted for some bras or something. You women like to shop. Do that. Or call up your boyfriend and put it on him all weekend. You got a boyfriend?"

"You got a girlfriend?" I shot back, looking at him like he was crazy.

"A woman I've been seeing for about six months," he admitted.

"Good, so take her shopping for bras. Let me see which ones you're taking," I said to Isaiah as he walked up holding a large folder. He handed it to me and I turned it upside down so the pictures could fall out in my hand. I flipped through the stack quickly, aware that they were both staring at me impatiently. I didn't give a damn. "Why do you need this one?" I asked. I held up a picture of Isaiah and me when he was fourteen. It was a fun themed portrait, with the two of us sporting matching shirts and smiles. I remembered that I had found my shirt in the boy's department and his in the men's.

"In case anybody asks about you. I need to be able to show 'em that my mama is a dime-piece, for real." He slid the picture from between my fingers and took the envelope from me.

"I don't like that, Isaiah." I was instantly irritated. Such silly phrases the kids used these days. "A dime piece? Come on and give me a hug. I'm at least a dollar bill." I went up on my tiptoes and wrapped my son in my arms. "Be good and do what Smoke says, and—"

"I know all that, Mama." Isaiah sighed. "You act like I'm going to Iraq or something."

"Did you pack decent clothes?"

"Supervised that myself," Smoke added.

"Oh . . . well, OK. You drive like you've got solid gold in the car, Smoke. No drinking, and no—"

"Lord have mercy, woman. Let us out of here already."

I rolled my eyes at Smoke and turned back to Isaiah.

"Call me as soon as you get there too. You love me?"

"Yeah, Ma." He breathed dramatically and tried to hide a blush, looking at the floor.

"I love you too. Be safe."

They left me a few minutes later, but I stood in the doorway, looking in the direction they had disappeared a long time afterward. This was worse than Isaiah's first day of kindergarten, when the teacher had to ask me to go ahead and leave. I had almost punched the cross-eyed bitch. In my mind there was no such thing as being overprotective.

I took Smoke's advice and got a manicure and pedicure, and went to the salon to have my locks touched up on Friday evening. Saturday morning I did a little shopping, starting with groceries and ending with three pairs of shoes and two pairs of slacks, and felt a little better. Still, I felt guilty about the indulgence and I stopped by the center to finish up some paperwork before the weekend staff left for the day. I stopped and picked up a salad for lunch, and ate it at my desk.

I was wiping up a dollop of ranch dressing from a spreadsheet when my cell phone rang. I dragged my purse across my desk and fished it out.

"Hello?"

"Anne, it's Smoke. And before you start screaming at me, Isaiah is fine."

"Okaaay," I said slowly. He was right. I was about to start screaming. "How is everything going there? He's not being mistreated, is he?"

"Hell, my mother hasn't stopped kissing him since he got here. Does that give you any indication as to how things are going? We walked in and I got a pat on the head and then it was all hail king Isaiah. I'm feeling a little mistreated myself, to tell you the truth."

"I'm glad. Where is he now? Can I talk to him?"

"He left with Don and Jeff a couple of hours ago. I don't know where the hell they are, and I'm about to send out a search party."

"Who's Don and Jeff, and why don't you know where my son is, Smoke?"

The sound of his laughter reached my ears, strong and deep.

"Relax, woman. Don is my oldest brother, who happens to be a policeman, and Jeff is my nephew. He's Isaiah's age, and they've been stuck like glue since we got here. It doesn't take two hours to go get ice, though, does it?"

"I would say not. Does he have a lot of cousins?"

"Enough. What are you doing right now?"

"I'm at the office. Why?"

"There's been a slight change of plans, and I need to run something by you."

"The answer is no, you cannot keep my son, and, yes, I will press criminal charges. So don't even think about it."

Smoke burst out laughing so hard he took the phone away from his ear. I heard a woman in the background and my ears perked up.

"Is that her, boy?" the woman was saying. Smoke was still laughing. He must have shook his head because she said, "What is so doggone funny? Have you asked her yet?" Then Smoke, "I'm getting around to it." Her voice came closer. "Give me the phone, Alec. Long distance costs too much for you to be wasting time cackling and carrying on." It sounded like a light scuffle took place over possession of the receiver and then Smoke was mumbling under his breath.

"Smoke?" I said into the phone. *What the hell?* I wasn't footing a long distance bill, but the call was all over my cell phone minutes.

"What is it you're saying?" the woman asked Smoke. Then, "Oh, OK, that's what I thought. I know you weren't trying to get smart." Two seconds later she was giggling like a schoolgirl and breathing in my ear. "Hello, is this Anne?"

I was caught off guard.

"Um, yes. Who is this?"

"This is Beverly Avery, Isaiah's Big Mama. Girl, that boy is a knockout. I thought I was back in time when I first saw him. He looks so much like Alec. Just like him. I'm so glad you let him come see me. He's so sweet, too."

"Are we talking about the same Isaiah?"

Her laugh boomed through the phone and brought a smile to my lips.

"You know you can never tell if they listened to a thing you taught 'em until they get away from home and do you proud. I'm so crazy about him I don't know what to do with myself. Oh, and thanks for the pictures. I put 'em on my shelf with the rest of the family pictures. Plus, I'm on my third roll of film already. What?" she asked someone who I guessed was Smoke. Her voice changed directions. "Don't be rushing me now. Go in the kitchen and check on my pies if you need something to do. I'm back, baby," she said to me. "Now what was I saying? Oh yeah, dinner usually starts at three, and then we sit around and socialize for a while. Maybe play some cards or something."

I was wondering if she was older than I had imagined and sort of mixed up in the head.

"That's nice," I said. "I'm sure Isaiah will enjoy that. He's good at Spades."

"I started teaching him how to play Bid Whist last night. You play?"

"No ma'am. I never learned."

"It'll be easy enough to teach you too. Just wear something casual. We ain't fancy when we're trying to eat, OK?"

"OK." I had no idea what she was talking about. I glanced at my watch. Fifteen peak time minutes gone.

"All right now, Anne. I'll see you."

"Sorry about that," Smoke said a few seconds later.

"I'm a little lost. Dinner is at three and Isaiah is learning how to play Bid Whist and pretending to be sweet. What did I miss?"

"That's what I was getting around to telling you. My mother wants to meet you. In person. Tomorrow."

"*What?*"

"That's what I said, but Isaiah was telling her about you and she decided that she needed to see who you were for herself."

"Smoke, I can't just drop everything I'm doing and hop on a plane to Indiana."

"When was the last time you've been home, Anne?"

"My home is here. Make up an excuse, tell her I'm too busy. Why does she need to meet me?"

"She wants to meet you because you raised my son single-handedly and did a good job in the process. I don't think she's planning on letting you finish the job alone from here on out, though. Hell, I'm not either, for that matter. It's just dinner, Anne."

"Dinner with your whole family. I don't need that kind of stress right now."

"It was originally Isaiah's idea." I sucked in a sharp breath.

"That was low, Smoke. Even for you."

"There's a flight leaving Chicago at seven tonight. You'll get here at eight-thirty, no later than nine. Me and Zay will pick you up from the airport."

"And where am I staying for the night?" I wanted to know. I was starting to warm to the idea. It didn't sound so intimidating if *Isaiah* truly wanted me to meet his family.

"At my house?"

"Absolutely not."

"There's a Holiday Inn right next to the airport."

"No."

"A Marriott down the street from the airport?"

"I don't think so."

"Damn. A Sheraton Elite a little farther down the street from the Marriott?"

"Better," I conceded.

That was how I found myself racing around my house, packing a change of clothes, and throwing toiletries in my carryall. I checked for the third time to make sure I had everything, locked up my house, and drove like a bat out of hell all the way to the airport to make my flight. I left my Lexus on a secured pay-to-park lot and made it to the gate just as tickets were being taken and passengers were boarding the plane I needed to be on. I reminded myself to thank Smoke for reserving a ticket for me and having it waiting at the counter when I trotted up, breathing hard and cursing the three-inch heels I was wearing.

It was dark outside when the plane landed. I waded through the crowd and stood by the luggage carousel, waiting for my garment bag to appear. I slung my carryall higher on my shoulder, looked to the left, and focused in on Smoke's face.

"The prodigal daughter returns," he drawled, walking over to me. He reached for my carryall and I gave it to him.

"You were supposed to be at the gate."

"I was. You were moving too fast for me to catch up, so I followed you here. Interesting skirt."

I looked down at the denim skirt I was wearing, puzzled. It stopped just above my knees and matched the thigh length crocheted sweater and V-neck top I had paired with it.

"What's wrong with it?"

"Not a damn thing. Is this your bag?" He pointed to a Louis Vuitton Garment bag and leaned over to snatch it up before I could tell him that it was. It matched the carryall he was holding. "Is this everything?"

"Yes, but wait a minute." I unzipped a side pocket on the carryall and stuck my hand inside. "I stuck some nuts from the plane in here. Let me get them."

"You want to stop and eat?"

"I can eat later, at the hotel."

Outside I whistled when I saw Smoke's truck. It was a man-size Dodge Ram pickup, one of the sporty ones that sat high off the ground with fancy looking tires and tinted windows. The paint was what caught my eye, though. It started off being black, and gradually faded into silver, like . . . smoke.

"Is this another one of your rentals?" I asked as he helped me up into the cab. I decided to ignore the fact that his hand was riding my hip. He walked around and hopped in next to me.

"No, this one's mine. This is my *other* baby's mama. You like her?"

"I can see that you do, so I guess that's all that matters." I pulled the seatbelt around me and buckled up.

"I let Isaiah drive the rental I had yesterday morning for a little while," he confessed as he adjusted the rearview mirror and shifted into drive. He caught my veiled look and scoffed. "I waited until we were out of the city and traffic was light. I'll tell you right now, Anne, I will put your ass out on the side of the road if you start screaming and shit."

I figured he was joking, but I didn't want to press my luck. I held my tongue and chose to suck my teeth all the way to the hotel instead. Every once in a while I popped a roasted almond in my mouth and slid him a look. He seemed to think I was hilarious, and he laughed off and on until we were in my hotel room. I never cracked a smile.

"I told him he had to take driver's ed before he drove, Smoke," I said as I dropped down on the queen-sized bed and slipped off my shoes.

"Who better to teach a boy how to drive than his father, Anne? Stop hogging him and let me have some of him, too. You have to share now."

I sent him a baleful look and shrugged out of my sweater. I took my swimsuit from the carryall and laid it on the bed.

"I know that. It's hard, that's all. Did he do OK with the truck?"

"Rode her like a man." Another baleful look. "Speaking of which, I need to get back to the house. Jake was teaching him and Jeff how to play poker. I'm partnering with Don."

My eyes got big, neck snapped back.

"What?"

"Would you chill out? Everything is under control. You going swimming?"

"Yeah. I don't have to wear a bra for that, do I?"

"No, but please tell me you brought one." We stared at each other.

"Get out, Smoke."

I was worn out after twenty-five laps in the pool, breathing hard and feeling like every ounce of energy had been zapped out of me—seriously out of shape. Not so long ago I could've done fifty laps without breaking stride. Sugar to shit, that's what was happening to my health regimen. I still ran a couple miles each morning, but I hadn't been to the gym in I didn't know how long, nor was I particularly careful about what I ate lately.

Case in point was the spinach dip I ordered later from the hotel restaurant, then used every one of the fried tortilla chips on the platter to clean the dish. After that I had a basket of hot wings and seasoned fries. Cleaned the damn bones and used a half a bottle of ketchup. I was feeling completely wiped out by the time I made it back to my room. I took a long, hot shower, moisturized my locks, and took my tired ass to bed. I decided I was getting a pool installed in my backyard real soon.

"Anne!"

I jumped like I'd been shot, rolled over on my back, and squinted my eyes open. I put up a hand to block the sun coming through the window across from my bed, and saw Smoke stalking through my hotel room like he was looking for a fugitive from the police.

"Smoke, what the hell are you doing in my room?" I pulled the sheet up, probably a second too late, and glared at him. I felt my blood pressure spiking.

"They gave me two keys when I checked you in. And good damn thing they did too, because I've been calling you for the last three hours. What did you do, go out partying last night or what?"

"Shut up and close those damn curtains," I snapped. He went over to the window and pulled the curtains closed. When I could see again, I used both hands to hold the sheet up and looked at him from head to toe. "And leave that extra key on the dresser too. That was foul as hell, what you just did."

"I thought you were hurt or something." The key clattered onto the dresser. "How come you're not up and dressed?"

"What time is it?"

"Eleven-fifteen."

"*Pffft*, I've still got a few more hours. She said three, right?"

"Right, but Isaiah had me come get you early, and here you are lying up on your ass like sleeping beauty." He started tugging on the sheet from the foot of the bed and I shrieked, which made him laugh.

"Isaiah should've called first, and so should you. He's just at batty as you are. Stop it, Smoke!" I know I looked silly, kicking out at him and twisting all around on the mattress, but I had to do something. He was pulling on the sheet, and I was naked underneath it. I had the sheet in a death grip as I narrowed my eyes at him threateningly. "Smoke, I swear to God . . ."

"God ain't got shit to do with the fact that your titties are looking me in my face. Nipples hard as hell too. So that's what they look like, huh?" He tilted his head to one side, staring.

"Don't even think about it." I put up a hand to stop him from coming over to the bed, but he ignored me and sat down next to me anyway. We locked eyes and I started scooting in the opposite direction. "Go away, Smoke."

"In a minute," he promised.

ALEC

I told her I would go away in a minute and then I leaned sideways and fastened my mouth on a nipple, drew it deep into my mouth, and lapped it with my tongue. I wet it up and it slipped out of my mouth. I stared at it, bouncing in front of my face, and blew on it softly. I think I heard buzzing in my ears, but I couldn't be sure since Anne's whimpering blocked it out. I liked the sound of it better than the buzzing anyway.

I braced myself on my hands and went after the other nipple. Anne flattened her palms against my shoulders and wasted her energy pushing me away. A baby could've used more force, and the sounds coming from her throat told me what I needed to know. I took my tongue to the undersides of her breasts, flicked it across, up and down, and around the tips of her nipples, then bit and sucked at her breasts until the hands on my shoulders turned to fists. That was when I quite literally lost my mind. Seriously. Rational thought ended, right then and there. Somehow I ended up in bed with my son's mother and it happened like this.

Anne cried out when I pulled the sheet aside and cupped her between her thighs. She fell back against the mattress and let her eyes slide closed as the heel of my hand found sensitive spots and began applying rotating pressure. Her head fell sideways, away from me, as I slid a finger inside her heat and captured her clit under my thumb. Seconds later she was fucking my hand, slowly and intensely, and floating her way to orgasm. I decided to help her even further along.

I snatched my hand away and replaced it with my mouth. My tongue vibrated down the length of her sex, dipped inside of her, then zeroed in on her clit. I tickled it, teased it, sucked on it noisily, and took her all the way through an orgasm that shook the bed. I slid my tongue all the way up her body and buried it in her open mouth.

We kissed a long time, changing the angle of our heads, testing out everything from sucking each other's lips to sucking the tips of each other's noses. I was all over her neck, hoping I wasn't leaving teeth marks, but knowing I probably was. I squeezed her breasts, dropped more kisses on them, and hissed through my teeth as her mouth went to work on my neck.

"Take this off," Anne whispered in my ear as she tugged on the hem of my pullover. She followed up her request by darting her tongue in my ear. I moved back far enough to grab her eyes with my own and comply. I was so hard it was uncomfortable inside the jeans I was wearing. I unzipped them gratefully and felt my dick pop out and tighten.

I braced myself on the mattress, enjoyed the silk of her thighs around my waist for a few seconds, and then, like a heat seeker, I was inside her. My eyelids dropped like automatic shutters when I discovered just how hot and wet she was. And tight. Incredibly goddamn tight, like a fist. I gritted my teeth against the selfish urge to take and then explode. I had to be still for long seconds while I tempered my urges. Then I began to move.

Fifteen minutes later we were the reason for the headboard knocking against the wall like an insistent guest. I was pumping into Anne wildly, giving her every inch of me and taking no prisoners, and she was telling me to do it. In between throaty moans, high-pitched shrieks, and gasps that threatened to cut off her air supply, she whispered to me what she wanted. Ten minutes ago she told me to flow deep and slow, and I did. Five minutes ago I was pulling her ass back against me as she sobbed into the pillow under her head. Now I was on top of her, about to lose my mind, and tonguing her deeply.

It was music, all of it was. A nasty, erotic kind of music that sent the musty smell of sex up into the air, made the sheets damp and twisted, and pulled them away from the mattress at the corners. I can't lie and say I didn't add to the rhythm, because I did. I was the bass drum, beating out hoarse shouts, throwing my head back, and growling like a bear. She was driving me fucking crazy. She was driving me. Fucking me. And making me crazy with the need to cum.

"Close 'em," I growled in her ear. She slid her thighs closed around my dick and came a third time. Less than a dozen strokes later I was bucking out of her and spilling my milk all over her belly. I squeezed my eyes shut when she took me in hand as I came. In the end I did give in to my selfish urges and slipped back inside her to finish spilling. I was still lying on my back, catching my breath when she crawled out of bed and went into the bathroom.

I toyed with the idea of joining her in the shower, but the closed door made me think twice. It was a statement just as surely as if she had given me the finger. So I stayed put until she came out.

We didn't talk as we dressed. I don't think we even looked at each other. Well, she didn't look at me, I know that much. I looked at her plenty. I took a quick shower and came out of the bathroom buck naked, and nothing, not even a glance. I got dressed and moved up behind her at the dresser, zipped up her dress, and borrowed some of her lotion. And still nothing. *So that's how we're playing it, huh?*

I tried to provoke her by letting her see me use her toothbrush, but she just sucked her teeth, snatched her purse from a nearby chair, and went to stand by the door. I joined her there a few minutes later. I reached around her to pull the door open, and grabbed her eyes.

"You're a sexy little woman, you know that?"

"You think?" she shot back, and it was my turn to suck my teeth.

A little conceited too, I thought, but didn't say.

By the time we pulled up to the curb in front of my mother's house, I had decided that I'd had enough of the silent treatment. I shut the truck off and sat back, staring at the side of her head until she gave me her eyes. She made me wait fifty-leven minutes for those big eyes of hers, and I thought about strangling her.

"OK, so . . . about what happened back there," I began.

"Nothing happened back there, Smoke."

"The people in the next room might have a differing opinion."

"They might, but they would be wrong."

"Oh, so you're in denial now?"

"Could we just pretend nothing happened, please?"

"We could." I thought about it for a second. "I guess that's a good plan. We did not damn near break the bed, and you did not cum at least four times. Nothing happened."

"I didn't mean to do that, Smoke," Anne blurted out suddenly. "I was horny, and you were sucking . . . things. It set me off."

"How long since you've been with somebody?"

"A while."

"How long?"

"I dated a man in Mississippi, but I broke it off when I moved." My eyebrows shot up.

"Over four years? Damn, woman."

"So you can see why I did what I did. I don't need you thinking I'm some kind of tramp or anything like that."

"I wasn't thinking that, Anne. Actually I was thinking that explains why you were so tight."

She closed her eyes and shook her head like I was a hopeless cause.

"Smoke, *please*. I'm trying to tell you that what we did back there was a mistake. I don't need sex to survive. And I especially don't need it from you."

"That's a lie and a half, but we'll roll with it," I said, laughing. "I won't bring it up again if you don't. It's done. Over. Finito. Feel better now?"

"You promise?"

"Promise. You want to pinky swear on it?"

Chapter 7

ISAIAH

My mind was all over the place, taking it all in. I was still forming my opinions and impressions, but so far everything was all good. Dude, I mean, Smoke swooped me up Thursday and took me back to his hotel with him. We sat up half the night, playing cards and talking 'bout all kinds of shit. It was all right. I brought along a few of my stories, the ones I thought were the best, and let him read them. When I fell asleep, he was still reading. One thing I liked was that he didn't grab a pen and start trying to check my shit. I hated when people did that. Like I asked them to check shit instead of just reading it.

We checked out of the hotel and hit the road at ten Friday morning. A few hours later I asked Smoke if I could drive, and I damn near shit on myself when he pulled over and turned over that sweet ass truck to me. The conversation we had tripped me out, though.

"Driving a car is like riding a woman, Zay. You have to listen to how she purrs to know how hard to push her. You feeling me?"

I checked my seatbelt and pressed on the brake.

"I think I know what you mean."

"You do, huh? You had some pussy yet?"

I choked on my own spit, started stammering and shit. I couldn't believe he was asking me some stuff like that. My head snapped around on my neck.

"What?"

He gave me one of those lopsided grins I was still trying to perfect.

"You heard me. *Have you had some pussy yet?*"

"Yeah, once." I cleared my throat.

"When?"

"I don't know, six or seven months ago, I guess. Dang, can I drive now?"

"Check your mirrors and pull on out. And stay under the speed limit, too. So what have you been doing since then? Jacking off?"

"I'm trying to drive, if you don't mind, Smoke."

"It's Smoke now, is it? That's cool. It's cool if you jack off too. That's some healthy shit. Ain't nothing like the real thing, though. Were you careful?"

"Huh?"

"Don't play dumb with me, little nigga. Did you use a rubber? Check your speed."

I glanced at the dash. Sixty-five. I was cool, but I eased up a little.

"Yeah. When I started dating this girl named Denise, my mama went all crazy and started throwing boxes of rubbers at me left and right. I had to sit through another birds and bees talk, too. She kills me trying to say dick with a straight face." Smoke laughed loudly.

"She actually said the word dick?" I shook my head.

"Naw, penis, but that's even worse."

"True, true. So, you screwed her and dumped her?"

"She dumped me for another dude. She's a ho."

"Good thing you used a rubber then. But remember

this, youngblood, always treat a female like a lady, regardless of what you think she is. You never know where you might run up on her again and if she'll have something you'll want when you do. Plus, it's just a good policy to have. What's up with the thicky-thick little cheerleader your mother pointed out to me? Aisha."

"We're just talking right now," I said.

"Well make sure you use a rubber if you decide to do more than talk. Each time and every time, Zay. AIDS and all that other shit ain't to be played with, and I'm too young to be a grandfather. Slow your heavy-footed ass down. Right up in here is a speed trap."

I slept some of the way, and Smoke woke me up when we got to his mother's house, around three in the afternoon. It was a single story house with a chain link fence around the front yard, and covered trashcans sitting at the side of the house. The front door had a big oval of glass in it that I couldn't see through, and rose bushes were all over the place. I decided that it looked safe enough.

Smoke led me to the front door with a hand on my neck. But he couldn't get his key in the lock good before the door was snatched open.

"Isaiah, this is Big Mama," I heard Smoke tell me.

Big Mama was really a little bitty lady, just about as big around as my mama, and about the same height. She was the same color as me and Smoke, and her hair was dyed a bright shade of red-gold, pulled back in a ponytail. I stared into her eyes as she stared into mine. She showed me the gap between her front teeth, and I showed her mine. She clapped her hands and put them under her chin and just kept on staring for the longest time. I glanced at Smoke to see what I should do.

"Smoke, if this ain't you at his age, I will eat you up and spit you out. Come here, baby, and give Big Mama some sugar." I hadn't kissed an old lady on the lips since my Aunt Bobbi was alive, but I bucked up, smacked my lips against hers, and hugged her back as she squeezed the breath out of me. "Sixteen years is a long time, boy. We got a lot of catching up to do. You come with me." She stopped long enough to peck Smoke on the lips and then she took my hand and dragged me along behind her.

Family was everywhere. I met my uncles, Jake and Don, who both looked like Smoke and me. It was strange looking into eyes like mine everywhere I turned. I found out that Smoke was the youngest of the three of them, and the wildest. Don was a police officer and Jake was an electrician.

I met three female cousins and we all stood around trying not to stare at each other until Smoke came and rescued me. Then I met Jeff. And relaxed. It was smooth sailing after that. I spent a lot of time with Big Mama, talking and playing cards and stuff, and it didn't take me long to figure out why they called her Big Mama. She had a set of lungs on her that wouldn't quit. I thought about what Smoke had told me about her clowning in court and cracked up. That shit was true. I just knew it.

Smoke took me by the Robinwood Projects, his old stomping grounds, he said, and where my mama grew up. He pointed out the building she used to live in with Aunt Laverne and Grandma Alice, and then showed me some of the places he used to stand around in. I met a cat named Deeter, and that fool was wild. He came out of a burned up building hollering about chicken and biscuits. Smoke handed him a bag of extra crispy, a shirt, and some Fruit of the Looms, and told him that I was his son.

Deeter made me get out of the truck so he could see me good.

"I'm yo' cousin on yo' Big Mama's side. Her brother was my daddy," he said, grinning like a fool. I couldn't help but grin back. "Boy, you yo' daddy up and down. Who yo' mama?"

"Anne Phillips." I looked in his face to see what his reaction was gone be. I didn't have no problems with punching his ass in a hot minute, but he just kept grinning and nodded.

"She was all right with me. Cool people."

We hung out with him for a while and then jetted.

"What's his deal?" I asked Smoke after we drove off.

"Crack," was all he said.

I stayed at Smoke's house with him. It was different than what I was expecting, but still cool. I thought I was gone have to step over shit to sit down the way I did in my room back home, and I was surprised to see that his house was straight laid out. Some more of that GQ shit, I guessed. I could see myself chilling there in the summers.

I was having a ball. One thing was missing, though. My mama. I wanted her to meet my folks, so I mentioned it to Big Mama, and together we told Smoke to call her and make her come.

I would've went with Smoke to the airport to pick up my mama, but I was running the streets with Uncle Don and Jeff. They took me to their house so I could meet Aunt Liz, who was nice too. She made me eat two slices of cake and took I don't know how many pictures. I made sure I was there when Smoke came back with my mama Sunday afternoon, though. I was helping Big Mama in the kitchen and keeping an eye on the door at the same time.

"Yo, Zay, I think Uncle Al just pulled up outside with your mama. They ain't got out yet, though."

"They *haven't gotten out*, Jeff," Big Mama called out. She was on me about using slang too. Me and Jeff slid glances at each other as I went to the door and pulled it open.

My mama came into the house, looking sharp in a

sleeveless dress and just enough makeup. I nodded approvingly and looked at Jeff just before I let her hug me like she hadn't seen me in a hundred years.

"Have you been behaving yourself, Isaiah?" my mama asked, embarrassing the hell out of me.

"He ain't did nothing but take his rightful place," Big Mama hollered out, coming out of the kitchen and walking up to my mama. "Turn that boy loose and give me a hug."

Mama got hugs from everybody, and I could tell she was caught off guard by how friendly everybody was. She looked kind of dazed, like she was wondering if she was in the middle of a dream. But she was cool, though, answering questions and laughing at Uncle Don's stale ass jokes.

"Keep an eye on my mama," I told Smoke when she got sucked into the crowd in the living room.

"I got it covered, youngblood."

He better.

Next thing I knew we was all sitting around the table eating some of the best pot roast, carrots, and potatoes that I ever tasted. But I wasn't so caught up in my food that I didn't notice Smoke sitting next to my mama and whispering in her ear every five minutes. I wondered what his ass was up to. Me and Jeff locked eyes across the table and grinned. I thought I knew when she rolled her eyes at him and punched him in his thigh under the table.

Later on I ate three pieces of sweet potato pie while Jeff and I whipped Uncle Jake's and Smoke's asses in some Spades. My mama was deep in conversation with Big Mama and Aunt Liz, and the big screen was showing a movie. Everybody looked up when the doorbell rang. Smoke laid his cards down and went to get it.

He came back with a fine looking shorty in tight jeans and a halter-top. I sucked in a breath and told my dick to go back to sleep. *Down, boy.* I actually whispered that shit out loud, and Uncle Jake burst out laughing and slapped me on my back. I had to swallow twice.

"I'm sorry to barge in," sweet thing said and smiled all around the room. "I was passing by and I thought I'd stop in and get a look at the son Alec is always bragging about. How are you, Miss Avery?"

"I'm doing fine, Diana. Come on in and have a seat. See if you can pick out Isaiah. Where is he anyway? Is he even in here?" One of the other kids said yes and she waved a hand. "Shoot, he looks so much like everybody else, it's hard to tell. Gone ahead, Diana. Pick my baby out."

Diana's eyes settled on my face and her eyes got wide and round. She put a hand to her chest and looked at Smoke.

"Am I seeing double or what?"

Smoke motioned for me to come over, so I laid down my cards and stood up.

ALEC

I made the mistake of mentioning to Diana that Isaiah would be with me over the weekend, and I must've mentioned to her that Anne was coming during our phone conversation the day before, because here she was, looking all trussed up and pretending like she was just passing by. She had been to my mother's house a total of two times before, and briefly at that. But it was cool. I played along. My mother did, too, which was surprising because I knew she wasn't particularly fond of Diana.

I motioned for Zay to come to me and dropped an arm around his shoulders.

"Isaiah, this is a friend of mine, Diana Daniels. Dee, this is my son."

"Nice to meet you." Isaiah smiled and extended a hand to her. I think my chest inched out a little. I bit back a grin at the star-struck expression on his face.

"I've heard some good things about you, Isaiah. It's nice to finally put a face with a name."

"Yes, ma'am. Thank you."

"And so polite," Diana gushed, staring at Isaiah.

"That's all his mama's doing," Big Mama announced. "Lord knows Alec doesn't have any manners, because if he did he would've remembered that Isaiah's mother is sitting right here and introduced her, too."

I wanted to choke Beverly Avery.

Still, she had a point. I took my eyes over to where Anne was sitting and saw her uncross her legs and stand. Images of her breasts in my mouth flashed across my mind as I watched her walk across the living room and slip her hand inside Isaiah's.

"I'm Anne Phillips, Isaiah's mother," she said in that husky, breathy voice of hers. Her face was carefully neutral, but I thought I could see her thoughts as they ran across her mind. *Why were you fucking me this afternoon when you could've been fucking this creature?* she was wondering. She shifted and looked at me.

"Nice to meet you, Miss Phillips," Diana said. Was it just me or was she suddenly sounding strange?

Me and Zay glanced at each other and I knew I wasn't the only one feeling a little bit of a freeze coming off of Diana.

"Anne, please. Miss Phillips is my mother."

"Oh, well, Anne, then. I'm sure we'll be seeing each other again sooner or later if Alec has his way."

"I look forward to it. Do you need me to finish your hand?" Anne asked Isaiah.

"Nah, you can't play anyway, Ma. Thanks, though. You still need me here, Dad?"

I understood that it had just slipped out, but I still grabbed on to it and held it to my chest. I locked eyes with Zay and tipped my head toward the kitchen. I had to clear my throat before I could speak in a normal voice.

"I don't think so, but let me see you in the kitchen for a second. Excuse me a minute, Dee."

"Come on in and have a seat, Diana. You want something to eat or drink?" my mother asked, and I could've kissed her.

I kissed Zay instead. As soon as we cleared the kitchen doorway I pulled him to me and hugged him tight. I pressed a kiss to the side of his face and let out a long breath as I felt his arms come around me. I didn't know I was waiting to hear my son call me Dad until he said it, and then something in my chest exploded. Tears filled my eyes and I closed them to keep them from spilling over. Never before had I been so aware of the value of time. Sixteen years had passed without me knowing that he was in the world, and I hated that with everything in me.

"Is everything all right?"

I opened my eyes and looked at Anne, standing in the doorway with a concerned expression on her face. She came in and touched Isaiah on his back softly, shot a look at me.

I set Isaiah away from me.

"We were just having a man to man talk."

"Looked more like a baby to baby talk to me." She turned Isaiah toward her and helped him wipe his face. "Are you OK? Do you want me to kick his ass for you?" We all burst out laughing, which was a necessary tension breaker.

"I'm cool, Ma."

I took a few steps back and laid my head back to crack up when she snatched a tissue from the table, held it up to Isaiah's nose, and told him to blow.

"Mama, please." He snatched the tissue from her and balled it up. I shook my head as he stomped out of the kitchen and turned off in the opposite direction of the living room. I figured he was going somewhere to get himself together, and let him go.

Anne was a different story. I cuffed her arm when she went to walk out of the kitchen, and pulled her close to me so I could whisper in her ear.

"A word with you, madam," I said.

"You have company, Smoke. In case you've forgotten." She tried to wiggle her arm free, but I wasn't having it.

"That did slip my mind, what with my son calling me Dad and everything. Powerful stuff, that was. Let me tell you what else was powerful."

"How many beers did you drink?"

"Two." I paused. "OK, four, but that's beside the point."

"What *is* your point, besides proving that you can't hold your liquor worth a damn? And stop breathing that mess down my neck. What do you want? Do I have to call Don or Jacob in here to get you together? Or what about Flossine?"

"Diana," I automatically corrected.

"Whatever. Let me go, please."

"In a minute."

"Where have I heard that before? Come on now." She choked out a laugh even though she was trying to be hard. "You don't need nothing else to drink, seriously."

"I'm not drunk." I was feeling OK, though.

"Not even a little bit?" Anne shrieked sarcastically. "Because I felt sure you—"

I dropped my voice a few octaves and parked my lips next to her ear.

"I was feeling drunk when I was riding you today, though."

"*Gaaawwd.* Get your paws off me, Smoke."

I looked up as my mother came through the doorway. It occurred to me in that moment that I just might be a little drunk. It could've just as easily been Diana who walked in. I loosened my grip on Anne's arm and tracked her progress as she escaped.

"Isaiah?" I asked.

"He's fine. Don is in my room with him, talking. You know what about?"

I shook my head and lied with a straight face.

"Don't have the foggiest." Don was my oldest brother and my best friend. I'd told him about Anne and about me, and about how Isaiah had come to be, knowing that he would take it to his grave. Whatever he was saying to my son would only be beneficial. He thought the same as I did about Anne, that she was an incredibly brave and strong-willed woman. It wouldn't hurt Isaiah to hear that from someone besides me.

"Did you forget you got company?"

"How could I do that?" I treated her to one of my lady-killer smiles and went back to the living room.

Diana was sitting on the couch sulking, and I took a breath for patience. I was not in the mood for any shit tonight. I really wanted to go find my son, but, as usual, she needed to be dealt with first.

ISAIAH

My Uncle Don was the type of brotha who said a lot without saying a word, but when he got started, look out. I went in Big Mama's room and sat on the bed to get myself together, and when I heard the door open, I just knew it was my mama with another tissue or something crazy like that. I turned around to tell her that I didn't need to blow my nose, but it wasn't her. It was Uncle Don.

"I used to wish I had a daddy," I blurted out as he sat on the bed next to me.

"You got one now," he said.

Next thing I knew I was crying like a big ass baby and Uncle Don was holding me against his chest. Once I started, I couldn't seem to stop. I felt like a buster, blubbering all over him and sobbing like a bitch. I hoped didn't nobody else walk in, 'cause this shit was ridiculous. Straight up ridiculous.

"Let it out, son," Uncle Don told me, and I did.

When I finished, he looked me dead in my eyes.

"Smoke told me about your mother."

"What the hell he do that for?" Just that quick, I was mad as a motherfucker.

He put up his hands like he thought I was about to rush him.

"Relax, I said he told *me*. Nobody else knows. Not Big Mama, not Jeff, not even my wife. And they won't. Curse at me again and I'ma turn you over my knee. You ain't too old."

"Sorry." I looked at the floor.

"It's cool," he said. "I understand reflexes and spontaneous reactions. That's what happens when you say crazy shit to your mother, right? You forget who you're talking to or some silly shit like that?"

"It ain't that, Uncle Don. Sometimes I just get so mad at her."

"Because she makes you do chores and gets on you about your grades?"

"Because of what she used to do. I can't believe she would be so stupid."

"Do you think it's any easier for her to believe, looking back on it?"

I hadn't thought of it like that. I shrugged.

"No? Then tell me this. Why do you make it worse on her by bringing it up and throwing it in her face?"

"She don't trip off the stuff I say."

"You'll find out when you have kids one day—one day a

long time from now, I hope—that the shit your child says to you can hurt you like nothing else can. That's a fact there, boy. The people you love the most are the very ones who can kill you. Did Smoke tell you about my mother falling out in the courtroom when he went before the judge?" I nodded and we cracked up. "She ain't never clowned so bad in her life. I'm telling you ain't nothing like a mother's love. You lose it and you're fucked up."

"I feel you, Uncle Don."

"Do you? Because what I really want you to understand is that you could be in foster care somewhere or living from hand to mouth, or you could be somewhere in a corner, praying for the kind of mother that you got right now. But you're not because you got a good woman in your corner, and I'm trying to figure out why you're doing your best to kick her out of it. Any woman who is smart enough to pull herself up short, get herself together, and *keep* herself together doesn't deserve to be treated with anything less than the utmost respect. What do you think?"

"You're right," I mumbled. He was making me feel like shit and I think he knew it.

"Damn right, I'm right. Now tell me what you think about this. How stupid is it for you to be using drugs and drinking and shit if you're so disappointed in your mother for being human and making the same mistake?"

I opened my mouth to say something and started crying again. I was still crying like a bitch when Smoke came in the room. *Damn.* Now it was two against one. A brotha didn't stand a chance around these cats.

"Everything all right in here?" Smoke asked.

Hell naw, everything wasn't all right. I couldn't get my shit together for nothing.

Suddenly I had all these people hugging me and touching me and wanting to be in my life. It was a lot to take in, but it made me feel good, like I belonged somewhere.

Now I could tell my friends back home about my people, my cousins and uncles and shit. My daddy. It wasn't just me and my mama no more. It was me and my mama and everybody else.

Big Mama was talking about me coming to spend the summer with her, and Jeff was planning on introducing me to his friends. My uncles were talking about me spending some time at their houses. And Smoke was teaching me how to drive and talking to me about shit that I been wanting to talk to another man about, lining up my neck for me, and talking about how we was gone do things together in the future. The family reunion was coming up this summer, and I was gone be there. Big Mama was taking pictures all over the place and calling all her friends to tell them about me. My picture was on the refrigerator right along with all the other grandkids. And I still had some more family to meet.

This was some serious shit. I didn't think Smoke was planning on going anywhere, anytime soon. At least, I hoped he wasn't.

Damn. I started to pinch myself just to make sure I wasn't dreaming. I used to dream about stuff like this. Not the crying part, but the other stuff.

Smoke sat down on the other side of me, put his hand on the back of my neck, and put a tissue to my nose.

"Blow," he said.

ANNE

Where the *hell* was my son? Why was this bitch *staring* at me like she was crazy? Where the *hell* was Smoke? Why was Big Mama trying to bulldoze me into agreeing to come to the *family reunion*? What *planet* did these people come from, with all this hugging and kissing, and who's little girl was this sitting *in my lap*? *When* did I start braiding the ends of her ponytails? Again. *Why* was this bitch staring at me like she was crazy?

I glanced at my watch and sighed. Nobody had to tell me that we were going to miss our flight. Isaiah would have to miss another day of school, but at least it was close to the end of the school year, and it wasn't like he really gave a shit anyway. I could see that he was in hog heaven here with all these clones of him. Big Mama was going to be the ruination of him yet, with her itty-bitty self.

Should I go see what was going on? Should I back up and let Smoke handle Isaiah? Why was Jeff staring at my chest? And why didn't I at least *bring* a freaking bra? I had one at home somewhere.

Big Mama must've sensed my bewilderment because she asked if I wanted to help her and Liz in the kitchen. I set the little girl on her feet—she was a cute little thing—and hit the floor running like a runaway slave following Harriet Tubman. Almost started singing "Go Down Moses."

Since we were leaving tomorrow afternoon instead of tonight, as originally planned, Isaiah stayed the night at Don's house to hang out with Jeff—titty staring Jeff. I said my good-byes, promised to keep in touch, and hopped in the truck with Smoke long after midnight. The first thing I did was kick off my shoes and make full use of the headrest on my seat. The second was to punch Smoke in his thigh.

"Can I help you with something over here?" he asked, pulling out into traffic.

"That was for leaving me alone with Flossie. She stared at me the whole time. You always did like those red-boned strumpets."

"Wait a minute. Which one is it, Flossie or Flossine? And why does she have to be a strumpet?"

"Did you hear me say she was staring at me like she was crazy? If it hadn't been your mother's house, I'd have asked her what her deal was."

"She probably just wanted to ask you what you did to keep your skin so smooth and tight. I don't think she was expecting you to be competition."

I looked askance at Smoke and rolled my eyes. I hadn't rolled my eyes so much in ten years.

"I'm not," I snapped.

"True. I was just speaking on the female psyche."

"Well don't, because you're not a female, so you don't know what the hell you're talking about. She probably just smelled pussy on your breath and wondered if it was mine." He laid his head back and roared with laughter, and I giggled, too.

"Yeah, you got me. I'll give you that one."

I hopped out of the truck as soon as he pulled up in front of my hotel and took off down the walkway with him hot on my heels. I unlocked my door, let myself in, and sent the door flying closed behind me. The delayed response time told me that he was in my space. Again.

"Go home, Smoke." I disappeared into the bedroom, kicked off my shoes, and dropped my purse on the table. I struggled with reaching around behind me to pull the zipper down on my dress. Smoke moved up behind me and relieved me of the task, then slipped his hands inside and around to cup my breasts. His fingers played with the tips of my nipples and sent warm tingles through my body. I ignored him and the tingles, and took off my earrings. I tossed them on the dresser and lowered my arms so the dress could fall. His mouth was open and wet on my neck. I stepped away from him and headed into the bathroom.

"Go home, Smoke," I repeated.

"In a minute."

I started the shower, adjusted the water temperature, and slipped out of my thong, stepping under the punishing spray. A few minutes later Smoke violated my shower. He took control of the sponge I was using and soaped my back. I turned so the water could rinse me, and collided with his mouth.

"Go home, Smoke." I gasped as he lifted me by the waist and braced me against the shower wall. I took him in slowly and opened my mouth for his tongue when he offered it to me. I locked my ankles around his waist and my arms around his neck, and took the kiss deep.

"In a minute, Anne. I want to give you something else real quick."

A minute turned into an hour, and an hour turned into two. Sometime after three hours, I lost count. The sun was shining when Smoke gave me one last orgasm and did what I'd asked him to do in the first place. Went home.

"Let me give you this."

I jumped away from the ticket counter as Smoke walked up behind me and whispered in my ear. I'd had enough of what he had to give to last a lifetime, and whatever it was, I didn't want it. The counter clerk handed me my ticket with a slightly amused look, as if she had an idea what I was thinking. I took it and shoved it in my purse.

"A little jumpy, aren't you?"

"What is it, Smoke?" I didn't see a damn thing funny. I looked around for Isaiah, saw that he was engrossed in conversation with Jeff, and met Smoke's eyes. He was standing too close, wrapping me up in Cool Water cologne. I remembered that Isaiah liked the shit, too, and I decided right then and there that I was tossing it out as soon as I got home. I didn't care if I never smelled Cool Water again. He handed me a folded piece of paper that I immediately recognized as a check. "You already gave me my check back," I told him.

"That's one from me to you, for Isaiah. He's a growing boy. He needs things."

"Give it to him then."

"So he can buy space age looking sneakers and help keep Tommy Hilfiger in his mansion? I don't think so. Put it up for him or something. Whatever."

"If you insist." Hell, he did need things. All the time. "I should probably tell you that I closed the file with Child Support Enforcement, so you won't be hearing anything else from them. You can rest easy."

"Good. We didn't need them in the middle of our situation anyway. Call me when you get home so I'll know you made it safely."

"I'll make sure that Isaiah does."

He searched my face leisurely, then took his eyes to the tarmac outside the glass walls. He watched porters pushing luggage carts back and forth for long seconds, then chuckled and brought his eyes back to me.

"It was good, Anne."

"It was." No sense in lying. The truth didn't need no support, and if it did, he could easily cite all the moaning and groaning I had done as evidence. The screaming and gasping was pretty damning, too. And the fingernail scrapes across his back sealed the deal. I wondered how he was going to explain those to Flossie. "It was also stupid, Smoke. Definitely not one of my better judgment calls."

"You knew all that from jump, so why'd you do it?"

"Curious, I guess. Nobody was looking, and I acted out a little."

"You weren't acting alone. I'll take a little of that rationale, too. Kind of like throwing a ball in the house when your mama's not home to see you doing what you know you shouldn't be doing."

"Exactly like that. She comes home and the ball is put away, but you have a juicy little secret she'll never know."

"Until your big mouth little brother tells on you because you won't let him see your favorite toy."

"Well luckily there's no toy here. Just a juicy little secret that I want to forget I ever knew."

He put on a fake, insulted look.

"Damn, you just said it was good."

"It was good," I said. "Real good, but still . . ."

"I have no choice but to remember what I know, at least until your claw marks fade. You think I can convince Diana that I ran into a wall and get her to put some ointment on them for me?"

I lifted a hand and massaged my tired eyelids. They were heavy from lack of sleep.

"Sorry about that," I mumbled.

"No sweat. I'm glad you enjoyed yourself. We'll call it even since I *was* trying to break you off a little something." He cracked himself up. "Ended up getting broke off, though."

"Smoke . . ."

"I'm serious, Anne. You had a brotha's eyes rolling back in his head." He caught the look I sent him and put out a hand. "But we won't talk about that. Let's just say it was a pleasant little interlude and leave it at that."

"I just don't want you thinking that sexual favors come along with access to Isaiah, because they don't. I'm not that girl you screwed anytime you felt like it, just because you could, anymore. I did what I did because I wanted to, not because you've got some kind of magical powers over me. I won't be lifting my skirt whenever you come around.

From here on out, you lift Flossie's skirt when you need your eyes to roll to the back of your head."

Smoke scratched the back of his neck and hissed through his teeth.

"I wasn't thinking that, Anne. You don't mince words, do you?"

"I try not to."

"I should be choking the hell out of you right now, but I'm not because I can see where you're coming from, how you could think what you do. However, let's be clear about one thing. I'm going to be in my son's life no matter what, no strings, no expectations. Regardless of what you say or do. You rubbed the magic lamp and here I am, so get used to it. I'm still a little pissed over the fact that you waited this long to come to me, but that's neither here nor there. The other thing is this, you lifted your own skirt because you wanted to, as you said. So stop pretending you didn't have a leading role in what happened. Matter of fact, you were the star a few times."

"All right, Smoke. I get the point."

"I don't think you do, Anne. Because if you did, you would know that all I was trying to tell you was that I enjoyed the hell out of this weekend, and that I find you attractive. That was it, the whole point. Now I'm not the worst looking man in the world, so I don't think I'll have to hang around waiting on you to lift your skirt when times get hard. No pun intended."

"So what, you think you put me in my place or something?" I narrowed my eyes and considered him, wondering if that's exactly what had just occurred.

"What I'm going to put you is on this plane, in a very few minutes. And then I'm going to call when I think you've made it home, to make sure everything is OK. Not because I want you to lift your skirt for me, but because we have a son in common and talking to each other regularly just makes sense. Don't you think? And get your hand off your hip. You're not scaring anybody."

I said the only thing I could think to say.

"Go home, Smoke."

"I'm about to. You're working my nerves like you wouldn't believe."

"Excuse me?"

"Excuse me?" he parroted sarcastically. He moved closer and dipped his head so that we were eye to eye. "Running around talking shit about not needing sex and then carrying on like you weren't knee-deep in it when you got some. You're grown, and I am too. I wanted to give it to you and you wanted to take it, so get over it. Go home, go straight to the store, and buy some damn bras, too." He looked up when the overhead PA system crackled, and he breathed a sigh of relief. "That's your flight. Please get on it."

"That's what you said last night," I reminded him bitchily, and a corner of his mouth tipped up as he searched the crowd over my head.

"You remember that, huh? You've got a damn good memory for someone who claims they want to forget. Want to know what I remember?"

I rolled my eyes and walked off. I went to join the line for boarding my flight while Isaiah said his good-byes. I remembered my manners and turned to wave at Jeff before I disappeared down the passageway. I found my seat and dropped into it gratefully. I was sleepy, tired, and sore in my lower regions. Tangling with Smoke was a completely different type of exercise in flexibility, and I was at least four years out of practice. The muscles in my inner thighs screamed as I crossed my legs. Smoke's fingers had left a bruise on my hip, and it had the nerve to complain as I fastened my seat belt. By tomorrow I'd probably need a wheelchair, for all I knew.

Isaiah boarded the plane and came down the aisle toward me. I searched his face for signs of distress, but I couldn't find any. He looked calm and peaceful, more like the little boy I used to know before his face took on a permanent scowl and scared me enough to start the wheels in motion that had brought us to this point. Seeing the change in him made me glad I decided to barge into Smoke's life and offer him my son. He couldn't have Isaiah, but I was getting used to the idea of having to share him. He folded his long frame into the seat next to me and gave me one of his patented I-want-something smiles.

"Whatever it is, the answer is no," I said, heading him off at the pass.

"See, I wasn't even gone ask for nothing, so there. I was just gone ask you if you had a good time. You like Big Mama?"

"She seems nice. Do you like her?"

"Yeah, she's cool. She told me she thought you was pretty."

"That was nice of her," I said. "I'm more interested in what she thought of you. Did you remember to thank her for having you?"

"Mama, please. I was on my best behavior, as always." I slid him a knowing look and got a shit-eating grin for my trouble. "Dad thought you was looking good, too."

"Please don't tell me you're harboring a fantasy about a fairy tale ending at your age, Isaiah."

"Nah, I'm just saying. What did you think of Diana?"

"She seems nice." I looked out the window.

"Mmmm. They ain't been together that long."

"Did you pack all of your stuff? You didn't forget anything, did you?"

"Yeah. I mean, nah. You remember all your stuff?"

"I think so. I checked fifty times before I left the hotel." I jumped in my seat and slapped a hand to my waist, checked to make sure my belt was around my waist and not back at the hotel.

"You wasn't too bored at the hotel, was you?" I shook my head.

"I went swimming and relaxed. Caught up on my rest. You could have come and kept me company if you were worried about me being lonely."

"I wasn't worried. Smoke kept disappearing and I figured he was with you, keeping you company."

My head whipped around on my neck. Did he just say what I thought he'd said?

"What did you say, boy?" I sputtered, staring at his profile. But his headphones were already fastened on his ears with the volume pumped up on his portable CD player. 50 Cent was blaring into his brain and his head was bobbing enthusiastically. A few seconds later he started bobbing his fists to the beat, pausing his rhythm just long enough to give me an innocent smile before he closed his eyes and laid his head back.

I wanted to twist his big ear.

Chapter 8

ALEC

I hated Tuesday morning faculty meetings even more than I hated okra and beets. I usually came in late and took a seat against the back wall so that Principal Bradley, who did smell badly, wouldn't have any reason to call on me to talk about shit. I preferred to sit, watch, and listen, take a few notes if I felt I needed to, and be left the hell alone.

I sat there and thought of a hundred things I needed to be in my classroom doing before the school day started. I still had a few exams to grade, I needed to run off some copies of a worksheet that I was planning to assign for homework that night, and I needed to do a quick review of conversion equations before I attempted to lecture on it throughout the day. Damned if the shit hadn't slipped my mind a little since the last time I'd taught it, this time last year.

I scribbled a few lines about changes in student hallway etiquette on the notepad I'd brought in with me, and capped my pen. I sat back in my chair and focused on a woman sitting three chairs ahead of me at a long table.

She taught art, and as I stared at the bird's nest of braids and twists piled on top of her head, I wondered if she considered the mess on her head a work of art, something like a walking advertisement for art appreciation. I hoped not.

My stomach growled and I had an unreasonable craving for chicken marsala. I took a sip of coffee from my favorite mug, shifted in my chair, and locked eyes with Diana. Her lips tightened just enough to let me know that she was pouting, still unhappy with the fact that we hadn't spent any real time together since last Sunday, when she'd invited herself over to my mother's house. I had to give her kudos for pulling that off, because it was a bold move. Problem was, I had never really liked bold women.

But I wouldn't say I was punishing her for doing what she did. My avoiding her was more like a savvy strategic maneuver. When we were alone together she liked to end up in bed, which was usually fine with me, but I still had a few pesky scratches on my back to deal with. For the most part, they were nothing but surface scrapes. But there was one from the time I had . . . anyway, one was being stubborn. I figured it would be best to give it time to fade into oblivion before I got naked with Diana again. Didn't take a rocket scientist to tell you some things, especially where women were concerned.

A more complicated and complex creature never existed than a woman. Take Anne, for instance. Just for instance, because it wasn't like I was dwelling on her. But every now and again I did rewind the tape of last weekend and go over it in minute detail. I was having trouble determining exactly what had happened, how we had ended up in bed together. I knew the basics—something about a breast peeking out, my mouth on said breast, and so on. But that's where common sense and awareness left off, and complete confusion stepped in. We had tried to fuck each other's brains out, and I couldn't, for the life of me, figure out what had brought it on.

Don't get me wrong, of course I noticed that Anne was shapely and petite, lean and athletic looking. Who wouldn't notice that she never wore a bra? I liked the look of her in snug fitting jeans, same as I did in skirts and shit. She was a tasty looking little woman, and any man with at least one working eyeball could see that she was attractive. A dime-piece she was.

But, so was Diana and millions of other women. Who the hell was Anne that she could have me sucking and licking all over her like I was starving and her chocolate skin was the last meal on earth? It was crazy. She was my son's mother. Period. Maybe if the circumstances were different and I had met her for the first time recently, I'd feel more comfortable about the fact that my dick wanted to be hard whenever I looked at her. But I was well aware of the circumstances, as was she.

It had to be curiosity. I knew her when she was at her worst, physically and mentally, just like she knew me when I was at my worst, mentally. Back then we were two bad elements circling around each other and serving each other's purposes. She had changed, and I had too, thankfully both for the better, and we were curious to see what the change was all about. We were kids then, and now we were adults.

I think I wanted to insinuate myself into her life so that I could get a closer look at the person she presented to the world. She was a mysterious woman with a shady past, walking tall and confident, proclaiming herself to be something other than what I knew her to be, and I couldn't rest on my laurels until I'd had a closer look. I wasn't consciously looking for evidence to discredit her, but I could admit to myself now that I wouldn't have been surprised if I had found some.

In the back of my mind I still saw Breanne Phillips. *Black Breanne, hair so thick, hair so wild, looks like a Zulu child.* I didn't give a shit about the black part. Hell, we were all black when it came right down to it. And truthfully, I found the color and texture of her skin extremely sensual, like chocolate silk. It was what the chant represented that stuck in the back of my mind, the drugs and the accompanying lifestyle with which I had issues.

Some would say that I hadn't had any issues with pleasuring Anne, and I would have to agree. I'd already established that neither of us were thinking straight at the time. Hell, all twelve times. But I was thinking straight now, and Anne had the right idea. Forget about it. Move on. It was murky water under the bridge.

I cleared my mind and remembered that I was in the middle of a staring contest with Diana, whom I *had* met recently and who did *not* have past problems with drug abuse. I grinned at her and took another sip of coffee. She wanted to be complicated and complex, but she wasn't. She was pretty, half-assed shallow, and spoiled rotten. No surprises there, and those were things with which I could deal with one hand tied behind my back.

Diana was waiting for me in the hallway after the meeting wrapped up. Still no surprises. She trailed me to my classroom, shut the door behind her, and pushed herself into my arms.

"I missed you yesterday, Alec," she purred. I had called off from work yesterday so I could take Isaiah and Anne to the airport. And because I was worn out from rolling around nonstop all Sunday night and into the next morning with Anne. I was nowhere near as resilient as I used to be.

"Isaiah decided to stay until Monday," I said, leaning down for the kiss she was offering. I turned it into a soft peck and eased out of her arms.

"When is he coming back?"

"Spring break, definitely, but probably for another weekend between now and then. He thinks you're hot," I told her with a smile.

"He's got good taste, just like his daddy. It was interesting meeting his mother and seeing what your tastes used to be like. She's . . . cute."

I kept right on erasing my board. *Here we go.*

"She thought you were too. Cute, I mean."

"Ah, so she said something about me?"

"Not really, Dee. She already knew I was seeing someone, and when she met you, she just commented that you were attractive." These were the conversations men avoided like the plague, and here I was wading in head first and without a life jacket. *Damn.*

"You just said she said I was cute. Dogs and bunny rabbits are cute." Apparently the distinction was important.

"You just said she was cute," I pointed out. I was starting to be a little irritated.

"Why are were arguing about this?" She looked at me quizzically and tilted her head. Her hair swung to one side and fluttered in the air. I wondered if she had practiced the gesture in the mirror until she perfected it.

"I don't know. Why are we?"

"You tell me, because I can think of better ways for us to be spending our time. What are you doing after work?"

"I hadn't planned on too much of anything. I'm still a little worn out, and I need to put my house back together. My son tore through it like a tornado." A small lie, but I was certain Zay would understand.

"I could come over and keep you company while you clean up," she suggested silkily.

"Can I take a rain check, Dee? I don't think I'll be the best company this evening."

"That's the fourth rain check you've taken, Alec. Should I be taking a hint?"

"You know I don't play around like that. If I wanted you to know something, I would tell you. Right now I'm just rearranging some things and concentrating on my son. Can you understand that?"

"I'm trying to, but who's concentrating on you while you concentrate on your son? You have needs, too." She moved closer and toyed with the buttons down the front of my shirt.

I probably wouldn't have any needs for the next two weeks. Women weren't the only ones who could be sore, that was for damn sure.

"Give me a few days and I'll get back to you with an answer to that question," I said, squeezing her shoulders gently. I leaned down and took another soft kiss. One for the road. I needed my space right now.

The warning bell rang and I went to open my door. Students would be dragging in any minute now. I was supposed to be standing in the hallway monitoring the flow of traffic, making sure no one suddenly decided to drop their books and have sex against a locker or something, but Diana wasn't making it easy for a brotha to attend to business. She pressed up against me from behind and slid by me like a pussycat, even though there was plenty of room in the doorway.

"I might surprise you and show up on your doorstep, Alec," she whispered. "I have needs too."

I watched her walk down the hallway, strut really, and shifted my attention after she turned a corner. I shot an appraising glance around me and locked eyes with one of the seniors who was loitering around his locker, talking with another student. We shared a brief grin, acknowledging the dime-piece we'd both been staring at just a moment ago.

Then it was down to business. Students started coming at me from all different directions, popping gum and huffing and puffing their way through the door. *Why did everybody hate math?* I wondered. I was relieved to see that Miss Jacobs was wearing an appropriate shirt and that Byron was in attendance, sans the iPod. When I was satisfied that I had all the captives assigned to me in the room, I pulled the door closed and walked over to my desk. I was shuffling through a stack of papers that needed to be passed back when the tardy bell rang and one last student came stumbling through the door.

I looked at the goofy looking boy and shook my head. "You forget your watch this morning, Lonnell?"

"Nah, Mr. Avery, I missed my bus and I had to wait till my mama was leaving for work so she could drop me off. You gone give me a demerit?"

"We'll discuss it after class," I said, already knowing that I wasn't. I gave him the evil eye as he walked past me. He did a double take and then a triple take, staring up at me like he was crazy. "Problem, Lonnell?"

"No, sir. I don't have one, but I think you might. When you start wearing lipstick and shit?" Lonnell asked and the rest of the class cracked up. I touched two fingers to my lips and looked at the purplish tinge they came away with.

"Have a seat," I barked, and they laughed louder. I found a tissue and wiped my mouth, irritated as hell. Then I gave it up and laughed myself.

ISAIAH

"What's up, Zay?"

I felt Hood's hand gripping the back of my Allen Iverson jersey two seconds before he caught up with me and stuck his face in mine. I looked around him at the school bus I needed to be on, hoping it didn't roll off without me.

"You got it, Hood," I said, pumping fists with him. "You wasn't in last hour. Where you been?"

"Man, fuck Mr. Golliday and his motherfucking math. The question is, where your ass been? You ain't been hanging on the weekends no more. What's up with that shit? You don't know a nigga no more?"

"Nah, it ain't like that. I been studying and shit, so I can get my grades back up. Tired of my old bag breathing down my neck, acting all crazy and shit." He put his arm around my shoulders and steered me away from the bus. "Dude, I'ma miss my bus."

"Fuck that bus too. Roll with me and I'll drop you at yo' crib later. Marcus got some more of that fire ass yayo."

I wasn't really feeling like dealing with Hood, but he wasn't exactly the type of brotha you could say no to most of the time. We walked across the parking lot to his car. The top was down and Marcus was already sitting in the backseat waiting for us. I pumped fists with that fool too, and dropped my backpack on the floor in the backseat before I got in the passenger seat. Hood took off, driving like a fool, and damn near rear-ended a school bus that was pulling off the lot.

I looked back at Marcus.

"You mean to tell me your ass ain't claim the front seat when you had the chance?"

"Uh-uh, I'm sitting right where I need to be, trust me." He smirked and then went to work spreading out his supplies. The smell of fresh weed was strong. "How thick y'all want this motherfucker to be?"

"Hook it up, playa. You know how you do," Hood said.

I didn't have time to think about the silly ass look on Marcus's face and what the hell he meant by what he said, because Hood turned on the stereo and blasted the damn thing—some old ass LL Cool J, rocking some bells and sounding kind of good. I was nodding my head to the beat when he leaned over and pulled a forty-ounce from under his seat. He handed it to me.

"Pop it on open, Zay. In honor of you coming back into the fold, I'ma let you have the first pull. That's that St. Ides there. Have you on yo' ass in a hot little minute. Gone head."

I looked at the bottle and then at Hood. He was turning into the park, so he didn't see the expression on my face. I took the bottle from him and waited until he parked behind some trees to give it back to him.

"I'm cool," I told him.

"You cool?" Hood stared at me like I'd just told him that I was white or some shit. "Nigga, you better open that shit so I can whet my throat. I'm thirsty than a motherfucker. And what's taking you so long with the blunt, dude?" He turned in his seat and looked at Marcus.

"Man, I'm sealing this bad boy now. Hand me a lighter."

I opened the forty-ounce and passed it to Hood. They got the blunt going and I turned my head to avoid a nose full of smoke. Marcus nudged me on my arm and motioned for me to take the blunt, but I shook my head.

"I'm cool," I said again.

"You ain't smoking, you ain't drinking. What's up, Zay? You suddenly going to church or some old bullshit like that now?" Hood took a toke and pulled back to look at the blunt like it was too good to be true. "Marcus hooked this mug up right too. Here, quit fucking around and hit this shit."

He tried to put the blunt to my lips, but I slid to the side.

"Hood, man, gone with that shit. I'm chilling right now. Y'all gone head and handle that."

"You think you too good for us now, nigga?"

"Nah, it ain't like that. I told my old dude I wouldn't smoke no more for a little while, so I'm chilling."

"Where that nigga at now? How he gone know you smoked?"

I was starting to get a little bent in the head from all the smoke swirling around me.

"That ain't the point. I told his ass I wouldn't, so I'm not."

"Well you told me you was gone do some shit, and you ain't did it yet, so what the fuck?" He was sounding like he wanted to get ignorant, and I looked at him like, what? Out of the corner of my eye I saw Marcus sit up in his seat and start smiling like he was stuck on stupid.

"What shit am I supposed to do?"

"Nigga, you know what you said you was gone do. Don't play with me. I ain't forgot that shit either. I'ma hook you up in a minute, so you can get on about yo' business with the shit."

Maybe I was the one who was crazy, or maybe it was all the smoke preventing me from thinking clearly, but I didn't have the slightest clue what Hood was talking about.

"Marcus must've put something in that smoke, 'cause you talking crazy. I ain't said I was gone do shit."

"Can you believe this shit?" Hood asked Marcus. "This nigga trying to play me like I'm some kind of buppy ass sucker." Then he looked at me. "Nigga, I'll punch you in your motherfucking grill, for real. You think I'm some kind of joke? One minute you riding in my shit and smoking up my herb, and the next minute you acting like you don't know nobody. Cause yo' punk ass daddy got you wrapped. You got me fucked up, Zay."

"Nah, that weed got you fucked up and talking crazy, Hood. My old man ain't got shit to do with this, either."

"He the reason you talking crazy and shit."

"How you gone get mad at a motherfucker 'cause they don't want to smoke no weed or get drunk, for once? I ain't got to do shit I don't want to do, dude. I ain't no damn kid."

"You fuck around and don't do what you said you was gone do and I'ma beat yo' ass like you a kid, Zay."

I waved a hand and shifted in my seat so I didn't have to look at his crazy ass. I glanced at my watch and hoped they would hurry the fuck up so I could get on home. Shoulda never gotten in the damn car with his ass in the first place. Now the nigga had me ten damn blocks from the house, stuck in the car listening to him talk crazy. *Wait till I tell Smoke about this shit.*

"Nigga waving his hand at me and shit, trying to play me for a fool," Hood was mumbling under his breath. Next thing I knew he raised his foot and kicked me in my thigh. "Get the fuck out, bitch."

My head flew around on my neck.

"What?"

"You heard me. Get the fuck out and walk yo' bitch ass home."

"Oh, it's like that now?"

"It's like that now. Get the fuck out of my shit. And hurry up before I decide to put some heater through yo' speaker, for real."

"You gone shoot me now?" I couldn't believe this shit.

"Just get yo' sorry ass out, dude."

"A'ight." I got the hell out of his car and grabbed my backpack from the floor behind the seat. "Holla at me when you sober up, Hood," I said before I starting walking off across the grass.

"Nah, nigga, I'ma holla at you when it's time for you to do what you said you was gone do," Hood hollered at my back.

I kept on walking. I wracked my brain and tried to figure out what I had told that fool I was gone do, but it wouldn't come to me. I must've told him some shit when I was high or drunk and talking out the side of my neck. Whatever it was had him tripping too. I thought about Smoke and how he told me that Hood wasn't really my friend. At the time I didn't see what he was saying, but I saw that shit now. As long as I was smoking and drinking, shit was cool. A brotha wanted to study and do some shit right, and it was a problem.

I walked across the park and came out on Salisbury Street. If I kept walking south I would probably be home in a minute. Yeah, right, more like an hour. Problem was I didn't really feel like walking all the way home, dragging no damn backpack and sweating like a pig. It was hot as hell outside and I just had to wear some jeans today instead of some shorts, and my feet was straight up sweating inside my Nikes.

I walked down to the gas station on the corner and used the pay phone. I dialed a number and listened to the phone ring seven damn times before my mama finally picked up.

"Ma, where you at?"

"I'm on my way home. Where are you?"

I told her and she started asking fifty-leven questions. I had to cut her off. I didn't know how many minutes a quarter got you, but I didn't have no more quarters.

"Ma, hold up. I need you to come pick me up. I'm at the gas station on Salisbury and Southwestern Drive. Nah, I ain't hurt or nothing. I'm cool. I promise, Ma. You coming?"

She swerved onto the lot ten minutes later, looking around all nervous and shit. She was so busy looking for me that she didn't even see me walk up and pull the passenger door open. I climbed in and tossed my backpack on the backseat. I guessed she could smell the weed smoke in my clothes because her nose tuned up, forehead got all wrinkly. She stared at me for a minute.

"Are you high, Isaiah?"

"No, Mama." I reached down and adjusted the seat so I could stretch out my legs. "I know you probably smell weed on me, but I'm not high."

"But you've been smoking?"

I looked around, trying to figure out why we were still sitting there and not rolling.

"I was with Hood and Marcus and *they* was smoking. *I* wasn't. That's why you had to come get me, 'cause I didn't want to smoke."

"That lousy son-of-a-bitch kicked you out of his car?"

I couldn't hate on my mama for being mad, because now that I thought about it, I was a little mad myself. But she killed me when she got mad, started snapping and talking all proper.

"Yeah, something like that. Can we roll now? I'm hungry."

She started to pull off, then slammed on the brakes. I shot forward in my seat and fell back.

"Hungry because you've got the munchies?" she asked.

"Mama, please. I'm hungry because they was serving them old tired ass nachos for lunch and I didn't eat."

"Did you just curse at me, boy?"

"I wasn't cursing at you. It just slipped out. What I meant to say was that I'm starving like marvin, but I ain't even a little bit high."

"You swear?"

"Ma, I told Smoke I wouldn't mess around with drugs and be drinking no more, so I didn't. Hood got mad and started talking crazy, so I had to walk over here and call you. Should've gotten on the school bus like I started to."

She nodded and pulled off.

"Yes, you should have." She got quiet and concentrated on driving for a minute. "You told Smoke that, huh?"

"Yeah, he was riding my ass, I mean my butt, so I promised I wouldn't mess around anymore so he could be quiet."

"That's good, because drugs will ruin your future." She cut across a grocery store lot to avoid a stoplight and shot a glance at the rearview mirror, looking for one-time. She got a ticket for that same shit not too long ago.

"They didn't ruin yours," I said.

"Damn near. I'm proud of you for keeping your promise, Isaiah."

Here we go. I knew my mama. Next, she was gone be sniffling and crying and shit. I graduated from kindergarten and she cried. I got on the honor roll and she cried. I fell off my bike and she cried. I found out it wasn't no Santa Claus and she cried. She cried about every damn thing with her cry-baby ass.

"You 'bout to start balling and carrying on? 'Cause if you are, let me out right here, please."

She cracked up.

"You need to stop."

"I'm serious, Ma. You know I don't like it when you cry."

"Crying is good for the soul," she had the nerve to say. "It's not healthy to keep everything bottled up inside. How are you planning on handling this situation with that jackass Hood?"

I didn't even have to think about it.

"I'm through with that fool."

"Good, because I didn't like him. I want you to stay away from him. I tried to tell you he was no good a long time ago, but *nooooo* . . ."

"Oh, OK, here we go. Gone head and say I told you so." We pulled into the driveway at home and I got out of the car. I walked around to her side and helped her out, then opened the back door and got my backpack. "I know you be knowing what you talking about most of the time, Ma, so I'ma gone head and save you the trouble. I'm a little hardheaded, I admit it. Now what else you got to say?" I looked down at my mama, thinking about how small she was. I shook my head and hooked my arm around her neck to walk her to the door. I kept my arm around her as we went inside the house.

"You should listen to me more," she chirped.

"I do listen to you. You just don't know it."

"Could've fooled me. Everything I say seems like it goes in one ear and out the other. Now let *Smoke* tell you something and you're all ears. It must be a man thing or something, and I know I'm not a man, but—" I waved a hand to cut her off.

"Ma?" She kept talking, mumbling under her breath and rolling her neck like Thelma from *Good Times*. "Ma? Can I say something?"

"What is it, Isaiah? I have asked you not to interrupt grown folks when they're talking, haven't I?"

I scratched the back of my neck and whistled through my teeth. My mama was something else.

"I just wanted to tell you that I'm proud of you too."

"Oh . . ."

"I thought maybe you might be tripping off of that stupid stuff I said a while back, so I'm saying now that you shouldn't trip off of it because it was stupid. I probably hurt your feelings too, and I'm sorry about that. I didn't mean none of what I said, but you know that, right?"

I thought she was gone start hugging and kissing all over me and I was gone have to run upstairs to get away from her, but she didn't. My eyes got big as hell, watching her put a hand on her hip and roll her eyes at me. She tried to be hard for a minute, and then she rubbed her face and stomped one of them high ass heels on the floor. *What the hell?*

"Damnit, Isaiah," she said. Next thing I knew she was

running in the bathroom and slamming the door in my face. She turned on the water in there to cover up the sound of what she was doing. But I already knew what she was doing. Probably sitting on the toilet, crying. I heard that clear enough, water or no water. Cry baby ass.

What the hell was up with women, anyway?

Chapter 9

ANNE

I was supposed to be doing some paperwork and putting some stuff together to give to my grant writer so she could get started on thinking up creative ways to catch the government's attention come grant giving time, but I wasn't. I was in my office, with the door closed and my feet up, reading Eric Jerome Dickey's *The Other Woman.* Vonetta had loaned it to me a couple of weeks ago, and I was just now getting around to cracking it open. I was caught up in the fact that the cheater's wife and the other cheater's husband were now cheating on the original cheaters, together. And the sad part about it was that I was actually rooting for them to end up together. How sick was I?

The lovemaking scenes were sucking me in, and I was deep undercover when my desk phone buzzed. I growled under my breath all the way over to my desk and snatched up the receiver.

"This is Anne Phillips."

"Bree, it's Laverne," my older sister said. I massaged the wrinkles from my forehead and moved around the desk to drop into my chair. "You still there?"

"Yes, I'm here. Is everything all right?" She hardly ever called just to talk and neither did I.

"Everything is fine. Mama's good, in case you were wondering. You want to talk to her?"

You called me, I wanted to scream.

"Not right now, no. I'm at work. I'll call her later."

"No, you won't, and you know it, and that's why I called. I want to see my nephew, and Mama wants to see her grandson."

"Right now?" What was it with the drop everything you're doing and come running phone calls?

"No, not right now. Are *you* all right? We were thinking you could bring him up over spring break. You could stay here with me. He's what, a senior now?"

I closed my eyes and breathed slowly.

"A sophomore. He turned sixteen in January. The seventh."

"Oh . . . well, I was close. Hell, we'd know how old he was if we ever saw him."

"No one's keeping you from coming to him, Laverne."

"You don't exactly make us feel welcome."

Us and then me. That's how it had always been. Them and then me.

"I don't recall anyone ever asking about coming to visit. And anyway, spring break won't be a good time. Isaiah will be with his father."

"His father?"

"Yes. He'll stay the week with him there in Indiana. I guess I could have him call you when he gets there and you two could arrange to visit."

"I didn't know you knew who Isaiah's father was, Bree. When did all this happen? I mean, you were—"

"I know what I was," I bit out. "I've always known who my son's father is. Always. Even when I was all drugged up I knew who I was fucking, Laverne. Anyway, that's where he'll be, so I guess you and Mama will have to wait another six years to make an attempt to see him."

"Bree, I didn't mean—"

"I know what you meant, Laverne. It's fine. Is that all you called for?"

She blew out a long breath in my ear.

"This is bad. We can't even have a civil phone conversation, can we?" she asked.

"I thought we were being really civil here myself. You said you wanted to see Isaiah, and I said he'd be with his father. You said you thought I didn't know who his father was, and I said I did. It's all been very civil. I mean, we've had worse conversations."

"I still want you to come, Bree. Come up when he comes and bring him for a quick visit or something. I want to see both of you."

"I was just there last month," I blurted out.

"Last month? And you didn't call or come by?"

"For what, Laverne? What did I need to come by for?"

"To see your mother, and to see me. My youngest is two now, and you've never even seen her."

"My youngest is sixteen now, and you haven't seen him since Aunt Bobbi's funeral. He was around eleven then. What's your point?"

"My point is that you have more family than just Aunt Bobbi, Bree."

"Could've fooled me."

"How do you think Aunt Bobbi knew to come and get your ass, huh? Who do you think called her, Bree? She wasn't psychic."

A low-grade migraine was kicking up just behind my eyeballs. I looked at the phone and thought about setting the receiver back in the cradle, disconnecting the fruitless call before I lost my mind.

"You don't know anything about Aunt Bobbi. You never liked her, and she knew it."

"I liked her enough to search through Mama's shit and find her number, Bree. I liked her enough to tell her that you needed help. And I loved you enough to convince Mama to let you go. So don't tell me what I don't know. I also know you can afford to take a couple of days off from that goddamn center and visit your mother and sister. You do that and the next trip will be on us. We'll come to you."

"I don't want you to come to me."

"But I want you to come here, Bree. We . . . no, *I* want to see you. I know Mama does too. But this is me talking right now. I miss you."

"You don't even know me well enough to miss me."

"Well, can I get to know you?"

She wouldn't let me off the phone until I agreed to visit, and I finally did. I told her I'd fly to Indiana with Isaiah when he went there for spring break, and then spend the day with her and my mama at her house. She pressed for my spending the night, but that was where I drew the line. I absolutely would not spend the night. After damn near twenty years of separation, I wasn't sure I could handle that kind of forced intimacy. Hell, I wasn't even sure if it would be safe to close my eyes under the same roof as the dynamic duo. Hell no, no overnight stays. If time somehow got away from me and I needed to stay in Indiana overnight, I would find a hotel room to crash in, and then haul ass all the way back home at first light.

I called Smoke to bring him up to speed on the slight change of plans. I got his cell phone voicemail and left a message for him to call me at either of my numbers, depending on what time it was when he got the message. I forgot that he was probably in class, teaching math. Ugh.

He called me back at the end of the school day from his cell phone.

"I got your message woman. What's up?"

"How's your back?" I asked.

"Ready for another round. You volunteering?"

"No. I was just concerned, that's all."

"Right. Is my son OK?"

"Yeah, but that's kind of why I'm calling, Smoke. Spring break is next week and—"

"Don't even try to tell me you're not sending him, because I might come through the phone on your ass, Anne."

"Shut up. He's coming. Just not Friday evening like we planned."

"Why not?"

"I need to fly in with him, but I don't want to do it until Monday. I thought maybe we could switch up weekends and he could stay with you through the following weekend instead of the previous one. Would that be too much trouble? Did you have plans with Flossie or something?"

"You are so obvious, you know that? What's happening on Monday that you need Isaiah to back you up?"

It occurred to me to tell Smoke that it was none of his business, but then it occurred to me that I didn't give a shit if it was his business or not. I was still reeling, and I needed to tell somebody about it.

"My sister suddenly decided she wants to see her nephew. I'm invited, too, of course. I told her Isaiah would be with you, but she wouldn't take no for an answer. I was planning on running him by there for a quick minute, and then leaving him with you."

"Your sister, huh?"

"Yeah."

"And you said you haven't seen her since your aunt died?"

"I'm surprised you remember that, but, yes, it's been that long. Suddenly she misses me."

"I remember everything you told me. So you're going to

jet in, toss Isaiah around a little bit, and then jet back out?"

"That's my plan."

"That's cold, Anne. You think I should meet you over there when you're ready to leave, so I can meet your sister and mother?"

"For what?"

"For Isaiah. You had to meet my family, so I guess it's only fair that I meet yours. I think I vaguely remember your sister, though."

"Please tell me you didn't screw her, Smoke."

"Never even tried to. Feel better?"

"Marginally. You should be prepared to hear a few insensitive comments, though, if you decide to come."

"I've already decided. What does that mean, insensitive?" I didn't say anything for a few seconds. "Anne?"

"Apparently I wasn't supposed to know who my son's father is. She was shocked that I had the foggiest idea."

"Ok*aaa*y . . ."

"I've only been with two men in my entire life, Smoke. Why the hell wouldn't I know whose child I was carrying?"

We were silent for what seemed like hours, but was really only several minutes. A complete waste of cell phone minutes in my opinion, but it was his dime. I needed the time to collect my scattered thoughts anyway. I hadn't planned on going there with Smoke, but now that the words were out, I couldn't take them back.

"Two men, Anne?" he finally asked.

"Come on, Smoke. The point of me saying that was to say—"

"The man you were seeing in Mississippi—that's one."

"I can see why math is your forte," I drawled. "I started dating him when Isaiah was seven or eight I guess. Until then I wasn't thinking about men and relationships. I felt like I had so much ground to cover and lost time to make up for that I couldn't be bothered. He was persistent, though."

"What was he like? What did he do?"

"He was a little older than me," I said. "About fifteen years, I think. He's a professor at Jackson State, or at least he was when I left."

"Was he good to Isaiah?"

"I wouldn't have dealt with him if he wasn't."

"Humph, I believe that. Taught you everything you know, huh?"

"I was a willing student."

"And a quick study." Smoke chuckled sneakily. "I took your virginity."

"I gave it to you. Look, don't start waxing poetic and shit. We both know I was a little mixed up at the time. It's old news. Old and tired as hell."

"It's new to me. I can't believe I didn't realize that I broke your cherry, Anne."

"I think you did at the time." The genuine remorse in his voice was like a balm. "You said something like, 'damn, you tight.' " I mimicked what I thought his voice might've sounded like, and he laughed ruefully.

"You remember that?"

"I wasn't high all the time, Smoke. Just some of it."

He soaked that up, then said, "All those years with the man, and you just walked off?"

"I told you, I don't need sex."

"You're full of shit. When are you bringing my boy to me?"

"We'll get there sometime Monday morning and spend a few hours with Laverne, and then I'll have Isaiah call you when he's ready. Is that OK?"

"I'll keep things loose and have my cell phone with me at all times."

"I appreciate this, Smoke."

"No sweat. I'll see you Monday."

* * *

I rented a car at the airport and drove around for an hour looking for Laverne's house. I'd never been there, and I left the city when I was a teenager, so I wasn't familiar with the area she lived in. Isaiah was working my nerves, complaining about being hungry, and I had to prolong the agony of inevitable confrontation long enough for him to get a freaking value meal and supersize his Coke. I nibbled on a Filet-O-Fish as I drove. Had to give him half of it because his Big Mac was long gone and he was begging.

A little after noon I turned into Laverne's driveway and shut off the car. Isaiah was unusually quiet and I looked at him.

"Remember your manners," I started in. "And don't—"

He waved a stiff hand.

"I know all that, Mama. You hooked me up right. I'ma go in here and smile and act nice, but don't be expecting me to be all lovey-dovey, 'cause I'm not."

"Why would I expect your sour butt to be lovey-dovey?" I joked, smiling at him. "We'll do this quickly and painlessly. Rip the bandage off in one jerk, scream like crazy, and then relax. OK? Stop looking uptight, boy. This is your grandmother and aunt, not the dentist and the shot doctor."

I was hoping to get him to crack a smile, but he wasn't giving an inch.

"I'm serious, Ma. I'm going in here and do what I need to do, but don't start that 'give so and so a kiss' stuff like you used to do when I was little. I ain't feeling them like that."

"What's your problem?"

"My problem is that they treated you wrong, called you names and shit, and that ain't cool. Probably was just jealous because you all that. Last time I seen Aunt Laverne she was OK, but she ain't got nothing on you. And that's all it is to it. I'm telling you, don't start that kissy-kissy stuff, 'cause I'ma clown."

I sat back in my seat and looked out the windshield. I thought, somewhere in all those double negatives and slang talk was a compliment, and I was speechless. The last compliment my son had given me was when he was nine or ten and he'd told me that I was a good mama. Of course, I'd just agreed to let him have four of his friends stay overnight, but a compliment was a compliment. With kids you had to take them where you could get them and be glad about it.

"You can't blame people for their ignorance, Isaiah. Sometimes people don't know the power of their words and actions," I said.

"I think you the prettiest woman I ever seen, Mama."

I pressed a hand to my heart.

"You slay me, boy."

"I'm really gone slay you if you start that kissy-kissy mess," he snapped and pushed the door open to climb out of the car. I got out too, and followed him along the concrete walkway to the front door. I rang the doorbell and stood back to wait.

I didn't have to wait long. Laverne came right to the door and pulled it open like she was expecting the Publisher's Clearing House Prize Patrol. I looked upon my sister in the flesh for the first time in half a decade. She hadn't changed much, maybe put on a little weight around the middle, but she was essentially still the same. She wore her relaxed hair in a sleek bob cut with a part on the right side of her head, and there were glasses perched on her nose. Those were new.

I barely had time to say hello before she was pulling Isaiah down for a hug and planting smacking kisses on his cheeks. So much for the kissy-kissy threat. The entrance door brought us into the center of the living room, and that's where I stood, rooted to the spot. I looked around at the comfortable furniture and smattering of discarded toys, the rerun of *Friends* playing on the television.

Laverne was going on and on, fluttering around Isaiah nervously, rubbing his arms and face, and making him blush ridiculously. Then she turned to me and I fought a fierce battle to keep from cringing. She squeezed me tightly, and I looked at Isaiah over her shoulder. I managed to guide my hands to the vicinity of her shoulder blades and leave them there.

"It's so good to see you, Bree. And look at this nephew of mine, just as tall and fine as he can be. I'm so glad you came. Sit down, sit down. Isaiah, you want something to eat or drink? You, Bree?" I wondered if she could see that I winced every time she called me Bree.

"No, ma'am, but thank you. I just had a Big Mac," Isaiah said graciously.

"And half of my sandwich." I sat next to him on the couch. I felt around under my left butt cheek and extracted a toy figurine, leaned forward, and set it on the coffee table. "I'm fine too, thanks. You look good, Laverne."

"Me? Girl, it's all you. The locks really become you. I like it. A lot, Bree. You look beautiful."

"Thanks." I glanced at my watch. "Um, is Mama here?"

"Yeah, she was in the back trying to put Tracey down for a nap. Last time I checked Tracey wasn't cooperating, though," Laverne said. She settled on the adjacent loveseat and took to staring at Isaiah and me like we were visiting royalty. She seemed to realize that she was staring and shook herself. "Mama, Bree and Isaiah are here!"

A few seconds later the sound of running feet reached my ears. The little person that I assumed was Tracey burst into the room like a tornado and skidded to a stop when she saw that her territory had been invaded by strangers. She sized up Isaiah for long seconds, and then turned her little, wise eyes on me. I stared right back at her. She inched her way forward, shooting cagey glances at her mother in the process, and decided that Isaiah's lap was where she needed to be. Laverne roared with laughter as Isaiah struggled with settling the child on his lap in a manner that met with her approval.

"She's a cute little thing," I said, reaching over to fiddle with her bare toes and stroke her fat little thigh. Dimples winked out of her face when she grinned at me.

"She's beautiful," Laverne proclaimed. "Look at that smooth, chocolate skin. When she popped out and I got a good look at her, the first thing I said was that she was the spitting image of you, Bree."

"There might be some similarities," I hedged, seeing none. Tracey had my bangle bracelet in a death grip, so I took it off and gave it to her rather than have my shoulder dislocated.

"That little gal is you all over again. She doesn't have your disposition, though. Seems like you were always quiet and passive. That one there hits you like a house fire. She got that pretty dark skin same as you, though."

I went completely still as my mother's voice assaulted my senses. She came into the room a little at a time, emerging from the shadows like a ghost, and made her way over to where we were sitting. I looked into her butter colored face and registered the tentative smile there. Didn't know what to do with it.

I felt Isaiah's eyes on the side of my face for a fleeting moment, and then he was up and moving.

"How are you doing, Grandma Alice?" He hugged her and let himself be hugged, with one arm out to the side balancing Tracey. I rose slowly.

"Hello, Mama."

ISAIAH

Damn, Aunt Laverne done gained some hella weight. And what the hell she go and do her hair like that for? Made her face look fatter than it already was. How did this little girl get in my lap, and didn't nobody see her pulling on my buttons like she done lost her mind, slobbering all over the damn place? I was gone have to change shirts when I got to Smoke's house, for real. I was glad my mama didn't have no more kids, 'cause this one here was 'bout to worry me to death.

Aunt Laverne was staring at me like she crazy and falling all over my mama like she Queen Latifah or some damn body. Shit, she didn't need nobody to tell her she was pretty. She ought to know that, 'cause she was. And Grandma Alice coming in like she ain't know we was here all the time. I wanted to tell her she should be hiding her face for the shit she did to my mama, but I didn't. I just got up and gave her a hug and let her kiss all over me.

I was so tired of kissing old ladies I didn't know what to do.

I was checking out my mama. She was sitting there like she was waiting on somebody to hit her or something. Everybody looking at each other like they was strangers just meeting for the first time. Hell, I guessed they was strangers in a way. I couldn't imagine not seeing my mama for years and years.

This was some dysfunctional shit here, for real.

ALEC

I almost felt guilty for picking up Isaiah and leaving Anne there to deal with her mother and sister alone. Don't get me wrong, though, they seemed nice enough. I stayed long enough to make a little small talk and for them to see that I was in my son's life for the long haul, but then it was time for us to take our leave. I could see that Anne was trying to do the same thing, but her mother wasn't making it easy for her. She was on her every step she took, right there. Touching her in some way or asking questions, I suspected just to keep her talking. It would've been endearing if Anne's face hadn't been frozen into a look of intense confusion.

Isaiah filled me in during the drive to the movie theater. We were doing a double date type thing with Don and Jeff, checking out the newest and last installment of *Star Wars*, *Revenge of the Sith*. What the hell? I was still waiting on somebody to tell me what a sith was. But, whatever.

Based on what I knew about Anne's relationship with her mother and sister, I knew she wasn't having the easiest time. I figured that by the time the movie was over, she would have gotten the hell out of dodge. After the movie ended, Don and the boys decided that dinner was in order, but I begged off. I left them to it and headed home. I wasn't particularly hungry, and catching some Zs sounded much more appetizing.

So why did I call Anne?

I didn't know, but I did. I pumped fists with Isaiah, started up my truck, and bogarted my way into traffic, dialing her cell phone at the same time. She picked up after three rings.

"Where are you?" I asked.

"Just getting the hell out of dodge," she said, echoing my thoughts. I heard a car door slam and then the irritating tingle of a no seatbelt warning.

"How did it go?"

"It went. Where are you?"

"Headed home. I just left Isaiah with Don and Jeff. They're going out to dinner."

"You weren't hungry?"

"Not really. Have you eaten?"

"I had half a sandwich earlier, but I couldn't eat right now anyway. I'm too jittery, too . . . something. I don't know. I just want to sleep right now."

"You going back tonight?" It was after eight.

"First thing tomorrow morning. I wasn't planning on being here this long."

"Where are you staying?"

"Hell, Smoke, I don't know. I can't think straight right now. I'll get a room someplace and crash, I guess."

"All right then," I said. "I just wanted to make sure you were OK."

"I am, thanks. Talk to you soon."

"Yep." I closed my cell phone, tossed it in the passenger seat, and concentrated on driving.

I'd been home five minutes when I decided to take a shower. Twenty when Isaiah called to see if it was OK if he hung out a little longer with Jeff. Don was taking them go-cart riding or some shit. "Cool," I told him. I knew he was in good hands. Another thirty minutes passed before I rolled across my bed and picked up the cordless phone from the nightstand.

"Where are you now?"

"At the airport trying to decide if I want to go ahead and go home tonight," Anne said. "I don't think I can deal with a strange mattress tonight. There's a flight leaving at ten-twenty."

"It's nine o'clock now."

"Duh."

"Come over and hang out with me for a little while, Anne."

"And do what, Smoke?"

"Shit, I don't know. I'm not thinking straight either. We

could make toast or play checkers. I could whip your ass in some checkers."

"Yeah, right. You got a chess game?"

"Of course."

"Where do you live?"

I gave her directions to my house and rolled back across the bed to wait.

When she arrived I had her pull her car into the garage and I let her in through the kitchen.

"This is nice, Smoke," she said, looking around my kitchen. Her nose took her farther into the house, through the living room and into the den. She nodded approvingly and dropped her purse on the couch. She ran her hands through her locks and shook them out.

I moved up behind her and put my hands on her shoulders, started kneading the kinks out. She groaned from deep in her throat.

"That feels good." It was all the encouragement I needed. I lifted the sweater she was wearing from her shoulders and helped her out of it. Then I slipped my hands underneath the straps of the tank she had on and put in some real work.

"You said it went . . ." I prodded softly.

"On and on. I didn't think I would *ever* get out of there. And then you took my armor from me and left me hanging. Harder, right there." I chuckled.

"Sorry about that. They seemed nice. Here? Like this?"

She gasped. "Yeah. Damn, did you take a class or something? They *were* nice. Too damn nice, if you ask me. I counted how many times each of them called me pretty or beautiful. Ten for Laverne, and six for my mama."

"No, I didn't take a class. I'm listening to your body." I was in the middle of her back, using the pads of my thumbs. "You are beautiful." I was conscious of the erection steadily rising inside my pajama pants.

"They want something, Smoke. I just haven't figured out what it is yet. Maybe a kidney or something." I pressed my thumbs into the small of her back, right at the tops of her ass cheeks, and watched her head fall forward.

"Could that something be your forgiveness, Anne? Maybe to be in your life more than they have been?"

"You should just come right out and ask for something like that. You can't bullshit your way around it. Just makes people even madder if you do. It's insulting. What are you *doing* back there?" she asked as I pressed in again and made her knees buckle. She reached around behind her to feel for herself, but she never got the chance to find out. I took her hand and wrapped it around my dick.

"I'm not sleeping with you, Smoke."

"We don't have to sleep." She squeezed me and my hips rocked forward, eyes slid closed. My forehead dropped to the crown of her head. "Let's go to bed, Anne."

"I'm too distracted to tangle with you right now." She pushed her hands down inside my pajama pants and gripped me.

"Let me help you focus, then."

I tugged on Anne's hand once and she came with me into my bedroom. I closed the door and tongued her softly, deeply. I sat on the edge of the bed and pulled her between my thighs so I could deal with her belt. She balanced herself with a hand on my shoulder as she stepped out of her khakis. I tongued her through her thong as she pulled the tank over her head and dropped it on the floor. The sounds she made egged me on, pushed my thought process to a completely different level. I was ready to eat her up in three quick bites and one long gulp.

"Isaiah?" she whispered, sinking onto the bed.

"We've got at least an hour," I estimated. I hoped. "Damn, Anne," I hissed as her lips closed around me. Her fingertips skimmed my ass, ran up and down my thighs like a feather, and drove me insane. I couldn't take more than a few minutes of the smackdown she was putting on me before I had to concede defeat and pull away. She looked up at me with a knowing grin. "I told you about my eyes rolling, didn't I? You thought I was playing?" I pulled the covers back and nudged her between the sheets. "This time pay attention."

I slid in after her and tried to choke her with my tongue. She was on top of me, all over me, and I was loving every minute of it. I watched her take me in and then sit back to ride me wildly. I let her do it for long seconds, grit my teeth, and filled my hands with her breasts. She was off on her own, driving herself toward orgasm and probably caught up in the distractions she mentioned.

She gasped in protest when I lifted her off my dick and sat up to drag my tongue along the valley between her breasts, up the slope of her neck and over her chin. I fisted my hands in her locks and pulled her face so close that our noses were crushed together.

"Uh-uh, I'm supposed to be helping you focus, remember?" I rolled over and pulled her underneath me. "Stay with me now," I suggested hoarsely.

Two hours later, the erection I was busy coaxing inside of Anne went stone cold limp when Isaiah rolled up into my bedroom and busted me and Anne in bed together. I don't know who was more shocked, me or him, but I'm guessing him if the size of his eyeballs was any indication. I was extremely thankful we were completely hidden underneath the covers. Ten minutes sooner and the shit would've really been off the charts, if I recalled correctly exactly what I had been doing to Anne that many minutes ago.

He couldn't see anything risqué, though. As if the sight of his mother in bed with his father, obviously naked, wasn't bad enough. Then there was the unmistakable imprint of raised and spread knees underneath the covers, of supine legs and poised ass cheeks ready to contract and thrust, to consider. Nothing about what was happening could be mistaken.

I froze, which alerted Anne to the fact that something was different. Neither of us had heard Isaiah come into the house because I'd had the brilliant idea to turn on some music sometime between our first and second orgasms. It was fucking me up that Atlantic Starr was crooning about secret lovers right at that very moment.

"Yo, Da," he said just before pushing the door open and skidding to a halt.

Anne immediately went into hysterics.

"Oh my God!" she cried, voice high and tight. She tried to roll from under me, but I thought it was a little late for that, and didn't budge.

I looked at Zay.

"Rule number one. Knock. Anne, please settle down. I think it's safe to say the jig is up, OK?" She was wriggling and squiggling, working my nerves.

"My bad. I didn't know . . . um, you was busy . . . what's up, Ma?"

That did it. I dropped my head and cracked up. The little nigga had jokes at a time like this. Marvin Gaye on the radio singing about sexual healing and he had jokes.

"Smoke, move!" Anne sounded like she was close to tears.

I felt the little girly pushes at my chest and laughed some more.

"Be still before you damage something vital," I told her.

"It's cool, Ma. . . . I mean, you ain't gotta cry or nothing. I understand these things," Isaiah was saying. "All I want to know is are y'all being careful? Because you know that's how I got here, right?" The grin on his face was devilish, just like the one I was wearing. I couldn't help it. This was some crazy shit.

"Boy, carry your ass on out of here," I said. "And close the door. Don't come back in here, either." I watched him until he was gone and the door had clicked shut. Looked down at Anne. "I forgot I gave him a damn key."

"You said we had an hour, Smoke!"

"Newsflash, we've been going at it for over two. Are you OK?"

"Let me up, fool!" She pushed at my chest and I let her up. She rushed around the room, scrambling into her underwear and clothes. "I cannot believe this shit!" She noticed me sitting on the side of the bed, bent over at the waist with my face in my hands, silently cracking up. "You think this is funny?"

"A little bit. Hell, it might as well be since we're already caught. OK, OK, calm down." I recognized the signs of spontaneous combustion and rose from the bed to do some damage control. "One good thing is that he didn't come in an hour ago, when we had that sixty-nine going. That would've been—"

"Smoke!"

"All right, all right. This is a little awkward, I can see that." I reached for my pajama pants and put them on. Janet Jackson was crooning about it being funny how time flies. I looked at the stereo, did a double take, and went over to switch the shit off. Enough was enough. I came back to Anne and saw that she was holding one of her shoes, hefting its weight like she was trying to judge how much damage it could do. "Don't even think about it."

"Smoke, I swear to God . . ."

I took the shoe and dropped it on the floor next to the other one.

"Woman, put your shoes on so we can go out here and handle this mess." I pulled a drawer open and yanked out the top to my pajama pants, put it on, but left it unbuttoned. It wasn't like we were fooling any damn body anyway. She straightened her clothes and I ushered her toward the door.

I reached around her for the doorknob and stayed like that until she gave me her eyes. We stared at each other for a minute, then I went in for one last taste of her tongue. Took her a minute to give it up, but she did.

"Please don't go out here screaming and clowning," I said.

"Please don't make me kill you," she replied.

"So we understand each other then. Just tell me this. Are you focused now?" She rolled her eyes at me and yanked open the door herself. Isaiah was sitting on the couch in the living room, flipping through a magazine.

Waiting for us.

ANNE

I have never been more embarrassed in my life. This kind of mess didn't happen to me. I've never been the kind of mother who entertained a man in that way when Isaiah was in the vicinity. I never went in for the let's-go-in-the-room-and-close-the-door routine when my son was up and about. Any fooling around I did was done while he was asleep or out of the house completely. I always made sure he saw me going to bed alone and waking up alone. Whatever I did between those two occurrences was none of his business. I always felt that, without a wedding ring, openly sleeping with a man in front of my son was inappropriate as hell.

Of course, the one time I'd found myself in a sexual relationship with a man, Isaiah was younger and well trained. He had set bedtimes that he had actually adhered to, and he never seemed to have a problem taking his ass to sleep. But things were different now. He was running around freely, using keys he had in his possession, and barging into rooms without knocking.

And none of this would've happened if I'd stayed at the airport instead of letting Smoke lure me over to his house. I knew what I was coming for. I wasn't crazy, for real. Who in the hell plays checkers? And don't even talk about chess! The problem was that I'd gone without intimacy for so long that I was suddenly horny. Had Smoke never touched me in the first place I would've been fine, would've never come out of hibernation. All the hard work I'd done to curb my desires, and one touch from that fool had me flaking out.

No relationship—not that I wanted one—no expectations, no nothing. Just straight up good loving. And it *was* good. That was a problem, too. It was *too* damn good. If his pecker was three inches long, this wouldn't be happening. If he didn't know what to do with his pecker, this wouldn't be happening. If he was ugly as the crack of my ass, this whole scenario wouldn't even be feasible. But none of the above was true. I would not be waking up any minute from a nightmare. Smoke's pecker was more than I could handle, he was quite skilled at working that thing, and Ray Charles wouldn't call him ugly. So this scenario was real, playing out in living color, and embarrassing as hell. Lord help me.

"OK, so . . . about what you just saw in there." I pushed my arms into the sleeves of my sweater. "It wasn't what you think." Smoke slid past me and took a seat in a chair across from where Isaiah was sitting. And I do mean *slid*, because he didn't have to be that close when he did it. I shot him a look and sat in another chair.

"Are y'all planning on getting together or something?" Isaiah asked, looking from me to Smoke with a blank expression on his face.

"No," Smoke and I said at the same time. We cut our eyes at each other, both surprised by the speed and intensity of the other's response.

"You answered that rather quickly," he drawled, cocking a brow in my direction.

"Your hand was right on the buzzer too, so shut up." I rolled my eyes when he started laughing and focused on Isaiah. "You know I was having a hard time with the whole Grandma Alice and Aunt Laverne thing, right? So I came over here to talk to Smoke about it, and one thing led to another. That's all there is to it."

"So it didn't mean anything?"

"No," I told Isaiah. "It was stupid and careless, and it meant nothing to me. I shouldn't even be here. I don't know what the hell I was thinking." Out of the corner of my eye, I saw Smoke sit all the way back in his chair and cross an ankle over the opposite knee. He set the chair to rocking and stared at me as he rocked.

"You know," Isaiah hedged, dropping his eyes to the magazine in his lap and flipping a page idly, "you always told me not to be careless, Ma. You said I should—"

I cut him off, waving a hand irritably.

"Think about the consequences of your actions before you act, and decide if it's worth the risk," I finished for him. "I remember quite clearly what I told you, Isaiah. I don't need a crash course, OK? You're getting handy as hell with the quotes from yesteryear, I see. It's funny how they don't seem to apply when you're sneaking in the house at three o'clock in the morning."

He raised his hands in surrender.

"Don't get mad at me because you and Dad got busted."

"There was nothing to bust, boy." I was getting madder

and madder by the minute, more at myself than anyone else, but still. There was more than enough madness to go around. I looked at Smoke. "Would you tell your son that there was nothing to bust?"

"I think you're doing a fine job of telling that lie all by yourself," Smoke said. He stopped rocking and sat up, propped his elbows on his thighs. "Here's the deal, Zay."

"Don't tell me he's got you calling him that silly mess, too," I mumbled. I fell back in my chair, crossed my arms under my breasts, and stared at the wall. Smoke and Isaiah were looking at me like I was crazy but I didn't care.

"Here's the deal," Smoke repeated. "Your mother was upset and she came over. I was here. Like she said, one thing led to another and you walked in. We were both feeling emotional and we acted on those emotions. *And you walked in.* We needed each other tonight. *And you walked in.* Are you seeing a pattern here?"

A lopsided grin tilted Isaiah's mouth.

"Something about me walking in?"

"I think that's what's got your mother upset the most. Having you see her like that."

"It was embarrassing," I put in. I jumped to my feet and started pacing back and forth in front of my chair. "In sixteen years I have *never* subjected you to this kind of shit, Isaiah. I set standards for how I wanted you to be raised, and I stuck to them. I tried not only to teach you right from wrong, but to show you too. And now, in one stupid night, it's all down the drain. *Shit.*"

"I know you're human, Ma."

"Yeah, but—" I said.

"That's right, but—" Smoke said at the same time.

"Smoke, I'm—"

"Can I talk?" he asked softly, cutting me off. We locked eyes. After a second, I nodded and took my eyes back to the wall. "I'm not even going to play and tell you that your mother and I weren't making love, because we were. We're both adults and it was what we wanted to do. It seemed harmless enough at the time and, as you said, human. But in no way do I want you to leave this conversation thinking that it's OK to be careless, especially when it comes to sex, Zay. I think we owe you an apology for setting a bad example because we weren't thinking."

"It's cool," Isaiah said. "I ain't mad or nothing. I was just surprised, that's all. I didn't know you and Ma was getting down like that. I mean, I kind of suspected you was, but I didn't know for sure. Now I do."

"Wait a minute. We aren't getting down like anything," I lied in a shaky voice. "This was a one-time mistake." Smoke looked at me and sucked his teeth. "Smoke is in a relationship with Flossie, and I'm not the least bit interested in anything with him, anyway. What *I* don't want you to leave this conversation with is the impression that anything is going on, because there's not."

"Who is Flossie?"

"Smoke, tell him who Flossie is," I said flippantly. I couldn't be bothered with minor details at a time like this. "And while you're at it, tell him about the virtues of being faithful when you're in a committed relationship."

"Feel free to jump in at any time on that too. You can tell him about being on the lookout for temptations, which might cause him to forget that he's in a committed relationship, and people who fail to remind him of that fact until *after* the fact," Smoke added and I wanted to scratch out his eyes.

"Y'all tripping." Isaiah laughed and shook his head.

"Who's tripping? I'm not tripping. I don't know who you think you're talking to, boy, because I'm not two seconds off of you as it is." I looked up when the phone started ringing. I took off in the direction of the kitchen without thinking. "You know fat meat is greasy, right?" I snatched the cordless phone off the kitchen wall. "What is it?" I barked into the receiver.

There were several seconds of silence, during which I realized that I wasn't at home, and that this wasn't my phone to answer.

"Um . . . maybe I dialed the wrong number. Who is this?"

How rude.

"Who is this?" I asked.

"This is Diana. Is this Alec Avery's residence?"

"It sure is. Would you like to speak with him, or do you have more questions for me?"

"Who did you say this was?"

"Did you say you wanted to speak with him or not?"

I felt the freeze all the way across the phone lines.

"Yeah, put him on . . . please."

I walked back into the living room, right up to Smoke. Stopped in the V of his thighs and dropped the receiver in the general vicinity of his penis.

"Smoke, Flossie's on the phone."

He stared at me, slightly amused and chewing on his thumbnail. Several humming seconds passed before he lifted the receiver to his ear.

"Hello?"

I found my purse and dug the key to my rental out, tossed it to Isaiah.

"Pull my car out of the garage and don't get any ideas about joy riding. Park it in front of the house." Isaiah made no move to do as he had been told. Instead he sat there looking at me like he didn't recognize me. I didn't care for the silly grin on his face, either. I shifted my weight onto one foot and propped a hand on my hip. "You need me to get ethnic with you?"

"Wait a minute, wait a minute, hold on, Diana. Where do you think you're going at this time of the night?" Smoke asked me.

"To the airport. Carry on with your business and get out of mine, please. I'm talking to my son."

"And I'm talking to you. I keep telling you, you don't scare anybody. You're fifty pounds soaking wet. What are you going to do to keep me out of your business?"

"Isaiah, go get the car."

"Sit down, Isaiah. What? Yeah, I'm still here. I'm just . . . Anne, get somewhere and sit down. Isaiah, see about 'cha mama. I'm going to have to take a rain check on that, Diana. Yeah, I know."

"Listen to me carefully, Isaiah," I said, looking my son directly in the eyes. "You're only here for a week. You have to come home sometime, and when you do I'll be there waiting. I will make your life a living hell, and you know I will. It'll be like I'm PMSing every freaking day, I swear to God. Get the car, boy." I stepped back and folded my arms across my chest, imminently satisfied with the way he hopped off of the couch like a bunny rabbit. He knew what I was talking about, and he knew I had the power to drive him up one wall and down another if I wanted to.

"Oh, now see, you're wrong for that." Smoke was incredulous. "What? No, she's not staying here. I can't . . . hold up, Zay . . . can I call you back, Dee? Shit is getting out of control over here. I will. No, I'm not. I said I would, didn't I?"

"Oh, please." I marched back over to Smoke's chair and snatched the phone away from his face. He hissed through his teeth and watched me press the end button. I dropped the phone in his lap. "There. Now what were you saying?"

His head rolled around toward Isaiah as he came to his feet.

"Bring your mother's suitcase and broomstick in, Zay.

Leave the black cat in the car." It rolled back around to me. "That was foul, Anne."

"Flossie was getting on my nerves."

"And you ain't working mine? What are you doing answering my phone, anyway?"

"The ringing was breaking my concentration. I was trying to *focus*." And for no reason at all, I punched him in his chest.

"Do that again," he said, stepping closer. I took a step back, but I didn't make a move to punch him again. "Come on, Miss Bad Ass, do it again."

"All right, Smoke. That's enough," I suggested evenly. I took another step backward.

"Don't try to punk out now, Anne. You think you can take me?"

"It's not a matter of thinking, it's a matter of knowing. I could have you flat on your ass just like th—aaahhh!" Smoke flexed at me and I skidded around and took off running with him hot on my heels. I tried to close myself in his bedroom, but he was too fast for me. Next thing I knew, I was spinning through the air and landing on my back on the mattress. He came down on top of me and tickled me until I was crying, begging him to stop.

I never laughed so hard in my life.

ISAIAH

I knew my mama wasn't no virgin. Hell, how she think I think I got here? Yeah, I was caught off guard when I walked in on her and Smoke doing the damn thing, but I wasn't totally shocked. I had peeped out the way he checked her out when he thought I wasn't looking. I could tell that he thought my mama was fine. Shit, everybody did. I didn't like for just any old buster to be gawking at my mama, but it was cool with me if Smoke stole a look every now and again. My mama could handle herself.

I knew she thought that I thought she was being a freak or something, but I wasn't thinking that crazy shit at all. Matter of fact, I had been wondering what her deal was with men anyway. I ain't never really seen her with a man, other than that cat in Mississippi, but she barely even touched him when I was around. Sometimes I couldn't tell if they were going together or what. In a way, I was kind of relieved to find out that she was just like everybody else after all.

Not that the sight of Smoke riding my mama didn't shake me up a little. I was still tripping off of that shit. Homeboy looked like he was getting ready to handle his business, for real. Anybody besides my mama and I might've tried to sneak a peek, see if I could pick up some techniques for whenever I finally did manage to get some again.

But not with my mama. That shit was sick. I was just glad that they was under the covers. *Ugh.*

That dude my mama used to mess around with in Mississippi was all right, though. He used to bring me books and let me read to him, which was cool because I liked to read and write back then, too. And he used to do fun stuff with me. I think he wanted to marry my mama, but for some reason they didn't end up hooking up like that. I was glad about that now since Smoke was in the picture. No telling what the hell was gone happen now.

I wondered if they really thought I believed that bullshit about them cutting the cake being a one-time thing. Like I said, Smoke was missing in action for a hot minute the last time my mama was in town, and he wasn't with Diana, 'cause she was calling round the clock. I didn't answer the phone, just looked at the caller-ID and saw that it was her. Plus, they was acting strange when he brought my mama to Big Mama's house. Him whispering in her ear and her punching him under the table. Not no hard, leave-me-alone punches either, but them pitty-pat ass punches girls give when they want some attention.

I didn't know what was up with them, but if they said it didn't mean shit, then that was fine with me. I just hoped they believed it, 'cause from what I could see, there was something stirring up. I wasn't no young buck, thinking all this shit was gone end up like a storybook, that they was gone get married and all that silly shit, but I could see that they was feeling each other.

I sat on the couch and looked back and forth between them, from him to her, watching them clown with each other—my mama playing around on the phone and calling Diana Flossie, knowing Diana could hear her, and Smoke sitting back letting her show her ass on the phone. He could've beat her to the phone and answered it his damn self if he really wanted to. But he didn't. He just sat there shaking his head, thinking it was funny. I was like, *what the hell?*

When my mama started talking that PMS shit, wasn't no question about me moving her car out of the garage. She wasn't no joke when it was that time of the month, fussing and nagging and hollering all over the place, even worse than usual. I didn't play with her when she was going through her female time. Just like I didn't play when she threatened to torture me when I got back home. She could do that shit if she wanted to.

I got up. Sat back down. Got up again. Went to get the car. Then I had to stop and trip off of the two of them, straight up acting a damn fool. I couldn't believe it when my mama took the phone from Smoke and hung up on Diana. He was right. That was foul. I leaned on the kitchen counter and watched, shaking my head. Anybody could see that they was digging on each other, playing just a little too much if you asked me.

My mouth dropped open as my mama screamed and ran through the house. First of all, I never heard her scream before. Second of all, seeing Smoke running through the house after her was too much. They wrestled over the door and then I heard my mama cracking up. I never heard her laugh like that either. She was up in there begging Smoke to stop doing whatever he was doing, and apparently he wouldn't because she kept right on laughing.

This was some wild shit. Like romper room up in here. I shook my head and went to get my mama's suitcase out of the car, wondering where she was gone sleep.

The shit got even wilder when I peeped out of the crack of my eye and saw Smoke creeping down the hall in the middle of the night. My mama was sleeping in the guest room at the end of the hall. Ask me how I knew that was where Smoke was headed. I rolled over and looked at the alarm clock. It was after three in the morning. They was tripping, for real. I wanted to be nosey and go see what they were doing just for the hell of it, and the fact that I had to pee was reason enough to ease my ass out of bed and go see what was up.

I passed right by the bathroom and tiptoed my way down the hall, sticking close to the wall. I didn't know what I was gone do if Smoke suddenly came out and caught me tripping. I got closer to the guestroom and heard Smoke laughing, low, so his voice wouldn't carry too far. Then I heard my mama whispering something, but I couldn't make out what she was saying. Whatever it was made Smoke laugh again. The door was open. I got even closer and peeked in.

My mama was in bed under the covers, and Smoke was lying right behind her, spooning. Only he was on top of the covers and still wearing the pajama pants he put on after his shower. One of his legs was draped over my mama's leg, and even from where I was standing I could see that his hand was underneath the covers by my mama's breasts. My mama was saying something, and Smoke laid his cheek against hers so he could hear better.

He laughed and pushed her locks out of the way, and kissed her neck. Next, he kissed her shoulder.

"What did you say when she said that?" he asked.

"I didn't know what to say. I had no idea she was the one who called Aunt Bobbi. But now that I think about it, I did wonder how Aunt Bobbi knew to come."

"So old Laverne wasn't all bad?"

"She was bad enough back then. This new person she is threw me off, smiling and laughing and putting this little chocolate baby in my face, saying how pretty she was. And she is. I don't mean she's not, but it just messed me up, that's all. I didn't get to meet her husband and oldest girl, but I saw pictures, and he's even darker than I am."

"Freaked you out, huh?"

"Mmm. That and all the compliments. I damn near threw up. How can they all of a sudden think I'm so wonderful when they treated me like shit back then?"

"People change, Anne."

"People don't change that much."

"You did. I did. Plus, they've had years to think about all the shit they said and did. You're an educated woman. You know about social brainwashing or whatever it's called. I know the social worker in you understands the whys and hows, especially where black folks are concerned."

"Stick to math, Smoke. Don't be trying to psychoanalyze me. It's too late at night."

"Sure the hell is. I need to be in the bed."

"How come you're not then? You came in here and woke me up, and I was sleeping good."

"I'm trying to be in your bed."

"No, you're not, not with my son down the hall."

Smoke laughed again.

"Did you see his face when he walked in on us? That was some funny shit."

Oh snap! I remembered then that I forgot to mention that Uncle Don was in the house when I first walked in on them. I guess he figured out what was going down and left quietly, because he was gone by the time I got kicked out of the room.

"That was not funny. Embarrassing as hell, but not funny. Ouch. Stop biting me, Smoke." Is that what he was doing to her shoulder? I couldn't see clearly. "How are you planning on explaining yourself to Flossie?"

"Let me worry about Flossie. Can I get under the covers with you?"

"No."

"It's a little chilly out here, Anne."

"Then go get in your own bed, Smoke. You shouldn't be sleeping around on Flossie anyway."

"I'm not sleeping around on Flossie. I'm sleeping with my son's mother."

"Is there a difference? And you're not sleeping with me."

"No, not much sleep to be had, you're right about that. What is this you put on your skin to make it smell so good?"

"Soap?"

"You know what I mean, woman. Don't play with me."

"Oh, you mean like moisturizer?"

"Yeah."

"African shea butter cream. Smoke, please stop. That tickles. Get out of my room."

"You really want me to leave?"

"You should."

"Yeah, but do you want me to?"

"Smoke . . ."

"OK, OK, but give me a kiss first."

I watched Smoke kiss my mama like he was playing in a movie or something, looking like Queen Latifah in *Set It Off*, tonguing that one fine ass chick. Tongues all over the place, mouths all open. *Ugh.* I didn't think my mama knew how to kiss like that. Shit, I didn't even know how to kiss like that.

I tipped back down the hall and got back in bed. I forgot all about needing to pee. Plus, it would be obvious as hell if I went now. I figured I'd wait until Smoke walked back down the hall to his own room, then I'd go.

By seven o'clock when he finally came his ass down the hall and passed my room, I was about to bust. I danced my ass to the toilet and peed for ten minutes straight.

Nothing going on my ass. I wasn't a rocket scientist, but I didn't need to be one to know when people were in denial like a motha.

ALEC

I hustled my ass back to my own bed after seven in the morning. I messed around and fell asleep lying next to Anne. I should've left when she told me to the first time, but *no*, I had to be hardheaded. I pushed and prodded until I was under the covers with her, spooning and shit, dozing off like I was in la-la land. This was going to have to stop.

I crawled in bed and spread out like an eagle, immediately smelled the scent of Anne's shampoo on my pillow, and caught myself inhaling it. This shit *really* had to stop. No sense in lying to myself and saying that the sex wasn't mind-blowing, but I was thirty-six years old, old enough to know better. It wasn't like I was purposely trying to run around on Diana. Hell, I'd had more than enough trim that, at this stage in the game, dealing with one woman wasn't hard to do at all. It was just that for some reason, Anne was a little irresistible to me. A brotha lost his mind looking at those tiny, perky tits, that handful of a waist, and that little onion of an ass. Two good handfuls, that's what it was. Add all that to the fact that the package was wrapped in some of the smoothest, loveliest skin I'd ever seen, and how could I help myself? She was on point. Working my nerves and running off at the mouth just enough to open my nose wide and have me sniffing after her like a dog in heat. I never did like sassy-ass women, but Anne was something else altogether.

If she wasn't so sassy in bed, we might not have a problem. I wanted to track that old dude down in Mississippi and slap him on the back. After I checked him out, of course.

I fell asleep telling myself that I was putting Anne's delectable little ass on a plane and sending her home as soon as I woke up. One of us had to be sensible, and I voted for me.

I woke up after nine and hopped in the shower. Then I pulled on jeans and a summer weight sweater. I was slapping on cologne and pushing my bare feet into Bass loafers when Isaiah knocked on the door and stuck his head in my room. I looked at him and shook my head.

"Close, but not good enough," I said, grinning. He grinned back and I waved him in. "Tell me the truth," I said as he sat on the side of the bed and got comfortable. "Were you upset by what you saw last night, Zay?" He shrugged nonchalantly.

"Nah. Like I said, I figured something was going on. I forgot to tell you, though, Uncle Don came in with me last night."

"Ah, good old Uncle Don. Where's your mother?"

"Still sleeping, I think. She ain't came out yet."

"Well go tell her to wake her ass up, would you? The

last thing I need is Diana popping up over here showing her ass. You feel me?"

"Yeah, that's the last thing you need," Isaiah agreed, choking on a laugh.

I narrowed my eyes at him.

"You think this shit is funny? Just wait a few more years and then you'll be calling me wanting to know what the hell to do. See how funny it is then. This just goes to show you that unexpected shit can happen. What are we doing today?"

"Big Mama's making me and Jeff do some stuff in her yard. Uncle Don is supposed to pick me up around noon and take us over there. It's on you after that. You coming over to Big Mama's with us?"

"I'll come, but I'm driving my own shit because Uncle Don likes to get lost," I said as I fastened my watch.

"You ain't never lied. Had to stop thirty times last night."

We shared a knowing chuckle and headshake. I slipped my wallet in my back pocket and turned to run my hand across the top of my son's head.

"Looks like we need to stop off at the barber shop too. Get your fade together. Come on, let's go get the enemy out of the house and then it's men only for the rest of the week."

"What about Flossie?"

"Let me worry about Flossie."

Isaiah and I huddled in the kitchen and came up with scrambled eggs and decently crisp bacon for a late breakfast. I put a few slices to the side for Anne before he could inhale them, in case she woke up acting ignorant because she was hungry, and then glanced at my watch.

"Does she usually sleep this late?" I asked Isaiah when it got to be eleven-thirty.

He looked at me over the top of the sports section. All I could see were his eyes, but that was enough.

"Nah, she ain't usually up so late, though."

I couldn't think of a damn thing to say, so I didn't say anything.

Don rang my doorbell at exactly twelve noon and came busting up in the house with Jeff right behind him, like the house was on fire or something. Isaiah pumped fists with Jeff, faked like he was going to punch Don in the gut, and got cuffed around the neck for his trouble.

"What's up, Uncle Don?"

"Yeah, where's the fire?" I asked, coming out of the kitchen.

"Thought I might have to break up a catfight or something. Everything cool in here?"

"You're funny."

"Nah, bruh, you're funny. Had me cracking up last night." He looked around like he was just remembering that we were in mixed company. "Look here J, Z, y'all go on out to the car. I'll be out in a minute. And don't touch my radio, either."

I pulled out my wallet and motioned for Zay to come over.

"You got some money?" I asked.

"I'm cool."

I knew he was lying, and I held out my hand for him to give it up. He dug in his pocket and gave me three abused looking one-dollar bills. I looked at them, then at him, raised my right eyebrow, and left my hand out there. Eventually he came across with another five. I situated the bills in my wallet and traded him a twenty for them.

"Soon as I raise the dead, I'll be on through there," I told him. We pumped fists and then he disappeared out the door with Jeff. I forgot to tell him to keep his lips zipped about the happenings in my house last night, and I hoped that he was past the motor mouth stage.

I sat on the arm of the couch and looked at Don.

"What's up?"

"You tell me. You and Anne, huh?"

"Nothing to tell. She came by, things got out of hand, and then they got back in hand. You planning on giving me the birds and bees talk? Because it might be a little late for that, I think."

"I'm just being nosey. I mean, you told me all the other shit, but you didn't tell me you were interested in her."

"I'm not. Like I said, things got out of hand."

"So you're sleeping with a woman you're not interested in? Come on, Smoke."

"Damn, you *are* nosey," I said. "You got a vested interest in this shit?"

"I've got a vested interest in my nephew, so, yeah, I want to know what the hell is going on. I don't think he'd like you playing with his mother."

"Zay knows I'm not playing with Anne, Don. And stop talking to me like I'm seventeen or some shit. She knew what she was doing, just like I did. That's all there was to it, no whirlwind romance and no strings attached. Straight spontaneous sex. Period. Isaiah walked in and we handled the situation accordingly."

Don stood there looking at me, searching my eyes. I didn't know what he was looking for, but I was certain he wouldn't find it.

"What are you doing with Anne, Smoke?"

"What are you doing with Liz, Don?"

"I thought enough of Liz to marry her, so that's neither here nor there. Somehow I don't get the impression that you think enough of Anne to marry her, so what are you doing?"

"I'm sure you've got it all figured out, so why don't you tell me what you think I'm doing?" I was starting to be tired of the conversation, but I kept a pleasant expression on my face just on GP. It was the principle of the matter. I stopped having these kinds of conversations with motherfuckers when I started washing my own dick. "Don't clam up now. Spit it out."

"Not too long ago you were telling me how stunned you were to find out that you have a son with a junkie—your word, not mine—and now you're dipping into the wick. I'm just trying to figure out the method to your madness, that's all. And don't think I didn't put two and two together when she was here the last time. Shit, I think Mama did too. Hell, even Diana picked up some vibes."

"Ain't shit to put together, Don. I'm with Diana, for now anyway. There's nothing between me and Anne except Isaiah. She knows that, and I do too."

"So you were just taking her for a test drive."

I nodded.

"Something like that. More like curious to see what she was about."

"Assessing the differences between then and now."

"You're a psychologist now? Yeah, maybe that was what I was doing. Seeing if there was a fire behind all the smoke. I wasn't planning on screwing her, but it happened. Meanwhile, I found out what I needed to know, for my son's sake. She's got her shit together as far as I know, and now I can concentrate on getting to know my son without having to worry about her still smoking that shit."

Don was incredulous, although I didn't see what he had to be so shocked about. He shifted from one foot to the other, folded an arm across his chest, and used it to balance his elbow so he could point at me as he talked.

"Let me see if I understand you right. You're telling me that you suspected the woman of still using drugs, but you slept with her anyway? Just because it just happened?"

"I didn't say I suspected her of anything. I just said I was checking things out. But if I thought for a minute that her shit wasn't right, I'd have her ass in court fighting for custody of my son so fast even I wouldn't believe it. I'm glad things didn't have to happen like that. That's all I'm saying."

"I don't believe this shit. Here I am telling Isaiah that he should respect the hell out of his mother, and you don't even respect her."

"Now how are you going to say some shit like that?"

"Nah, how are you going to say some shit like you just said? You're taking the woman to bed every chance you get, and, knowing you, fucking her six ways to Sunday—"

I shot up off the couch and put out my hands.

"OK, I'm done, man. You're all up in my business—" He kept talking, raised his voice, and rolled right over my words.

". . . and deep down you still think of her as a crackhead!" he shouted.

I lost it.

"She was a crackhead!" I shouted back. "How the fuck was I supposed to know that's what I'd get as a mother for my child, huh? Hell, thanks to her and that shit she was strung out on I didn't even know I had a son until he was fucking sixteen years old! Half grown and shit. So what if I fucked her? She fucked me a long time ago, Don. So now we're even, if you want to keep score. I'm running around trying to figure out what the fuck to tell people when they ask me about my son's mother. Should I tell them that she was this crackhead I used to trade sex for drugs with? Huh? No? Should I say that never in my worst nightmares could I have imagined that my shit would be going down like this? What? I can't even truthfully tell my own mother where I met the damn woman! I thought I left that life behind me years ago, and now here it is, slapping the shit out of me every time I turn around. Hell, I'm damn near forty fucking years old. I'm supposed to be married with a few kids out of the deal. At the very least, divorced with kids I can explain away with the truth."

"Married to who? Somebody like your first wife or empty-headed Diana?"

"Diana's not a drug addict. That's one thing she has going for her."

"You—" Don's eyes shifted away from me and went somewhere over my shoulder. His face cleared and his eyes softened. He dropped his interrogation pose and pushed his hands in his pockets slowly. "Hello, Anne."

My chin dropped to my chest, eyes slid closed on a long hiss. *Damn.*

"Hi, Don. How are you?"

"I'm good, and you?"

"I'm good too, thanks. Where's Isaiah?"

"He's out in the car with Jeff. My mother recruited us for yard duty."

"Oh . . . well, that's good. Tell her I said hello. Smoke, I need you to open the garage so I can pull out. There's a two o'clock flight, and I intend to be on it." Don stepped around me and took her suitcase from her. He set it by the front door. "Thanks," she mumbled.

I smelled her as she passed by me on her way to the door. A light and fruity scent, kind of spicy. She pushed open the storm door with her arm and hefted the suitcase with a soft grunt. Don moved to help her, and she stopped him with a look.

"I can handle it, Don, but thanks, though. The garage door, Smoke?" And then she was gone.

"I didn't know she was still here, Smoke," Don said by way of apology.

I massaged the bridge of my nose and sank back down to the arm of the couch.

"And I fucking forgot," I said slowly.

I sat there for a minute or two longer, feeling like shit. Then I pushed up from the couch and went to push the button that opened the garage door. *How did I manage to forget that Anne was in my house?*

I followed Don outside. I was planning on bringing Anne back inside with me so that we could talk about what I was sure she'd heard. Don was parked in the driveway, so I left him at his car and turned into the garage, thinking that she was loading her suitcase in the car and fiddling around like women usually do before they get in a car.

"Anne," I called out, approaching the car. It was a sporty little Volkswagen Jetta and it was a good thing I had excellent reflexes. She might've taken both my knees out if I hadn't jumped back in time. She backed the car out of the garage, stopped just short of ramming Don's brand new Taurus, and then pulled forward again. I thought I had her. She was trapped. She couldn't move until Don moved his car, and he was still standing by the driver's door watching me.

I didn't have her, though. I scrubbed a hand down my face as I watched her wrestle with the steering wheel until she had it just where she wanted it. Then she backed the car out, around Don's car, onto the grass alongside my driveway—the neighbors' grass—and steered the car back onto the driveway behind Don's car. Quite calmly she backed into the street and shifted into drive. Isaiah stuck his head out the back passenger side window and waved as she drove off. She hit a button inside the car and let her window down to wave back and blow him a kiss. She put her fingers up to the side of her face, signaling him to call and sent him the prettiest, most serene smile I'd ever seen in my life. Then she drove off.

Damn.

* * *

I probably called her about ten times over the next three days. I got her voicemail at home and on her cell phone, and left at least two messages on both, but she didn't return my calls. Not that I really thought she would, but I tried anyway. I mentally reviewed my conversation with Don and I thought I could pinpoint the exact instances where I'd said something seriously fucked up. I wanted to give Anne the opportunity to curse me out and to call me whatever names she could think of, so I wouldn't feel so bad about what happened. But she wouldn't take the opportunity I extended.

Friday morning rolled around and I started a fresh round of phone calls, this time targeting her office. Three calls later and I still wasn't having any success. The receptionist cheerfully asked who I was, I gave her my name, and then she informed me that Anne was in a meeting. All three times. I started to smell a conspiracy.

I waited until Isaiah woke up and came stumbling into the kitchen, scratching himself and looking disoriented, and handed him the receiver.

"Call your mother," I said.

"I just talked to her last night, right before we went to the game." He was clearly confused. "Something happen since then?"

"No, nothing happened. Just call her and give me the phone when she answers." It was a simple request and I wasn't seeing what the problem was. If he kept on playing with me, I was going to pop him upside his head.

"Oh, I get it. Y'all ain't talking, and she won't get on the phone if she knows it's you, right?" I cocked a brow and he started dialing. A few seconds later, he said, "Ma, yeah, it's me. What 'chu doing?"

I bum-rushed him and took the phone. She was in the middle of explaining something about something that I wasn't even trying to listen to. I jumped right in.

"What exactly *are* you doing that you can't return my calls, Anne?"

I heard her suck in a sharp breath. Several seconds of silence.

"I see you thought up another way to use my son against me, Smoke. Hats off to you. What did you need to speak with me about? Is there a problem with Isaiah?"

"You know what I want to talk about."

"I think I have an idea, but I don't really see the point. You said what was on your mind, and I heard you loud and clear. I just wish you had been more forthcoming with me in the beginning. I might've made better decisions. As it is, I'm embarrassed enough, so can we please move on from here?"

"What exactly are we moving on from?" I glanced at Isaiah, saw that he was pretending to read the back of a cereal box as he ate, and carried the phone with me out of the kitchen.

"From nothing. From one colossal lack of judgment on my part, and on yours too. You wanted to see what I was about, and you did. Let's leave it at that."

"I feel like I should apologize to you. Some of the things I said were pretty strong, and I can see how you would be upset. I—"

"Upset?" she asked sweetly. "Why would I be upset?"

"Are we talking about the same conversation here?"

"Yeah, we are. The conversation you had with Don, right? I'm not upset about that, Smoke. I told you once before that you don't have the power to upset me, because I haven't given it to you. You said what you felt, and I'm glad you were honest, even if you weren't man enough to say those things to me. This whole situation would've been so much simpler if you had been."

She aimed a pointy little arrow right at the center of the bull's eye on my chest.

"Hold up, Anne—"

"No, you hold up, Smoke. You wanted to apologize? Fine, apology duly noted, but it's not accepted, because I don't need it. What I *do* need is for you to be good to my son and to respect him. I could care less if you don't respect me. I don't need that either, because I respect myself. At least I did until I let myself be talked into bed with you, but that's beside the point. You helped me *focus* more than you know, and now my *focus* is on my son, where it should've remained in the first place. Oh, while I have you on the phone, what time do I need to pick up Isaiah from the airport Sunday?"

"What?"

"What time do I—"

I shook my head to clear it. Was she for real?

"I heard you the first time. I'm just trying to keep up. So that's it? That's all you have to say about what happened?" I took the phone from my ear and stared at it for a second.

"Smoke, I'm at work and I'm busy. The only thing in the world I can think of that we need to talk about is my son. What time is his flight?"

"Seven. Gate sixteen. American."

"OK, tell him I'll be there."

I understood that the call had been completed when I heard a click in my ear. I stood there for a minute, running the conversation through my head for clarity's sake. Somewhere in there I'd lost track of what I was planning to say, and lost control of the conversation.

I wasn't buying that *I'm not upset* shit. I didn't know one woman who really wasn't upset when she made a point of saying that she wasn't. Usually they were seething, waiting for the chance to exact their revenge when a brotha least expected it. Move on from here, my ass. She'd blow up sooner or later and maybe then we could resolve this shit once and for all.

I waited for Anne to take her chance every time I spoke to her for one reason or another.

For instance, when she called to tell me that Isaiah had made it home safely.

"Smoke, it's Anne."

"What's up?"

"Nothing much. I just called to let you know that Isaiah is here in one piece. I just picked him up." I heard muffled gangsta rap in the background. "Isaiah, please turn that mess down. No, I don't know who Memphis Bleek is, and where did you get that mess from anyway?" She listened for a moment. Then, "Thanks a lot, Smoke."

"He used his own money," I said helplessly. Hell, track number eleven *was* a jam. "How are you?"

"I'm good. You?"

"Good."

"Did you want to holler at Isaiah?"

"Um, yeah. I guess so. I think he tipped his ass out of here with my Armani belt."

"Probably so. Hold on. Here he is." And that was that.

Then there was the time Isaiah left me a message to call him back. Something about needing money to rent a limousine for the prom. Anne answered the phone, sounding out of breath.

"Hello?"

"Did you just come in from running?"

"Yeah, who is this?"

That pissed me off. Just a little.

"Who do you think this is?"

"Smoke?"

"Who else would it be, Anne?"

"Don called earlier, and then Jeff, and you all sound alike. You need to speak to Isaiah?"

"Actually I wanted to talk to you. I got his message

about needing money to rent a limo for the prom, and I'm trying to figure out what the hell he needs a limo for."

"That's what I asked him. He said some mess about a bunch of them going in a group, but I think he really just wants to floss." Her voice changed directions. "Isaiah Avery Phillips!" I thought that maybe she had pressed the receiver to her breasts because Isaiah's response was muffled when it came a few seconds later. "Before I give him the phone you should know that I declined to waste money on a limo. I offered to drive him and that Aisha person myself, and I happen to know that her father did too." Her voice changed directions. "Because he called me, boy," she snapped at Isaiah when he questioned her. "Keep on and you're going to have a fat lip. Smoke?"

"I'm still here," I said, chuckling. "His middle name is Avery?"

"I thought you knew that."

"No, I didn't."

"Well, it's getting ready to be *dead* if he doesn't watch his mouth. I don't appreciate him calling you behind my back and pulling some mess like this."

"I don't either. Let me talk to him."

"And did he tell you about the C he's getting in math?" Anne wanted to know. She sounded like a tattle-telling sibling. Isaiah was huffing and puffing in the background. Then it sounded like there was a low-grade scuffle over the phone.

"Da, listen . . . ouch, Mama!"

"You trying to play me and your mother against each other, Zay?" I knew that was exactly what he was doing and had to laugh.

"Nah, see the C is getting ready to be a B, for real. And what do I look like pulling up to the prom with my mama driving? Come on now, you gotta help me out here."

"Put your mother back on the phone, boy." He had a point. A sketchy one, but still.

"She's gone back out the door."

"Oh, well, have her call me and we'll see what we can come up with."

She never did take her chance, and she never called me either.

I ended up calling her two days before the prom.

"Did you get the check I mailed?" I asked as soon as she picked up the phone.

"Yes, I did. I deposited it in his savings account. Thanks."

"Why do you always thank me for doing what I'm supposed to do?"

"Because you don't have to do it, and I appreciate it."

"If I didn't do it voluntarily, you could make me do it," I reminded her. "You almost did."

"I wasn't going to go through with that, Smoke. The goal was to find you, and I did. I would've asked for ten dollars a month, just so you could see Isaiah. I probably make three times what you do anyway, so it was never about the money."

I let that roll.

"So you just take it and put it in the bank? All of it?"

"Well, I did buy myself a pair of boots last week. They were on clearance, though, because it's summer time. But basically that's what I do, yeah. I don't buy crack with it, if that's what you want to know."

"That never crossed my mind."

"Didn't it?"

"No, it didn't. But since we're on the subject . . ."

"Don't go there, Smoke."

"You just took it there."

"You're right, and I'm sorry. Were you calling for Isaiah, because he's not here."

"What did you decide on for prom transportation?"

"I let him rent the damn limo." She sighed dramatically. "I got to thinking about teenagers and drinking and driving, and I decided that I didn't want to risk him having to get in a car with someone who might be drunk or high or just plain old can't drive. It's a cheapie, though. Doesn't even have a radio, and everything is manual."

"Pushover."

"Whatever. Should I have Isaiah call you back when he comes home? Should be in a minute or two. He went with some four-eyed boy to pick up their tuxes."

"Yeah, have him call me back."

Still no showdown, and her perpetual friendliness was messing with my head.

Chapter 10

ISAIAH

I left Aisha talking to a bunch of her silly friends and went to find the restroom. I had to pee, bad. A few minutes ago I was slow dancing and feeling all over her booty, and I couldn't even enjoy myself for holding a bladder full of piss. Her booty was righteous, and I needed to be able to concentrate on getting my hands on it properly, which meant that the piss had to go. Now.

The prom was in a hotel banquet room. They had it decorated decently, with balloons and streamers and little white lights on the ceiling. The music was cool and the chicken they served wasn't as good as my mama's, but it hit the spot. But what I couldn't figure out was why they didn't have bathrooms nowhere near the damn banquet room. I had to go up a flight of stairs and walk down a long hallway to find a spot to pee. I was seriously thinking about letting loose in a potted plant when I rolled up on the men's room. Finally.

That was the last thing I remembered clearly, thinking about pissing in a potted plant.

I was standing at a urinal, watching myself pee, and

wondering what good the little plastic deodorizer in the bottom of the urinal was doing when the door busted open behind me.

"Yeah, nigga, I told you not to play me, didn't I?"

Hood ran up on me and punched me in the back of my head. I turned around to defend myself, but I didn't have a chance to throw a punch. Two other motherfuckers were on me before I could even blink. I was taking punches from every direction, and pissing on myself as I slid to the floor.

Somebody was hitting me with something more than a fist. I looked around just in time to see Hood coming down on me with a bat. He cracked the damn thing across my shoulders, but I managed to grab the urinal so I wouldn't go all the way down.

"Man, what 'chu doing?" I choked out.

Nobody answered me. They just kept on punching. Then they started kicking me. I came off of the floor swinging wildly. One of them niggas was gone catch my fists some kind of way. I know I punched Hood in the mouth at least once, and another dude got punched in the side of his head. I felt the skin on my knuckles split, which meant that somebody's teeth took a lick, too. I was trying to fight my way to the door with my dick hanging out and everything.

"Fuck, this nigga done busted my damn lip," Hood yelled.

"That's what you get, motherfucker," I told him and kept swinging.

"Hold him!"

They bum-rushed me and grabbed my arms. When they had my arms pinned behind my back, Hood started punching me in my stomach, one punch after another until I threw up the chicken I ate all over the front of my tux.

"Punk, motherfucker. Let his ass go."

I was wobbling on my feet, staring at him. He had blood on his lip and I raised a hand to point at it, and smiled at his sorry ass.

"You need two other motherfuckers to fight me, and you calling *me* a punk?"

I felt myself spinning around in empty space and saw the little squares of tile on the walls fly past my eyes for a second. Then I was falling face down toward the floor. I would've had a clean fall if it wasn't for the urinal sticking out from the wall, right where my forehead could get to it. I ain't never had a seizure in my life, but I think I started having one as my brain went sloshing around inside my skull. And then I was out.

"Shit! Hood, man, let's get the fuck out of here!" somebody said.

Them motherfuckers ran out of the bathroom and left me lying there with my dick hanging out and piss all over my pants, like I was playing with myself and fell asleep when it started to get good.

ALEC

Diana was all over me, doing her damnedest to get my attention, and I was trying to give it to her. I swear I was, but my mind was otherwise occupied. I was thinking about my son going to his first prom, even though he was only a sophomore and a little young to be butting in on the seniors' action. But his main squeeze Aisha was a senior, so that alone got him in the door. I wondered what was in store for after the prom, and then I wondered if he'd remembered to slip a few condoms in his pocket. I had talked to him about that shit. I could've called him on his cell phone and checked in, but he didn't have one, thanks to Anne. She didn't think kids needed cell phones unless they could pay the bill themselves. Damned if I didn't half-ass agree with her, but it still would've been nice to be able to check in.

She had taken pictures of my boy and his date before they left for the prom and e-mailed them to me. Handy little creations, those digital cameras were. He looked damn good in his tux, grinning from ear to ear with his ears sticking out. His bowtie and cummerbund were a funky shade of purple that matched his date's low cut dress perfectly. Her little half-grown titties were popping out all over the place. I could almost hear Anne sucking her teeth and see her rolling her eyes as she took the pictures. Picturing the look that had probably crossed her face had me laughing out loud before I knew what I was doing.

I was sitting on the couch and Diana was straddling my lap, tonguing my neck and undoing the buttons down the front of my shirt. She pulled back and looked at me curiously.

"I must be doing something wrong if you're laughing."

I opened my mouth to tell her what I was thinking, and then I thought better of it. Anne was a touchy subject. I shook my head and cupped her breasts.

"It's nothing, baby. I just thought of something funny." I caught her look and rushed to soothe her. "And it damn sure ain't you. Where were we?" She went back to her tonguing, and I went back to my thoughts.

Anne had been in a few of the pictures, standing beside Isaiah wearing a completely different grin than the one he was wearing. While his was cocky and self-assured, hers was slight and feline looking, as if she knew a secret that nobody else was even close to figuring out. I found myself wondering what the secret was. Then I found myself looking to see if she was wearing a bra. *Not,* I decided after several seconds of intense staring.

Diana was wearing one, though, and it needed to be

dealt with. I slipped my hands under her shirt and went to work while she switched from unbuttoning my shirt to unbuttoning hers. When she was done and I had a mouthful of breast, she reached down and cupped me between my legs. A frustrated groan filled the room when she discovered that I wasn't hard yet. Nowhere near it, actually.

"Do I need to help you out with that?" She slipped off of my lap and headed downtown.

I was wondering if I should call Anne and find out if she'd given Zay a curfew when the phone rang. I eased away from Diana, sent her an apologetic look, whispered that I'd be right back, and went to the kitchen to answer it.

"Hello?"

"Smoke?"

"Anne?" Her voice sounded strange. "What's wrong? Did something happen to Isaiah?" She started crying and my patience flew right out the window. "Stop crying and tell me what's up, Anne." I listened for a second. "I can't understand a thing you just said. Stop crying and tell me."

Five minutes later I hung up the phone and walked back into the living room.

"I have to go," I told Diana. I glanced at my watch and then looked toward the kitchen, wondering what the hell was taking Anne so long to call me back with specifics. All I knew so far was that someone had called her from the hotel where the prom was being held and said that Isaiah was hurt and was on his way to the hospital. She was finding out which hospital and calling me back. *When?*

"You have to go?" Diana's head rolled around on her neck and I saw storm clouds gathering. "Damn, Alec. Who was that, your other woman?"

"That was Anne . . ."

"That bitch again. What is it with you and Anne? What, is she stranded here again, and on her way over?"

I wasn't feeling like this shit, not when I didn't know what the hell was wrong with my son, and I would have to travel hours away to find out for myself. I buttoned my shirt and straightened my zipper, fastened my belt.

"Isaiah was in an accident and it sounds pretty serious," I said on my way to my bedroom to throw some clothes together. I needed to call the airlines and see when the next flight to Chicago was leaving. I needed to—

The phone rang again. I walked around the bed and picked it up on the second ring, put the receiver to my ear, and listened to Diana intercept the call. *What the hell?*

"I need to speak to Smoke," I heard Anne say.

"Who the hell is Smoke?"

"Um . . . Alec. I need to speak to Alec. It's an emergency."

I opened my mouth to tell Anne that I was on the phone, but Diana beat me to it.

"I'm starting to think it's always an emergency with you. He was busy when you called the first time, so—"

"Listen, bitch, put Alec on the phone right now, OK? I don't have time for this shit."

"I'm here, Anne," I snapped. "Hang up, Diana."

"Why do I have to hang up? She can say whatever she has to say with me on the phone."

"Smoke, you *really* need to exert better control over your whores. This reflects badly on you as a pimp. Get Flossie's ass off the phone, or I'm hanging up on the count of three, and not calling back."

I took a breath for patience.

"Diana . . ."

"I got your whore, bitch."

"Fuck you," Anne said sweetly.

"No, I'm fucking Alec, which I think is your whole problem."

"Then that makes two of us, doesn't it? Smoke, I'm not

up for this shit. You need to handle your business. One . . . two . . ."

I heard Diana suck in a sharp breath. This shit was crazy.

"Diana, hang up the phone."

"What the hell does she mean, that makes two of us, Alec?"

". . . two and a half . . ."

"Hang up," I said.

"I asked you a—"

I stomped over to the doorway.

"Hang up the fucking phone, Diana!" I heard a click and went back to throwing clothes on the bed. "What did you find out?" I said into the phone. I saw Diana leaning in the doorway ready to do battle as I took a stack of boxers from a drawer.

On my way to the closet for pants, I stopped and dropped my chin to my chest. I listened carefully for a few more minutes and then I pinched my nose and breathed deeply.

"Where are you now?" She told me she was in her car on her way to the hospital. I filed the name and location of the place in the back of my mind. Right outside of Chicago, not far from the airport. I glanced over at Diana, wondering who she was, and then I remembered.

"I'll be on the next flight," I told Anne. "I'll meet you at the hospital. You said Incarnate Word, right? OK, hang tight. I'm on my way, but I'll have my cell on if you need to reach me before I get there. Matter of fact, call me every half hour and keep me updated." I dropped the cordless on its base and pulled my carry-on from a shelf in the closet.

"Start talking, Alec," Diana demanded from the doorway.

"Start talking about what?"

"I can't believe you're going to play dumb. Are you fucking her or not?"

"Haven't we had this conversation before?" *Where the hell is my favorite belt? Shit, that's right. That damn Isaiah stole it.* I twirled the belt rack inside my closet and yanked off my second favorite one.

"We have, but there's always two sides to a story, and hers is that you're fucking her."

"I don't think that's exactly what she said, Diana," I said, knowing that was exactly what Anne had said. That was what she meant anyway. "She was trying to piss you off, and judging from the look on your face, it worked. She wasn't expecting you to answer my phone." I spared her a meaningful glance as I headed to the bathroom to gather up toiletries. "Neither was I."

"Oh, she can answer your phone, but I can't? And what's this Smoke stuff?"

"Childhood nickname."

"I never knew about it."

"You never knew me as a child. Should I even bother asking you to take me to the airport?"

"You can, but if I drive you, I'm going with you."

I looked at her like she'd suddenly taken leave of her senses.

"For what?" I didn't mean to phrase the question quite like that. The words had just slipped out ever so ungraciously.

"Because I'm your woman, and if something's happened to your son, I should be with you." She waited for me to respond, and several seconds of silence passed. "Shouldn't I?"

I zipped the bag and set it on the floor at the foot of the bed. I was ready to roll out, but as always, Diana needed to be dealt with.

"This probably wouldn't be the best time for you to

come with me to Chicago, Dee. A lot of shit is going on, and I need to be able to concentrate on that."

"Is it that, or is it because Anne will be mad that you brought me?"

"I'm going to have to say door number one. Come on, Dee, I need to go. Can we take a—"

"Raincheck? You owe me about fifty of those damn things, Alec. Or should I call you Smoke?"

"Don't call me Smoke." I moved past her and out of the room, and she was right on my heels. I picked up my cell phone from the coffee table, checked to make sure that it was on and charged up, and dropped it in my pocket.

"But Anne can call you Smoke, though, right?"

I shifted and looked at Diana. I studied the curve of her lips and admired the slope of her full breasts, appreciated the roundness of her hips, and finally met the mutinous gleam in her eyes. She was so jealous that I could've sworn her skin was taking on a greenish hue. But I didn't know how to help her out with that. Not right now anyway. I wished I could snap my fingers and magically transport myself to Chicago.

Instead of trying it, I said, "I need to go."

My plane landed in Chicago at precisely one AM. I had called ahead to the rental car office inside the airport and had them reserve a Saturn Coupe for me. Not my usual style, but I needed wheels, and I wasn't willing to wait while they located a luxury sedan and had it delivered for me. After I gave him my credit card information over the phone to speed things up, I told the agent to make sure that the car was gassed up and ready to go when I got there. I scribbled instructions to the hospital on the back of the rental agreement, and drove off while the agent was still telling me to have a nice day. Or night, as the case was. I punched in Anne's cell phone number as I drove.

"Any news?" I asked as soon as she answered. She was

whispering. Probably because she wasn't supposed to be using a cell phone inside the hospital.

"No, not yet. He still hasn't woken up. They don't know when he will."

"What floor is he on?"

"Five. They may not let you up here this time of night."

"I'm pulling into the emergency room parking lot now. Come down and get me," I said and snapped the phone closed. I needed to see my son, and quickly.

I waited by the receptionist's desk for ten minutes and then I finally caught sight of Anne coming down a corridor in my direction. She was wearing a tailored two piece suit and skyscraper heels. The cool shade of coral sat nicely against her chocolate skin. Her locks were arranged in a chignon at the crown of her head, and tasteful diamond solitaires winked in her ears. Her shoes were taupe sling-backs, and even with the three inches they loaned her, I still had to drop my head to look in her face.

"The doctor started hemming and hawing when I told him that I was staying and that you were coming up, but I told him I'd kick his ass if he even thought about putting me out," Anne announced after stopping six inches away from me and tipping her head back.

My eyes roamed all over her face.

"Tell me again what the hell happened."

"Let's walk and talk." I followed her back the way she'd come. Even though my nerves were shot and I was worried about my son, I noticed the subtle sway of her hips and the controlled contraction of her calf muscles as she walked.

She stopped in front of a row of elevators and pressed the up button.

"Leonard was one of the prom chaperones, and he's the one who found Isaiah in the men's restroom. Apparently Aisha noticed that he hadn't come back after a reasonable amount of time, and she asked Leonard to go in the men's room to see if Isaiah was still in there. He thought maybe a group of boys had sneaked off to drink or something."

Several pairs of elevator doors opened at once and people spilled out of them, heading in all different directions. I stepped aside so a man dragging an oxygen tank behind him could pass. *Why aren't patients sleeping at this time of night?*

"Anne, is that you?"

She halted in the act of stepping onto an elevator and turned around expectantly. A dark haired white man wearing a long lab coat and a stethoscope draped around his neck approached her with his hand extended. She slipped her hand inside of his and shook briskly.

"Smoke, could you hold the door, please? Lewis, it's good to see you."

The ID badge hanging around Lewis's neck said that he was Dr. Lewis Hanrahan, but she had called him Lewis. I caught my ears perking up to listen carefully, and felt no shame at all about it.

Lewis moved in and kissed Anne's cheek, dangerously close to the corner of her mouth.

"You look wonderful, as always. What are you doing here this time of night? Finally decided to take me up on that invitation to dinner?"

She had the nerve to blush. I stopped the door from closing with one hand and ran the other one around the nape of my neck slowly.

"I told you I'd be happy to go as long as we can bring along your wife."

"Ah," Lewis said, smiling ruefully. "Pesky details. How is Isaiah?"

"Actually, he's not doing so good right now. That's why I'm here. He's on five, unconscious and refusing to come out of it."

"What happened?" Lewis put a concerned expression on his face.

That's what I was in the process of finding out before we were so rudely interrupted, I thought cryptically. I wanted to grab Anne and shake the shit out of her for making me wait while she flirted. She started explaining to Lewis what she hadn't even explained to me, and I cleared my throat irritably. She glanced over her shoulder at me and continued to talk, which sent my blood pressure soaring into murderville.

"This is Isaiah's father," she finally said. "Alec Avery, Dr. Hanrahan."

"Lewis, please. It's nice to meet you. Isaiah's a fine young man. I hope he pulls through."

"Same here, and thanks," I said and gave his hand an extra squeeze. His eyes shot to mine, then skidded back to Anne. He heard me loud and clear.

"Be sure and call me if there's anything I can do, Anne. Meanwhile, I think I'll give Dr. Belcher a call and alert him to the fact that we've got visiting royalty in the house. I'll tell him to let you stay as long as you want."

"I already told him I'd kick his ass if he tried to put me out," Anne said, giggling.

"I'll tell him you meant that too," Lewis said, preparing to shove off. Another handshake and another kiss on Anne's cheek that was too close to her lips, and he was gone.

"So . . . he hit his head on a urinal?" I picked up where we'd left off as the elevator doors closed us in. Thankfully, there was no one in the car except us.

"Or either he was hit on the head with something."

"What?"

She took a deep breath and gave me her eyes.

"You haven't seen him yet, so you don't know, and I didn't want to upset you by telling you over the phone.

He's got bruises all over his face and some swelling, which tells me that he was in a fist fight. He's got a few cracked ribs, too."

I didn't make a living as an accident reconstructionist, but it was clear to me that my son had been jumped.

"Somebody, or a group of somebodies followed Isaiah into the restroom and caught him off guard while he was taking a leak. Is that where you're going, Anne?"

"It's the only thing that makes sense to me. His knuckles are scraped up, so he was defending himself against somebody. I just wish he'd wake up and tell me what happened, so I'd know what to do next."

"What are they doing to alleviate the swelling around his brain?" It occurred to me that we were sitting still. Neither of us had remembered to push the button on the panel for the fifth floor. I removed a hand from my pocket and reached around Anne to do the honors.

"They've got him on anti-inflammatory meds and an IV drip. It's gone down some, but there's still a ways to go."

"Do we have any idea who did this to Isaiah?" We stepped off the elevator and she led the way down the corridor. She shook her head as she walked, and I understood that that was my answer.

"Prepare yourself," she warned me and pushed open the door to Isaiah's room. She went immediately to his bedside and picked up the hand closest to her to hold.

I rounded the bed and stared in shock. My son's eyes were swollen shut, his lips were twice their normal size, and purplish bruises peppered his face. There was a long, wide bruise across the width of his forehead, which confirmed that he'd either hit his head on something, or he'd been struck there. Either way, the force of the blow was the reason for his supine state. It had caused swelling around his brain and had sent my son into a deep slumber.

Rage welled up in my chest and damn near choked me.

I felt unsteady on my feet, like I was under the influence of a hallucinogenic drug. I stared at my son and waited for him to suddenly pop upright and announce that he was fine, ready to go home. But he never did. A machine at his bedside monitored his heartbeat and blood pressure. There was an IV needle thrust into the skin on the back of his hand, and he lay there impervious to all of it. I wondered if he could hear what was going on around him and, if so, what he was thinking.

Something caught my eye and I winced and pointed.

"Is that a . . . ?" She followed the direction of my finger.

"A catheter? Yes." I wobbled on my feet and she noticed. "Smoke, maybe you should sit down."

Sit down while my son was *unconscious*? Isaiah was the victim of a brutal attack and he was damn near in a coma because of it, and she wanted me to sit down? I wanted to punch holes in the nearest wall or stalk the corridor looking for somebody to inflict pain on, and she thought that maybe I should *sit down*? She was standing, but *I* should sit?

"Was he conscious when they found him? Who did you say it was again?"

"Leonard, his coach, and, no, he wasn't. He told me that Isaiah was probably in the middle of relieving himself when he was attacked. He was . . . exposed, if you know what I mean, when Leonard found him. He fixed his clothing before the paramedics arrived and anyone else could see him like that."

I thought about what Anne said, pictured it in my mind. When I thought I had an accurate picture of it in place, I scrubbed both hands down my face and breathed into my hands. My legs buckled and I sat my ass down.

Every hour or so a nurse came in to check on Isaiah and to shoot encouraging glances at me and Anne. "The body has a way of shutting down to recuperate and rest when it needs to," they said in whisper soft voices. *Fuck that*, I thought. I wanted my son to open his eyes and be all right, not resting and out of it. He was in a place where I couldn't reach him, and the helplessness was slowly driving me crazy. I paced the floor in his room restlessly.

By contrast, Anne seemed cool, calm, and collected. A second chair had been brought in, and she alternated between getting up to stand at his bedside, stroking his face, or holding his hand, and sitting in the chair with her legs crossed, staring out the window. At times I doubted she even realized that I was in the room. She withdrew into herself and stayed there for long stretches of time.

Dr. Belcher had given us a fairly good prognosis. He was confident that the swelling would continue to go down and that Isaiah would awaken from this episode without the added burden of brain damage. All the scans were normal, he said, and Isaiah's vital signs were steady and strong. There was no lasting internal damage, which was the initial concern. For all intents and purposes, my son was sleeping off his trauma.

"How long does something like this normally last?" I asked at one point when he came into the room to check on Isaiah. It was after four in the morning and we were both looking tired and worn out. Anne was back to staring out the window. She turned when she heard the door open, but was content to let me do the talking this time around.

Dr. Belcher shrugged his shoulders and replaced the chart he was scanning.

"It's hard to tell with these kinds of things, but Isaiah is young and healthy, which helps a lot. It could be two more hours, or two more days. The important thing to remember, Mr. Avery, is that he is not in a coma, and the swelling is going down steadily. It's about half what it was when he first came in, so the meds are working wonderfully. We just have to wait and see, but my guess is he'll wake up when he's ready."

Knowing my son, he'd wake up this time next year, simply because he knew that by then I would be crazy. Completely batty. Anne and I sat in our chairs and watched. And waited.

As the sun came up the next morning, I ran my tongue around my teeth and fished my cell phone from my pocket. It would need to be charged soon, but there were two bars left, enough for me to make the calls that I needed to make. I called my school and apprised the principal of what was happening, told him that I needed the rest of the week off. Then I punched in my mother's number. I was between the third and fourth digits when Anne suddenly came back from the dead.

"Are you calling Diana? If so, give her my apologies. I didn't mean to go there with her, but she was working my nerves."

"She was working mine too, but you *were* a little off the chain, Anne," I said just to see what her reaction would be.

She waved a hand.

"Whatever. She was fucking with me at the worst possible time. I don't fuck around when it comes to my son, and I told her the call was important. All she had to do was give you the fucking phone and that whole scene could've been avoided."

I punched in the fourth and fifth digits, and looked at her.

"You curse too motherfucking much, you know that?" We laughed and some of the tension slipped. "I'm not calling Diana, but I'm sure she would appreciate your apology."

"It's not heartfelt."

I finished dialing and sat back in my chair. Our eyes locked across the width of the room.

"I wasn't under any illusions that it was," I said.

ANNE

The waiting and watching was killing me. My son, my baby, the only person in the world that I loved unconditionally was lying unconscious, and there wasn't a damn thing I could do about it. Worse, I had no real clue how he'd ended up that way. He left my house with that glossy looking half-dressed girl, going to the prom, and the next thing I knew my cell phone was blowing up right in the middle of the last ten minutes of the stupidest stage play I'd ever had occasion to view. Something about the idiotic girl's mama not liking the man her daughter was about to marry, but by some cruel twist of fate, the mama had ended up sleeping with the man behind her daughter's back. I guessed the moral of the story was that forgiveness and family loyalty were important. I didn't get it, though. Forgiveness was largely overrated, and what did family loyalty really mean, in the broad scheme of things? It was a black play and I was thinking that black folks needed to quit while they were ahead with all the silly drama shit. It was past tired.

I was thankful that Leonard had found Isaiah when he did and called an ambulance. Otherwise, he might've lain in that bathroom half the night. I didn't even want to think about what could've happened if Glossy hadn't noticed that my son was missing in action. I reminded myself to make sure that I thanked her for that. If my son had died, I think I would've gone somewhere and hanged myself. There would've been a double funeral, a homecoming for both Isaiah and me, because I would've been completely done. I mean, through.

I was barely holding it together as it was. Smoke kept looking at me, probably wondering why I wasn't falling out, screaming, and cursing God, instead of sitting in a chair staring off into the great beyond. I understood that I was supposed to be clowning, knew I was considered to be behaving strangely because I wasn't, but it wasn't in me. I had done all the crying and screaming I could handle for the time being, earlier, when I'd called Smoke. Now I questioned doctors and nurses with an even, polite voice and earned a few raised eyebrows in the process. My step never faltered, not even when they finally let me see Isaiah and I set eyes on his beautiful face, swollen and bruised from senseless violence.

None of them knew what I did. They had no clue that I was shouting and ranting and raving on the inside. I needed to scream so badly that my throat was clogged with it. Death, I knew firsthand, was a slow and excruciating experience, because every minute of the past several hours had taken a little more of my life and proven that to me. I couldn't even cry, not the way I needed to. Not yet. I always cried when Isaiah accomplished something and made me proud, I cried when I watched sentimental movies, and I cried when I was so angry that I didn't know what else to do and still be within the confines of the law. But crying right now just wouldn't happen. I felt frozen, like a block of ice, so maybe that was why. My tear ducts were locked up.

A doctor walked in the room while Smoke was whispering into his cell phone. She shot him a warning look, which he pretended not to see, and then checked on Isaiah's progress. I stood at the bedside so I could see everything she was doing and ask questions that I already knew the answers to. The ID badge hanging around her neck said her name was Dr. Heather Newman, and I watched her neatly clipped, clean nails poke and probe at my son, and saw him grimace in response. At one point he moaned in obvious pain. I caught myself reaching out to push her hand away from him and pulled up short. She saw me and smiled reassuringly.

"He's coming around," she said, showing me large teeth and a silver tongue ring. "Just last night he wasn't responding to pain at all. Looks like his nap may be wrapping up soon. Next time it could be him trying to push me away. Let's hope it is."

"Everything still looks good, right?" I searched her eyes, looking for signs that she was keeping something important from me.

"Great, actually. Except for his obvious injuries, he's physically fine. The impact to his head was jarring, but the swelling is almost gone, and his vitals remain good. All we need him to do now is wake up."

"She said that all we need him to do now is wake up," I told Smoke when Dr. Newman was gone and he was off the phone. I walked over to him and stopped between his open thighs, looking down at him. "Do you think a good, stiff slap would do the trick?"

"You slap my son and it's going to be me and you," Smoke told me. "You look like you need to be sleeping too."

I imagined I did look a little rough around the edges. I glanced at my watch. Almost one o'clock in the afternoon. Over twelve hours gone already. I needed a shower, no, a long bubble bath and a toothbrush loaded with Aquafresh. A few hours of sleep to recharge my batteries. I took in his wrinkled khakis and yellow Polo oxford shirt. He was looking a little worse for wear too.

"I can't leave him alone here," I said.

"You mind if I ask why you're dressed like a congresswoman? And he's not alone, or did you forget that I'm here too?"

"I didn't forget," I snapped. I left him and went to stand at the window, looked down at a parking lot full of cars. I did forget a little bit. Sixteen years was a long time to have someone all to yourself, and then suddenly have to share them. I remembered his question and looked back over my shoulder. "I went to a play last night. That's where I was when Leonard called me."

"Good old Leonard. Look, why don't you go home, get some rest, and eat something. I'll stay with Zay."

"What if he wakes up while I'm gone?"

"Then we'll both see you when you get back."

I thought about that for a split second.

"I'm not leaving my son."

Smoke went to the cafeteria a little while later and brought back food—sandwiches and iced tea. I ate half my sandwich and picked at the other half, knowing I needed to eat it, but not finding the energy to do so.

"Didn't your mother ever tell you not to waste food?" he joked when he caught me lifting the wheat bread and spying at the meat inside. "Give me the damn sandwich if you're not going to eat it, Anne."

I took it to him.

"You going to drink the rest of your tea?" I asked. I looked at his half-empty cup longingly. My own tea was long gone. He sighed and handed it to me.

"Go home, Anne. Get some sleep."

"No." I sank down in my chair and looked at Isaiah. My eyes were dry and gritty feeling, and I closed them briefly to alleviate some of the discomfort. In a minute I planned to get up and find something to do to keep me busy.

I didn't remember falling asleep.

* * *

It was half past seven in the evening when I woke up to the sound of Smoke's cell phone ringing. I shifted in my chair and opened my eyes to find him staring at me. I scrubbed my hands over my face and caught a whiff of my breath, frowned. I could tell by the change in his voice that it was Flossie calling. The conversation was short, terse sounding on his end, and I raised my eyebrows as he snapped the phone closed.

"What, does she think we're getting it on in the hospital broom closet or something?"

"Thanks to you, she probably does."

"Ah, the turmoil of relationships. Thank God I don't have to deal with that. So what, you're angry because I had to get her straight?"

"You *had* to?" He looked at me suspiciously. "You didn't sound too put out about doing it. You knew what you were doing, Anne."

"So did you when you were hopping from one bed to the other. Don't be mad with me because you didn't cover your ass along the way. You're too old for this kind of mess anyway."

"And you had nothing to do with it, I suppose?"

"Not really. It was all you, dude," I said and laughed.

"So I forced myself on you?"

"I'm not saying that, but you were the one with the ulterior motive. Without that, we wouldn't have ended up in bed, and Flossie wouldn't be breathing down your neck now."

"I'm not sure I really had an ulterior motive, past getting between your thighs and working one of those juicy little breasts of yours into my mouth, that is. The rest is blurry."

"You're full of shit." I uncrossed my legs and then crossed them in the opposite direction, clasped my hands at my waist, and slid down in my chair to watch him talk his shit. "That's not what you told Don, Smoke. You said you wanted to see if I was really who I said I was. I still don't get how you thought sex would help clarify things, but that's what you said."

"I know what I said."

"Good, so tell me why you bothered to pretend that you were concerned about me, like you enjoyed being with me, if you were entertaining the idea of challenging me for custody of my son? The one *I* raised for the first sixteen years of his life."

"I wasn't pretending, and I'm well aware of the fact that you kept him from me for sixteen years. Why are we getting into this now? When I wanted to talk about what happened, you said you didn't. Suddenly you want to duke it out?"

"I lied. I wanted to talk about it, but I wanted to talk about it when *I* was ready to talk about it, not when *you* said we should talk about it, Smoke. You're still trying to manipulate things to suit your purposes, and I've been manipulated enough. I slept with you because I find you sexy and I always have, but you'd be mistaken in thinking that I give a flying shit what you think about me. You seem so hung up on the fact that I used drugs for a few years of my life that you just can't fathom that I was a child then, hurting and gullible. Well see if you can fathom this," I said calmly. "If using drugs makes me such an irredeemable crackhead—your word, not mine—then what does selling the fucking drugs make you?"

He shot to his feet, glaring at me.

"This isn't the time for this shit, Anne. I'm stepping outside for a minute. You need me to bring you anything back?"

"I need you to sit your ass down before I make a scene.

That's what I need you to do. You're not the only one with an opinion, you know. Used to be a time that when you spoke, people listened. Well now I'm talking, and if you try to walk off without listening, I swear to God I'll tear this fucking room up and say you did it. Have your ass hauled off to jail . . . again. Damn societal derelict."

He hissed behind his teeth and tried not to be insulted. "You wouldn't."

My eyes jumped up and locked with his.

"Try me." We stared long and hard at each other. He finally lowered himself back in his chair and rubbed his eyes tiredly.

"You're off the chain, you know that?" he asked.

"Another one of your opinions that I don't give a shit about," I said. "What I want to know is why you kept jumping between my thighs if you think I'm nothing but a crackhead? It kind of makes you look bad, don't you think?"

"I don't think that, Anne. Look, the conversation with Don was intense. He was coming on strong and I reacted strongly. Some of that shit came from way back, just popped out before I could think about what I was really saying. I was mad as hell."

"Because you just found out about Isaiah." It wasn't a question.

"Exactly. You can't miss something that you never had, but after I met my son and got to know him, I realized what I missed. And as a man, it hit me doubly hard. For sixteen years I had a son in the world, growing up without a father, and that didn't have to be the case. I was angry about that, and at the same time, attracted to you. Things got out of control."

"So your plan was to pay me back by fucking me to death?"

"Hey, sista, some of the death wish was coming from your direction too."

I held up a hand and laughed, caught.

"I'll give you that."

"Damn right. You gave me something else too. Willingly and many times."

"I don't have a problem giving as good as I get. Why did you take it if it repulsed you so much?"

"Repulsed isn't quite the word I would use," he said rhetorically, like he was explaining the purpose of a complicated mathematical equation to a confused student.

"What word would you use then?"

"There is no one word, Anne. Look, we had some of the best sex I've had in a minute. If I was repulsed by anything it was the fact that I couldn't get enough of you. Ain't nothing like lovemaking done right. You know that yourself."

"You and Flossie weren't doing it right?" I tilted my head and studied him curiously.

"I'm not talking about Flossie right now. I'm talking about you and me. You wanted to have this conversation, so don't start talking crazy now. I said some things to Don that I shouldn't have said, and I want to go on the record right now as saying I'm sorry."

"You were thinking them. Even if you had never said them, you were thinking them, which is just as bad."

"Maybe I thought some of those things when Mr. Charlie slapped me with child support papers in the middle of my classroom, yeah. I barely remembered you and what I did eventually remember, you said yourself wasn't very complimentary on either of our parts. No, I wouldn't have wanted a child with the Breanne Phillips I used to know, and you can't penalize a brotha for that. You might want to, but you know you can't." Smoke leaned forward in his chair and braced his elbows on his knees. He licked his top lip, glanced at Isaiah, and pursed his lips.

"That's what you got, though, a child with Breanne Phillips."

"No, I didn't. That's what I thought I was getting, but the picture didn't gel. I'm still trying to figure out who the hell you are, but you're not Breanne Phillips."

"She's dead," I reminded him.

"So is Smoke."

"No, he's not."

His brows shot up, surprised.

"How do you figure Breanne gets to be dead, and Smoke can't be?"

"I've been looking at Smoke every day for the last sixteen years," I said, nodding my head toward the bed where Isaiah lay.

"I guess you've got a point," Smoke breathed and sat back in his chair. He watched Isaiah sleep for a while and then brought his eyes back to my face. "I said what I said because I was angry. Hell, I don't even remember most of it."

"I wish I could say the same thing," I told him just before the door swung open and Beverly Avery marched in.

Smoke and I traded startled looks and turned to look at her. She set a small suitcase by the door and went over to Isaiah's bed. She fussed with the covers around his waist and straightened the sleeves on his hospital gown, laid a hand on his forehead. I wasn't sure she even realized that we were in the room.

Smoke was the first to speak.

"Mom, I told you, you didn't need to come."

"Bullshit," Big Mama snapped, sending a sweeping look around the room to include me and Smoke before she rolled her eyes and waved his words away. "When have you ever known any of my babies to be sick or hurt and me not come to see for myself what the problem was? I should punch you in your mouth for telling me not to come, Alec. Don and Jake are driving in first thing in the morning too, so shut up and start talking. What are the doctors saying?"

Chapter 11

ANNE

Isaiah told me a couple of times before that Big Mama was a force to be reckoned with, but I hadn't paid him any mind. Until now. I let myself in my house and slipped out of my heels, wondering just how she had managed to talk me into agreeing to leave the hospital. Probably the same way she'd talked me into coming to Indiana a few months ago. She left no room for arguing or excuses. She simply told you what you were going to do, and you did it, without even considering the fact that you had other options. She told me that I was going home to get some rest, and here I was. Smoke was next on the relief list. When I went back, he would go and do the same. Left with no other choice, I gave him the spare key to my house and told them that I'd be back in a couple of hours.

I dropped my purse on the kitchen table and scourged through the refrigerator for something to eat besides cold cuts. I found a leftover slice of apple pie and ate it in two bites, drank about a half a gallon of milk, and then followed that up with a can of condensed chicken noodle soup. Didn't even add water, just sucked the salty concoction down right out of the microwave.

On my way out of the kitchen I looked at the phone and thought about making a few phone calls myself, the way Smoke had done from the hospital. He had called his mother and she'd passed the word that one of the herd was in trouble. Pretty soon they would all converge on the hospital and surround my son with family. I thought about calling my own family and tried to guess what their reaction would be. Would Laverne laugh and ask what I wanted her to do now? My mother would probably hem and haw, and find any excuse not to come. Either way, it was no more than I expected or probably even deserved.

I hit the light switch and left the kitchen without making the call. Some bridges were better left burned.

I sank into a tub full of lavender scented bubbles at ten o'clock and didn't rise to pat myself dry until after eleven. I experienced a moment of anxiety, worrying about Isaiah, and then I remembered that Big Mama was in charge and I let the anxiety slip away. Ten minutes passed as I punished my mouth with my toothbrush and scraped my tongue until it stung. Gargling with Listerine for thirty whole seconds set my mouth on fire. I set the alarm clock to wake me up in three hours' time, at three-thirty in the morning, and whimpered like a baby as my skin made contact with the cool sheets on my bed. I didn't bother with a gown or pajamas, and it was like floating on a cloud. I slid a pillow under my head, curled another one against my body, and let the cloud take me away as it floated into oblivion.

ALEC

Anne's house was quiet and cool, and smelled like a fading flower garden when I walked inside. I was expecting her to have a light burning somewhere so I could see where I was going, but it was completely dark. I found the stairs and went up slowly. I thought I remembered where Zay's room and Anne's lair was, but that was about it. I tipped down the carpeted hallway and stuck my head in rooms as I went.

I came to Anne's room and walked in like it was my room too. She was lying on her stomach, face pushed in a pillow, and one leg curled on top of the covers. I remembered that she was a wild sleeper as I considered the slope of her naked back. Her dreads were spread out on the mattress like ropes, her mouth slightly open. The woman was knocked out, even snoring lightly, which tipped up the corner of my mouth.

I expected her to hear the shower blasting and come stalking down the hallway to see who had invaded her house, but she didn't. She slept right through me scrubbing myself and then brushing my teeth. I went down to the kitchen wearing absolutely nothing and peeked inside the refrigerator. I spied a pizza delivery box and reached in to crack the lid.

"Bingo," I said as I took the box out of the refrigerator and switched on the oven. I made as little noise as possible in my search for a pizza pan or cookie sheet, but I still created more than a little bit. I looked through the doorway and down the hallway, expecting Anne to appear any minute to curse me out.

I desperately needed a stiff drink to wash down the four slices of pizza I ate, but I wouldn't get one in Anne's house. There wasn't a drop of anything remotely resembling alcohol as far as the eye could see. Times like this a brotha needed a stiff drink. It wasn't every day that your only son ended up in the hospital and you felt like straight up murdering somebody. Some Jack Daniel's would've gone down nicely. I gulped down two glasses of fruit punch and took three Oreo Double Stuf cookies with me out of the kitchen.

My muscles were tight and knotted with the need to float like a butterfly and sting like a bee. I was feeling a little out of sorts, kind of aimless and heavy with worry for my son. Big Mama had run me out of his room too, but I wanted to be there with him, even if I couldn't do anything but watch and wait. We'd nearly elevated to the point of shouting at each other before I finally came to my senses and remembered who I was damn near shouting at, conceded defeat, and left the hospital. For the time being, anyway. My plan was to catch a few Zs and then go back and kick her ass out, and see how she liked it.

I tossed the last cookie in my mouth and cleaned up behind myself in the bathroom—neatly folded the towels I'd used, and wiped down the vanity. I gathered up all of my shit, took my bag to Anne's room, and set it on the floor by the dresser. Then it started.

I looked down at my dick in the darkness and tracked its slow rise. I wondered what Diana would say if she could see me now, needing no help at all to become aroused. All I had to do was look at Anne, and all she had to do was let me look at her, and it was on. That's as far as my thoughts of Diana went. She skidded out of my head like a vague memory, and I felt bad. I really did. I wanted thoughts of her to propel me out of Anne's room. There were two other rooms besides Isaiah's where I could stretch out and sleep, but I didn't go to either one of them.

I followed the leader and climbed in bed with Anne.

She was lying on her back now, arms over head and her face turned toward me. I moved up against her and pushed my tongue in her mouth, giving her a taste of the Oreos I'd just eaten, and hoping that she liked chocolate. I pulled back when she gasped and jerked away. Waited while her eyes adjusted to the darkness and stared into mine.

"Smoke? You scared the *shit* out of me!" Her face was close to mine, so I went back in for another kiss. She put my tongue out of her mouth and pushed at my shoulders.

"What are you doing?"

"Trying to give you something," I said as I dove in for her neck. I was about to cum just smelling the scent of her skin. I took her hand and brought it down to where I was throbbing, and wrapped her fingers around me.

"Uh-uh, Smoke. You can't do this shit. Get out of my bed and go in Isaiah's room or something. *Ahhh.*" She moaned and turned her head when my tongue found the spot on her neck that she didn't know I knew about. I applied more pressure, brought my teeth in on the act, and closed my hand around hers on my dick, showed her what I needed.

And I did need it, I realized. It was a shock to my system just how much I needed it. Wanted it too. I wanted this shit like I hadn't wanted anything in a long time. I rolled my tongue around her neck, started in on the other side, and hissed when I figured out that she didn't need my hand to coach her anymore. She evaded my lips.

"Stop running and let me put my tongue in your mouth," I whispered in her ear.

"Why, Smoke? What kind of game are you playing now? What is this, more curiosity?" I sucked a breast deep in my mouth. "I hate you for this shit, you know that?" Let it snap out and watched it jiggle in front of my face. Did the same thing to the other one. I let the deep groans coming from the back of my throat be my answer. "I'm serious, Smoke, you need to leave. I mean it." A high-pitched scream came out of her mouth as I slipped my hand between her thighs and sank my fingers into her flesh. She started having spasms, threw back her head, and made a sound like a hiccup.

I took advantage of the situation and tried to touch the back of her throat with my tongue. Everything went still as we kissed. Her hand on my dick, my hand on her clit—everything. It was deep, the kiss we were sharing, messy and wet, but so damn satisfying that I lost myself in it. I opened my mouth as wide as I could and tried to suck her in whole. It wasn't enough, though. I had to be inside Anne like yesterday.

She went over on her back and I went with her, spreading her thighs wide. We both sucked in air as I eased into paradise and took root like I never planned to leave. I braced myself on my elbows and stared down at her as I stroked her long and soft.

I dropped a kiss on her parted lips.

"Put your hands on me."

"No. This is wrong, Smoke."

"Wrong feels right as hell. Touch me somewhere. *Damn, ahhhh.*" She skimmed her fingers across my back and then palmed my ass. I sucked on her bottom lip and whimpered like a fucking baby. I was almost embarrassed. "You're doing some voodoo shit to me, you know that? Got me losing my mind."

"You better get it back because this is going to stop." Her walls contracting around me took most of the sting out of her whispered words. She tilted her hips up and squeezed her eyes shut.

"Good to you?"

"Yeah, but not good enough for you to keep . . . *ooooh* . . . playing with me, though. I hate your ass."

I was listening to her body.

"Like this?" She nodded with her eyes still shut like she was afraid to look, like she thought she might see the boogey man or somebody. I guessed I was the boogey man.

"Look at me," I hissed.

"No."

"Look at me, Anne."

"Fuck you, Smoke." She pounded on my back with her fists. Girly, powder puff licks, and I didn't miss a beat stroking her.

"Open your eyes, punk," I teased her. "Look at me." When she did they were wet and glossy looking. Too wet, I thought. And too glossy looking. Damned if she wasn't about to cry. I froze and stared at her. I realized that she was breathing harder and clenching her bottom lip between her teeth. I blew out a long stream of breath. "Damnit, Anne."

She shook her head, telling me not to go there. The hands on my ass squeezed, wanting me to keep stroking and ignore what I was seeing, but I couldn't do that. The look on my face must've told her that I couldn't do it, because she turned her head and swallowed so loud that I heard it.

"I said look at me, Anne."

"You said . . ." She tried to give voice to the words running around in her mind. Shit I'd said without thinking, and shit she couldn't stop thinking about, regardless of what her mouth said.

"Shhh, fuck that, fuck what I said, OK?" I pushed my hands under her head and lifted her up for my lips. I pressed kisses down the side of her face and across the curve of her shoulder. The first sob came out and my body jerked right along with hers, like somebody had sucker punched me. She wasted two tears on me, and I smoothed them into her skin with the tips of my fingers, caught her chin, made her look at me, and started stroking her again.

"I'm sorry," I whispered as she squeezed me from the inside out. "I'm sorry," I repeated as her thighs tightened around my waist and her nails dug into my skin. "You hear me, Anne? Yeah, that's right. Cum for me. Take that shit out on me. *Ahhh.*"

"Fuck," gasp and jerk, "you," gasp, gasp, and then her head fell back. "Smoke, I hate your ass."

"I know, baby. I know." I knew something else too. My hand streaked down between our bodies and zeroed in on her clit. I watched her wobble and fall over the cliff.

"Stop." She was vibrating like an electric wire. "Stop, Smoke, I can't take anymore." I made her take a few more seconds, and then I pushed my face in her locks and spilled for ten seconds straight.

The alarm clock buzzed at three-thirty and had me popping up in bed, looking around like I was crazy. I looked at Anne to see if she knew what the hell was going on and couldn't do nothing but laugh. She was spread eagle on the bed, face pushed into a pillow. The noise penetrated her fog and she started moaning and whimpering like she was about to cry.

"No, no, *nooooo*," she whined pitifully. She lifted a hand and nudged me none too gently. "Make it stop, Smoke."

It took me a minute to figure out that the noise was coming from the alarm clock on the nightstand next to me. I reached over and fiddled with the damn thing until it fell silent. Who the hell needed an alarm clock that played CDs, tapes, and told the temperature outside too?

"What time is it?" Anne asked.

"Three-thirty in the morning, and it's seventy-four degrees outside," I said, sliding back under the covers.

"I'm going back to the hospital . . . soon as my eyes uncross."

"No, you're not. Big Mama said we couldn't come back until the sun was shining."

"She's your mother, Smoke, not mine."

"All right, then take your bad ass back to the hospital and see what you get." I reached out and pulled her back against me until her ass was in my lap. "You going?" I asked when she didn't move.

"I like Big Mama," she said, yawning and snuggling in.

"Yeah, that's what I thought."

Chapter 12

ISAIAH

I opened my eyes and looked right into Big Mama's face. Oh, shit, I was dead and now I was in heaven! She was laughing, staring at me, and nodding her head like I had just answered a question right. I turned my head and looked dead up in Uncle Don's grill. *Damn.* Was heaven like some Wizard of Oz shit or what? And you was there, and you and you, and even you, Toto. What the hell was this? All my Indiana peeps crowded around, looking long in the face, come to see me off. Uncle Jake saw me staring at him and smiled. I was trying to figure why the hell he wasn't shaved and shit, looking like a straight up grizzly bear. I didn't see Jeff nowhere. God must've decided to take me and leave that nigga to grow old and get all the pussy he could stand. That shit wasn't fair. One taste of pussy and a nigga had to be snuffed out.

OK, Zay, calm down. God don't like cussing and shit. You can't bust up in heaven running off at the mouth. Fuck around and be shaking hands with Lucifer. And anyway how did I know I was going to heaven? All the shit I'd done, I could just be in a holding place until they got my furnace ready. Big Mama and them could be here to say so long, sucker.

OK, OK, breathe. No sense in shitting on myself just yet. I was probably just . . .

Maaaaammmaaaaaaaaaaaaaaaaaaaaaaaaaaaa aaaaaaaaaaaaaaaaaaaaaaaaaaaaa!

I cracked my lips open.

"My mama?"

"I'm calling her right now, baby. I made her go home and rest 'cause she was about to fall over on her face. Your daddy went to make sure she was OK. You had us all worried about you," Big Mama told me. She kissed me on my cheek and then hustled around the bed to the phone.

"Finally decided to wake your butt up, huh?" Uncle Jake leaned over me and scratched his beard. "Wish you would've thought to do that shit before we drove all the way here."

I tried to smile, but my lips hurt. Then I went back to sleep.

ANNE

Smoke told me my baby was awake and asking for me, and I literally jumped into a pair of jeans and pulled a shirt over my head. I was drying off and pushing Smoke out of the bathroom when the phone rang. When we heard that Isaiah had opened his eyes my mind had quickly shifted from entertaining notions of a quickie to rushing to my son's bedside. Smoke hung up the phone, finished fastening his belt, and watched me lace up my sneakers.

"She said he just went back to sleep, mumbling something about Dorothy and Toto." He laughed. "I told her we'd be on our way as soon as you decided which earrings to wear."

"I would've been ready half an hour ago if you hadn't been in the bathroom meddling while I was trying to take a bath." I decided on medium-sized silver hoops and put them on, and then I went to work arranging my locks in a ball at the crown of my head. I caught Smoke watching me in the mirror. "What?"

"Last night was damn good."

"Last night was a disaster of monumental proportions, but I'm glad you thought it was good. Hold on to that memory, because I'm bidding your dick a fond farewell." I saw him coming toward me. "Hands off, Smoke."

"You want me to dump Flossie for you? Is that what the issue is?"

"You don't want to dump Flossie for me, and I'm not asking you to." I dodged his hands and circled around him as I stuck the last bobby pin in place. "Besides that, with her you won't have to worry about what other people think, or if they're wondering where you know her from. She's a little more respectable, though barely, if you ask me."

"Anne—"

I spritzed on some Oscar de la Renta and cut him off.

"Take me to my son, Smoke." I walked out of my bedroom and left him standing there, and then I ignored him all the way to the hospital.

Isaiah was sitting up in bed talking with Big Mama, who had let the guardrail down and was sitting on the side of the bed when I rushed into the room. I skidded up to the bed, looked at Big Mama, and then I looked at my son. He tried to smile, but it looked more like a frown, and that was enough to break me. I didn't have any problems falling across his chest and bursting into tears.

"Ouch, Mama!" Isaiah complained. I had forgotten that a couple of his ribs were cracked. I tried to ease my hold on him, but I just couldn't seem to do it. "I'm all right, Ma. I'm all right. Aw, man, she's crying."

"That's all right," Big Mama said. She laid a hand on my back and rubbed gently. "Mothers have a right to cry any time we feel like it, so you let her get it out of her system."

"Anne, please," Smoke said like I was being unreasonable. I felt his hands on my shoulders, massaging the kinks out, and didn't offer too much resistance when he lifted me away from Isaiah. "Go on over there with that noise." I thought he was about to nudge me out of the way, but he turned me in his arms and pulled me against his chest instead. I didn't have any problems with that either. I slid my arms around his waist and pressed my face into his shirt to finish crying. The feel of his hands smoothing up and down my back was soothing, and I hiccupped like a baby.

"Glad to see you up," Smoke told Isaiah. "Had me worried I was about to lose you after I just found your little tack-headed ass, boy."

"Nah, dude, you stuck with me." Isaiah laughed. I heard the sound of palms slapping.

"Oh, we're back to dude now, huh? You must've really hit your head hard."

"You got jokes, right?"

"A few. You feel all right?"

"Head hurts a little, and Mama just finished breaking my ribs, but I'm cool."

I stuck my hand in Smoke's left pant pocket and pulled out the handkerchief I'd seen him fold and put there as he was getting dressed. I used it to wipe my face before I turned around and gave Isaiah a watery smile. That's when I noticed that Don and Jake were standing at the foot of the bed. Dark as my skin was, I think I turned three shades of red.

"I'm sorry, Don, Jake. I didn't see you standing there. How are you?" I could hardly look Don in the eye.

"I'd be better if I hadn't had to ride all the way here listening to nothing but B.B. King," Jake said, coming around the bed toward me. "But it's Tupac all the way back, I'm telling you that now." He kissed my cheek and squeezed my hand. "Looking good, as always."

I thanked him and offered my cheek to Don when he came closer.

"Liz said for me to make sure that Isaiah was all right, and then for me to get that recipe from you. She said you'd know which one, so please don't let me forget it or else I'll be the next one in the hospital with a head injury."

Everyone laughed.

"Don't be making fun of my baby. I'm sorry you all had to come all the way here for something like this."

"That's what families do, Anne," Jake said, looking serious. "Big Mama put out the call, and we came running. Or creeping, in the case of Don's driving."

I looked at Isaiah.

"I hope you know how lucky you are to have a family like this, boy."

"I do, Ma. The doctor came in and tried to make everybody leave, and Big Mama told him she'd put her foot in his butt if he didn't get on out of here."

I shook my head, wondering why black folks always had to be setting some mess off. The hospital staff probably couldn't wait for Isaiah to go home.

"I knew I liked you," I said to Big Mama.

"Girl, like recognizes like. You hear me?"

Smoke's hands were back on my shoulders, massaging, and I glanced at him with a question in my eyes.

Why are you touching me?

Oh, now you don't want to be touched? his eyes shot back at me.

"What time did you two get here?" Smoke asked Don and Jake. They mumbled something about five AM and he tilted his wrist so he could look at his watch. "You had breakfast yet?"

"Who could think about food when my sugar baby was lying up?" Big Mama wanted to know.

"Actually"—Don scratched his head—"I could go for a sausage, egg, and cheese biscuit right about now myself."

Jake slid him a thinly veiled look of agreement.

"I'm feeling a little *peaked* too."

"If I recall correctly, you didn't eat breakfast this morning either, Anne."

I shifted and glared at Smoke just as Big Mama said, "You trying to get rid of us or something, Alec?"

"Yeah, so take the hint and get out. I want to talk to my son. *Alone.*"

"I'm not hungry." I sniffed and folded my arms across my chest. "So I think I'll—"

"Anne . . ."

I stood there for another ten seconds with everybody watching me to see what I would do. Would I give in to Smoke's subtle domination and leave? Or would I stand up to him and check him like he needed to be checked? *Take the hint and get out.* What the hell? And who exactly did he think he was anyway? Like nobody else wanted to talk to Isaiah but him? We had all been worried sick about my son. He'd only just opened his eyes a little while ago, and we were supposed to take the hint and get out. *Fuck you, Smoke.*

"You want me to bring you something back?" I asked sweetly.

ALEC

"Whatever you decide to bring will be fine," I told Anne, a smile playing with my lips. She thought I hadn't seen the little conversation she was having with herself, but I could read her like a book. *Fuck you, Smoke.* I could almost hear her thinking it. "As long as you bring me something to drink." I looked up and caught Don's eye just before he ushered everybody out and closed the door behind him.

I pulled up a chair to Isaiah's bed and sat down, propped an ankle on my knee, and grabbed his eyes with mine.

"Are you in pain? You need me to call the nurse or doctor?"

"Nah, they ain't been too long left. I'm cool."

"What about your head? Everything still in it that needs to be there?"

"I think so. They didn't give me a lobotomy or nothing." I cracked a grin.

"So . . . you want to tell me what the hell happened?"

"Some niggas jumped me while I was taking a leak. I was—"

"Hold up." I put up a hand. "Some niggas jumped you. OK, start at the beginning so I can put myself there and see exactly what happened."

"You Sherlock Holmes now?"

"I'm listening, Zay."

"A'ight. I was at the prom, dancing with Aisha, and I had to pee, so I told her I would be right back and went up on the second floor to the bathroom. I was peeing when them niggas came in. It was three of them. They just bum-rushed me and shit. I was fighting back, but wasn't nothing I could do with three of them."

"Did they hit you with anything besides fists?" I was picturing this shit in my head and getting madder and madder by the second. I kept what I was feeling out of my face, though.

"A bat once or twice. I hit my head on a urinal when that nigga got that last punch in."

"What nigga?"

"Hood," Isaiah said. The expression on his face told me that he still couldn't believe Hood had played him. "I thought that nigga was cool people."

"Hood did this to you?"

"Yeah."

"You said there were three of them. Who else was with him?"

"Marcus and this other cat named Lo-Lo."

"Lo-Lo? What the hell kind of name is that?"

"His real name is Lawrence, Da. We call him Lo-Lo because of the shit he does on the court when we're shooting hoops."

"And Marcus is that other idiot who was in the car the time I rolled up on you in the park, right?" Isaiah nodded. "What was the beef about?" Not that I really gave a damn about the particulars.

"That's what I don't know. Hood was mad, clowning and shit 'cause I wouldn't smoke no weed with him or drink nothing, but I told him that me and you talked about it and I was gone leave that shit alone." He lifted his hands, grimaced from the pain the motion caused, and let them fall slowly. "I didn't think he was tripping that hard. We got into it a little bit and he put me out of his car. I had to call Mama to come pick me up, and she was all crying and shit when I told her what happened, saying she was proud of me. You know how she does."

"I'm proud of you too, but I'm not getting ready to cry, if that makes you feel better," I said. I did know how Anne did. All that crying and carrying on knocked a brotha off his game. "What else?"

"I thought that was it. That nigga was mad at me, and I didn't really give a shit anyway, so it was over. He kept talking about me playing him, not doing something that I told him I was gone do, but I don't know what the hell he was talking about. He was tripping, for real."

"You told him you were going to do something that you can't remember telling him you were going to do?" I sat up in my chair. "He slings dope, right?"

He seemed to see where I was going, and his eyes got wide with comprehension.

"Yeah, but I don't mess around with that shit. Mama would kill me."

"And you never told him you wanted to start slinging for him or anything, that you'd make a run for him or something?"

"I don't think I did, naw. Why would I say some shit like that?"

"Maybe because you were under the influence of alcohol and/or drugs, and not really cognizant of what you were saying, Zay." I couldn't keep the frustration out of my voice. He picked up on it and glanced at me sharply. I closed my eyes and pressed my fingers into my eyelids. "I know one thing, if I even *hear* about you looking at a blunt or catching a *whiff* of somebody's breath who's been drinking, let alone drinking yourself, it's all over for you. You understand what I'm saying?"

"So what, you mad at me now?"

"You haven't answered my question."

"Yeah, I understand, but you ain't answered mine either."

"No, I'm not mad, just disappointed. You need to use better judgment when you're deciding whom to hang around with. Everything that looks good ain't good, Zay."

"Hood was cool before this shit happened."

"Hood was never cool. I told you that shit too."

"Man, you told me a lot of shit. You told me you used to sling dope too. So how are you going to hate on somebody else for doing the same thing?"

"How do you think I can speak on this shit, boy? When I tell your knuckle-headed ass something, I'm speaking from experience. I told you to always use condoms because I've been around a lot longer than you have and I know you know I like a fat ass just like the next man. I told you to always have your shit together when you leave the house because I learned the benefit of that a long time ago. I told you to value education because that's the one thing nobody can take from you once you have it. And I told you to always respect your mother because I don't know what the hell would've happened to me if mine hadn't been in my corner. None of that shit is fairy-tale, make-believe shit, Zay. Just like you can believe I'ma put my Vigliano loafers so far up the crack of your ass you'll be speaking Italian like a native if I *ever* run up on you drunk or high again."

I was strung so tightly I couldn't sit still. I hopped up from my chair and paced the floor.

"I'm not going to lie to you and say that I was nothing like Hood when I was his age, because I was. I sold drugs and I stacked money like King Midas, but fuck that shit. One thing I never did was try to talk niggas into jumping into the game with me. Plus, I wasn't a punk motherfucker like Hood, either. I—"

I looked at the door as it cracked open, and I locked eyes with Anne. My mother and brothers were standing behind her, looking into the room like they thought something was really going on.

"I'm still talking," I told Anne. I watched the crowd back out of the doorway, then I turned back to Isaiah.

"What was I saying?"

"You was saying how you wasn't no punk motherfucker," Isaiah reminded me.

"I told you about the cursing and shit, didn't I?" I went and sat back down. "Look, niggas like Hood don't want shit, never had shit, and ain't trying to have shit, for real. They see a young brotha like you, full of potential, good looking and smart, and sit back trying to figure out ways to bring you down to their level. Next thing you know, he'd have been trying to talk you into smoking a little crack or shooting a little heroin in your arm. 'Come on, Zay, this is some good shit. Try it,' " I mimicked what I was certain Hood would sound like.

"That shit ain't funny, Smoke. You know the deal with my mama, so why you playing like that?"

"Ah, so you see how easily it could happen, right? Some people are masters at taking a thing of beauty and snuffing it out. That's what happened to your mother, because she didn't have anyone to talk to her like I'm talking to you. You can't do nothing but kiss her fucking feet for making herself into what she is today, Zay. But that's your mother. I'm talking to you right now. You haven't had me for the past sixteen years, but ain't shit we can do about that now. You got me now, though, and I'm asking you, what are you going to do with me?"

I tilted my head to one side and checked him out. He was looking out the window, trying not to let me see the tears in his eyes. I moved closer to the bed.

"I know you're not over here crying and shit," I teased him. He swiped at a tear running down his cheek and I chuckled. "Did Daddy make boo-boo cry?" I tried to touch his face, but he pushed away my hand. That really made me crack up.

"This ain't funny, Da," he told me, still wiping at tears, but trying to look cool about it. I faked like I was going to touch him again, and he jumped. "Stop, now. Gone."

"Nah, youngblood. You're stuck with me, because I'm not going anywhere." I palmed the back of his peanut head and made him look at me. "You know I love you, right?"

I left his room a few minutes later, left him crying like a

baby. My baby. I wondered if I would ever be done with the foot-up-your-ass speeches. Then I thought, probably not.

Now where was my baby's mama with my food?

I found my family in the waiting area, with food spread out on a coffee table, arguing over the television remote.

"Don't nobody want to watch the news, Jake," Big Mama was saying. "Put it on Dr. Phil."

"That's what's wrong with black folks right today," Don testified, biting into a biscuit. "Always looking to the white man for information."

"Kiss my ass, Don, and pass me some strawberry jam too." Big Mama sat up to snatch a condiment packet from Don. Jake put the television on Phil Donahue. "I said *Doctor* Phil, Jake. Oh hell, I guess that's close enough. I don't feel like trying to figure out what Dr. Phil is saying anyway. That accent kills me."

Anne was sitting in a corner with her feet curled under her, watching the play-by-play like she was engrossed in a television movie. She took a bite of hashbrown and looked up, saw me standing in the doorway staring at her. She picked up a cup of orange juice from the table next to her and held it out to me. I walked in and took it gratefully, and sat in the chair next to her. I rifled through the bag of food and pulled out a thick sandwich.

"What did you say to my son?" she asked.

"What I said to *my* son is between me and him. Man talk. Mind your business, woman. Put the news on, Jake."

Big Mama and Anne caught each other's eyes with some of that silent female communication nonsense.

"I think we've been outnumbered, Ms. Beverly," Anne said.

"None of these fools would be here if it wasn't for me and you, Anne. Long as they remember that, we can never be outnumbered. Now, Jake, I'm gone say it one more time. Put the television on Dr. Phil, boy." Jake cleared his throat and changed the channel.

Some of Isaiah's classmates skipped school and came to visit him after lunch, which I thought was thoughtful, but Anne thought was irresponsible. And she wasted no time slipping into mothering mode, lecturing the poor kids until they were all red in the face and hemming and hawing. I introduced myself and hurried up and slunk away before she could find something to start nagging me about. I cracked up when she graciously thanked them for coming before they left. Like she hadn't taken a bite of each and every one of their asses just a few minutes earlier, even threatened to call a few parents. She was something else.

The hospital staff must've thought a circus was in town when Isaiah's basketball team members, complete with horny ass Coach Leonard, descended on the floor, talking loud and walking even louder. They disappeared into my son's room, and a few minutes later, the doctor, two nurses, Anne, my brothers, *and* Big Mama came stumbling out, looking like they'd been hit with a stun gun. I sat back and watched. And laughed.

I wasn't laughing when Leonard brought his ass out of the room and cornered Anne, though. He was just a little too touchy-feely for my tastes. Didn't take long for me to become irritated as hell at the way he kept stroking Anne's arm and touching her shoulders. Even I could see from where I was sitting in the waiting area that he wanted some snatch, and he wanted some bad. Too damn bad the snatch he wanted wasn't up for grabs. I grit my teeth as he moved in for a hug and his hands lingered a second longer than they needed to around her waist, and hers a little too long around his.

I was about to get up and go introduce myself *again*, when Don dropped into the chair next to me.

"You didn't tell me you were in love with Anne, Smoke," he said in a low voice.

"I'm not in the mood for your shit right now, Don." I slid him a glance to let him know that I was serious as a heart attack.

"I'm just saying, little bro. You talked all that other shit, but you didn't tell me what the real deal was." Don chuckled quietly. "You checking out the coach with his tongue dragging the floor and shit?"

"Mmmm," was all I had to say about that.

"That's a good looking little woman. Smart. Sexy too. You could do worse."

"You could mind your own business too. Talking to you is what got me in trouble in the first place."

"Nah, see that's where you're wrong. Not being able to control your dick is what got you in trouble. Then you started trying to rationalize everything instead of just going with the flow. You talked to her about that yet?"

"Little bit. It's complicated." I had a stellar view of Anne's tight little butt, and I took full advantage of it. Good looking didn't even begin to describe what she was.

"Which means she busted your balls and handed you back prunes, right?"

"Them mugs was sun-dried and dehydrated to perfection," I added and we cracked up.

"You planning on telling her how you feel anytime soon, because old coach looks like he's on the prowl. I wouldn't sleep on that if I were you." I looked at him.

"Jeff got you listening to rap music again?"

"Don't tell Jake. I pulled that B.B. King shit on purpose. Nigga owes me fifty dollars and ain't came across yet. I think I'ma jam some Muddy Waters on the way back, just to drive his ass crazy." I laid my head back and laughed long and hard. "Seriously, though, what are your plans?"

"I don't have the foggiest idea. I care about her, I like being around her, I think about her when I'm not around her, and the sex is—" I had to stop and think for a minute. Couldn't come up with a word, so I just blew out a long breath. "I don't know about love, though."

"But you're sitting back here thinking about putting a beating on Isaiah's coach 'cause he's salivating all over your woman? Man, you better wake up and smell the Folgers. You still hung up on some shit that happened twenty years ago?"

"Not really," I said. "Do you know she had the nerve to accuse me of being just as bad as her because I sold the shit she was using?"

"Told you she was smart."

"If she didn't get it from me, she would've gotten it from some other menace to society." I felt that was an important point to make.

Don shrugged. "Maybe, maybe not. Either way she was, what, thirteen when she started, and eleven when she quit? Don't nobody give a shit about that no more, Smoke. Except you, I guess. Hell, if I wasn't happily married, you might have more than Mister Charlie to be worried about."

"Oh, it's like that, huh?"

"It's like that, little brother. You going to quit making up excuses and stake your claim or what?"

I cornered Anne alone in a small alcove where the hospital had a coffee machine and a microwave set up for visitors' use. At this point we were more like tenants than visitors, but I poured myself a cup of coffee anyway.

"What's up with you and horny ass Coach Leonard?"

"Excuse me?" She reached around me, shook powdered

creamer in her coffee, and looked up at me, all sweetness and light.

"You heard me."

"What's up with you and Flossie?"

I had to laugh. That Flossie shit cracked me up. I wondered if she was aware of what she told me every time she said it. Probably so.

"I asked you earlier if you wanted me to stop seeing Diana, and you never did answer me."

"Yes, I did. I reminded you that Diana is what you consider to be a respectable, publicly acceptable woman. That's what you want, right?"

"You're all that too, so maybe I want you." I put it out there.

"So what if you do, Smoke? Does that mean I should automatically want you back?"

"You make love to me like you want me back."

"Don't confuse sex with lovemaking. They're two different things, as you know."

"Let's go to bed and find out, shall we?" She froze and we locked eyes. I blew on my coffee. For once, it was hot. "I thought so. How long are you planning on making me pay for the stupid shit I said, Anne?"

"I'm not making you pay for anything. I'm just making sure I don't forget. It's good to know where you stand with people, especially one you're sleeping with. That way you know what to give and what to hold back for someone who deserves it." I cocked a brow.

"You holding back for Coach Leonard or Lewis or some other chump like that?"

"Smoke . . ."

"Smoke," I imitated her perfectly. "What, no answer? You like saying my name, don't you?" I moved toward her and backed her against the wall. A doctor passed and I watched him go, waited until he was out of earshot. "You say it a lot when I'm riding you too."

"Oh no, you didn't go there. You're really in fool mode, I see. Get up off me and quit clowning."

"We need to sit down and talk, Anne."

"No, we don't, Smoke."

I opened my mouth to push the issue and say something that was sure to bring her around to my way of thinking, but the door to Isaiah's room swung open just then. Everybody in the hallway jumped as the team's group chant rang out. I shook my head. This shit was getting ghetto as hell. Doctors and nurses looked askance, and Anne gasped. Down the hall, Don shook his head and Jake cut short his mack session with a cute little Latino nurse.

The team filed out of the room slowly, with Coach Leonard bringing up the rear. I made sure he saw me and Anne in the position we were in before I stepped back and turned my attention to the other issue at hand. I waited until the team had walked down the corridor and was about to turn the corner, headed for the elevators.

"Lo-Lo," I called out cheerfully, like we were old friends.

Several heads turned in my direction, but it didn't take me long to zero in on punk ass Lo-Lo. He was the one shuffling around, looking at the floor. He finally looked up and caught my eyes. I gave him no expression at all, just raised my coffee cup and saluted the young brotha. He had the nerve to come and visit my son, the nerve to show his face after the foul shit he had helped to do. Probably thinking that the shit was all over. *Right.*

Wrong.

Anne was gone when I finished looking my fill and turned back around. She probably thought the shit was over too. Wrong again.

Chapter 13

ANNE

I wasn't taking no for an answer, because it was the least I could do. I insisted on Smoke taking his mother and brothers to my house so that they could rest and get cleaned up. They were planning on checking into a hotel for the night and heading back to Indiana in the morning, but there was no way I was letting them pay money for a hotel when I had room to spare in my house. Plus, I thought that they might like to see where Isaiah lived and how he lived. I didn't want any of them thinking that I wasn't handling my business.

Smoke took my SUV and used the spare key to let them in while I stayed at the hospital with Isaiah. There was talk of him possibly being discharged in the morning, but the doctor wanted more X-rays and a follow-up CAT scan to make sure that there wasn't any brain damage or internal injuries that had been overlooked the first time around. I waited in the room while they took Isaiah down to the third floor to do the X-rays and scan.

He came back laughing and joking with the nurses, and that was when I knew he was really going to be OK. I found out for sure from the doctor, the one with the tongue ring—Dr. Newman—that they had removed his catheter and that, other than two cracked ribs, there was no internal damage.

"Looks like you'll be coming home in the morning," I told Isaiah when I came back in the room from the hallway where I'd been talking to the doctor. The tail end of our conversation had veered toward her asking me where I'd bought my shoes, and me asking the same about the earrings she was wearing, a sure sign that my boy was out of the woods.

"Yeah, and I can't wait to get in my own bed. These mattresses are hard as my head."

"I think your Uncle Jake might be in your bed right now, so you might have a problem." I fussed with the blanket covering his legs, and he swatted my hands away.

"You kill me picking lint and straightening stuff, Ma. I'm cool. I'm sorry you was worried too."

"I'll worry about you until you're eighty years old, boy. So let me pick and straighten, OK?" I went back to the covers, spied a string on the sleeve of his gown, and yanked it off. "You want me to bring anything in particular for you to wear tomorrow?"

"My AI jersey and some jeans, I guess."

"AI is in the dirty clothes. What else?"

"Sprewell."

"OK." I paused a second or two. "What were you and Smoke talking about earlier?"

"Now you know I can't tell you that, Ma. That was between father and son. Man talk."

"Father and son, huh? That's the same shit he said. I remember a time when you used to tell me everything."

"That was when I was five and I ain't know no better. I still love you, though. You know you my boo."

"You're my boo too. That's why I'm staying here tonight." He rolled his eyes dramatically and groaned. "I don't care."

"I'ma tell Smoke to take you home when he comes back," Isaiah threatened, like Smoke was my daddy instead of his.

"Smoke can't make me go home, and you can't either."

"We'll see."

Three hours later Smoke pulled into my driveway and looked at me. I wanted to slap the I-told-you-so look off his face. Instead I snatched my keys from him and got out of my SUV. I was halfway to the door when I realized that he wasn't following me. I turned and went back to where he was standing in the driveway, walked right up to him, and put my hands on my hips.

"You coming in or what?"

"You're a sexy little woman, you know that?"

"Yeah, I know that. What's your point?" He leaned back against his rental car and pulled me between his legs with his hands on my ass. I tried to step back, but he held on tight. "Smoke, my neighbors might be looking at us and this is *not* cute."

"Look in my face and tell me if you think I give a damn about your neighbors. You need to be worried about Jake coming out here in his drawers to smoke a cigarette in the middle of the night instead of me touching your ass. Speaking of which, I'm sleeping with you tonight, so don't start talking loud when I sneak in your room later on."

"I don't think so," I said. "I don't need your mama thinking I'm Flossie the second. Sleep in the room with Don or something."

"Big Mama thinks the sun shines and sets on your tight little ass, Anne. Besides that, ain't nobody crazy. They all know I'm smacking it, flipping it, and rubbing it down, whatever you want to call it. Speaking of that too, get on in the house and start me some dinner. I got a feeling a brotha might be hungry when he gets back."

"Well then *a brotha* needs to get on in there and fix himself something to eat."

Smoke leaned down and kissed my lips, then he nudged me toward the house.

"I'll be back."

"Don't tell me you met a woman here in Illinois."

"Jealous?"

I didn't get a chance to respond. I looked around and Smoke was backing the Saturn out of the driveway. I took a minute to mentally prepare myself for a house full of people, and then I went inside.

"Where's Alec going?" Ms. Beverly asked as soon as I came through the door. She was standing at the living room window looking out. There was no sense in wondering if she'd seen Smoke pawing me in the driveway.

"He didn't say," I told her. "Probably sneaking off to meet his latest squeeze."

"Oh, no, honey, something tells me he's not done squeezing you." She winked at me and Don chuckled from his seat on the couch. He and Jake were watching the sports channel on cable.

I didn't know what to say to that, so I scratched my head and dropped my purse on a nearby table.

"I've been told to make dinner, so I guess I'll do that. Anybody have any special requests?" Don wanted chicken and Jake put in a bid for something involving rice and pan gravy, which I didn't know how to make, but I wasn't going to tell him that.

Ms. Beverly joined me in the kitchen a few minutes later and we fell into the groove of preparing dinner for men who were sitting on their asses watching television, an age-old tradition. As we worked, we talked and cackled like we'd known each other for years. We did the woman thing and talked about beauty and hygiene products—which ones we liked, which ones we didn't like, and which ones we loved but couldn't fool with because they didn't love our bodies in return. We talked about Isaiah and how thankful she was for the opportunity to be in his life. I brought out all of my photo albums and we poured over them while we waited for the chicken to finish baking. She dug out an old family portrait of her with her sons surrounding her, and compared the then four-year-old Smoke to a picture of Isaiah at that age. I had to admit that my son was the spitting image of Smoke, both then and now.

She *oohed* and *ahhed* over various aspects of my house—the spa tub that she had soaked in for over an hour, the furnishings and accessories, and the state-of-the-art kitchen. We traded decorating tips and debated the pros and cons of the home furnishings stores we liked to shop in. I was partial to Pier One and she leaned toward Spiegel. I conceded that Spiegel did have some things going for it, if you felt like digging through their junky ass warehouse. And then she wanted to talk about soap operas, which I had to admit, I hadn't watched in years.

Somewhere along the way I told her that I liked to cook, and that it was a kind of therapy for me. Then she turned those shrewd eyes on me and I ended up telling her about my mother and sister, about the messed up relationship we had. She said she'd been wondering why none of my family had come to the hospital. I put mixed vegetables on to steam and admitted that I hadn't bothered to call them.

"So all these years it's just been you and Isaiah?" She was genuinely confused.

"Up until Isaiah was twelve we lived in Mississippi with my Aunt Bobbi," I said, wondering why I was getting into this with her. "After she died we relocated here."

"What part of Mississippi? I think I've got some kin people down there somewhere."

Oh, Lord. Here we go. Black folks' geography.

"Right outside of Jackson. That's where I went to college—Jackson State."

"No wonder Isaiah wants to go to school there." She slipped a potholder on her hand and opened the oven. When she stood up again, I was looking at her like she'd just told me that Martians had landed in my front yard. "What?"

"Isaiah talked about going to school there?"

"You sound surprised. I'm not going to lie and say I didn't try to convince him to go to school next door to my house, but he said he was seriously considering Jackson State because that's where you went."

"Oh." Let my son tell it he was seriously considering taking a job at Hardee's and working his way up to fry machine manager. He didn't even want to discuss college.

"Did you like living in Mississippi?" I thought about that for a minute.

"After a while I got used to it. Things don't move as fast down South, and it took me a while to slow down and keep pace with it. It was good for me and Isaiah, though." I turned the eye under the vegetables off and went to the refrigerator for a can of dinner rolls. "My new life began in Mississippi, so I guess I wouldn't trade it for the world. Matter of fact, I know I wouldn't." I searched for my favorite baking sheet for three whole minutes before I finally spotted it in the sink with melted cheese all over it. "That damn Smoke," I mumbled, moving to the sink to wash it.

Ms. Beverly laughed, repositioned her potholder, and slid the chicken from the oven. We had thrown together a chicken and rice casserole. She sniffed appreciatively and set the dish on the stovetop.

"You knew my son when he was *Smoke*, Smoke . . . in your old life? Of course, he's always been Alec to me, but you know what I mean."

I glanced at her sharply, wanting to see the expression on her face, but she was transferring the vegetables from the steamer to a serving bowl and making a production out of it.

"Yes, ma'am," I finally said. Hell, in for a penny, in for a pound. "In my old life he was *Smoke* Smoke."

"You had to be pretty young then."

I grinned at her because I couldn't help myself. She was a mother through and through, nosey as hell and not ashamed of it.

"I moved to Mississippi when I was seventeen, three or four months pregnant with Isaiah." I thought that snippet of information would fill in the blanks in her mind. I spaced rolls on the baking sheet and waited while she silently formed complete sentences.

"Like I said, young. You have a hard time with my sugar baby?"

"No, I had my Aunt Bobbi, and she had me, if that makes sense."

"Makes perfect sense. Everybody needs an Aunt Bobbi in their lives. So what is this two-step you and Smoke, I mean Alec are doing now?"

I slanted a glance in her direction as I slid the rolls in the oven.

"Smoke told you we were doing something?"

"He didn't have to. I know my sons better than they know themselves."

"Well . . . right now Smoke is reconciling himself with my, shall we say, less than reputable past, and I'm letting him do that. My main concern is Isaiah."

She waved an irritated hand.

"When he reconciles himself with his own, *shall we say*, less than reputable past, then he'll be all right with yours. Girl, ain't men a trip and a half? They think they can do whatever, but let a woman so much as show her panties in public and they got their noses all out of joint. Don't stop 'em from sniffing after them panties, though, does it?"

I cracked up. I liked me some Ms. Beverly, and I was glad she was my son's grandmother.

"I don't think it does, Ms. Beverly."

"Stop with that Ms. Beverly stuff too. You call me Bev or Big Mama if you want to. And you listen to me. There ain't no dishonor in having a past, Anne. The thing is what we do with the future. We think we know where we are right now and we make plans for where we're going, but one thing we know for sure is where we've been. That's what makes us who we are."

The bread came out of the oven. I handed her a stack of plates and took some glasses down from the cabinet. I was thinking about what she'd said and wondering how we had moved so smoothly from talking about throwrugs to my past when she cleared her throat.

"Did I ever tell you what I was like before I met my sons' father, rest his worrisome soul?"

I shook my head and smiled, knowing that whatever she was about to tell me was going to be juicy.

"I don't think so. Is this gossip?"

"Girl, this is hot, stinky ass gossip. Come on over here, 'cause I can't talk too loudly. Now you . . ."

We stepped apart and our heads flew up when Don and Jake walked in the kitchen.

"What, are the sports off?" Big Mama asked.

"Nah, but we're hungry, and something smells good in

here," Don said. He looked from me to Bev with a suspicious glint in his eyes. "Are we interrupting something?"

"Remind me later where I left off," she said and winked at me.

Smoke slid into bed next to me after one in the morning. It was on the tip of my tongue to roll over and demand to know just where the hell he'd been, but then I reminded myself that it wasn't really my business. That was Flossie's domain.

I rolled over for completely different reasons when I felt him grow hard against my ass. We didn't waste time with preliminaries. He pulled me over on top of him and I positioned myself to take him in. The hands on my hips moved to my ass and squeezed insistently.

"Ride me, Anne," Smoke murmured. His fingers spread out and relaxed as I set a pace that sent a shiver through his body. "Yeah, like that." Two minutes into it, he was rolling his hips and meeting me halfway, making me ride him like I was on a horse. "*Ahhh*, yeah, like that." I listened to him sucking in air through his lips like he was slurping soup and came before I knew what was happening.

I wilted over him and sighed as he rolled over and pulled me underneath him. My thighs fell apart and then clenched his waist when he braced himself on his hands and drove into me. His strokes were long and hard, so fast that I could hardly catch my breath. The sounds coming out of his mouth were sharp and deep, loud. I had a moment to wonder if we could be heard on the other side of the closed door. Then I was cumming again, gasping like I was having an asthma attack, my legs trembling like a seizure was imminent. Less than a dozen strokes later, Smoke came and I didn't have to wonder if we could be heard because I was sure his hoarse growl had disturbed the neighbors' sleep. He took my mouth and tongued me for long seconds.

"I'm sorry, baby," Smoke panted in my ear as he curled up behind me and pulled the covers over us. His head dropped onto the pillow behind me and his breath went shooting down the back of my neck. "I needed that." Another throaty growl, then, "*Damn*, did I need that."

I parted my knees and let him slip one of his between them, took a deep breath, and went right to sleep. Apparently, I needed that too.

JAKE

What the hell are they doing in there? Not that I didn't know, but I'm just saying. I need to go smoke a cigarette before I take it on in for the night. I'm wearing my drawers too. Wish somebody would say something to me.

BIG MAMA

Big Mama let out a knowing chuckle. *That's right, honey. Send Dirty Diana packing. Never did like that one anyway. Now, how long before I can get some sleep? I really do like those curtains. I wonder if she got them from Pier One?*

DON

I told Smoke not to sleep on that. Glad to see he still listens to his big brother. What is she doing to him anyway? I know CPR. I wonder if I might have to use it?

ALEC

I pulled Anne's soft body back against me and fought to catch my breath. She had brought some shit out of me that I damn near forgot I had in me. Well, she didn't really bring it out, per say. It was spilling out when I walked in the house and tipped up the stairs to her room, but she took it and rolled with it like a trooper. I wasn't lying when I told her I needed it. Needed it bad too.

There was something about violence that tended to wake up a brotha's baser urges. I was still trembling with the need to do some damage, but I curbed it. I slipped a hand up and around Anne's breast and pressed my face into the curve of her neck, tongued her skin softly. Gradually the trembling eased and then stopped completely. Long minutes passed as I breathed in her scent and used it to help Smoke go back into his cave and resume hibernation. He had come out for a hot minute, which was a strange feeling after all these years, but I didn't fight him. I let him run wild, do what he needed to do, and handle his business.

What a lot of people didn't know was that there were two Smokes. Me, I was the Smoke that Anne knew, the one my son referred to, and the one that Don still slipped and called me from time to time. Everyday Smoke. The calm one. But that motherfucker fucked with my son, and I had no choice but to let the *other* Smoke loose, the one I'd killed off a long time ago. I was like Anne now. Smoke was dead.

Yeah, right. Smoke had to put some heads to bed tonight. One head in particular.

The rhythm of Anne's breathing told me that she was asleep. I closed my eyes and tried to do the same, but I had to review first. I had to make sure that I had made my point sufficiently.

Zay really didn't know what he was telling me when I casually asked him about the places that he used to hang out in with Hood. The park—I already knew about. But I had specifically asked about all the other spots. There was the pool hall down on Lindbergh, across from the junior high school, the little hole in the wall strip club over on Seventh (I had slapped Zay upside the head about that shit), and the dope set over on Sullivan Strip (Zay swore he hadn't been there, but he knew about it anyway. "Everybody knows where the dope house is, Da."). Those were the main ones.

Now a brotha wasn't about to step inside a dope house, especially not in my Cole Hahn loafers, my Bulghari trousers, and my Armani collarless silk shirt. I never did roll like that, and it was a good thing I didn't end up having to start. Hood thought he was a big-time dope slinger, but he didn't have the slightest idea who he was fucking with. If his cousin was still alive, he could've told him. Shit, we could've held a séance and bitch ass Yogi could've told Hood *why* he was dead, and on whose orders. He thought Zeus was a god, but what he didn't know was that Zeus was merely my replacement. That chump had started off working for me, and he had only stepped up because I had stepped down.

I sat outside the strip club and made a few quick calls. By the time I got out of my rental and went inside I was confident that stupid ass Hood was going to be having some serious problems with his supply in the very near future. I let the big, ugly bouncer wave his magic wand up and down my body, and locked eyes with him when he heard a beep.

"You Smoke?" he asked me with a cigarette hanging out the side of his mouth.

"Yeah. Dino call you?" I knew Dino from way back. Before I knew Anne, and before Isaiah was even thought about, Dino was the slippery nigga who had put that first sack of rocks in my hand and started me in the dope game when I got tired of waiting on my mother to get paid, so she could figure out how she was going to buy me the sneakers that I wanted, and pay bills too. Dino was the slippery nigga that I forgot I knew when one-time kicked in and locked up my silly ass. Dino was the first one to give a brotha a thumbs-up when Uncle Sam shipped that ass off. Wasn't it coincidental that he was in town right about now? Yeah, OK, coincidental. Whatever.

I still hollered at Dino from time to time, just to see how he was doing and all that, but other than that my nose was strictly clean and had been for the past umpteen years. Dino couldn't do shit but respect that. Just like he couldn't do nothing but respect the fact that he would've been staring at least twenty years in the face had a brotha slept on him way back when. A brotha didn't sleep, though, and Dino had a good memory.

"Just got off the phone with that nigga," magic wand told me. The cigarette wobbled and dropped ashes. I looked down to make sure that they hadn't landed on my sleeve. He grinned. "Little motherfucker you looking for just took a skeezer in the Red Room. You got back at ten and two."

I thanked him and stepped inside the Honey Pot, Dino's club. *Silly name*, I thought as I nodded at ten and two—two thick-necked thundercats, who were there on Dino's orders, not mine. The Red Room was off to the left, toward the back of the club. I made my way past a thicky-thick sista, who was shaking her titties in a star-struck white boy's face, and smiled at a dark chocolate cutie with nipples the size of dinner plates. She lifted her breasts and squeezed them for my benefit, and I had a vision of Anne's breasts. I knew what I was about to get into as soon as I raised up out of here. I slipped Abraham Lincoln in her

G-string to thank her for helping me focus, and then pushed the heavy red curtain covering the doorway to the Red Room aside.

"Yo, Hood, let me holler at you for a minute," I said by way of introduction. He was in the middle of snorting a line of cocaine when I walked in, and I could tell from the expression on his face that the intrusion was not entirely welcome. *The motherfucker was a cokehead, too? Damn.*

"Man, who the fuck is you? The motherfucking FBI or something?" The coke had him pumped up and talking straight shit.

I looked at the sista standing next to him and blew her a kiss. I slipped a fifty-dollar bill from my pocket and handed it to her, thinking that kids were expensive as hell.

"I need a little privacy," I told her, and then I watched her ass jiggle as she hurried through the curtain.

Then I took Hood's head and smashed it into the glass plate in front of him. He tried to scramble to his feet, and I pushed my thumbs into his windpipe and helped him out. I hauled his ass to his feet and put my face in his face.

"Who am I, nigga? I'ma let you figure it out while I stomp your ass from one end of this room to the other."

That dude had heart. I had to give him that. He put up a good fight. But his coke-induced rage wasn't shit compared to the rage I felt. I didn't know that I could love someone like I had come to love my son, and because I did love my son, Hood had to feel the wrath.

I never really cared for scarring up my hands, so I picked up a chair and took his ass down with it. He eventually got back to his feet, and my elbow was waiting to take out a few of his teeth. I watched a couple fly out of his mouth just before he got a powerful jab across, right in my kidney. That shit hurt. I took a couple of steps back and did some quick reconfiguring.

Very quickly I came to the conclusion that I was going

to have to really get down with this fool. I worked his ass like I was George Foreman, Mike Tyson, and Evander Holyfield all rolled into one. Even threw a little bigmouth Roy Jones in, just on GP. Somewhere in the back of my mind I registered the fact that I was too damn old for this shit, but I was too far gone by then. I should've turned Hood and his flunkies over to the police, and let them handle it. Should've done a lot of things, starting with going in the house with Anne when I had the chance.

But I wasn't thinking straight. I was thinking crooked as hell, about to lose myself. I reigned myself in little by little. It was quite possibly the hardest thing I'd ever had to do in my life, but I did it. I could've easily killed somebody. I wrapped my hands around Hood's neck and pulled him up off the couch, looked him dead in his eyes.

"Don't make me have to tell you again, scrub," I said and let his ass go. He fell back on the couch like a rag doll, still talking much shit, but starting to have a clue.

I straightened my clothes and cracked my knuckles as I considered the damage I'd done to Hood. Missing teeth, a pretty little shiner, some ugly bruises, and with any luck, a few cracked ribs. I was calling myself all kinds of jackasses by the time I got ready to take my leave, and Hood was too.

"Fuck you, nigga! Fuck you!" His voice was hoarse, clogging up with tears that he thought he was too hard to shed.

"Don't sleep, youngblood," I told him. "I'll be watching you. Fuck with my son again and I'll be back. Spread the word."

I moved to the doorway and pushed the curtain aside, pulled up short as I came face to face with Dino. We stared at each other.

"You through handling your business in here, Smoke?"

He was still as bald as a cue ball, and as big as a two-family flat with a disarming baby face. I knew he was every bit of fifty years old, but you couldn't tell it by looking in his face. We pumped fists and leaned in for a quick embrace.

"For the time being," I said. "I'm too old for this shit, Dino." He nodded and grinned at me.

"That's what I know. So step aside and take your pretty ass on home. Can't have you fucking up my worker bees too bad. Not good for business, but I don't have to tell you that."

"Homeboy over there needs a little more on-the-job training, if you ask me. He's got a decent right hook, but somebody needs to tell him who to play with, and who ain't to be fucked with."

Dino looked over my shoulder and surveyed the damage impassively.

"You started it off right enough. I'll take it from here. You get on out of here and keep doing what you do."

It was some damn good advice, and I took it willingly. I was starting to feel twitchy—too much cigarette smoke and too many naked women. I took two steps toward the exit and heard Dino cackling and no doubt slapping somebody on the back.

"That nigga there, he like a son to me," he was saying, loud and ghetto as hell. "Taught him everything he knows. Boy, I'm telling you, that's the real deal there."

I shook my head, grinning and wondering if Anne was waiting up for me. Tripped off myself for a minute because I was seriously hoping she was.

Chapter 14

ISAIAH

The second Smoke and my uncles brought me home from the hospital, Big Mama started fussing over me and working my nerves like crazy, fluffing pillows and shoving food down my throat every time I cracked open my eyes. That was how come I faked sleep damn near the whole day. I figured I'd wake up the next morning after they drove off into the sunset.

The one time I was really sleepy, the Three Musketeers came busting up in my room, acting like they was just checking on me, but I could tell by the look in their eyes that they was really there to check *me.* I had to lie there and take it too. Smoke pacing back and forth, looking like he was 'bout to snap somebody in half, Uncle Don sitting on my bed staring at me like he was a Supreme Court Justice and I was on death row, and Uncle Jake standing in the corner turning red when Smoke got to cursing, and mouthing *sorry* when he thought nobody was looking. I think Uncle Don must've smacked him in the back of his head at least three times and told him to stop being so damn soft. Smoke had to step in between them twice.

Them dudes preached and lectured on and on about everything. Sex, girls, drugs, the fat content in pork versus beef. I'm like, y'all ain't got to go home, but . . . When they finally left, I kissed Big Mama (on the lips) and told her that I would see her when I came up there in the summer. I always wanted a more hands-on grandma, but telling me not to flush the toilet before she could check my shit for blood was just a little too hands-on for me. I made sure I was standing on the porch when Big Mama and my uncles hit the road, waving like a fool and grinning from ear to ear.

Smoke stayed with my mama and me for two more days, which was cool with me because he liked to sneak down to the kitchen in the middle of the night and pig out just like I did. Wasn't no conflict there. At least not with me, anyway. But him and my mama clowned with each other the whole time. She was on Smoke, every move he made. He took the trash out and she wanted to know where he was taking it, specifically. He told her he was hiding it in the garage to dig through later and see if we forgot to eat something. I cracked up. He pulled out the lawn mower and cut the grass, and she wanted to know what he was doing with the clippings. He told her that he was saving them to patch up the roof. I laughed so hard that I hurt myself. She found a pair of his boxers in the dryer with her clothes and asked him how they got there. He told her that they must've been tangled up with her clothes when she took them off the night before. I waited until she left the room to crack up over that one.

I didn't know why she was trying to act hard and carrying on like she was, especially since it was all a front. She knew it, I knew it, and Smoke knew it. They didn't think I could hear them in the room with the door closed at night, laughing and playing coochy-coo. Had to put a pillow over my head one night to block out the sound of the headboard hitting the wall. Nah, she wasn't fooling nobody. He wasn't either, for real. Always touching my mama, rubbing her shoulders, or swiping a hand across her ass when he thought I wasn't paying attention. *Pleeeease.*

A couple of times Diana called, and what the hell she do that for? My mama started slamming shit around and huffing and puffing. Smoke tried to make the phone calls quick, but he couldn't make them quick enough for my mama. Even I was starting to get tired of all the flouncing around she was doing. I couldn't help but wonder how Smoke was going to handle that situation. Didn't take a rocket scientist to figure out that juggling two women wasn't easy to do. I could've gotten mad because my mama was one of the women, but I was seeing for myself that she didn't need my protection. Looked like to me she was handling Smoke pretty damn good all by herself. From what I was hearing at night, he was trying to climb the walls or some shit.

Yeah, everything was going fine as far as I could see. That was until Smoke fucked up and came up with the brilliant idea to wash his ass before he left for the airport.

ANNE

"What the hell happened to your back, Smoke?" I set the stack of clean laundry I was carrying on my bed and gently fingered the dark purple bruise on his lower back. I could've sworn the damn thing was throbbing all by itself. I knew we'd been going at it pretty regularly, but I didn't think I'd gotten so caught up that I had done that to him.

He was standing at the dresser, brushing his fade and scrutinizing the perfection of his shave. We locked eyes in the mirror.

"I had a little altercation," he said and kept brushing.

"An altercation with who?"

"Just somebody that rubbed me the wrong way, Anne. It's no big deal." But he wouldn't look me in the eyes as he said it, which made me think that whatever happened *was* a big deal. Suddenly studying the exact wave pattern in his hair was extremely important.

"You don't even live here, so how could someone rub you the wrong way in a week's time? What did you do, Smoke?"

"I didn't do anything that didn't need to be done. Can we leave this alone, please? Talking about it is giving me indigestion. Could've been that stir fry you made for lunch, now that I think about it." The clothes he'd laid out to put on after his shower were lying on my bed. He snatched up his undershirt and pulled it over his head.

"You shouldn't have gone back for thirds then. Who did you get into a fight with?"

"I said altercation. I said nothing about a fight." He held up a finger to emphasize the difference.

"OK. Who did you get into an altercation with and get your ass kicked by?" I crossed my arms under my breasts and shifted my weight onto one foot, waiting for an answer. "Don't tell me you got caught hitting on some woman and her husband had to bounce you around a little bit."

"You underestimate me, Anne. You know as well as I do that the only person bouncing me around is you. I'm crushed." He put on a phony hurt look and straightened the collar of his shirt.

"Don't try to get me off track. Who were you fighting?"

"I wasn't fighting. I was having a calm, man-to-man discussion with Hood, and it got a little out of hand, that's all. By the way, I ran out of deodorant, so I had to use some of yours. I hope it really is strong enough for a man."

"Hood? That jackass Isaiah runs around with? Why were you fighting with him?"

"I keep telling you, I wasn't—"

"Smoke . . ."

"Look, Anne, the situation is under control, OK? It's nothing for you to worry about." He stepped into his slacks and tucked in his shirt. "I don't think Isaiah will be running around with that punk anymore, but if he does, do me a favor and let me know, will you?"

"What is it you're not telling me, Smoke?"

"There's nothing to tell. Isaiah was hurt and I took care of the situation. End of story. It's over. He shouldn't be having any more problems but, again, if he does, put a bug in my ear."

"Wait a minute." I walked over and stood in front of him, propped my hands on my hips and looked up into his face. "Let me see if I'm following you. You somehow discovered that Hood was responsible for what happened to Isaiah and you went after him? Am I right so far?"

"You're getting warmer. Have I mentioned that you're looking especially sexy in those shorts you're wearing today?"

I waved his words away with an irritated hand even as my groin tightened.

"Why would you do that, Smoke? Why not discuss what you knew with me and then we could've gone to the police?"

"Baby, this wasn't a situation for the police to handle. This had to be handled in the streets, where it started."

"I see." I didn't really see clearly at all, but I was starting to see shadows, like the bandages were being removed and I was opening my eyes for the first time. "And how did you know where to find Hood? Did you just happen to run across him at Chuck E. Cheese?"

"Leave it alone, Anne."

"No, really, I'm curious. What, are you psychic?"

"I still know people. I found out what I needed to know easily enough. You mind stepping aside so I can finish getting dressed?"

"Yes, I do mind. You still know people, huh? Is that code for I still hang in the streets?"

"No, it's code for I still know people that I used to hang in the streets with a long time ago." He stepped around me and went in the bathroom. I was right on his heels. He glanced at me over his shoulder and shook his head. "Anne, please. I'm strung tight enough as it is."

"Is that why you came in the other night rutting like a bull? Because you were strung tight?" Realization came slowly and had my eyes widening. "That's when you went after him, isn't it?"

Smoke picked up his toothbrush and aftershave, looked at me in the mirror, then set them back down carefully.

"Yeah, I went after his ass. You want all the gory details, Anne? OK, let's see. He sells drugs, so I made a few calls and tracked his ass down at a second rate strip club across town. I went in there and beat his ass for having the audacity to put his hands on my son. That's the whole story."

I was mystified, stunned.

"That's not the whole story, though, is it? Because clearly you have no idea what you've done."

"What have I done besides protect my son?"

"You should've let the police handle the situation instead of charging in and stirring the pot. What do you think is going to happen to Isaiah the next time he runs into Hood or some of his friends? They could kill him, and all because of what you did." I whirled around and ran out of the bathroom. It infuriated me to no end that Smoke could be so calm, taking his time in the bathroom, gathering up his toiletries like he had all the time in the world. "Did you hear what I said?"

"I heard you. The whole fucking block probably heard you, so would you lower your voice, please? I'm not trying to bring Isaiah into this, because it's none of his business."

"You can stand up and repeat that at his funeral." I dropped down to the edge of the bed and buried my face in my hands.

"There won't be a funeral," he said.

I hopped up with murder in my eyes, thinking that he was right. There wouldn't be one funeral, but two. He must've read the intent in my eyes because he quickly put up a hand.

"Listen to me. You can't communicate with people like Hood through the police. If we had gone to the police, Isaiah would've been labeled a punk, and he would've been a walking target for Hood and anybody else who felt like they had something to prove. Like I said, I took it to the streets because that's where it started, and that's where it had to end. So Hood won't be bothering Isaiah anymore, and there *will be no funeral*, and stop saying that shit. I'll admit I lost control for a minute, but that only helped to prove my point. Everybody knows who everybody else is now, and the situation is under control."

"Oh God. Should I put my house on the market and start packing now, Smoke? What the hell have you done?"

"I think you're overreacting."

"You brought violence to my door, and *I'm* overreacting?" I couldn't fathom how he could go about calmly packing and darting glances around my bedroom, looking for things he might have missed. "You haven't changed a bit, have you? You're still cocky ass Smoke from Robinwood. You cover it up well, I have to give it to you, but the old Smoke is still in there, acting a damn fool, throwing your weight around and loving every minute of it. Hiding behind a classroom full of teenagers, pretending like you're legitimate and looking down on the derelicts of society."

"Look, don't start screaming and falling out, because I'm really not in the mood for it right now."

I picked up a wad of socks and threw it at him.

"All this time you've been pointing your finger at me and reminding me of my past every chance you got, like you had a right to judge me, and you're still a street running thug. While *I*, on the other hand, at least had the courage to truly leave my past behind and start a new life for myself." I saw his eyes go from hazel to smoke, but I didn't give a shit. "One of us is a hypocrite, Smoke, and it isn't me."

"Was Isaiah unconscious, or were you?" he snapped. He zipped his suitcase, lifted it from the bed, and let it drop soundly on the floor. "I'm thinking it was you, and while you were out, you were in a damn dream world. You can't solve all of your problems by running away and hiding from the world. Everybody doesn't have the luxury of secluding themselves in a cushy little dream world the way you have. Some shit you have to stand up to. Let's take Hood, for example. People like him don't understand reason, and they don't respect punks, either. I wasn't leaving here letting that motherfucker think that he had a new whipping boy. You and I both know that Zay isn't cut out for the kind of shit that fool would've tried to lure him into doing. I understand Hood perfectly, not because I'm still in the streets, but because I've been where his sorry ass is right now, in that other life you're always talking about. The difference between me and you is that I accept that I lived that other life instead of hiding from it all the damn time. And if I had to take a few steps back and do some shit that I never thought I'd do again to save my son, then that's what I had to do. But don't keep talking shit to me about me bringing violence to your house, because it's already been here. What I did was make sure it doesn't come back!"

"That doesn't make sense to me. Violence begets violence, Smoke. You of all people should know that." I pushed shaky hands through my locks and gave him my back. A few seconds later I started pacing the floor. "And I don't live in a dream world. You were wrong for that."

"You don't think I know who I used to be? I remember every damn thing I did, and probably just about everyone that I did it to. I never had to worry about a motherfucker jumping me or trying some shady shit because people knew not to fuck with me. It may not have been the best reputation to cultivate, but it was useful at the time. This was one of those times when it was useful again. Call me what you want, but I made sure my son wouldn't find his way down the same path I took. If you don't believe me, then watch my smoke. No pun intended."

"I don't live in a dream world!" I shouted. For some reason that had really rubbed me the wrong way. How dare he criticize my life? It was safe, predictable, and trouble free, just the way I liked it.

"Pissed you off, huh? The truth has a way of doing that, Anne. Why don't you talk to your family? Why haven't you ever invited them here and tried to build some sort of relationship with them? Why don't you ever venture outside of Illinois?"

"Go to hell."

"I've been there already. Satan put me out."

"You—" His cell phone rang. We both turned to look at it, where it was lying on the nightstand plugged into a travel charger. I scrubbed a hand across my face while he answered it. It didn't take me long to figure out that it was Flossie calling.

"Yeah, I was kind of in the middle of something,"

Smoke said into the phone. He listened for a few seconds and then, "Yes, I know you called last night, Dee. You're right, that was on me. I agree completely." A few more seconds. "Look, can we talk about this when I get home?" Longer seconds. I thought I heard her screaming. "I'll call you when I get there, OK? Bye." He snapped the phone closed and we looked at each other.

"You know, you really do treat her like shit," I said.

"Now you're concerned about the way I treat Flossie?" The expression on his face told me that he was perplexed and maybe even a little amused. He cocked a brow smugly.

"I don't give a damn about Flossie."

"Oh, because I was getting ready to say, you sure have a strange way of showing care and concern."

I looked at him like he was crazy.

"It occurs to me that you like this crap. Two women arguing over you and spreading their legs for you, too." I scratched my head and whistled. "I guess it would be flattering and convenient as hell, now that I think about it."

"I didn't have two women until you came along, which I think you know. This thing with you and me just happened. I never planned on being attracted to you, or you to me. The timing is jacked up, though. I agree with you on that."

"I'm not attracted to you."

"Are you scratching road maps in somebody else's back?"

I couldn't stand the smile on his face.

"Fuck you, Smoke."

"You already do that, often and well, so that's a moot point. Come at me with something else, smart ass."

I lost it.

"See, that's your whole problem! . . ."

Smoke sliced a hand through the air and took a step toward me, and I shut right up.

"My problem is that I'm trying to think up every way I

can to tell you that I want to be with you, but you keep blocking me out."

"*What?*"

"I'm not saying that shit again, Anne. I know you heard me the first time."

"What kind of sick game are you playing now? First you seduce me, then you call me a crackhead. Then you seduce me again and tell me that you didn't *mean* to call me a crackhead. And now you want to *be with me*?"

He stared at me for several seconds, then he shook his head like he needed to clear it. He threw up his hands, shrugged nonchalantly, and walked over to the dresser.

"You know what? You're right. This is a ridiculous situation, and I don't need this shit. My life was fine before we started dealing, so I'm going to get back to it and carry on with business as usual. And for the record, don't presume to tell me what I do for my students, because you have no clue, OK?" I flapped a hand at his reflection in the mirror and rolled my eyes. He chuckled softly. "Call me when you're ready to talk like two adults, instead of one adult and one—"

It was my turn to do the cutting off.

"Crackhead?"

"Uh-uh, woman, you're not tangling me up with that bullshit again. Like I said, call me if you want to talk like two adults."

"There's nothing to talk about. We had a fling and now it's over. So I won't be calling."

"Whatever, Anne. I'm going to go check in with Zay, and then I'm heading out." He slipped his wallet in his back pocket and fastened his watch on his wrist, staring at me the whole time.

"Good. Check in with Zay, and then be gone. Give Flossie my best." He had the nerve to laugh, which only pissed me off more.

"You're like a little chocolate devil or something."

"Better than being a high-yella hypocrite."

"Recluse."

"Two-timing sex fiend."

"You like it."

"I did, but I don't anymore. Flossie can have you all to herself now, because I'm done with you."

"Because you don't need sex, right?"

"Get out of here, Smoke." I watched him pick up his suitcase and walk out of my room and, I hoped, out of my life.

All in all, I thought I had handled that pretty well.

Chapter 15

ALEC

"Earth to Alec." Diana leaned across the armrest and snapped her fingers close to my face. "Or do I need to call you Smoke to get your attention?"

I took my eyes away from the street long enough to slide them in her direction for the space of three seconds, long enough to make my point.

"You snap your fingers in my face again and you're going to need something, but I doubt you'll want it." I made a last minute right turn and lifted my ass slightly off the seat to resituate my groin.

"Is that your way of telling me that you plan on getting rough with me later on?" she purred suggestively.

I glanced at her again. She was seriously working the long denim skirt she was wearing, and her blouse was unbuttoned just low enough to give me a tantalizing view of cleavage. I should've been turned on, considering how long it had been since I'd been intimate with a woman. Two weeks and counting. The scratches on my back were long gone, and I could've segued from sleeping with Anne right back into sleeping with Diana, smoothly and with a minimum of complication. But it wasn't quite that simple.

We'd caught a movie and then had a late dinner. Neither of us had to work the next day because school was out for the summer. The perfect nightcap could be going down in mere minutes, either at my house or her apartment. Problem was, I knew I had to handle my business. A brotha was wrong and had been for the longest time. Not only was I foul as hell for dealing with two women at the same time, but I had allowed my son to see me doing it. That wasn't cool at all.

"That's my way of telling you not to snap your fingers in my face," I said carefully. "Were you saying something and I missed it?"

"I've been saying a lot of things that you've been missing, Alec. You want to tell me what's going on?"

"Nothing is going on. Just got a few things on my mind, Dee." So much so that I almost ran right through a red light. Probably should have since I finally stopped in the middle of the damn intersection anyway. I spotted one-time at the three o'clock position and made a point of reversing my truck until I was safely behind the white line.

"Is Isaiah OK?"

"Fit as a fiddle."

"Well, if he's OK, then what's wrong?"

"Nothing is wrong, Dee."

"Something is, Alec. We've hardly seen each other in weeks, and when we do, you're off in la-la land somewhere. When was the last time we made love? Do you even remember?"

I honestly couldn't say that I did. *Damn.* I had to get my house in order, for real. I glanced in the rearview mirror, hopped in the next lane, and cruised down the ramp onto the interstate. I opened my mouth to say something, I didn't know what, and put my foot so far down my throat

I was surprised I didn't end up with all sixteen ounces of the steak I'd savored for dinner in my lap.

"Anne brought something very important to my attention not too long ago, Dee, and I think we need to discuss it."

I felt the temperature inside the quad-cab drop ten degrees.

"Anne? Why do we need to discuss your baby's mama, Alec?"

"We need to discuss *my son's mother* because she's a big part of what's going on with me and you. I need to go ahead and be truthful with you."

"Please don't tell me you've been fucking that black bitch all this time. I know damn well you're not getting ready to tell me that."

I let the black bitch comment slide because I couldn't think of a way to point out the foulness of it without possibly causing a ten-car pile-up. This was definitely not the time to stand on ceremony, not at seventy miles an hour.

"I'm not going to insult your intelligence and tell you that nothing happened between me and Anne, because I think you already know that something did. I'm just trying to be honest, Dee."

"And Anne had to suggest that you be honest for you to figure out that you needed to be? Well, that's jacked up."

"Can we leave Anne out of this?" A day late and a dollar short, I knew. But, still.

"I knew that chick was going to be a problem when I first laid eyes on her," Diana told me. "And you knew you were in a relationship, so why would you even go there with her?"

"It just happened. I didn't plan it, and neither did she. One of those things, I guess."

She shifted in her seat and stared a hole into the side of my head.

"So what's happening between you two now?"

"Nothing." At least that was the truth. "Nothing at all."

"So it was just a fling?"

I thought about that for a minute as I exited the interstate.

"Something like that," I finally said.

"How many times did you fuck her, Alec? Once, twice, what?"

"Do we really need to go there?"

"Hell, yeah, we need to go there. Tell me this, then, what is it about her that made you stray from this?" She looked down at herself, then back up at me with a look of complete and utter disbelief in her eyes. "She's cute enough if you like those dark sistas, but she ain't got shit on me. So what was it?"

I caught myself chuckling before I knew it. Somebody needed to tell this sista a little something-something. It wasn't going to be me, though. I was still driving.

"Let's concentrate on what it wasn't, and it was not meant to disrespect you. I didn't set out to do that, Dee, and I want to apologize because I know that's what I did anyway."

"You had help," she snapped.

"No, I didn't. I knew what I was doing, and I take full responsibility for my actions."

"Are you planning on seeing her again?"

"Not that I know of, unless it involves my son."

"That's how all this shit started in the first place. She pops up out of the blue with a long lost son and suddenly you forget to keep your pants zipped up, so that doesn't tell me what I want to know, Alec. You better try again."

I took a breath for patience.

"What is it you want to know, specifically, Diana?" Her neck rolled. *Here we go.*

"I know you're not sounding like you have an attitude. You fucked around on me, remember?"

Quite clearly, I thought. I steered my truck around a car full of rowdy teens too busy clowning to drive properly, and came out ahead of them. Diana's apartment complex was just down the street and around the corner.

"I don't have an attitude, and I know I fucked up. I'm just trying to find out what it is you want to know."

"Are you planning on seeing her again?"

"That's not in the plan, no."

"And whose decision was that?"

"Come on, Dee. I'm telling you it's over. I told you it started, and now it's over. Cut me some slack with the twenty questions, please?"

"I guess that means it was her idea, right?"

"No, that's not what it means," I lied calmly. I pulled to a stop in front of her building and left the engine running, a fact that was not lost on her.

"Oh, so you're not coming in?"

"I thought I would give you some time to think about what happened, and take some time to do the same thing myself."

"What if I don't want time? What if I want us to move past this bullshit and work on our relationship?"

"You might feel differently in the morning," I suggested.

"Or you might. Is that what you're saying?"

"I don't know what I'm saying, but I do know that we need to chill for a minute and see where things go from here. You might be willing to overlook the fact that I cheated on you, but I'm still dealing with it. Shit is still up in the air."

"With you and Anne, you mean."

"I—" My cell phone rang. I shot Diana an apologetic look and held up a finger, asking for a minute as I checked the caller ID. I put the phone to my ear. "What's up, youngblood?" It was my son. "No, I'm not picking your narrow ass up from the airport. Don and Jeff will be there to get you. That's cool?" I listened to him hem and haw for a second. "Nah, I've got a job interview I need to attend. None of your business, chump. Yeah, I'll tell you about it when I see you. Everything cool there?" More hemming and hawing. "No problems? Good. Yep, me too. What? See if she wants to talk to me about it herself."

I jumped when the truck door slammed so hard that the glass rattled. I followed Diana's progress up the cobblestone walkway with my eyes, made sure that she got inside safely and felt like shit.

"Oh, she doesn't want to tell me herself, huh? That's fine. Talk to you later then. Peace." I snapped the phone closed and threw it up on the dash, wondering if I'd just bitten off my nose to spite my face.

I guessed time would tell.

Anne would never come to the phone when she knew it was me calling, so I turned into a crank caller, started calling when I knew Zay was asleep and she would have no choice but to answer the phone when it rang.

One time I called and said:

"What are you doing?"

She sounded like she'd been knocked out for hours, but I didn't care.

"What do you want, Smoke? Isaiah is asleep, which I'm sure you know."

"I called to talk to you."

"About *what*?"

"I was thinking about you."

"You mean there's room in your head for thoughts of something besides yourself?"

"I was asleep and I rolled over and smelled you on my sheets."

"Then you need to do laundry."

Another time I called and said:

"What's new at the Olive Branch?"

"You have *got* to be kidding me, Smoke. It's after one in the morning!"

"I know what time it is, Anne. I was lying in bed, thinking about the center, and I wanted to know what was new."

"Well then, call the center tomorrow and have them send you some information."

"I might do that. Have you thought any more about what we talked about?"

"What did we talk about?"

"Me and you shaking the sheets and making some more babies."

Long, drawn out, disgusted sigh.

"Good night, Smoke."

The last time I called to harass Anne, the day before Isaiah was due to arrive to spend part of the summer with me, I said:

"Wake up. I called to tell you something."

"Why am I not surprised? It *is* after one in the morning. What do you have to tell me, psycho?"

"I'm not seeing Diana anymore."

"Goodie for you. Are you sad?"

"Nope. Are you?"

"Why should I be sad?"

"Probably because your days are numbered."

"Excuse me?"

"I'm putting you on notice, Anne."

"Putting me on notice about *what*? Are you sure you never tried your own supply?"

"If you want me, you better come and get me before somebody else sweeps me off my feet. I did what I needed to do. Now are you woman enough to do what you know you need to do?" I hung up without waiting for an answer.

Part of me didn't know what the hell I thought I was doing. But the other part of me was well aware that I was seriously digging Anne. And it wasn't just about the sex, either. It had something to do with the way she moved, the way she talked and laughed, the way she kept me on my toes and always paying attention. I could've attributed the strength of my attraction to the fact that she had done a damn good job raising my son on her own, and had provided a good home and stability, but that wouldn't have explained the fact that I'd gotten a woody the very first time I laid eyes on her, strolling down the driveway in those tight jeans. I was a man. I could admit that I wanted to lay my hands on her in something other than a religious way right from the start, that I wanted to know her in the biblical sense, if for no other reason than simple curiosity. And once I'd gotten a hold on Anne, I thought, *OK, now you know. Curiosity satisfied. Now you can push on. Yeah, right.*

I went back for seconds, thirds, and twenty-thirds, and I still wanted more. The woman had a brotha all twisted up, trying to figure out exactly when my nostrils had started flaring from a whiff of her scent. When had I stopped picturing *Breanne* Phillips and started really seeing *Anne* Phillips? Probably right after she'd checked me on that shit the first time.

I'd said some jacked up shit to and about Anne. I knew that. Most of it I wanted to believe because then I wouldn't be calling her in the middle of the night and harassing the hell out of her, just on GP. I wouldn't be tripping at all, fiending like a youngblood in the throes of his first crush on a tackhead that he knew he couldn't have. But I *was* fiending, and my attempts at trying to hold on to a tired, old ass past had failed miserably. Next thing I knew I'd be scribbling her name in the margins of my lesson plans and sending her love letters with hearts drawn around the edges, calling her saying, "please, baby, baby, pleeeeeease."

"Snap the fuck out of it, Smoke," I told myself. My whole thought process was so out of order it wasn't even funny. A brotha really needed to get his house in order.

ANNE

If I believed in omens I would've known something in the cosmic balance was off when everything started going haywire at around the same time. One thing right after another, popping off like gangbusters. I could hardly put out one fire before another one started. And after a while, I wondered if there was enough water to go around.

The center was thriving, so much so that we had added two more women's groups and another jazzercise class to the weekly schedule, which meant that I had to interview and hire two more group facilitators to handle the extra load. I wasn't counting on two of the women in the new group discovering that they were both sleeping with the same man and coming to blows in the middle of a session. It took three group members, both facilitators, and a man from the AA/NA meeting going on in the room next door to separate the women and restore order. The newly hired facilitators both quit on the spot and left us in a helluva predicament. I'd had to work more evenings than I cared to count over the last couple of weeks while we searched for replacements.

But it was a good thing I was working some evenings, because somebody with an ounce of common sense needed to be on hand to stop the overflowing toilet in the men's restroom from spreading and ruining the carpet in the lobby. The one man on staff, a maintenance worker, was long gone for the day, and the ladies were hesitant about going into a men's restroom. I called them all wusses and charged in, plunger in hand.

I saved the night. And the day when every computer and printer in the building shut down for no apparent reason. I called the software company, held the line for thirty minutes, and then cursed up a blue streak until they agreed to send someone out immediately to troubleshoot. I think I even threatened to call Harold Pattino from the Channel Twelve News "It's Your Money" segment. Nobody in their right mind wanted Hound Dog Harold following them around with a microphone and cameraman if they could help it.

OK, so replacements were found, a new toilet installed, and the computers were running like tops. Everything was in order. Or so I thought.

I managed to find the time to take off and take Leonard up on his invitation to dinner. After the fact I decided that I should've gone on ahead to work. He was perfectly nice and we had a pleasant conversation throughout the meal. That wasn't the problem. He was surprisingly funny and earnest in his conversation. I found myself thinking that we could be great friends and I might've mentioned that to him if I'd had time. I opened my mouth to tell him how much I enjoyed his company, and ended up choking on a mouthful of tongue. *Oh, my.* For a split second I let myself participate in the kiss, out of pure selfishness. Then I remembered who I was kissing and why, and pulled back. He was one of those wet and sloppy kissers, one of the ones who surrounded your lips with theirs and rendered you useless, which I hated, and I knew that there was no way I could deal with that, no matter how nice he was. I refused to explore the possibility that I was making up excuses, or, worse, comparing him to the one who shall remain nameless.

Then Isaiah called with his nonsense.

"Ma, it's me," he said as if anybody else on God's green earth called me Ma. "You busy?"

"If by busy you mean am I in the middle of refereeing an argument between two of my staff over a can of Pepsi that was left in the break-room refrigerator, then yes. Is everything all right there?" He'd been with Smoke since a week after school ended for the summer, which now totaled over a month away from home.

"Yeah, everything's straight."

"Speak English," I requested. "Are you all right or not? Eating enough? Going to bed at a decent time?"

"And you know this." He chuckled, knowing that I knew no such thing. "That's why I'm calling. I'ma go ahead and stay a little while longer, maybe until school starts."

"Excuse me? Who put you in charge of deciding when you come home and when you don't, Isaiah? Hold on for a second." I put my hand over the mouthpiece and stepped out of my office. "Darlene, Nita, why don't you split the damn soda and quit fussing about it? To tell you the truth, neither one of you is entitled to it because *I* bought it!" I slammed my office door and went to sit behind my desk. "Now what is this nonsense you're talking?"

"Come on, Ma. Me and Jeff was going to do some more stuff this summer, and Smoke said—"

"Smoke said? Who asked Smoke? And why are you even calling me with this mess, Isaiah? You know we agreed that you would help me landscape the backyard this summer. You can't do that if you're in Indiana."

"I know, Ma."

"So what I'm hearing you say is that my hedges and shrubs and those little rocks that I wanted to put down aren't important?"

"You're killing me. I'm just saying I want to stay a little longer, instead of coming home next Saturday. Plus, that's the day of the family reunion, and you know Big Mama wants me to be there, Ma. You planning on explaining to her why I'm not coming?"

"What about the plans we made for the summer, huh? You said you wanted to go to Vegas and I was moving stuff around on my calendar so we could take a weekend trip. Now I'm going by myself, I guess."

"What weekend was we going?"

"I don't know yet, but we were going." He laughed at my fumble. I propped an elbow on my desk and dropped my face in my hands. "I guess you don't miss me. Is that it?"

"Aw, now don't start that, Ma. You know I miss you. I called you, didn't I?"

"Yeah, you called to tell me that you're kicking me to the curb."

For some reason he found that hilarious. I listened while he cracked up in my ear.

"Kicked to the curb went out five years ago, Ma. What 'chu been doing while I been gone? You got a boyfriend yet?"

"No, and stay out of my business. Where is Smoke? Did he put you up to this?"

"Nah, he don't even know I'm calling. He said I could stay as long as I wanted, though. I was thinking I might want to go to school here next year too."

"*Whaaaat?* Oh now I know you're on something. Put Smoke on the phone, boy." Suddenly I felt like I was about to blow my stack.

"Hold on, Ma." I heard a muffled exchange. I pressed my ear to the phone so that I could decipher what was being said, but I couldn't make out a thing. I drummed my fingers on the desktop. "Ma?"

"What is it, Isaiah? I told you to put Smoke on the phone."

"I know, but he said he don't want to talk to you right now."

"He *don't* want to *talk* to me *right now*," I mimicked Isaiah's dialect perfectly, which made him laugh again. I wanted to go through the phone. "Ain't that some shit? Tell Smoke to get the damn phone."

"He said no."

"*No?*"

"He said you don't never want to talk to him when he calls, so he don't want to talk to you now."

"Boy, I said—" I caught myself before I really got ethnic. I hopped up from my chair and started pacing, massaging the bridge of my nose. I had to think clearly in order to out-think Smoke. He was playing childish games and I had to be better than him to get his goat. OK. One, two, three breaths. In and out. Count to ten.

"Isaiah?" I asked calmly.

"I'm still here, Ma."

"Would you ask Smoke to please come to the phone? Tell him I said *please* and that I asked nicely." He did and I waited patiently to hear Smoke's voice come over the line. More muffled conversation.

"He said that you should say *pretty* please, and for me to tell you that he has a craving for devil's food cake. What do y'all have me up in the middle of?"

"Tell him a hypocrite's favorite color is yellow."

"Mama, please. Hold on," Isaiah said and covered the mouthpiece to relay the message. He came back to the phone a few seconds later. "Smoke wants to know if you ever heard of a spider called the Brown Recliff. *What?* Oh. Recluse. S'cuse me. Ouch, Da!"

"Tell him Brown Recluses are poisonous." He told Smoke.

"He said to come bite him and see what happens. Oh now, see, this is wack. Is this some of that foreplay stuff I'm not supposed to know about?"

I could hear Smoke howling with laughter in the background.

"Are you coming home or not?" I asked.

"Not right now, Ma. I—"

I cut him off, fuming.

"You better look for me in the sunset, boy. Because it's on when I get there. You hear me?"

ISAIAH

Damn, I should be the next James Bond 007 or some damn body. Mission accomplished like a mug. I didn't have no doubt that my mama was going to be on the next plane, hauling ass to Indiana to have it out, first with me and then with Smoke. I was hoping that while they was having it out they would go ahead and admit that they was digging each other.

I wasn't no little kid, thinking my parents were going to have a big fairy-tale wedding and suddenly live happily ever after. But I had eyes in my head, and I could see for myself that they were acting a damn fool with each other because they wanted to be together some kind of way. I didn't consider myself meddling, just lending a helping hand. Somebody had to do something to get my mama to Indiana so she could handle her business.

Smoke was playing dumb, acting like wasn't nothing up, and my mama was right along with him. Like they didn't have a big, loud ass argument that woke up a brotha from his nap right before Smoke left. My mama liked to drove me crazy around the house until I finally got the hell out of dodge. Nagging about every little thing and leaving the room whenever Smoke called, like one of those cartoon characters that took off so fast that you could still see feathers floating in the air after they was gone. It was funny as hell.

I figured my mama was used to being on her own. She didn't have no family that she dealt with, and since that one dude in Mississippi, she didn't too much fool with men. She was one of them *independent women*, which was cool up to a point, but I could also tell that she was a little too alone. She didn't have a lot of friends, and she didn't go out of her way to make any. She was like a hermit or something, except for when it came to getting up in my business and running the center that she founded. She probably didn't even know she was scared.

Deep inside, I knew she was scared to trust people, especially since she went through all that shit with Aunt Laverne and Grandma Alice. They hurt her bad and she didn't come out of her shell too much because of it. I came to the conclusion that Smoke made her come out of her shell, and that was why she sent him packing. Probably had something to do with the way they met and ended up making me, but I felt it was mostly because of what she went through with her peeps.

There was something between my mama and Smoke that needed to be resolved, and that was why I called her and made her think I wasn't coming home. I knew she would come after me and end up having to talk to Smoke. I just hoped he was up on his game enough to take over from there. There was only so much I could do.

My mama ain't never been the kind of woman to let any old body in her bed. Hell, before Smoke I never saw her doing nothing close to sexual with a man. That right there told me that Smoke was different. That was how come I didn't clown when I caught them getting busy that time. It hit me differently than it would've if it was some other buster ass nigga. I don't know, it was just different. Maybe because they were my parents, but maybe not.

Another thing I noticed was that Smoke wasn't dealing with sweet thing Diana no more. I asked him why she didn't come around, and what did I do that for? I had to hear a whole long lecture about being honest with women and playing fair. He went on and on and on about how he should've been honest with Diana about his feelings for my mama, and honest with himself too. I was sitting there like, *who do I look like, Dr. damn Phil?* I asked a simple question and got all that for my trouble.

I got something else too, though. I got that Smoke was feeling my mama, for real. A brotha just had to wait and see what was going to happen. I guess it *would* be nice to have both of my parents in the same house, now that I was straight up thinking about it.

ANNE

I skidded to a stop in Smoke's driveway and stomped up to the front door. I had my hand raised to ring the doorbell when the door flew open and Isaiah came stumbling out. He almost knocked me down. His eyebrows flew up and a surprised smile sliced his face in half.

"Ma, what are you doing here?"

I lifted my cheek for the hasty kiss he planted there and narrowed my eyes at him.

"I came to smack some sense into your thick head. Where do you think you're going anyway?" He was holding a basketball against one hip and bouncing from one foot to the other, like he was anxious to be off. I could've sworn he was a couple of inches taller than he was the last time I'd seen him. Either that or I had shrunk.

"I'm going to shoot some hoops in Kenny's backyard."

"Who's Kenny, and where is his backyard?" I looked at him from head to toe, noticed the new Jordans on his long feet, and the fresh haircut on his head. He didn't look too depraved or neglected. Looked like he'd been lifting weights too. My baby had little biceps going on. I felt my eyes misting.

"That's Kenny's crib right there, Ma." I followed the direction of his finger and studied the neat house sitting directly across the street. "And that's Kenny looking out the window watching you front me off."

"I haven't fronted you off yet, boy," I said. "Where's my hug anyway?" He hugged me so tightly that my feet came off the ground, and then he kissed the side of my face.

"There. Is that better?"

"For now. You're still not staying here, though. Where's Smoke?"

"Inside, in his room, I think."

"You *think*? If you don't know where your father is, does he know where you are and where you're going?"

"Well . . ."

"Get out of my way, Isaiah." I nudged him from in front of the doorway and yanked the storm door open. "Now how long are you planning on staying over at Kenny's? Or is it really Kim's? Don't play with me, boy."

He gave me a long, drawn out sigh that told me he would've been perfectly content with my staying in Illinois.

"It's Kenny, Ma, and I'ma be home in a few, OK?" He took off across the street and left me standing in the door, looking after him like an overprotective mother bear. I knew I needed to learn how to let go, but I wasn't quite ready yet. And, hell, would I ever truly be ready?

A blast of frigid air from inside the house reminded me that Smoke probably didn't want to cool off the whole neighborhood. I pulled the storm door closed and shut the front door softly. At first I left it unlocked for when Isaiah returned, and then I locked it because I remembered that he had a damn key. I went to find Smoke so I could kill him.

He wasn't in the kitchen or the lower level. Nor was he in the garage or the bathroom off the hallway. That left the one possibility that I dreaded, which was his bedroom. I took slow steps in that direction, looking at the closed door like it was a cobra about to strike. I prepared myself to walk the green mile.

I turned the knob and stepped into the room quietly. The blinds were drawn against the sun and it was semi-dark and cool. Smoke was sprawled on his stomach in bed with a pillow bunched under his head and facing away from me. He slept in blissful ignorance of the fact that I was standing there salivating at the mouth, eyeing his sleekly muscled back. Except for a dark blue sheet pooled around his hips, the covers were thrown off and back, and his breathing was deep and even.

"Smoke," I hissed, rooted to the spot. He didn't move. "*Smoke*," I said a little louder and he still didn't move. "Smoke!" I barked, stamping my foot.

He jerked and rolled over, peering at me through slits.

"Anne?"

"It's the chocolate devil in person. I came to have it out with you about Isaiah," I said.

"What about Zay? He do something I don't know about?" His voice was gruff with good sleep.

"He called me talking about he was staying here for the rest of the summer and planning on going to school here when it starts back."

A slow smile spread across Smoke's face. I rolled my eyes when I saw the gap between his front teeth.

"He said that?"

"Like you didn't know. And why are you in bed this time of day anyway?"

"I was messing around in my mother's backyard this afternoon, so I'm recuperating from the three heat strokes I know I had. And no, I didn't know anything about Zay staying here. But it's fine if he wants to. Get undressed and come in with me, Anne."

"What do you mean it's fine if he wants to?" I propped my hands on my hips and glared at him.

"Just what I said." Smoke stretched long and hard, like a sleek panther. Growled like one too. The sheet slipped down a notch, exposing the top of the crack of his ass to my searching eyes. "Look, we can talk about it later. Right now, take off your clothes and come in with me."

"I don't think so. I want my son on a plane home next weekend, no exceptions."

"You came all the way here to say that?"

"You wouldn't come to the phone." I pointed a finger. "Which was childish as hell, by the way."

"Whatever." He rolled to his side, facing me, and didn't even try to catch the sheet when it slipped even farther. "Look what you're making me do here." I glanced at his erection and turned my head.

"Would you please be serious?"

"I am being serious."

"Well put that thing away." I waved a vague hand in his direction and kept my eyes on the wall.

"I'm trying to, but you're playing hard to get. At least come sit down and rest your feet. Those are, what, four-inch heels? I know your dogs are barking right about now. Come here so I can massage your feet for you." He patted the edge of the bed and raised his eyebrows.

"I'm too old for booty calls. Games too."

"So am I. I missed you, Anne."

"You missed the sex, Smoke."

"That too, but I missed you. I think I already told you that I wanted to be with you. You ready to talk about that now?"

I shuffled my feet around for a minute, pushed my hands through my locks, and scrubbed them across my face anxiously. His scent was thick in the room. Cool Water cologne mixed with the unique, sexy scent of his skin, the moisturizer he used in his hair, and the soap he used. It was making me dizzy.

"I might be," I heard myself say. "What, specifically, do you mean by *be with me*? Casual bed partners? Friends with benefits? What? I need to know, so I can make informed decisions."

"Casual bed partners? *Hell*, no. And anything with the word friends in it is automatically out too." He caught my eyes and stared me down. "If we decide to explore something with each other, I'll have to have a commitment from you, Anne. Monogamy."

"Like you had with Diana?" That was an important point to make, I thought. He nodded and lifted a hand to press his fingers to his eyelids, released a stream of strong breath.

"The situation with Diana was messed up. You're right."

"How can I be sure you won't do the same thing to me, Smoke? I mean, as far as I could see, she was more than enough for you to handle. And I *know* I'm more than enough for you to handle, but if you're one of those greedy men who has to have two or three women at any one time, I can't deal with that shit."

"Can I say something?" I kept talking.

"The thing is, I'm not in the market for games and drama and all that other crap. I have enough to deal with on a day-to-day basis without having to worry about where my man is and what he's doing. My tolerance level is very low too."

"Diana was a nice lady, Anne, but she wasn't you. I was a little late breaking up with her, you're right, but all I can say is that I didn't know what I wanted then. And for the record, after we started making love I wasn't intimate with her again. Hell, I couldn't be. You made a brotha impotent." He chuckled softly and scratched his fingers through the hair trailing down his abdomen. It crackled in the silence and drew my eyes there.

"And do you know what you want now?" I asked.

"Yeah, I know."

"Tell me."

"I want you, Anne. Even though I can't quite figure out why, with all your nagging and worrying and screaming and crying all the damn time. I think I can work with it, though. You think you can work with me?"

"You cheat on me and I'll kill you in your sleep. I'm telling you that now."

"OK, but I reserve the right to the same privileges."

"What about the distance?"

"We can work with it . . . for now. You coming to bed?"

"Not quite yet. I thought you were angry with me because I waited so long to tell you about Isaiah?"

"I was, but I'm not anymore. I've made my peace with everything that happened, and I understand why you did what you did. You still mad with me for saying the stupid shit I said?"

"I was, but I'm not anymore," I said softly. "I guess I can understand why you said what you said. This won't work if you still feel that way, though."

"I don't, Anne." He sighed and threw off the sheet, giving me an unobstructed view of his naked body. "You got me feeling all kinds of things, but mad isn't one of them.

Come here so I can show you a little bit of what I'm feeling."

"Wait, Smoke, what are we telling Isaiah?"

"I don't know what you're telling him, but I'm planning on telling him that he might have some brothers and sisters in a hot little minute or two."

I blew out a shaky breath and wrapped my arms around my middle, walked around in a perfect circle. Digesting and processing, that was what I was doing.

"No games, Smoke," I warned him one last time.

"No games, Anne. Now?"

I unbuttoned my blouse and lifted it off my shoulders slowly, let it fall to the floor. My skirt was next. Then I slipped my heels off my feet. He was right, I could use a massage. I walked on my knees across the bed toward Smoke. He came to his knees and met me halfway, reaching around to slide my panties down as he put his mouth on my breasts.

"Yeah, now," I whispered in his ear and heard him chuckle. A moment later, our mouths met and we sighed at the same time.

ALEC

Now I knew what Gerald Levert's whining ass was always singing about in his songs. "Baby, hold on to me," was right. I was losing myself in the scent of Anne's skin and thinking, *I wonder what her spin is on more kids? At least one more, for sure. Another son would be good, or a little chocolate devil like her mama. Have me wrapped around her little finger.*

I already knew me and Anne made pretty babies together, and I planned on giving her another one as soon as possible. This one we were going to raise together. What she didn't know yet, but I already did, was that I wasn't going anywhere, anytime soon.

"That's right, baby, ride me," I hissed as she took me in and sat back to ride me slowly. My hands curled around her breasts, eyes slid closed on a long moan. "Been driving me crazy, making me wait on you. You know you got me, right?" She leaned over me and I grabbed her locks and pulled her face down to mine. We stared at each other for long seconds.

"Smoke," Anne whispered.

I swallowed her breath and gave her mine, ran my tongue across her lips. I saw the fear and uncertainty in her eyes, right along with the orgasm she was trying to hold back. She looked so pretty when she came, like she was floating on a cloud of ecstasy. Mouth open and eyes closed, her breath coming out in short, soft huffs. She tightened around me and I fought to keep my own eyes open. I wanted to see her ride it out. Wanted to give her a million more.

When her eyes opened, I closed mine and let her watch me take the ride. Then I kissed her, slow and deep, sucked on her tongue, and let her suck on mine. She giggled.

"Damn, your eyes really *did* roll back in your head."

"You thought I was playing?" I flipped her over on her back and came down on top of her. I pushed my arms under her and moaned as her arms wrapped around my neck to hold me close. She had the softest breasts in the world, and I laid my head on them and sucked in a deep breath. "Stay with me, Anne."

ISAIAH

I heard them as soon as I stepped in the house. A slow smile spread across my face and stayed there for the rest of the day until they finally came out and I played like I didn't know what was going on.

Smoke and my mama played around in the kitchen, cooking dinner and touching on each other. Did more touching than cooking, far as I was concerned. But I wasn't complaining when my mama slid a plate of mashed potatoes and gravy and smothered cube steak in front of my face.

I chewed slowly, checking them out the whole time. Then, when I couldn't take it no more because the suspense was killing me, I swigged some Dr Pepper and came out with what inquiring minds wanted to know.

"So, y'all getting together or what?" I waved my fork back and forth between them.

"Yeah," they both said at the same time, watching me closely. Smoke reached over and ran his hand up my mama's arm, then touched her neck, and she had the nerve to blush.

I went back to my steak.

"That's cool," I said nonchalantly. "Any more steak left, Ma?" *'Bout damn time. Wait till I tell Uncle Don about this shit. He owed me fifty big ones, for real.*

ANNE

We were arguing about where to go for lunch the next afternoon when Smoke's phone rang and I went to answer it. Isaiah wanted pizza and Smoke was talking noise about Chinese, but I was holding out for soup and salad. I picked up the phone and called out, "All you can eat soup and salad," before I put the receiver to my ear. It was Big Mama and we talked for a good ten minutes, which had Smoke and Isaiah moaning and groaning about being hungry.

Smoke finally came and took the phone from me. Then

I started looking crazy because *he* was taking so long and my stomach was starting to growl. I went and sat next to Isaiah in the living room to wait. Tried not to glance at my watch as ten more minutes turned into thirty.

I heard Smoke hang up the phone and skidded into the kitchen to light a fire under his ass. I came up short when I found him leaning against the wall with his arms folded across his chest, staring at the phone like it would tell him the key to solving world hunger.

"What? Is everything OK over at Big Mama's?"

"Everything is perfect at Big Mama's, Anne. Just like everything is perfect here, except for one thing." He searched my face intently and had the hair on the back of my neck standing up. I wracked my brain, trying to think of something that I'd done and had yet to confess. It was one of *those* looks.

"And that one thing would be?" If he started talking out of the side of his neck, I figured I was close enough to the knives that I could slice him up real quick.

Smoke locked eyes with me and lifted the receiver from its cradle, held it out to me.

"Call your mother."

I took two steps back and looked at him like he was crazy.

"*What?* For what?"

He shrugged casually.

"I don't know, to see how she's doing? Shoot the shit a little bit? Same thing you just did with Big Mama."

"You know it's not like that with us, Smoke." I stared at the phone and then at him.

"Call your mother, Anne. It's time."

I stood there for several seconds, looking around the kitchen frantically. I opened my mouth, closed it, and opened it again. I wiped the back of my hand across my forehead.

"What am I supposed to say?"

"You could start with hello." He caught my look, hung up the phone, and came away from the wall. The palms of his hands on my ass pulled me up against him chest to chest. I lifted my face automatically when he dipped his head for a kiss.

"Why are you doing this?" I asked. Talk about being caught off guard, out in left field somewhere. Just like that, completely out of the blue, *call your mother*. What was I supposed to do with that?

"Because I love you. You love me?" I nodded. "You trust me?" I nodded again and pushed a hand through my locks. "Call your mother, Anne. Shit, if you can give me a second chance to treat you right, you think you can extend your mother and sister the same courtesy?"

I thought about that for a long time while Smoke stared me down. He was holding the receiver out to me again and I had yet to touch it. I lifted my hand, then snatched it back. Lifted it again, and snatched it back again. I looked at Smoke, long and hard.

Then I took the phone.

"Hello, Mama," I said into the phone a few minutes later.

"Take your time, baby," Smoke told me. "We'll wait as long as you need." He slid past me and left me alone in the kitchen.

A few minutes into my conversation with my mother, Smoke's voice boomed through the house.

"Boy, be quiet, OK? You keep saying you're dying from hunger, but you ain't keeled over yet!"

I burst out laughing, suddenly feeling lighter around my shoulders and in my chest. My mama giggled too, and wanted to know what was funny.

"Nothing, Mama. Just Isaiah clowning, as usual. What? Oh, he's doing fine . . ."